THE
BLEEDING
EDGE

THE
BLEEDING
EDGE

WILLIAM W. JOHNSTONE
with J. A. Johnstone

PINNACLE BOOKS
Kensington Publishing Corp.
www.kensingtonbooks.com

PINNACLE BOOKS are published by

Kensington Publishing Corp.
119 West 40th Street
New York, NY 10018

PUBLISHER'S NOTE
Following the death of William W. Johnstone, the Johnstone family is working with a carefully selected writer to organize and complete Mr. Johnstone's outlines and many unfinished manuscripts to create additional novels in all of his series like The Last Gunfighter, Mountain Man, and Eagles, among others. This novel was inspired by Mr. Johnstone's superb storytelling.

All Kensington titles, imprints, and distributed lines are available at special quantity discounts for bulk purchases for sales promotions, premiums, fund-raising, educational, or institutional use. Special book excerpts or customized printings can also be created to fit specific needs. For details, write or phone the office of the Kensington special sales manager: Kensington Publishing Corp., 119 West 40th Street, New York, NY 10018, attn: Special Sales Department; phone 1-800-221-2647.

ISBN-13: 978-0-7860-2807-8
ISBN-10: 0-7860-2807-6

First printing: October 2012

10 9 8 7 6 5 4 3 2 1

Printed in the United States of America

One man with courage makes a majority.
—ANDREW JACKSON

CHAPTER ONE

Holding his straw Stetson tightly in one hand, John Howard Stark stepped out into the Texas heat. The glass door of the medical office hissed shut behind him on its pneumatic closer. Stark, a tall, broad-shouldered man with the sort of compelling presence that made people look at him twice, paused, standing there in the bright sunlight for a long moment.

Six decades of living had put plenty of silver in his thick, dark hair and in his mustache. But he still stood straight, an obviously powerful man despite his age.

Right now, however, something had etched furrows in his weathered cheeks. The things the doctor had told him had come as no surprise, and he had nodded stoically as he listened, but something inside him had drawn tighter.

Now he stood there looking at nothing, his gaze pointed out at the Texas town around him. Across the street from the brick complex of medical offices was an elementary school. Beyond that was the high school, the bigger buildings around it visible from where Stark stood whether he actually saw them right now or not. A block to his left, a nice Italian restaurant on the corner of the highway that also served as the town's main drag, with its multitude of fast food joints, auto supply stores, gas stations, and big box discount stores. Traffic along the road was a never-ending hum.

Stark ignored all of it.

Then something besides his own thoughts finally caught his attention. He lowered his gaze to something more immediate, the parking lot right in front of him. He'd had to park on the outer edge of the lot when he'd gotten here an hour earlier. His pickup still sat there.

And some damn fool was trying to break into it.

Stark's eyes narrowed. He put his hat on and stepped down off the sidewalk to cross the parking lot. The young man standing next to the pickup either didn't see Stark coming or didn't care. He continued trying to work the un-folded wire hanger down to the door lock. Stark's pickup was old enough that it didn't have electronic locks, just a little knob that had to be pulled up.

Old and out of date, just like me, Stark thought.

The would-be thief wasn't alone. He had two compan-ions, both dressed like he was, in baggy blue jeans and floppy shirts, with bandannas tied around their heads. One of them nudged the guy working on the lock and said, "Hurry up, Chuy. Somebody's comin'."

Chuy glanced over his shoulder at Stark and said, "It's just an old man."

Stark came to a stop near the back of the pickup and asked, "Can I help you fellas with something?"

"Go away, hombre," Chuy snapped. "This ain't none of your business."

Stark laid a hand on the sidewall around the pick-up's bed.

"This is my truck, so I think that makes it my business."

"It *was* your truck," one of the other young men said. "It ain't no more."

Disgustedly, Chuy slid the hanger out of the tiny gap at the top of the driver's-side window. He threw it to the pavement and said, "The hell with it. Gimme that pipe. I'm gonna smash the window."

"What's it matter to you, old man?" Chuy demanded. "Like Angel said, this ain't your truck no more. It belongs to us."

Stark shook his head.

"I don't think so."

"You gonna give us trouble?" Angel sneered and lifted his shirt to reveal the butt of a revolver tucked into the sagging waistband of his jeans. "You better run, man, 'fore I light you up."

The one standing next to Chuy grinned and said, "Better run, better run," in a singsong voice.

Stark lifted both hands, palms out.

"Take it easy, son. I'm not looking for trouble."

Angel curled his fingers around the gun butt.

"I ain't your son, you—"

Filth spewed from his mouth as he cursed Stark. He was so caught up in his creative obscenity that he failed to notice Stark edging closer.

When he finally noticed what was going on, he yelled, "Hey, man, don't crowd me!" and jerked the gun from his waistband.

Before he could lift it, Stark kicked him in the balls.

It was a swift, hard kick that made Angel scream and crumple forward. Stark closed his right hand over the revolver, gripping the cylinder so tightly that even if Angel managed to pull the trigger, the gun wouldn't fire. With his left hand he grabbed the front of Angel's shirt and heaved him against the pickup. Angel's head cracked against the metal.

Stark ripped the gun from Angel's hand. He was on the passenger side, with the pickup between him and the other two thieves. As they yelled angrily and clawed under their shirts for their guns, Stark bent low and quickly circled around the front of the vehicle, putting himself behind the sturdier protection of the engine block.

As Chuy and his companion opened fire, shooting wildly in Stark's general direction but not really coming close to him, Stark went even lower and triggered two shots under the truck. Each bullet found its mark, shattering bone and spraying blood across the pavement. Chuy and his companion went down howling in pain, each with a destroyed ankle. They would be lucky to ever walk normally again.

Still moving fast, with grace and agility that belied his years, Stark charged around the pickup and kicked away the guns Chuy and the other thief had dropped. Then he backed away so that he could see all three of the young men. Angel was on the ground, too, still stunned and senseless from having his head rammed against the pickup.

Stark reached in his pocket for his cell phone to call the police, but it wasn't necessary. The door of the doctor's office opened and the young woman who worked there as the receptionist rushed out, calling, "Mr. Stark! Are you all right?"

"Yeah, I'm fine, Bonita," Stark told her.

"I saw everything that happened. I already called the cops."

Stark heard a siren in the distance. He smiled and nodded.

"*Muchas gracias,*" he told the receptionist. "You better

go back inside now, in case these fellas try to cause any more trouble."

The two crippled thieves were lying on the pavement, clutching their ruined ankles and whimpering. Bonita looked at them and shook her head, saying, "I don't think they're going to be bothering anybody for a long time."

"We can hope not," Stark said.

Chuy twisted his head around to glare up at Stark. Panting breathlessly because of the pain, he said, "You're dead, man! You're . . . dead! You hear me?"

Stark ignored the threat. It wasn't like he and death hadn't been close companions for many years.

Lights flashing, a police car came around the corner off the highway, onto the side street where the medical offices were located. It squealed to a stop, and the uniformed officer inside got out hurriedly, crouching behind the open door and pointing his gun at Stark.

"Put your gun on the ground!" he yelled. "Now!"

Stark could tell the cop was young and inexperienced. Moving carefully and deliberately so there wouldn't be any excuse to shoot, he bent over and placed the revolver on the ground at his feet, then backed away from it and held his hands up at shoulder level, in plain sight.

"Now you get on the ground, too!" the cop ordered. "Facedown!"

"Oh, stop it," Bonita said in a scathing tone. "Don't you know who this is? This is John Howard Stark."

The cops eyes widened.

"One of the heroes of the Alamo?"

Stark tried not to wince. He had never thought of himself as a hero, and certainly not as a latter-day equivalent to Crockett, Bowie, Travis, and the other men who had died defending the Alamo in 1836. They were true heroes.

"That's right," Bonita said. She pointed at the three

young men on the ground. "And he was just defending himself from those three punks who tried to steal his truck. You shouldn't be yelling at him. You should be pinning a medal on him!"

Stark had to smile ruefully at that. With the way things were in the country now . . .

Well, the chances of anybody ever pinning a medal on the likes of him were pretty doggoned small.

CHAPTER TWO

The sleekly groomed and coiffed news anchor on the TV screen was saying, "This bloody shooting was merely the latest violent incident in which Mr. Stark has been involved. Known for his clashes with drug smugglers several years ago, which resulted in the death of his wife, and then later for his involvement with the so-called defense of the Alamo, Stark has been a lightning rod for controversy."

The shot cut to pre-recorded video footage of a handsome Hispanic man saying, "Given Mr. Stark's history of violence directed toward minorities, the refusal of the police to carry out more than a perfunctory investigation of this incident is an outrage." A graphic at the bottom of the screen identified him as Victor Martinez, attorney for the three young men charged with assault. Martinez went on, "I think it speaks volumes that my clients are the ones being prosecuted here, and yet they're the ones who are in the hospital while Mr. Stark, hale and hearty, walks free."

The live shot of the news anchor replaced the footage of Martinez. She said, "Representatives of the Justice Department in Washington have indicated that they will also be looking into the matter with an eye toward determining if any hate crimes occurred during the incident outside a local doctor's office." A bright smile lit up her face as the expression of grave concern vanished. "In other news, there are further indications tonight that the administration's efforts to bolster the economic recovery are succeeding as the national unemployment rate plummeted last month from 16.3 percent to 16.2 percent. This dramatic decrease in unemployment, coupled with the recent announcement that the national debt rose by only 1.2 trillion dollars in the first quarter of the year, prompted an administration spokesman to say that this is tangible evidence the country is on the right track."

Chief Dennis Feasco used his foot to nudge a trash can toward Stark. He pushed the button on the remote control that turned off the TV and said, "If you're going to throw up, do it in that, not on my desk."

"Why would I throw up?" Stark asked.

Feasco jerked a thumb toward the now-blank screen.

"Isn't that enough to make you sick?" he asked.

Stark chuckled.

"If I let the swill coming out of Washington bother me that much, I'd have been throwing up for the last ten years. I'm too busy with other things to get that worked up over it."

Feasco sighed and said, "You'll be busy making license plates and trying to protect yourself from the Hispanic gangs in prison if Martinez has his way."

"He won't," Stark said. "The district attorney's got the testimony of Bonita and half a dozen patients and employees from Dr. Browner's office that those three jumped me when I tried to stop them from stealing my pickup."

"That's not the story that Martinez is telling to anybody who'll listen. The way he tells it, his clients were just walking peacefully by the parking lot when *you* attacked *them*.

He's getting plenty of sympathetic ears for that version in Washington. The Justice Department is liable to bring federal civil rights charges, regardless of what the DA does here."

Stark shrugged.

"I reckon I'll deal with that when the time comes, if it does."

"I just wanted to give you a heads-up on this, John," Feasco said.

"Well, I appreciate that, Chief." Stark reached for his hat, which was sitting on the corner of Feasco's desk. "Is that all?"

"Yeah. Except . . . you'd better keep an eye on your back. As far as we know, there are no direct ties between those three and any of the cartels. They're just local punks, about as far down on the totem pole as they can get. But Martinez getting involved in the case worries me. He doesn't come cheap. Whoever's paying him to jump in may be somebody who has a grudge against you."

"There are plenty of 'em out there who fall into that category, I suppose," Stark said as he stood up.

Feasco grunted.

"Yeah. All the way from here to the White House."

"I never caused any trouble for the fella who's in there now."

"No, but you made his side look pretty bad a few times, and you know how those bastards hold a grudge."

Stark inclined his head in acknowledgment of the chief's point. He put his hat on, lifted a hand in farewell, and left the office. As he walked out through the police station, several of the cops who were there smiled and nodded to him. As a general rule, police officers didn't have much use for anybody who could be classified as a vigilante, but these cops, who had to deal every day with the increasing lawlessness along the border between Texas and Mexico, couldn't help but respect the way Stark had stood up for himself and others.

His pickup, the pickup that had started this trouble, was parked out front. Stark wasn't sure why those three had wanted it so badly. Sure, he kept it in fine condition, but it was old and wouldn't have brought much from a chop shop. Enough to buy some drugs, though, he supposed.

He got in and started the engine, listening to its well-tuned purr for a moment before he put the truck in gear. A few minutes later he was rolling out of town toward home.

Once, home had been the Diamond S ranch, a success-ful spread a hundred miles west of here. Following his wife's death in the war against the Mexican drug cartel that had tried to take over the ranch, Stark had kept the place going for a while. His sons, David, a Navy pilot, and Pete, a lieutenant colonel in the Marines, had come home for a while to help out, but eventually they'd had to return to their duties. David was on a carrier in the Indian Ocean. Stark didn't know exactly where Pete was, but he suspected Afghanistan even though American troops supposedly had withdrawn from that troubled country.

Stark didn't hear from either of them very often, and that was fine; they both had their own lives to live, and they were doing important work. Somebody had to help hold the line against an increasingly savage world, even when those in power in Washington seemed determined to kowtow to every two-bit, crackpot dictator on the other side of the globe in the name of "international cooperation."

Eventually, even though he hated to do it because the land had been in his family for generations, Stark had been forced to sell the Diamond S. He couldn't keep it up by himself, and people didn't want to work for him because they were still worried about possible retaliation from the cartel. He'd had to sell the place for much less than it should have been worth, but he'd been lucky to find a buyer at all. Most real estate within a hundred miles of the border was virtually worthless now because of the drug smugglers who had taken over. Even on the Texas side of the border, the gangs ran things. It was a pitiful state of affairs.

After selling the ranch, Stark had moved east along the Rio Grande, settling near the medium-sized city of Devil's Pass. He had a nice mobile home in Shady Hills Retirement Park.

At first he had wondered what in the world had prompted him to buy a lot there. The place was full of old geezers.

But then he realized that he fit right in there, and for the past few months he'd been relatively happy. Without Elaine, he knew he would never be completely content again, but he had his books, a satellite dish for the TV, and he'd even discovered that the Internet wasn't as bad as he had thought it would be. He'd even had a Facebook page for a while before he'd had to shut it down because of all the people who'd posted their liberal vitriol there. To a lot of folks he was a villain, a symbol of everything that was wrong about America as they continued their quest to transform it into a European-style welfare state.

He shook those thoughts out of his head as he reached the arched gate in the white picket fence that enclosed the twenty acres of the retirement park. He was home.

CHAPTER THREE

Located in South Texas, the Shady Hills Retirement Park was neither shady nor hilly. The former came closer to being true than the latter, because at least there were some small trees growing here and there among the mobile homes and modular housing that made up the park's residences. Those trees provided a little shade. But there wasn't anything resembling a hill anywhere in sight on these plains. You had to go farther west along the border to find that.

It was evening when Stark reached the park, a little after supper time. His doctor's appointment had been at one o'clock, he had come out of the office a little before two, and after the dust-up with Chuy, Angel, and the third would-be pickup thief, he had spent the rest of the afternoon being questioned by the police and the district attorney.

Then Chief Feasco had caught him on the way out of the station and asked to talk to him for a minute. Dennis "Fiasco," as he was sometimes called (as opposed to "Feesko," as he pronounced it), was a good man. Stark didn't know him all that well, but he was confident that Feasco was honest and did his best in a thankless job.

By now the sun wasn't quite down yet, but it hung big and red and low above the western horizon, and the heat of the afternoon was beginning to give way to the slightly cooler temperatures of evening. Some of the residents were sitting out on their covered porches and decks, sipping iced tea and getting some fresh air after supper. Others strolled up and down the neatly paved roads that divided the park into a grid. The park was owned by a retired aerospace engineer and his wife, and they did a good job of keeping it well cared for.

Stark pulled up in the parking area next to his gray doublewide. The mobile home was bigger than he really needed, but after living all his life on the Diamond S, he liked to have some room to spread out when he wanted to.

His neighbor to the right was Alton Duncan, who had been an insurance claims adjuster before retirement. The mobile home to the left of Stark's was occupied by Fred and Aurelia Gomez. Fred had taught high school math and Aurelia had been a bookkeeper, so they had a love of numbers in common. The Gomezes were sitting in folding lawn chairs on the little patch of grass in front of their home while Alton Duncan had the hood of his '64 Mustang raised and was doing something with the engine.

Fred was on his feet by the time Stark got out of the pickup. Even though Aurelia called after him, "Now, Fred, don't be a nuisance," he hurried over to Stark.

"John Howard, are you all right?" he asked. "We heard about you on the news."

"You and half the county, I expect, Fred," Stark said. "I'm fine. Didn't even muss my hair."

"Yeah, well, I wouldn't have to worry about that, no matter how much trouble I got into," Fred said as he ran a hand over his head and grinned. Except for bushy gray eyebrows, he was bald as an egg, and shaped about like an egg, too.

Alton Duncan came over to join them, wiping his hands on a rag as he did so. His hairline had receded quite a bit, but he still had a lot more hair than Fred. He said, "You shouldn't have put those punks in the hospital, John."

"Oh?" Stark said.

"No, you should've put 'em in the morgue. Lowlifes like that are a waste of perfectly good oxygen."

"Better be careful, Alton," Fred advised. "All of them were Hispanic. Racist talk like that violates their civil rights. The feds will be coming here to arrest you before you know it."

Duncan's eyes narrowed for a second before Fred grinned and punched him lightly on the arm, saying, "Hey, I'm just screwin' with you, man. I hate punks like that even more than you do. You think it's easy being named Gomez when it seems like every piece of gutter trash in the world is trying to drag your whole race down with them?"

"Yeah, I guess you're right," Alton said. He turned to Stark again and went on, "Seriously, John, are you gonna be in trouble with the law over this? Because if you are, I know a really good attorney—"

As if on cue, the front door of Alton's mobile home opened and an attractive woman with short blond hair came out onto the deck. She said, "I guess I'll be going now, Pop—oh, John Howard, you're back." Trimly built, wearing blue jeans and a silk blouse, she came down the steps and crossed the yard to join the group of men. "I heard about what happened. Are you all right?"

"I'm fine, Hallie," Stark told her.

Alton said, "I was just saying to John that if he needs a lawyer, I know where he can find a good one."

"Thanks for the vote of confidence, Pop," Hallie Duncan said, "but I think I liked it better back in the old days before lawyers were allowed to advertise."

"Hey, that's not advertising," Alton protested. "That's just good word of mouth."

"Your dad's got a point, Hallie," Fred said.

Stark enjoyed the banter, even though he wasn't really the sort to take much part in it, being more the quiet type. The strong, silent type, like Gary Cooper, Elaine had sometimes teased him.

He was aware that Hallie was watching him. She visited her father often, nearly every day, and cooked a lot of meals for him. Stark knew that she was in her early fifties, although she looked at least a decade younger than that, and that her husband, who had also been a lawyer, had died of a heart attack several years earlier. She had always used her maiden name in their law practice, Alton had told Stark, so after she was widowed she just kept on using it.

She was a pretty woman, and she looked at Stark with an interest that made him a little uncomfortable. He wasn't searching for romance, but if he had been, he could have done a heck of a lot worse than beautiful, intelligent Hallie Duncan.

But he'd been happily married for a long time, and although the pain of Elaine's tragic death had faded somewhat, he knew it would never go away completely. His memories were companion enough for him.

"I heard on the news that the Justice Department is going to investigate the incident," Hallie went on. "Why do you suppose Washington is taking such an interest in a simple vehicle theft, John Howard?"

"You know why," Alton answered before Stark could say anything. "The man's got some powerful enemies up there. They had to lay off him for a while because he was such a hero to people, but they figure enough time has gone by now that most folks have forgotten about what happened before. Those bureaucrats didn't forget how you stood up to the government, though, John, and they never will."

"My dad's right," Hallie said. "This has all the makings of a vendetta."

"That's crazy," Stark said. "The government wouldn't come after an innocent man that way, just to make a point."

Hallie, Alton, and Fred all looked at him as if they thought he had to know better than that. And truthfully, he did. The politicians running things now, and their willing accomplices in the mainstream media, liked to tout their sweeping, progressive ideas, but at the same time they could be as petty, spiteful, and vindictive as five-year-olds.

They threw tantrums about like five-year-olds, too, when they didn't get their way.

"Right now, all I know is that the district attorney isn't going to pursue any sort of case against me," Stark said. "If that changes, or if anything else comes up, I'm liable to be giving you a call, Hallie."

"I hope you mean that, John Howard." She leaned over and gave her father a kiss on the cheek, then told him, "I'll see you tomorrow."

"You don't have to come over here and cook for me every day, you know," Alton told her.

She laughed.

"If I didn't, you'd live on Vienna sausages and Froot Loops."

"Throw in some beer and it's a perfectly balanced diet," Alton insisted.

Laughing, Hallie waved at the other men and headed

for her car, which was parked next to her dad's vintage Mustang.

"Hell of a girl," Alton said as she drove away. He glanced at Stark. "And she likes you, John."

"You're only about twelve years older than me," Stark pointed out. "You wouldn't want an old geezer like me for a son-in-law."

"Don't be so sure about that."

"Hallie just regards me as somebody to be looked after, the same way she thinks of you."

Alton shook his head and said, "That just shows how much you know."

Alton might have a point there, Stark thought as he said his good nights and went on into his mobile home.

As crazy as the world was getting, he wasn't sure he knew much of anything anymore.

CHAPTER FOUR

Washington, D.C.

The most powerful man in the world leaned back in the chair behind the big desk and cursed bitterly under his breath as he looked at the flat-screen TV mounted on the wall. The huge screen was broken up into eight windows, each showing a feed from a different newscast. All the major broadcast and cable networks were represented.

And every one of them was talking about John Howard Stark.

"Were all these running at the same time?" the president asked the attorney general as he used the remote to mute the audio on the TV. The two men were alone in the Oval Office.

"No, we put the feeds together," the AG said. "I thought it might more effectively demonstrate the threat this way."

"One old man in Texas is not a threat."

The AG shrugged, making it clear that while he wasn't going to openly challenge the president's statement, he didn't agree with it, either.

"What do you think we should do?" the president asked. He hated asking questions like that, nakedly begging for advice. But he had to because deep down he knew that despite the trappings of the office, despite the very real power that he possessed by virtue of being commander-in-chief, he was out of his depth here. A few times early in his career, he had run for president, but he had never really, truly believed that he would *be* president.

And he still wouldn't be if one of his predecessors hadn't gotten so carried away with his messiah complex that he believed he could order a nerve gas attack on American citizens and get away with it.

The past decade had been a political roller coaster, with the country split almost evenly down the middle between right and left. The stranglehold that the left had on the news media and the courts, though, had been enough to ensure that they held nearly all the reins of power during that time. They should have been able to consolidate that power even more so that they would be assured of never having to give it up, but a series of unfortunate events had prevented that from happening.

The first one had involved the very man whose face looked out now from that big screen, John Howard Stark. He had stood up to the Mexican drug cartels, stood up to the federal government as well, and embarrassed the president. That debacle had been followed by others along the U.S.–Mexico border, and the situation had gotten bad enough that the party had dumped the incumbent and elevated her vice president to the top of the ticket for the next election. He had won, of course, and then proceeded to make things even worse with his smug, arrogant, heavy-handed demeanor and his tendency to think that he could get away with anything because he was so adored by the public.

That had all come crashing down with the trouble in the little town of Hope, Texas, and the revelation that the government was funding a secret biological and chemical weapons laboratory in the mountains of West Texas. When the president had ordered the unleashing of one of those weapons on American soil, with the intention of killing American citizens, it had almost ruined everything. He had been impeached and ultimately arrested when he refused to surrender power. Of course, he hadn't been imprisoned but had been taken secretly out of the country. Now he lived in a luxurious villa in the south of France—paid for by the American taxpayers, naturally— and was writing a book about how he had been the victim of a sinister right-wing conspiracy.

His vice president had taken over the presidency only long enough to resign, which meant the Speaker of the House had ascended to the office. She was hated virulently even by members of her own party and had been told in no uncertain terms that she would *not* be running for reelection when her term was over. The party was doing its best to distance itself from the extremes of the past two chief executives, and so they had turned to an obscure congressman who had been around just long enough to have some decent national name recognition.

He'd had no business winning, and he probably wouldn't have if not for the constant barrage of vicious attacks on the opposition candidate by the news media. It was a rip job, pure and simple, and a particularly savage one, and it had worked.

And so the country had a president who sat in the Oval Office and didn't have any earthly idea what he was supposed to do next.

He could tell that the look the attorney general gave him was a pitying one, but there was plenty of scorn in the AG's eyes, too. The attorney general said, "We're already doing all we can do right now, sir. You haven't commented on the matter yet, and it would probably be best if you didn't. I'll issue any statements that need to be made through the Justice Department."

"Are you going to bring charges of civil rights violations against this man, Stark?"

"That will depend on what the investigation uncovers." The AG grimaced. "It won't be easy. There are several witnesses who have already told the police that the three suspects were trying to steal Stark's truck and attacked him first. There's, uh, even some security camera footage showing one of the men pulling a gun."

"The gun that Stark used to shoot the other two."

"That's right. The fact that the three suspects all have records of violent crimes in their past doesn't help, either. One of them, Chuy Mendoza, was on probation for the sexual assault of a minor."

"Good Lord," muttered the president. "It's going to be hard to portray them as innocent victims in all of this."

"Yes, it is," the attorney general agreed. "There's a good chance the matter never would have come to our attention if Stark hadn't been involved." The AG paused. "He's red-flagged in all the computers at Justice, State, the IRS. . . ."

"Well, I should think so." The president reached a decision, although it was a pretty noncommittal one. "All right, Charles, use your own discretion in pursuing this. I trust your judgment."

"Of course, sir. Thank you."

The attorney general got to his feet and left the Oval Office.

The president sat there watching the talking heads discuss John Howard Stark. The sound on the TV was still off. The president didn't really know a lot about

Stark, just what the general public knew: the war with the cartel, the tragic death of the man's wife, that well-intentioned but horribly misguided business about turning the Alamo back over to Mexico. . . . Stark claimed that he just wanted to be left alone, but he had been a thorn in the side of the liberal establishment for years now. Something needed to be done about him. Maybe not now, maybe not over this particular incident. This might not be the right time.

But soon, the president thought.

No man could be allowed to stand in the way of social progress.

CHAPTER FIVE

Several weeks later

Antonio Gomez didn't know what he wanted to do more, throw up or run. Maybe throw up, *then* run. That would work. That would get rid of the ball of sickness rolling around in his belly and get him out of here before things got bad.

But he didn't do either one of those things. He stayed right where he was, because he didn't want Ignacio "Nacho" Montez to think he was a coward. If that happened, Nacho would do one of two things: be disappointed in him, which was bad enough, or kill him, which was worse. Maybe.

Nacho had brought Antonio and two more young men out here to take care of a problem, as he put it. Antonio knew what that meant. Nacho was going to hurt somebody.

Their car was parked behind a shed so it couldn't be seen from the road. The four young men had gotten out of the car and stood beside it, waiting in the darkness. It seemed like they had been here forever, but Antonio knew it had been only half an hour or so.

Carlos Montez, Nacho's hulking younger brother who liked to be called Chuckie, like the evil doll in that old movie they had seen one night when they were all stoned, dug a joint out of his shirt pocket and opened his lighter to set fire to it.

"What the hell you doin', man?" Nacho demanded.

"I just thought it would make the time pass quicker," Chuckie said.

"You can't do that," Nacho said in a tone of mingled annoyance and tolerance, the way you'd talk to a little kid who didn't know any better. "You don't want anybody seein' the light, and you don't want Jimmy smellin' no reefer when he drives up and gets out of his car. He'd know somebody was here."

"Oh. Yeah, I guess you're right." Chuckie snapped the lighter closed and slid the joint back into his pocket. "Later, when we're done, okay?"

"Sure, man." Nacho laughed. "You brought enough to share, didn't you?"

"Yeah, I guess."

"He's screwin' with you, man," Jalisco said.

Antonio didn't know what Jalisco's real name was. That was all he'd ever heard anyone call the tall, pock-marked hombre. Unlike Antonio, Nacho, and Chuckie, who had all been born and raised on the Texas side of the border, Jalisco was from Mexico. He scared Antonio as much as Nacho did, maybe even more. He dropped hints that he was in good with one of the cartels, and Antonio believed him.

The highway that ran from Devil's Pass to San Antonio was about half a mile east of the isolated house where Antonio and the others waited. Antonio saw headlights going by on the road and wished he was over there in one of those vehicles. He wouldn't care where it was going, as long as it was away from here.

Nacho moved closer to him, nudged him with an elbow. "You nervous, Antonio?"

Antonio managed to shake his head and keep his voice level as he said, "No, man, I'm fine."

"You'll be finer when this is over. You'll really be one of us then. It's gonna be good. You'll see."

"You sure we're not gonna kill him? Just rough him up some, right?"

"Yeah, man. We don't want no real bloodshed. Just teach him a lesson, so he don't even think about holdin' out no more."

Antonio swallowed hard, hoping that Nacho wouldn't notice. He had to do something about the lump in his throat, though. He nodded.

"Sounds good," he said.

"You get in some good licks, that's all you gotta do. We'll know then you one of us."

Before Antonio could say anything else, Jalisco announced quietly, "Here he comes."

A pair of headlights had turned off the highway and were bouncing toward the house over the rutted dirt road. Once again Antonio fought down the urge to be sick. At least this would be over soon, he told himself.

The four men crowded into the thick shadows behind the shed. The approaching car's engine was loud, and so was the Tejano music blasting from its stereo speakers through the open windows. When both of those noises cut off abruptly, the night suddenly seemed painfully quiet.

A car door slammed. Antonio and the others started to emerge from their concealment behind the shed.

Another door slammed.

Jimmy Rodriguez wasn't alone.

Nacho paused for a second, muttered, "It don't matter," just loud enough for his companions to hear, and moved out again, pulling a gun from under his shirt as he did so. It was a Glock nine millimeter, and Nacho was proud of it and showed it off every chance he got, like it was his baby.

Jalisco had a gun, too, Antonio knew. He and Chuckie carried only knives. The guns were just to make sure Jimmy didn't put up too much of a fight, Nacho had said. He would have to take what was coming to him.

Two figures were moving toward the porch. Nacho called out, "Stop right there."

They froze, and at that instant, Chuckie clicked on the powerful flashlight he had taken from the car. Its beam washed over the two people standing there, hands raised in an attempt to shield their eyes from the unexpected, blinding glare.

Jimmy Rodriguez stood there, and next to him was his fourteen-year-old sister, Sonia. Antonio's stomach clenched as he recognized her. They hadn't gone to school together—Antonio had graduated several years earlier, and Sonia was only about to start high school as a freshman—but he knew her anyway. She was really pretty and sweet, and it wasn't her fault that her older brother had gotten mixed up with some bad hombres.

"Nacho—" Antonio began.

"Well, this is a surprise," Nacho said, ignoring him. "You bring your *hermana* along to protect you, Jimmy?"

"Sonia, get back in the car," Jimmy snapped.

She took a step, then stopped as Nacho said, "No, no, no, you stay right where you are, little one." He and Jalisco split up, Nacho going right, Jalisco going left, as they approached the two frightened teenagers. They stayed on the edges of the cone of light so that the guns they held would be visible.

Jimmy said, "Nacho, I don't know what you want, but Sonia's got no part in it. Lemme give her my keys. Let her drive away from here."

"Why, I can't do that," Nacho said in a tone of mock surprise. "She's only fourteen years old. She got no driver's license. You wouldn't want me to let somebody break the law like that, would you?"

"What do you want?"

"You been skimmin', man. You five grand short over the past couple weeks. The hombres can't have that."

"It's a lie," Jimmy said indignantly. "I been straight up. I always been straight up, you know that, Nacho. We go way back, you and me."

"Back far enough I know not to trust you."

Jimmy said, "Look, I got two thousand in the house. I'll give it to you, you give it to the hombres. I don't mind doin' that if it'll fix things, even though I never skimmed a cent, man. You'll do that for me, won't you, Nacho?"

Nacho grinned and said, "Oh, we'll take the two grand, all right . . . after we're finished with you and little Sonia."

"I told you—"

Nacho cut in on Jimmy's angry, desperate outburst by turning his head and calling, "Antonio!"

After another hard swallow, Antonio stepped forward. This was his part, he supposed. He'd give Jimmy a beating, and then they could get out of here. He hoped they wouldn't hurt Sonia before they left.

Hands clenching into fists, he said, "I'm sorry about this, Jimmy—"

"Hold on," Nacho said. "You'll need this."

He pressed the Glock into Antonio's hand. Antonio stood there shocked, unable to move.

"Shoot him in the head," Nacho said quietly, his voice

little more than a whisper. "Walk up to him, point the gun at his face, and pull the trigger. That's all you gotta do."

Sonia burst out, "No!" and then put her hands over her face in horror as she began to sob.

Antonio forced words out of his mouth.

"You said . . . you said . . ."

"You should've known better, man," Nacho told him. "Why'd you think we brought along the machete?"

Jimmy broke and ran.

He made it two steps before Jalisco drilled a bullet through his thigh. Jimmy cried out, grabbed at the wound, and tumbled to the ground, raising a little cloud of dust as he landed.

"Sonia, run!" he screamed through his pain.

She was too scared to move, though. She stood rooted to the ground between the car and the house.

"Go ahead now," Nacho told Antonio. "You can do it. He's squirmin' around, though, so you'll have to aim good." Nacho caught his breath. "No, wait! I got a better idea. We'll make him watch while I give Sonia to Chuckie. Then you can shoot him."

"I . . . I . . . I can't."

The Glock slipped from Antonio's fingers and thudded to the dirt at his feet.

Nacho's arm whipped up and around and his knuckles cracked viciously across Antonio's face. He screamed curses in Spanish.

"You drop my gun!" he screeched. "You drop my gun in the dirt, you—"

Jalisco's gun spat fire twice. Jimmy jerked as the bullets struck him. The little automatic he had dug out of the top of his boot fell from nerveless fingers, unfired.

The shots made Nacho stop his frenzy. He looked

expressionlessly at Jimmy's body as blood continued to well from the wounds in his chest.

"Well, I guess we won't make him watch after all," Nacho said.

"But I still get Sonia, right?" Chuckie asked.

Nacho jerked his head toward the girl and said with a sleepy smile, "Go for it, brother."

Sonia ran then, terror finally galvanizing her muscles, but she was much too late. Chuckie dropped the flashlight and lunged after her. The light hit the ground, and the brilliant beam broke the landscape up into weird shadows as it illuminated the chase. Within a few yards, Chuckie caught up to Sonia, loomed over her like a great bird of prey, and swooped down on her.

Antonio caught a glimpse of that terrible sight over his shoulder as he looked back. He was running, too, toward the highway, and he expected to feel a bullet from Jalisco's gun smash into his back at any second.

No more shots rang out, but Sonia started screaming and kept screaming. Even over the pounding of his heart, Antonio could still hear the sound all the way to the highway, where the rumble of passing trucks finally, thankfully, drowned it out.

Chapter Six

Stark was standing at the counter that separated his kitchen from the living room. He had just poured his first cup of coffee for the day and was breathing in the aroma of it when somebody knocked on the door of his mobile home. Carrying the coffee with him, he went over and opened the door.

Hallie Duncan stood there, looking trimly efficient and businesslike in a gray suit, yet still very attractive. She smiled and said, "Good morning, John Howard."

"Hallie." Stark lifted the cup. "Want some coffee?"

"No, thanks. I've got a latte in the car."

"Didn't offer you a milkshake," Stark said with a smile. "Asked if you wanted coffee."

She laughed and said, "You're determined to hang on to being a dinosaur as long as possible, aren't you?"

"They ruled the earth for a long time, depending on who you believe."

"And eventually they died out, too." Hallie grew more serious and said quickly, "I'm sorry, I shouldn't have said that. It didn't really come out like I meant it."

"Don't worry about it," Stark told her. "Come on in. A gentleman shouldn't leave a lady standing on his porch."

He stepped back to let her into the mobile home. As she came in, she asked, "Have you had the TV on this morning?"

"No, it's a little too early in the day for me to have my intelligence insulted."

"I suppose you'd say the same thing if I asked you if you'd been on the Internet."

Stark just chuckled.

Hallie reached into her purse and took out her phone. She touched the screen, started swiping her finger across it, and said, "I'm sure I can find the clip I want on Google News. . . . Ah, here it is."

She turned the phone so that he could see it as a video clip started playing. The sleekly handsome, smug features of a man Stark recognized as the attorney general of the United States were in close-up.

". . . concluded that there was no basis for any sort of federal prosecution in the incident," the attorney general was saying. "This is solely a matter for the state of Texas to handle, and I assume the local authorities will do so in a proper and prudent manner."

Stark went over to the front door, opened it, and stepped out onto the porch. He tilted his head back and surveyed the sky.

"What are you doing, John Howard?" Hallie asked with a note of exasperation in her voice.

"Lookin' for pigs," Stark said as he squinted upwards. "That was a federal official saying that there was something the state could handle better than the federal government, wasn't it?"

Hallie burst out laughing. She put her phone away and said, "It's not really funny, you big old galoot. The Justice

Department has cleared you of civil rights violations in the case of those three punks who tried to steal your truck."

"As well they should have," Stark said as he came back inside and closed the door. "I didn't do anything wrong by protecting my property and my own life."

"These days, a lot of people would disagree with you."

Stark shrugged.

"They can disagree all they want," he said. "That doesn't make them right."

"Maybe not, but you're still lucky. I'm convinced that they never would have been able to make a case against you with that many witnesses on your side, but they could have made your life very unpleasant for a long time if they'd wanted to. And one thing about a case going to trial . . . you can never be one hundred percent certain how it's going to turn out."

"Unless you've got a good lawyer, and I happen to know one," Stark said. He raised his coffee cup in a little salute.

"I've been keeping a pretty close eye on the investigation these past few weeks," Hallie said. "I have an old friend from law school who works in D.C. He's not in the Justice Department, but he's got a pipeline in there, and he's been monitoring the situation for me."

"He?" Stark repeated. "Old boyfriend? Somebody you used to go skinny-dipping with at Hippy Hollow there in Austin?"

He was just teasing her, but the pink glow that suddenly spread across her face told him he'd inadvertently hit the mark. She muttered, "You wouldn't think that a woman of my age who'd been married for twenty years of her life would be embarrassed by anything, would you? But yeah, I may have flirted a little on the phone with him. I figured it was for a good cause."

"Thanks, Hallie," Stark said. "I appreciate that, and I didn't mean to make you uncomfortable."

She waved that off.

"Don't worry about it, John Howard. What's important is that the whole weight of the federal government isn't going to come crashing down on you."

"I'm grateful for that too, don't get me wrong," Stark said. "There's no mess like a government mess, and I'm glad I don't have to deal with it."

"I just wanted to let you know." Hallie started to turn away, but she stopped and looked down at the newspaper sitting on the little table next to Stark's favorite recliner. She picked up the folded paper and held it so the main headline was visible. "Did you see this already?"

Stark nodded and said, "Yeah. Terrible business."

The headline read BODIES FOUND IN BURNED-OUT FARMHOUSE. That was bad enough, but the real horror was contained in the story below the headline. Stark had scanned it enough to know that volunteer firemen called to the scene of a blaze had found the bodies of a young man and a girl in the ruins of the burned house. It was pretty obvious, though, that their deaths hadn't been a result of the fire.

The heads of both bodies were missing. Someone had chopped them off, possibly with a machete, according to sheriff's department investigators. Despite that, the bodies had been identified, although those identities were being withheld pending notification of next of kin.

"We're just going to keep seeing more and more things like this," Hallie said as she set the newspaper back on the table. "Unless the government decides to secure the border and stop the cartels from moving in—"

"Might as well go check the sky for flying pigs again if you're gonna start talking like that," Stark advised her.

Hallie sighed.

"I'm afraid you're right." She put a smile back on her face. "I need to get to work. Congratulations on not being railroaded."

"I don't plan on getting too worked up about it," Stark said as he set his coffee beside the chair and opened the front door for her. "I'd like to think they backed off because they didn't have a case, but I can't help but wonder if they're up to something else."

"That's a good question," Hallie agreed. She paused on the porch. "Pop's going to be barbecuing Saturday night. I assume you and the Gomezes will be there?"

"You bet," Stark said. "I wouldn't miss one of your dad's barbecues—"

A shrill, horrified scream interrupted him.

Stark's head jerked up at the sound. The screams continued, coming from across the street. The neatly kept mobile home over there belonged to an eighty-year-old widow named Dorothy Hewitt. She had a small vegetable garden at one side of her lot, and thanks to her constant tending of it, the garden produced enough tomatoes, green beans, peppers, squash, and cabbage that everybody in this part of Shady Hills shared in the bounty.

Dorothy was standing at the edge of her garden, a hoe at her feet where she had dropped it, her hands clapped to her cheeks as she continued screaming.

Stark shouldered past Hallie and said, "Stay here!" He hit only one step on his way down to the ground. His long legs carried him at a run across the street. He heard Hallie's high heels clicking on the pavement behind him and knew she had ignored his order to stay put, which didn't particularly surprise him.

Other people were emerging from their homes, drawn by the sound of Dorothy Hewitt's screams. As far as Stark could see as he came up to the elderly woman, she was all right, just scared out of her wits as she stared into her garden. He took hold of her shoulders and turned her to face him.

"Dorothy, what is it?" he asked. "What's wrong?"

She couldn't find the words to answer, but she flapped a hand at the garden. Stark realized she was indicating a row of cabbage plants. Some of the cabbages nestled in their leafy bowers had grown pretty large.

But a couple of them were gone and had been replaced by one of the grisliest sights Stark had ever seen. Despite everything that had happened in his life, he was still shocked to the core as he stared into the empty, lifeless eyes of the two human heads that had obviously been placed with great care in Dorothy Hewitt's vegetable garden.

CHAPTER SEVEN

Hallie called her office to let her secretary know she would be late; then she took charge of Dorothy, putting an arm around the older woman's shoulders and leading her away from the garden. Stark posted himself at the edge of the street to keep everybody else away from the gruesome scene while he took his phone from his pocket and called 911.

His efforts didn't do a lot of good. People might not be able to approach the garden as long as he stood there glaring at them, but they could still look past Stark and see the grim, bloody "produce" being grown there. A few of the neighbors turned green and ran off to throw up, but more remained to stare in horrified fascination and babble questions.

Stark didn't want to look at the heads again, but he had already seen enough to know that they had belonged to a young Hispanic male and an even younger Hispanic female, and it didn't take Sherlock Holmes to figure out that they went with the two bodies that had been recovered from that burned-out farmhouse northwest of town.

Since the Shady Hills Retirement Park was located well

outside the city limits of Devil's Pass, Stark's 911 call was directed to the sheriff's department. He told the operator where he was and what Dorothy had found in her garden and was told to remain where he was.

"I don't plan on going anywhere," Stark said.

Fred Gomez and Alton Duncan came over to him. Alton said, "Hallie's got Dorothy over at my place trying to calm her down. That poor woman. What a terrible thing to find first thing in the morning."

"Or any other time," Fred added. "You know where they came from, John Howard?"

"I've got a pretty good idea," Stark said. "Have you read the morning's paper?"

Alton snapped his fingers.

"Those bodies in that house that burned," he said. "The paper said they'd been decapitated."

"This has to do with those drug gangs," Fred said, his voice trembling with anger and outrage. "You know it does."

"More than likely," Stark agreed.

"But why put them in the garden?" Alton asked. "Dorothy Hewitt doesn't have any connection whatsoever with those thugs. She's not even from around here. She just moved here after her husband died."

Stark knew the story. Dorothy and her late husband had bought a place at Shady Hills years earlier, when it first opened, thinking they would retire there. Then Dorothy's husband had died before they could do that, but she had moved in anyway, stubbornly carrying out the plan they had made back in a time when violence along the border hadn't been so prevalent.

"I don't have any explanation," Stark said. "Maybe it's just somebody's idea of a sick joke. They were driving around, looking for a place to get rid of the heads, and saw those cabbages. That could have given them the notion."

"It's a perverted notion," Fred muttered. "What's wrong with some people?"

"If we knew the answer to that and could fix it, I reckon the world would be a better place," Stark said.

Sirens wailed in the distance. A couple of minutes later a sheriff's department cruiser reached the park and turned in with a squeal of tires. People cleared the street as the car came up with its flashing lights.

A stocky deputy got out and hurried over to Stark, Fred, and Alton. He leaned to the side to look past Stark and exclaimed, "My God, those are human heads!"

"Didn't your dispatcher tell you that?" Alton asked.

"Well, yeah, but I thought I must've heard her wrong." The deputy swallowed and looked queasy. "I gotta get the sheriff out here. I don't want any responsibility for this." He started back to his car, then paused to say to the three men, "You guys stay right there."

"We're not going anywhere," Stark promised again.

During the next half hour, several more sheriff's cars showed up, as well as an ambulance. Once there were more deputies on hand, Stark and his neighbors were shooed away from the garden as the officers set up a crime scene perimeter. They went back over to Stark's mobile home, where they were joined by Fred's wife, Aurelia, and Hallie, who explained that the EMTs were checking out Dorothy Hewitt.

The five of them sat on lawn chairs in Stark's yard drinking coffee. Hallie dumped her latte and poured a cup of hot coffee from the pot in Stark's mobile home. Stark hadn't had breakfast yet, but he didn't have much of an appetite most mornings anyway, and even less of one today.

Once a couple of ice chests containing the heads were loaded in the back of the ambulance and driven away, Sheriff George Lozano came across the street. Stark had met the sheriff before and stood up to shake hands with him.

"I'd ask you how you're doing, John Howard, but after starting your morning the way you did, I expect the answer would be 'Not very good,'" Lozano said.

Stark shrugged.

"You'd be right about that, Sheriff," he said, "but I'm doing better than some."

"Yeah," Lozano said. "Jimmy Rodriguez and his little sister, Sonia."

Hallie said, "That's who those . . . those . . ."

"Yes, ma'am," Lozano said, not forcing her to finish the question. "That's not for public consumption, though. We've notified the Rodriguez family about the bodies that were found in that farmhouse, but they don't know about this yet. Neither does the news media." Lozano sighed. "Although I don't expect that to last long. I figure cell phone pictures and videos of the scene here will be showing up on the Internet in no time."

"I'd be surprised if they haven't already," Hallie said. "There were quite a few people standing around earlier."

"True," Lozano said with a resigned nod.

"I kept 'em back as much as I could," Stark said.

"That's not your job, John Howard, but I appreciate the effort anyway. Tell me what happened."

Stark went over the details of the story. It didn't take long, because he didn't really know much.

"I'm guessing those . . . remains . . . had been there for several hours," Lozano said when Stark was finished. "They must have been put in the garden during the night. Those plants around them were leafy enough that it would be hard to see them from the street unless you knew what you were looking for."

Alton said, "Quite a few people probably drove by this morning and never noticed they were there."

"That's right. But whoever put them there knew that somebody would come out to work in the garden sooner or later and find them." Lozano looked like he had bitten into something that tasted bad. "They didn't care what a shock it would be. They probably got a big laugh out of it."

"It was the drug gangs, right, Sheriff?" Fred asked.

"I can't even speculate on that right now, sir," Lozano told him.

"What about the Rodriguez boy?" Stark said. "He tied in with one of the cartels?"

Lozano shook his head.

"Sorry. I just can't get into that."

"Which means he is," Hallie said.

"You have the luxury of guessing, Ms. Duncan," the sheriff replied. "I have to concentrate on the facts our investigation turns up."

"The cartels are behind all the crime down here," Fred said. Stark heard the bitterness creeping into his friend's voice. "This used to be a decent place to live. A beautiful place. You couldn't beat the weather. Now the weather's still nice, but the criminals run everything."

Predictably, Lozano bristled.

"That's not true. They don't run the sheriff's department, and they never will as long as I'm in charge. We'll get to the bottom of this. I give you my word."

"You'd better be careful what kind of promises you make, Sheriff," Fred said. "If you give them too much trouble, they'll just get rid of you."

"Fred!" Aurelia said. "You shouldn't talk like that."

"It's true," her husband insisted. "We can't stand up to them. If we try, we end up like . . . like . . ."

He couldn't finish, but he turned his head to look across the street toward Dorothy Hewitt's vegetable garden, so they all knew what he meant.

Cross the cartels too much, and you might wind up in a cabbage patch.

Only part of you, though.

CHAPTER EIGHT

The uproar lasted the whole morning, but by afternoon all the official vehicles were gone. Dorothy Hewitt's lot had been staked and marked off with yellow crime scene tape, though, so nobody was going to forget the grim discovery that had been made there.

Nobody who had seen those heads was liable to forget them any time soon, anyway.

Fred Gomez knew he wouldn't, that was for sure. He hadn't gotten as close a look at them as Dorothy, John Howard Stark, and Hallie Duncan had, but he had seen enough to know that the grisly image was liable to haunt his dreams for some time to come. He was glad Aurelia had stayed back.

That evening she found him cleaning his gun. It was a Colt .45 automatic like the one he had carried in the Army, and as far as he was concerned it was the best handgun ever manufactured.

"What are you doing with that?" Aurelia asked.

"What does it look like I'm doing?" Fred said, then glanced up at her. "Sorry. I didn't mean for it to sound that way."

"You think you're going to need that gun?"

"It doesn't make you nervous, knowing that somebody put those . . . things . . . in Mrs. Hewitt's garden?"

"You said yourself that we can't stand up to the cartels. You think one gun is going to make any difference to them?"

Fred sighed.

"No, it won't," he admitted. "But I'm a man, Aurelia. I have to do *something*. I have to protect my home and family, or at least try to."

"You won't protect anything by getting yourself killed."

He knew she was right, but she just didn't understand. John Howard would, and so would Alton Duncan. Both of them would know why he felt this way.

He wouldn't be surprised if they were cleaning some guns tonight, too.

"I'll feel better if you put that away," Aurelia went on.

"As soon as I'm finished," Fred told her. "But I'm going to keep it handy."

"So you can have a shootout with some drug gang?"

"I'm hoping it won't come to that," Fred said.

He tensed suddenly as a knock sounded on the front door. Aurelia's head jerked toward the door. Her eyes widened in fright. Fred had removed the clip from the gun earlier, along with the round that was in the chamber. He slid the clip back in now and worked the slide as he stood up.

"Go into the bedroom," he told his wife.

She looked like she wanted to go a lot farther than that, but she shook her head stubbornly and asked, "What are you going to do?"

"I'm going to answer the door," Fred said.

"I'm not going to leave you in here by yourself."

He knew better than to argue with her. It would be a

waste of time. His hand tightened on the .45's grip. He wouldn't let anything happen to her, he told himself.

"Go stand in the kitchen, anyway," he said, and to his relief Aurelia did so. The counter between kitchen and living room wouldn't offer much protection, but it was better than nothing.

Whoever was outside had knocked only a couple of times. Maybe they had gone away, Fred thought as he moved closer to the door.

Even though the door was fairly sturdy, he knew it wouldn't stop a projectile from a high-powered weapon. It wouldn't even slow a bullet down very much. It was all he had, though. He leaned closer and listened intently, trying to tell if whoever had knocked was still out there.

The sharp rapping sounded again, this time only inches from his face. Fred jumped back. He couldn't help it.

"Who is it?" he called. He was glad his voice didn't sound as shaky as he felt. At least he hoped it didn't.

"Antonio."

That reply changed things immediately. Fred closed his eyes and heaved a sigh of relief as he recognized the voice of his grandson.

Aurelia heard it, too, and hurried out from behind the kitchen counter.

"Don't just stand there," she told her husband. "Let the boy in."

Fred lowered the Colt and undid the dead bolt and the chain with his other hand. He opened the door and said, "Antonio, what—"

That was all he got out before Antonio rushed past him, took hold of the door, and closed it quickly behind him.

Fred tensed again. Antonio was acting like trouble was right behind him.

And knowing the boy the way he did, Fred realized there was a good chance that was true.

He hated to think that about his own grandson, but he had to face facts. During the past few years, ever since Fred and Aurelia's son, Michael, and Michael's wife, Donna, had been killed in a tragic car accident, Antonio had fallen in with a bad bunch of people.

After the wreck, Antonio had come from San Antonio and lived here in this very mobile home with his grandparents for six months, since he wasn't of legal age yet, but as soon as he turned eighteen, he'd moved out to be on his own.

Fred hadn't thought that was a good idea and neither had Aurelia, but they hadn't been able to talk any sense into the boy's head. They had offered to help pay for Antonio to go to college, but he got a job in the automotive department of the local MegaMart instead and moved into an apartment of his own.

Most of the defiance Antonio had shown could be traced back to the way his father had felt about Fred and Aurelia. Michael had decided somewhere along the way that he was ashamed of his parents because they "weren't Hispanic enough," as he put it. They had spoken English at home nearly all the time Michael was growing up, and what sort of name was Fred for a proud Hispanic man, after all? That white guy on *I Love Lucy* was named Fred, for God's sake!

Their reasoning for making sure that Michael was equally fluent in both English and Spanish was so that he would never be held back in life by an inability to speak both languages. Fred had told Michael that, and Michael had seemed to understand at the time, but later he'd decided that was a betrayal of their native culture. He had listened to too many troublemakers who were more interested in being Mexican-American rather than just plain American. Michael had wound up marrying a girl who felt the same way, and they had raised their son like that. So naturally Antonio felt some resentment toward his grandparents, but they had always tried to do their best for him anyway.

They still would, Fred thought, regardless of what sort of trouble Antonio was in.

Antonio's face was drawn tight and haggard with strain. He looked older than his years tonight. The jeans and T-shirt he wore were dirty and torn, like he'd been crawling through brush. He said, "Has anybody been here looking for me?"

"No, not that I know of," Fred replied, shaking his head. He was baffled by what was going on here. "What's wrong, Antonio? Is somebody after you?"

Antonio laughed, but there wasn't a trace of humor in the sound.

"I need a place to rest for a little while, maybe something to eat," he said. "And in the morning I gotta catch a bus and get out of here."

Aurelia came over and took his arm.

"Sit down," she told him. "I'll bring you some food. And if there's a problem you'll stay right here. We'll help you."

Antonio shook his head.

"You can't help me. It'll just cause trouble for you if you try. I've got to get out of this part of the country. I need to go as far away as I can, as quick as I can."

"That's crazy!" Fred said. "Running away isn't going to solve anything."

"What are you gonna do, Grandfather?" Antonio demanded. "Fight?" He gestured at the .45 in Fred's hand. "With that old relic?"

Sudden anger coursed through Fred. He grabbed Antonio's arm and said, "Listen to me, boy. This gun may be a relic, but I am, too. That doesn't mean we can't still fight! We'll call the law. The sheriff was just out here today—"

Fred stopped short as a horrible thought blossomed in his mind. He couldn't even hardly conceive of it, but he couldn't banish the idea, no matter how much he wanted to. He had to ask in a husky half-whisper, "Antonio . . . did you have anything to do with . . . with those heads in Mrs. Hewitt's garden?"

Antonio frowned and looked genuinely confused, so much so that he didn't try to jerk his arm out of Fred's grip.

"Heads?" he repeated. "I don't know what you're talking—"

Before he could continue, tires screeched on the street outside. Antonio's head jerked up, and sheer terror flooded into his brown eyes.

CHAPTER NINE

Even though the doors and windows of the mobile home were closed, the air conditioner was humming softly, and the TV was on, playing a DVD of one of his favorite John Wayne movies, *Rio Bravo*, Stark heard the tires wailing on pavement, followed by the squeal of brakes.

Sounds like that were seldom, if ever, followed by anything good.

He pushed the stop button on the remote and got out of his chair. Another button push turned the TV off, killing the light that came from it. Stark reached over and twisted the knob on the lamp beside his recliner, turning it off as well. Except for the faint glow of a night-light coming through the open bathroom door, the mobile home was dark.

Stark went to the front window. He didn't have to be able to see to move around inside the mobile home. He'd always had the knack of knowing his surroundings. That had led some of the men he'd served with in Vietnam to claim that he could see in the dark, like a cat.

Stark used his right hand to flick aside the curtain so he could look out. His left reached down to close around the barrel of the shotgun he had leaned against the wall next to the door. He didn't have to be able to see to do that, either. He instinctively knew where his weapons were.

He didn't normally keep his shotgun by the door like that. Since moving here to Shady Hills he hadn't seen the need for it, although there was a loaded pistol in the night-stand drawer next to his bed. He knew that if he ever found himself in need of a gun, he probably wouldn't have time to rustle around and hunt one up, then load it.

After the gruesome business of the heads being left in Dorothy Hewitt's garden, though, Stark had decided it might be wise to take more precautions. Chances were that the murderous varmints who'd left the heads there wouldn't ever come back to the retirement park, but that possibility couldn't be ruled out entirely.

Somebody was here who wasn't supposed to be, that was for sure, Stark thought as he moved the curtain aside. Nobody who lived in the park would be driving like that.

Headlights set on bright blazed out from the car that had come to a stop in front of the Gomez house next door. In the reflected glow of those lights, Stark saw three fig-ures crossing the yard toward the mobile home. Two of them were slender, almost whippet-thin. The third was taller and bulkier, hulking like a bear. As far as Stark could tell they weren't armed, but he knew better than to believe that. The loose shirts they wore probably concealed pistols and knives.

Stark was willing to bet that the three men didn't have any business coming to the home of Fred and Aurelia Gomez. Their grandson, Antonio, was about the same age as these visitors, but Stark had met Antonio a few times and was sure he wasn't one of this trio.

Antonio might still have something to do with this, Stark thought. Fred had confided to Stark that he was worried about the sort of people the youngster spent his time with. These three certainly looked like bad news.

Fred and Aurelia might need his help, Stark decided. But if he went out the front door, he'd probably attract the attention of the three strangers.

Taking the shotgun with him, he went out the back door instead, moving with the sort of quiet intensity that had kept him alive on numerous occasions in the jungles of Southeast Asia.

He cut across the yard between the two mobile homes and crouched behind some shrubs. One of the strangers pounded on the door. Stark heard Fred's voice come from inside in response, but he couldn't make out the words.

"We're looking for Antonio," the stranger said.

This time Stark understood as Fred said, "He's not here."

"We know better, old man. Let us in. Antonio's our amigo. We just want to talk to him."

Stark didn't believe that for a second, and he figured Fred was smart enough not to believe it, either.

"You'd better leave now!" Fred shouted. "I told you Antonio's not here. I've already called the sheriff!"

"The sheriff?" The one who appeared to be the ringleader of the trio laughed. "What have we done, old man? We just asked if our friend was here, that's all."

"I've got a gun!" Fred's voice shook a little with fear, but it had determination in it, too.

That threat brought wheezing laughter from the biggest member of the trio. He asked, "You want me to kick the door down, Nacho?"

"No, the crazy old hombre might really have a gun. No point in any of us taking a chance on getting hurt." The one called Nacho paused, evidently to think over the situation. "Go around back and bust in that way, Chuckie. They won't be expecting you."

"Then what?"

"Then we take Antonio with us and teach him he can't run out on us, the—" Nacho added some vile curses in Spanish.

With the heavy footsteps of a big, clumsy man, Chuckie came down the steps from the Gomez porch and started around the mobile home. Stark drew back deeper in the shrubs, completely hidden in the thick shadows. Chuckie rounded the corner and started toward him.

Stark let the big man move past him. Then Stark stepped out, lifted the shotgun, and drove the butt stock against the back of Chuckie's head. He hoped Chuckie had a thick skull. Whether he did or not, the son of a gun was just too big to take any chances with.

The thud was loud enough to be heard out front, but the one called Nacho was talking again, probably to distract Fred and whoever else was inside from Chuckie's attempt to break in. That effort was going to backfire, because Chuckie had fallen to his knees and now pitched forward onto his face without making a sound.

Stark rested the shotgun barrel against the back of Chuckie's neck and reached down with his other hand to search for a pulse. He found one. Chuckie was out cold but still alive.

Stark straightened and glided to the corner of the mobile home. On the porch, Nacho called, "We're gettin' tired of waiting, old man. Open up and send Antonio out here now. Nobody gets hurt."

Stark stepped out into the open, brought the shotgun to his shoulder, and leveled it at the intruders.

"That's right," he said. "Nobody gets hurt as long as you leave now."

The third man, the one who hadn't said anything so far, turned toward Stark and his hand started toward his waist. He stopped short when he saw the shotgun pointing at them.

"Jalisco!" Nacho said.

"Not good," the one called Jalisco said. "He's too close. He can blow us both apart with one shot."

"That's right," Stark said. "I won't lose any sleep over doing it, either."

"Where's my brother?" Nacho demanded.

"Chuckie? He's sleeping. You'll need to come get him and haul him back to your car." Stark's voice hardened. "Then you need to haul ass out of here while you still can."

"You don't know what you're doin', *viejo*," Nacho said softly. "You don't know what you're gettin' in here."

"Maybe not, but I do know exactly how much pressure it takes on the trigger of this gun to make it go off . . . and it's not far from it." Without lowering the shotgun, Stark moved to the side, closer to the street. "Come get your friend. Now."

Enough light spilled over the yard from the headlights for Stark to see that Nacho was seething with rage at being defied this way. Jalisco was colder, more calculating, and therefore probably more dangerous, Stark thought. He watched both of them very closely.

Finally, Nacho said, "We'll go. But we'll be back."

"Don't bother," Stark told him. "There's nothing here for you."

"That's where you're wrong, old man." Nacho jerked his head at his companion. "Let's get Chuckie." He blustered at Stark, "He better be all right. He's my brother."

The two of them came down the steps. Stark tracked them with the shotgun's barrel as they went to the side of the mobile home, bent down to take hold of Chuckie's legs, and then dragged him across the yard to the car parked at the curb. With grunts of effort, they lifted the big, senseless form and let Chuckie tumble through the open door into the backseat. Stark kept them covered the whole time.

Jalisco slid behind the wheel. Nacho went around to the passenger door. He opened it and yelled across the top of the car, "This ain't over, old man! It ain't anywhere close to over!"

Then he jerked a revolver from the sagging waistband of his trousers and opened fire.

CHAPTER TEN

Stark had been expecting a move like that, so he was ready for it. He dropped to one knee as two shots blasted from Nacho's gun. The bullets were already going high because Nacho had rushed the shots. They whined well over Stark's head.

Stark was in the habit of always being aware of his surroundings and being aware of where he was in relation to other things. He knew that Nacho's bullets would pass harmlessly between his mobile home and that of the Gomezes. Backing up to both of their lots was a big sheet-metal shed where the owners of the park stored mowers and other equipment. The bullets would hit that shed without hurting anything.

The butt of the shotgun was socketed firmly against Stark's shoulder. He pulled the trigger an instant after the shots spouted from Nacho's gun. Buckshot smashed into the side of the car. Behind the wheel, Jalisco let out of a yell and tromped the gas. Nacho had to dive through the open passenger door to avoid being left behind as the car leaped ahead with its powerful engine roaring and wailing like a banshee.

Stark pumped the shotgun and fired again as he tracked the car. Both taillights went out as the buckshot smashed them to smithereens.

A door slammed, and Stark glanced over his shoulder to see Fred Gomez charging out of his house. Fred came to a stop, thrust out the .45 automatic he held in his right hand, and gripped his wrist with his left hand to steady it as he fired three shots after the speeding car.

If this had been a movie, the car would have blown up as one of those bullets struck its gas tank. Stark knew that in real life, that was practically impossible, so he wasn't surprised when the car careened around a corner with screeching tires and accelerated away into the night like the proverbial bat out of hell.

It was possible that one of Fred's shots had penetrated the back window and done some damage, though. Stark supposed they'd have to settle for that.

His ears were ringing a little from the racket. As the echoes of the shots began to die away, Fred said, "My God, John, thank you! I don't know what would have happened if you hadn't shown up when you did."

Stark straightened and pumped another shell into the shotgun's chamber just in case Nacho, Jalisco, and Chuckie came back. He thought that was pretty unlikely, but it was better to be prepared.

"People will be calling to report those shots," he said, "so I'll ask you this while I've got the chance, Fred. Is Antonio in your house?"

Fred opened his mouth to reply, then closed it without saying anything. Stark had a hunch his friend had been about to lie to him but couldn't bring himself to do it.

"Yeah, he's here," Fred said after a couple of seconds. "He showed up a little while ago. He's in some sort of trouble, John, and he needs help."

"With varmints like that after him, I'd say he must be. You know what it's about?"

"Not really," Fred replied with a shake of his head, and Stark thought he was telling the truth.

"Let's go have a talk with him and see if we can't figure something out."

Fred looked like he wasn't sure about that suggestion.

Before they could move, Alton Duncan came trotting up, carrying a .22 rifle.

"Hey, are you guys all right?" Alton asked.

"We're fine," Stark said. "Some fellas tried to break into Fred's house."

"A home invasion?"

"Something like that, I expect." Stark didn't want to spread word of Antonio's connection to the trouble until he knew what was going on. "I heard the commotion and stepped out to see what the trouble was."

"I already called 911, and I imagine plenty of other people did, too, when they heard that shooting. The deputies ought to be here pretty soon."

"We'll be glad to talk to them, but we don't know much," Fred said. "All I'm sure of is that those guys probably would have gotten in my house if John Howard hadn't showed up to run them off."

Alton nodded and said, "I'm glad it wasn't any worse than that. You want me to hang around and keep an eye out?"

"No, they took off in a hurry," Stark said. "They won't be back any time soon."

"I hope not." Alton scrubbed a hand over his face. "It used to be so peaceful around here, and then suddenly it's like . . ."

"A war zone?" Stark suggested as Alton's voice trailed off.

"Yeah. I didn't want to say it, but . . . yeah."

Stark understood the feeling. He hoped he was wrong, but he had a hunch things were going to get worse before they got better.

For the time being, though, he wanted some answers. Maybe Fred's troubles weren't any of his business, but he'd just been shot at, so he figured that gave him a few rights.

"Okay," Alton went on. "If you need my help, just give me a holler."

"Sure," Fred said. "Thanks."

He waited until Alton was gone, then continued, "Antonio's not going to like it if I bring a stranger into this."

"Antonio and I aren't strangers. We've met before."

"Yeah, but he doesn't really know you. And you're white. I'm afraid my son and his wife, God rest their souls, raised him to be suspicious of anybody who isn't Latino. I don't know if he'll open up with you around."

"Let's give it a try," Stark said.

"All right. Come on." Fred smiled faintly. "After what you did, the least I can do to repay you is offer you a beer."

"And I'll take it," Stark told him with a smile of his own.

They went up the steps and into the mobile home. Aurelia stood with her hands resting on the kitchen counter, looking scared.

"Are they gone?" she asked.

"Long gone," Fred told her.

"When you went charging out there with that gun like . . . like the Lone Ranger, I didn't think I'd ever see you alive again."

"You know better than that. Anyway, it was more like I was the Cisco Kid."

"Don't joke!" Aurelia said. "This is serious business."

"It is," Fred agreed, growing solemn. "Where's Antonio?"

"He's in his old room. He wanted to go out the back door and run, but I begged him to stay and tell us what's wrong."

"I hope he didn't climb out the window," Fred muttered as he led Stark along the hall toward the bedrooms. "When somebody gets scared enough, they don't think straight. They do just the opposite of what they ought to."

Stark knew that was right. He hoped Antonio hadn't fled into the night, too. They couldn't help him if he had.

Antonio was still there, standing in the darkened room. Enough light came in from the hallway that Stark could see the knife clutched in the young man's hand.

"It's just me, Antonio," Fred said. "It's all right. Those men are gone."

"They'll come back," Antonio said, his voice drawn tight with strain. "Who's that with you?"

"It's John Howard Stark, Antonio," Stark said. He kept the shotgun pointed at the floor. He didn't want Antonio to feel any more threatened than he already did. "We've met a few times. I live next door to your grandparents."

"John Howard saved us all," Fred said. "He ran those men off."

"They're still alive?"

"Yeah, as far as we know."

Antonio said, "Then all you really did was sign your death warrant, Señor Stark. Because they won't stop now until they've killed you."

CHAPTER ELEVEN

As the car roared through the night, Nacho Montez pounded the dashboard in frustration and ripped out curse after curse in Spanish. It was bad enough that they hadn't gotten their hands on Antonio, but to be chased off by some old gringo . . . it was a blow from which Nacho's pride would be a long time recovering.

The only way to fix it was to kill the old man, to kill Antonio and his grandparents, to kill everybody in that whole damned retirement park if they had to.

"Settle down," Jalisco said. "We know where he is now. If he tries to leave we'll know it, and we can take care of him then."

"We don't know for sure he's there," Nacho said.

"If he wasn't, his grandfather wouldn't have acted the way he did. Antonio's there, all right. That's why I called Señor Espantoso and asked him to have men watch the park all the time."

Nacho drew in a deep breath. Jalisco was right, he told himself.

In the backseat, Chuckie groaned. He was starting to

come around after being knocked out by the old gringo. He had a lot to be ashamed of, too, Nacho thought.

"If Chuckie had just put those damned heads in the right place instead of across the street—"

"He got a little turned around," Jalisco said. "It can happen, especially in a place like that where so many of the houses look the same."

The heads had been intended to send a message. A warning to Antonio that his grandparents would pay the price if his former friends were forced to hunt him down. He would hear about it and know that he'd better turn himself in.

Of course it hadn't worked out that way. Chuckie had left the heads at the wrong house . . . in a vegetable garden, of all things! Despite that, the grisly warning might have worked since it was right across the street from Antonio's grandparents' home. Obviously, Antonio had been lying low all day and hadn't heard about it.

Then somebody, one of the many sets of eyes who worked for Señor Espantoso, had spotted him heading for the retirement park, and Nacho, Jalisco, and Chuckie had been sent to get him. After all, it was their fault he had gotten away in the first place. It was their responsibility to bring him in before he could do any damage.

Not that he could really hurt the cartel's operation. It was too big for that now. Too many officials had been paid off, and too many people were scared. Antonio was just a minor annoyance, but he needed to be taken care of anyway.

Chuckie sat up in the backseat, muttering curses. After a moment, he said, "Wha' happened? Where's Antonio? Didn't we get him?"

"No, we didn't get him," Nacho snapped at his dim-witted brother. "You let some old man knock you out.

Then he threatened us with a shotgun and made us put you back in the car."

"Why didn't you just shoot him?" Chuckie asked. He sounded genuinely puzzled.

"We tried, you . . ." Nacho lapsed into cursing again.

"You shouldn't talk to me like that," Chuckie said. "I'm your brother."

"Don't remind me!"

Jalisco looked at the rearview mirror and said, "*Policia*."

Nacho twisted around in the passenger seat to look behind them. Flashing red and blue lights were coming up fast.

"I'm not surprised. That old gringo bastard blew out our taillights." He looked at Jalisco. "Pull over."

"I can outrun him," Jalisco said.

"No. Pull over."

"If they run the plates, they'll see they're not from this car. They'll see the damage from those shotgun blasts."

"Do you care?"

A smile curved Jalisco's thin lips. "Not really."

"Well, then, pull over."

Jalisco guided the car to the side of the road. The lights of Devil's Pass were visible in the distance, but this stretch of roadway was dark and deserted for the most part.

The sheriff's cruiser pulled up behind the stopped car. Two deputies were in it. The driver got out and approached Jalisco, resting his hand on the butt of his revolver as he did so. The other deputy got out of the car but stayed behind his open door. He played a handheld spotlight over the car. Nacho and Jalisco were visible, holding their hands in plain sight.

The deputy spotted the damage the buckshot had done

to the side of the vehicle. He said, "You fellas look like you've been in a war—"

Chuckie rose up from the floorboard in the backseat then, in response to a hissed command from Nacho, and cut loose through the lowered window with the automatic weapon that chattered and jumped in his big hands. The stream of bullets tore the deputy almost in half.

Even as the first deputy died, Nacho and Jalisco were out of the car, twisting and opening fire on the second lawman, who managed only to draw his revolver before slugs punched into his chest and drove him backward. He stumbled and fell. Nacho raced back alongside the cars and shot the deputy twice more in the head.

The whole thing had taken seven seconds.

When they drove away a few minutes later, after dousing the sheriff's cruiser with gasoline and setting it on fire, Nacho felt a little better.

He was ready to face Señor Espantoso now and tell him that Antonio Gomez was bottled up at the Shady Hills Retirement Park.

CHAPTER TWELVE

Tomás Beredo had gotten the nickname "Espantoso" when he was little more than a boy, because there were few places he could not get into and out of without ever being seen, like a ghost. Espantoso didn't translate literally as "ghost," but it referred to something horrible and dreadful, so many people used it that way. Beredo liked it for one simple reason.

The more people who were afraid of him, the better.

He had grown into a handsome man whose sleek good looks gave no real clue to the ruthlessness within him. Personally, he had killed seventeen men, four women, and six children. He had ordered the deaths of many more; he had no idea of the exact number. It wasn't worth keeping up with. Over the past ten years he had risen steadily in the ranks of the cartel for which he worked, until he had reached a position of responsibility for operations in a section of the border between Texas and Mexico that stretched for more than two hundred miles. The amount of narco-trafficking in this area was impressive, but it could always be better.

Now the men Beredo worked for had sent this . . . this

man Patel to him. This beast. Beredo was supposed to impress him with the efficiency of the cartel's setup, because there was an agreement pending between the cartel and Hezbollah, the organization Gabir Patel belonged to. The Islamic terrorists had already invested heavily in the Brazilian and Colombian cocaine industries. That was the way they all thought of it these days, in business terms. Now Hezbollah was considering expanding its reach into the Mexican cartels, an alliance that could make billions of dollars for both sides. *If* Beredo could convince Patel that it was a good idea.

Which meant it was a bad time for all this trouble among his low-level employees.

"Tell them to wait," Beredo snapped to the man who'd brought him the word that Nacho Montez, his idiot brother, and the gunslinger Jalisco were back. The only one Beredo had any respect for was Jalisco, who had been sent up here because he had killed too many federal officers in his hometown and his bosses there thought it would be wise to let the heat die down for a while. The Montez brothers were buffoons who were dangerous enough in a crude way, as long as they could smash their way through obstacles without having to actually think about what they were doing. But when it came to strategy . . . well, they wouldn't be in the trouble they were in if they were any good at that.

"If you need to speak to these men, by all means go ahead," Patel said.

Beredo shook his head.

"It can wait," he said. "A minor matter, that's all."

Patel scratched at his jaw, which always seemed to sport a dark patina of beard stubble even five minutes after he'd shaved, and said, "No, go ahead. I'd like to see how you handle your subordinates."

Beredo swallowed the anger that tried to well up his throat. Patel was infuriatingly smug, but the hombres in Mexico City wanted him kept happy, so Beredo would do his best.

He gave the guard a curt nod and said, "Bring them in."

They were in Beredo's new headquarters, a sprawling stucco ranch house several miles north of the border. The ranch had a number of barns and outbuildings that were good for storing drugs, as well as its own airstrip, and the house was luxuriously furnished. The increased smuggling and the attendant rise in other criminal activities had led the owner to sell it. The sale to a dummy corporation had been handled through Victor Martinez, and Beredo had moved in not long afterward. It made him feel good to know that he was operating on the Texas side of the border, right under the noses of the arrogant, idiotic Americans. If they only knew how futile their efforts to stop the smuggling really were! If they only knew how little so many of those in their own government really cared!

Patel seemed impressed with the surroundings. He and Beredo were sitting in the big living room with one wall of floor-to-ceiling windows that overlooked the swimming pool, which was lit up as bright as day so the men inside had no trouble admiring the sight of half a dozen beautiful, naked young women enjoying the pool. Later, Patel would have his choice of the women, since he was not so devout in his religion as to prefer such pleasures in the afterlife. He could even have all six of them if he wanted, although Beredo had serious doubts that the man possessed enough masculine ability to satisfy even one of them. So many of those Arabs seemed to be more interested in young boys, Beredo thought.

A pair of guards carrying automatic weapons brought the three visitors into the room. Despite the fact that the

Montez brothers and Jalisco worked for the cartel, they had been searched and disarmed before they were escorted in. Only Beredo's personal guards were allowed to carry weapons anywhere near him.

Beredo leaned back in the overstuffed chair where he sat, casually cocked his right ankle on his left knee, and made them wait while he sipped from a glass of sparkling water. In deference to his Muslim guest, he wasn't drinking tequila tonight. Finally he asked, "Has the matter been taken care of, Ignacio?"

Nacho Montez looked nervous. He licked his lips before answering, "We ran into an unexpected difficulty, señor."

Beredo sat up straighter and frowned in displeasure.

"What sort of difficulty?" he demanded.

"Antonio was at his grandparents' house, as we expected, but when we went there to get him, one of the neighbors interfered. We were forced to leave without Antonio."

Beredo suppressed the impulse to throw his glass to the floor so that it shattered. Such a gesture was too melodramatic, although it would have felt good.

"One man? One man forced you to fail at your assignment?"

"He had a shotgun," Nacho said sullenly. "We tried to kill him, but—"

Beredo silenced Nacho with a curt gesture.

"But you failed," he said.

Jalisco said, "We have men watching the trailer park. If Antonio tries to leave, they'll let us know."

Beredo was aware that Patel was watching him closely. He set his glass aside and stood up. Clasping his hands behind his back, he walked closer to the three men. The big one who went by the ridiculous name Chuckie looked like he wanted to run.

"Do you have any idea who this one man who made you flee was?" Beredo asked.

Nacho didn't answer, but Jalisco did.

"I got a good enough look at him to recognize him from the TV news. His name is Stark."

Beredo stiffened. He knew the name, but he wanted to make sure they were talking about the same man.

"John Howard Stark?"

Jalisco nodded and said, "Sí, Señor Espantoso."

Stark, the man responsible for the death of the legendary cartel kingpin Ernesto Diego Espinoza Ramirez, better known as the Vulture. Stark, one of the heroes of the so-called Second Battle of the Alamo. Stark, the man who only recently had defied three very, very low-level associates of the cartel and been hailed as a hero once again.

Nostrils flaring, Beredo drew in a deep breath, then smiled and said quietly, "Well. This changes everything."

CHAPTER THIRTEEN

"You'd better talk fast, Antonio," Stark advised in a hard voice. "The cops will be here soon, and if you don't tell me what's going on here, I'll have to turn you over to them."

"John, you wouldn't!" Fred exclaimed.

"I don't like being shot at," Stark said, keeping his voice flat. "Especially when I don't know the reason."

He didn't really plan on turning Antonio over to the authorities, and he would make that clear to Fred and Aurelia later on. He had sensed, though, that the young man might be stubborn about revealing the truth, and Stark wanted to shock him out of that stance. He knew he would stand a lot better chance of being able to help if Antonio would come clean with him.

Antonio still didn't say anything, so Stark made a guess.

"This has something to do with those heads that showed up in Dorothy Hewitt's garden this morning, doesn't it?" he prodded. "The men who put them there were supposed to leave them over here as a warning to your grandparents, but they got the wrong house."

A sigh came from Antonio. He said, "Poor Sonia."

"That's the girl who was killed?"

"Sonia Rodriguez. She . . . she didn't have anything to do with the whole business. She just happened to be with her brother, Jimmy, at the wrong time."

Stark could tell that the truth was ready to come spilling out of Antonio. It would be a relief to the young man. However, before he could ask any more questions sirens sounded outside, quickly growing louder and then stopping abruptly.

"Stay here," Stark told the young man.

"You're not going to turn me in?"

Instead of answering, Stark looked at Antonio's grandparents and said, "It was just a simple attempted robbery. Some men tried to force their way in, I heard the commotion and hurried over, and we ran them off. Right, Fred?"

Fred swallowed hard and nodded.

"Right," he said. "Thank you, John Howard."

"Let's go talk to the cops," Stark said.

They left the weapons inside the house and stepped out onto the porch to meet the sheriff's deputies who were crossing the lawn toward them with hands on their guns.

"Show 'em your hands, Fred," Stark said quietly. He stood with his own empty hands in plain sight. After what had happened here at Shady Hills this morning, it was likely that a report of shots fired would put the deputies on edge.

"Is one of you the homeowner?" one of the deputies asked as they came to a halt about a dozen feet away.

"I am," Fred said. "Fred Gomez."

"Who are you, sir?" the deputy asked as he turned his attention to Stark.

"John Howard Stark. I live next door."

"What happened here? We got a report that there was a lot of shooting."

"Some thugs tried to break into my house," Fred said. "They were yelling and threatening to kick down my door. Mr. Stark heard them and came over to help me. We chased them away."

"How many were there?" the deputy asked.

"Three."

"And they ran away from the two of you?" The deputy sounded dubious as he asked the question. He didn't actually call them old farts, but that was the impression Stark got.

"We were armed," Stark said. "I had a shotgun, and Mr. Gomez had a pistol. The weapons are inside if you want to examine them. I discharged two rounds, and I believe Mr. Gomez did, as well."

"The intruders returned fire?"

"No, we did," Stark said. "They started shooting first when they got back in their car. You can probably find some brass in the street."

"Is it all right if Deputy Conners goes inside to look at those weapons?"

"Sure," Fred said. "My wife is in there. Should she come out here?"

The deputy who'd been doing the talking nodded and said, "Yeah, we'll want to ask her some questions, too." To his companion he added, "Ted, go check out those guns."

Fred turned and called through the open door, "Aurelia, can you come out here?"

He glanced at Stark, who understood the worry he saw in his friend's eyes. Fred was concerned that the deputy would find Antonio hiding in there, which would cast doubt on their story. At this point, though, all they could do was hope that the deputy would just take a look at the shotgun and pistol and see that they supported the story Stark and Fred had told.

Aurelia appeared in the doorway, looking shaken and nervous. Nothing wrong with that, thought Stark. Anyone who'd just been the near victim of a home invasion would be upset. That was understandable.

Stark, Fred, and Aurelia went down the steps to talk to the first deputy while the other one went into the house. All three of them were relieved when he came back out almost immediately carrying Stark's shotgun and Fred's .45.

Both deputies examined the weapons for several minutes and seemed to be satisfied with what they found. They set the guns on the front porch.

Then the spokesman said, "Take me through the story again. Mrs. Gomez, why don't you tell me your version of it?"

Aurelia handled herself well, keeping things simple and sticking to the "facts," as Stark had laid them out quickly in Antonio's old bedroom. The story they told the deputies was in fact true, except that they didn't say anything about Antonio or the real reason the three intruders had shown up.

"You know, the sheriff's department was out here this morning on another call," the lead deputy mused. He inclined his head toward Dorothy Hewitt's place. "It was a pretty bad one, too."

"We know," Stark said. "We all talked to Sheriff Lozano while he was here."

"Do you think what happened tonight had any connection to that other incident?"

This was the first time they'd actually had to lie. Fred stayed calm and said, "I don't see how. But I'll tell you, I'm starting to wonder if I want to keep on living here. I mean, first that horrible business right across the street and now this tonight . . . things didn't use to be so bad around here, that's for sure."

"You're right about that, Mr. Gomez," the deputy agreed. "Can you describe the vehicle those men were in? You didn't happen to get a license plate number, did you?"

"No, it was too dark to read the plate," Fred said.

"You can look for a car with a lot of buckshot holes in the driver's side and the rear," Stark added dryly. "It was big and loud. A muscle car."

"And a low rider," Fred said. "Dark. Blue or gray, I'd say. Not black." He shook his head. "I'm sorry I can't tell you the make or model. I was too scared and upset to notice all those details."

Stark agreed with that. The deputy was making a few notes in his notebook when the radio squawked through the cruiser's open door. The other deputy went to answer the call, then a moment later popped out of the cruiser and yelled, "Bennie, come on! Officers down!"

The deputy snapped his notebook closed and said hurriedly, "You folks are all right now?"

"We're fine, Deputy," Stark said. "Go on and answer that call."

The deputy ran to the car. His partner was already behind the wheel. With lights still flashing, the cruiser swung around in a wide turn, causing some of the bystanders who'd come out to see what all the commotion was about to get out of the way in a hurry, and then roared back toward the park entrance.

"That went about as well as we could hope," Stark said. "Now let's go inside and find out the rest of the story."

CHAPTER FOURTEEN

Although Stark thought it was unlikely with the deputies right outside, there was a chance Antonio had climbed out the window and taken off. When they got inside, he was relieved to see that that wasn't the case. Antonio emerged tentatively from the bedroom when Fred called out that everything was okay.

"Not hardly," Antonio said, his face set in grim lines. "Nothing is okay."

"Let me get some coffee for everyone," Aurelia said. "Then you can tell us all about it."

Antonio still looked like he wanted to bolt, but he sat down on the sofa, perched nervously at the front of the seat cushion with his hands clasped together between his knees. Stark thought the boy looked like he'd been to hell and back.

Fred sat down beside Antonio, being careful not to get too close and crowd him. Stark took an armchair across from them. The shotgun and Fred's pistol lay on the coffee table in front of the sofa. Stark wouldn't have put the guns there, but Aurelia had said it was all right since the table had a cloth on it.

Aurelia brought cups of coffee for everyone, then sat down on the other side of Antonio. She patted his knee and said, "Whatever you have to tell us, you know it'll be all right. It won't change how we feel about you."

Antonio let out a hollow laugh.

"I wouldn't be too sure about that," he said. "I . . . I was there last night . . . when Jimmy and his little sister were . . . killed."

"Did you do it?" Fred asked. His voice was as hollow as Antonio's laugh had been.

"No!" Antonio shook his head firmly. "No, of course not."

Aurelia muttered thanks to the Blessed Virgin in Spanish.

"When I saw what was happening, I . . . I ran," Antonio went on.

"That's good," Fred told him. "I never thought you'd have anything to do with something like that."

"No, it's not good!" Antonio burst out. "Didn't you hear me? I saw them shoot Jimmy. I knew they were going to kill Sonia. And I ran! I just tried to save myself!"

Stark could see the torture the young man was going through. He didn't agree with any of Antonio's decisions, but he also knew it was impossible to walk in anybody else's shoes and inhabit his soul.

"Was it the three who were here tonight?" he asked quietly.

Antonio swallowed and nodded.

"Nacho Montez and his brother, Chuckie. And the other one, the one who . . . who looks like the grim reaper, he's called Jalisco."

"What would they have done if you'd tried to stop them?"

"They would have killed me," Antonio answered without hesitation.

"Then there would have been three folks dead instead of two," Stark said. "You couldn't have saved the girl."

"I could have *tried*!"

Stark knew that's exactly what he would have done, if he'd been in Antonio's place. But he didn't see what good it would do to say that.

"What was it all about?" Fred asked. "Was it drugs?"

"Of course," Antonio answered with a bitter edge in his voice. "That's what it's always about now, isn't it? Jimmy, he worked for the same bunch that Nacho and Jalisco do. He helped bring the stuff across the border. But the bosses—the hombres, Nacho always calls them—they thought Jimmy was keeping some of the money for himself. Not much, but some."

"And they can't abide that," Stark said.

Antonio shook his head and said, "No. Nacho told me we had to teach Jimmy a lesson. Make an example of him so nobody else would try to do what they thought he was doing. So he told me I was going to beat Jimmy up."

"You work for those monsters?" Aurelia asked, unable to keep the horror out of her voice.

"No . . . yes . . . I don't know! I thought Nacho was my friend. He kept trying to get me to work with him. . . . He said I could make a lot of money. . . . So finally I agreed to help them out with this job. It was going to be the first thing I did for the hombres. I thought it would be all right as long as I didn't have to hurt anybody too bad . . . But then when we got there, Nacho gave me his gun. He wanted me to . . . shoot Jimmy."

Aurelia covered her mouth with her hand. Her eyes were wide with shock and disbelief.

"I wouldn't do it," Antonio said. "I dropped the gun.

And then Nacho went crazy and Jimmy tried to run and Jalisco shot him . . . While that was going on I ran out into the brush and headed for the highway. . . ."

He let out a long, shuddery sigh, unable, for the moment, to go on.

The four of them sat in silence for several long seconds. Finally Stark asked, "When was this, last night?"

Antonio nodded.

"I hitched a ride with a trucker, but I had him let me off before we got to town. I know the cartel has eyes and ears everywhere. They even have little kids, schoolkids, working for them! I remembered this little creek with a deep gully, so I hid out there during the day. I knew they'd be looking for me. Then when it got dark I came across country to get here. I hoped I could get some money, maybe a little food, and catch a bus up north to someplace where they couldn't find me."

"You didn't think about the fact that they'd probably be watching your grandparents' place?" Stark asked.

"I was too scared to think. I just wanted to get away." Antonio looked back and forth between Fred and Aurelia. "I'm sorry. I never meant to bring trouble down on you."

"It's all right," Aurelia told him. She looked shaken but resolute. "We'll call the law now, talk to the sheriff—"

"No!" Antonio shook his head emphatically. "I can't risk that."

"Surely the sheriff can keep you safe," Fred said. "They can put you in protective custody."

"The sheriff's department is full of people who work for the cartel. I wouldn't last a day in protective custody."

"That can't be true," Aurelia said.

"It is," Antonio insisted.

Fred looked over at Stark and asked, "What do you think, John Howard?"

Stark drew in a deep breath and let it out.

"I think the boy's right," he said. "Maybe it's not quite as bad in the sheriff's department as he makes out. I'm convinced George Lozano's an honest man and tries to run an honest department. But these hombres, as he calls 'em, are bound to have men in there. And they can bring a hell of a lot of pressure to bear when they want to. It'd be dangerous for Antonio to turn himself in."

"You see?" Antonio said. "I need to run." He laughed humorlessly again. "That's how all this started, with me running. That's how it'll end."

"No, you're gonna stay put right here until we figure out what to do," Stark said.

"Here?" Fred asked.

"You may get tired of being cooped up, Antonio, but they can't be sure you're here," Stark went on. "If you stay out of sight, maybe they'll get tired of looking for you and figure you already left the country somehow."

"That's what I should have done," Antonio said bitterly. "I should have hitched a ride on a truck and not stopped until it was a long way out of Texas."

"That's no way to live," Stark told him. "Just hunker down for a while. I'll talk to a friend of mine. She's a lawyer, and she's pretty smart."

"What if Nacho and the others come back? They're not gonna give up, you know. And now they've got even more of a reason to want to cause trouble. They've got a grudge against you, Mr. Stark."

Stark chuckled.

"If I lost much sleep over everybody who's got a grudge against me, I'd be mighty tired," he said. He looked meaningfully at the guns on the coffee table. "If they come back, I guess we'll just have to be ready for them."

CHAPTER FIFTEEN

Señor Espantoso walked over to a large fancy table with a map spread out on it. Paperweights held down the corners. From the looks of it, the señor had been pointing out things on the map to his visitor, Nacho thought.

Nacho had never seen the man before. He was large and balding, though the hair he had left was thick and dark, only lightly streaked with silver. The same was true of the man's mustache. He stood to the side as Señor Espantoso motioned for Nacho and Jalisco to join him.

Chuckie wasn't paying attention to anything inside the room anymore. He was staring out through the glass doors at the naked women around the pool with a lustful expression on his face, totally enraptured by the sight. Since he was busy with that, Nacho didn't interrupt him. Besides, Chuckie wasn't really bright enough to grasp whatever it was Señor Espantoso intended to tell them.

"Look," the señor said as he jabbed an elegantly manicured fingernail at the map. "What do you see, Ignacio?"

Nacho leaned over slightly to study the map, proud that Señor Espantoso evidently was going to ask his opinion about something. He looked at the markings on the map and after a moment said, "Those are the routes we use to transport the drugs."

The señor drew his fingernail around an area on the map northwest of Devil's Pass where there were no marks.

"And this?"

Nacho's jaw tightened. He answered, "Shady Hills Retirement Park."

"Exactly." Señor Espantoso smiled. "You see how sometimes events converge? You want revenge on Antonio Gomez because he let you down, because what he did was tantamount to a betrayal of us and our cause. You want revenge on this man Stark because he defied you, and the hombres in Mexico City would like him dead as well because he has been a great annoyance in the past. And I . . ." Señor Espantoso tapped the map again. "I want this land. It sits in the middle of a corridor that is already mostly under our control. With it we could move our product more swiftly and efficiently. Do you follow what I'm saying, Ignacio?"

Nacho licked his lips. He thought he knew what the señor was getting at, but he wasn't sure. . . .

"Of course, señor," he said anyway. It wouldn't do to let this man know that he didn't understand.

"The people who live here in this . . . Shady Hills . . ." Espantoso's lip curled in contempt. "They are all old, true?"

"A few younger ones, I think, who take care of elderly relatives, but mostly yes, señor, they are old."

"Old and easily frightened. So that is your job, Ignacio. Frighten them." The señor's hand clenched into a fist and smashed down on the map. "Make of this Shady Hills Retirement Park a living hell so that its residents will flee. Those who survive, anyway. Can you do that?"

"Of course, señor," Nacho answered without hesitation. "What about Antonio?"

Espantoso waved a hand dismissively.

"Antonio Gomez means nothing anymore. Kill him if you find him. He makes a good excuse. But there are two things I really want." He pointed again. "This land." His hand clenched once more into a fist. "And John Howard Stark's head, so I can put it in a box and send it to the hombres who lead our cartel. Give me those things, and great will be your reward."

"It will be done, señor," Nacho breathed.

Or he would die trying.

CHAPTER SIXTEEN

After Stark went back to his mobile home, he spent the rest of the night in his recliner, dozing in the sort of light sleep that allowed a man to rest while he still remained fairly alert. The shotgun was in easy reach on the floor beside the chair, and he had loaded his own .45 like the one Fred had and placed it on the table close at hand.

If Nacho Montez and his compadres came back, Stark was ready to give them a warm welcome.

The rest of the night passed quietly, though, for which Stark was grateful. As dawn was breaking the next morning, he put some coffee on and then took a quick shower while it was brewing.

He was sitting on his front porch, appearing unarmed though he had the .45 tucked into the back of his jeans under the untucked tails of his shirt, when Hallie Duncan pulled up next door at her father's mobile home. She waved to him as she got out of the car.

"Hallie," he called to her, "can you come over here a minute?"

She walked across the yard—there was no fence between the properties—and leaned on the railing beside the porch steps.

"Good morning, John Howard," she said. "You're up bright and early."

"It was sort of an interesting night," Stark said.

Hallie's carefully plucked eyebrows rose.

"The sort of night that I might be interested in spending?" she asked.

"Not really." Stark paused. "The fellas who left those heads in Dorothy's garden came back."

Hallie's gaze darted around. The park appeared to be tranquil and quiet this morning, so Stark knew what she was thinking.

"Most folks don't know about it yet," he went on. "They were after Fred Gomez's grandson, Antonio. They were gonna break in to get to him, but Fred and I managed to stop them. The rest of the park thinks it was just an attempted robbery."

"So why are you telling me different?" Hallie wanted to know.

"Because Antonio's holed up inside Fred's place, and he's got some legal troubles. He could use a lawyer."

Hallie drew in a breath. She glanced along the front of Stark's mobile home toward the Gomezes.

"You know I have just a general legal practice, don't you, John Howard? I draw up wills, set up trusts, handle lawsuits and settlements, that sort of thing."

"You do some defense work, too," Stark said.

"Yes, but there are people who specialize in that. I don't."

"Antonio needs a lawyer he can trust. I trust you, and I think he'll listen to my advice if I tell him you should represent him."

"I just came by to fix breakfast for my dad."

"Alton would want you to help if he knew what was going on."

"That's my condition," Hallie said. "I'll consider taking the case, but only if you tell my dad what's going on, too. He has a right to know that he's living next door to trouble."

Stark couldn't argue with that sentiment. He nodded and said, "All right, if you want to bring him over here, we can talk about it."

"I have a better idea. Come with me over to his house, and I'll fix breakfast for all three of us."

Stark smiled.

"That's an offer I'm sure not gonna turn down."

As he stood up to go down the steps and join her, she asked, "Are you carrying a gun, John Howard?"

"Yep. Got a permit to do it, too."

"I know you do. I just like to know when people around me are armed."

A bad feeling had been growing in Stark ever since the trouble the night before. He said, "If you're gonna be coming to visit your dad on a regular basis, I think you'd better get used to it."

The smell of bacon and pancakes filled the mobile home. That was one of the sweetest perfumes in the world, Stark thought.

But to tell the truth, whatever scent Hallie was wearing smelled pretty good, too. Of course, he wasn't the sort to tell her that, especially not now.

As they sat at the kitchen table and ate, Alton said, "This is nice, John Howard. You should come over for breakfast more often."

"Pay attention," Hallie told Stark.

Alton took a sip of his coffee and said, "Somehow, though, I don't think this is exactly a social get-together. This is about what happened last night, isn't it?"

Stark nodded.

"I'm afraid so," he said.

"It was more than what you told me."

"I hated to lie to you, Alton, but at the time I didn't really know what was going on. I figured I'd better find out before I started spreading rumors."

"Well, I suppose that makes sense," Alton said with a shrug. "It wasn't that you didn't trust me or anything."

"Not at all."

"So now you're ready to tell us?"

"He'd better be," Hallie said, "if he wants us to help him."

"It's not me that needs help, exactly," Stark said. "It's Antonio Gomez."

"Fred's grandson?" Alton asked with a frown.

"That's right."

Stark told them the whole story. Hallie looked horrified when she heard about Antonio's connection to the two human heads that had been found across the street. Alton seemed to take it in stride, although his expression grew grim as he listened.

"The boy's there now?" he asked when Stark was finished.

"I suppose. I haven't been over there to check."

Hallie said, "He needs to turn himself in to the law. I can go with him to the district attorney—"

"He won't do that," Stark said, "and I don't blame him. If he's locked up in jail, like for drug dealing, the cartel can get to him like that." He snapped his fingers. "And who should he trust in the sheriff's department? If he guesses wrong, he's dead."

Hallie thought about it for a moment, then said, "All right, how about the Border Patrol or the DEA? Or even the FBI? You don't honestly believe that the cartel has infiltrated those agencies, do you, John Howard?"

"Probably not to any great extent, although you could have some renegade agents here and there."

"It's just that you don't trust the federal government."

"With good reason, I'd say," Alton put in. "Remember all the trouble they gave him before. Hell, they even sicced the IRS on him! You can't get any more inhumane than that."

"Then what do you want me to do?" Hallie asked Stark.

"I thought maybe you could talk to your friend in Washington," Stark said. "Find out if there's somebody we can trust who can do something for Antonio."

Hallie's blue eyes narrowed in thought.

"Anybody who can do us any good is going to want something in return," she said. "What can Antonio testify to?"

"He can pin the murder of those two kids on the Montez brothers and their buddy Jalisco."

"Yes, but how far up the ladder are those three?"

Stark grimaced and shook his head.

"One rung, maybe."

"In other words, they're nobodies. Dangerous, maybe, but in the larger scheme of things, nobodies."

"That's probably right," Stark said.

"And Antonio doesn't know who they work for?"

"You'd have to ask him, but that's the impression I got."

"Nobody's going to be interested in such little fish, John Howard. I hate to say that, but it's true. Even if they could use Antonio's testimony as leverage to flip this Nacho Montez, maybe, it's doubtful that anybody would want to invest the resources to do so. The payoff is too uncertain."

"So what can be done?" Alton asked. "Just throw Antonio to the wolves?"

"I didn't say I wouldn't make any calls," Hallie said. "I'll do what I can. But for now it looks like it may be up to friends and family to keep Antonio alive."

Stark nodded.

"That's usually what it boils down to," he said.

CHAPTER SEVENTEEN

Stark and Hallie walked over to the Gomezes', where Hallie spent an hour talking to a visibly nervous Antonio. She had already called her office and told her secretary she would be running late again this morning. She didn't have any court appearances scheduled today, she told Stark, so her secretary was able to rearrange her appointments.

Antonio didn't have much money in his pockets, so Fred had given him a hundred dollars to hand to Hallie as an attorney. That made their conversation privileged. She'd chased Fred, Aurelia, and Stark out of the room so that they couldn't be forced to testify to anything Antonio told her.

Of course, all three of them had already heard Antonio's story, but that constituted hearsay, she explained, and it was likely that she could get any such testimony suppressed if things ever came down to a trial.

Just hearing mention of a trial made Antonio look more nervous, Stark thought. As well it should. He had been loco to get mixed up with a bunch like that. Kids did loco things sometimes, though.

As did adults, Stark added to himself with a wry smile as he thought about some of the things he had gotten himself into. Holing up in the Alamo and fighting the dang Mexican army . . . nobody could call that sane.

But he'd had to do it anyway.

When Hallie finally came out of the house, she joined Stark, Fred, and Aurelia in lawn chairs on the porch.

"Can you do anything for him, Hallie?" Aurelia asked anxiously.

"I don't know, but I can certainly try. When I get to the office I'll call a friend of mine in Washington."

"Washington," Fred repeated with a note of scorn in his voice. "Do you really think any of those people are interested in helping anybody but themselves?"

"Some are," Hallie insisted. "Unfortunately, they're greatly outnumbered. But all we can do is try."

"And stay alert for trouble," Stark said.

"Do you think those men will be back?" Aurelia asked.

"I think there's a darned good chance of it."

Fred reached across his belly to tap the butt of the pistol that was snugged into a cross-draw holster at his waist, under his shirt.

"That's why I'm going to be armed from now on," he said. "I'm thinking about taking this .45 of mine into the shower with me."

"Don't be silly," his wife told him. "You don't have to do that while I'm standing guard with a shotgun."

Fred smiled sadly.

"Did you think we'd ever be saying such things? Our retirement here was supposed to be so nice and peaceful."

"Life has a way of throwing curveballs," Stark said.

Hallie headed for her office after promising to call them later. Stark went back to his mobile home. He didn't have anywhere he had to be today, so he spent his time cleaning his guns and reading.

And keeping an eye on the street outside.

He didn't hear anything from Hallie until the middle of the afternoon, when she called his cell phone.

"I just got through talking to Fred," she told him. "My friend in Washington said there was nothing he could do for Antonio, but he kicked it on upstairs. Since the three men who killed those young people were acting on behalf of an organization, there's a chance they might be able to open a RICO file on the case."

"That's organized crime, right?" Stark asked.

"Right. It won't be easy, though. The climate in Washington isn't very favorable right now to anything that could be construed as biased toward Hispanic Americans."

"You mean the political climate."

"That's the only kind that matters in Washington."

Stark didn't doubt that. He said, "Those cartel bosses, those hombres Antonio was talking about, they're not any sort of American. They're all Colombian and Mexican."

"I know that. But a lot of the people who work for them are American. Ignacio and Carlos Montez—Nacho and Chuckie—are legitimate American citizens, born in the United States."

"Were their parents here legally?" Stark asked.

"That doesn't matter," Hallie said, and Stark had the answer to his question. "They were born here."

Then they were natural-born American assholes, Stark thought as he remembered how those human heads had looked nestled among Dorothy Hewitt's cabbage plants. Country of origin didn't matter all that much to him. Evil was evil, no matter where it came from. Looking at it from that angle, Hallie was right, no doubt about that.

"So nobody wants to do anything about the cartel

because it might annoy the Mexican government," he said bleakly.

"I didn't say that," Hallie responded. "There are factions in the Mexican government that have been fighting against the cartel for years. It's just that they're outnumbered by the ones who either don't want to rock the boat or have been bought off or threatened into submission by the drug smugglers. So they act outraged by anything that can be perceived as prejudice, no matter by what twisted logic, and the Hispanic lobbying groups in this country are the same way."

Stark sighed. It wasn't in his nature to get discouraged, even after all the tragedy he had suffered in his life, but sometimes it was hard to feel any other way when you took a good look at the way the world really operated these days. Logic and decency no longer mattered. Power, spin, and the big lie were the only things that counted.

Hallie went on, "Hispanics are going to be the majority in this country before too many more years, John Howard. No one can get elected on a national basis without the Hispanic vote. It helps that they don't all march in lockstep and that there are some real conservatives among them, but still . . ."

"You don't have to say anything else," Stark told her. "What it amounts to is that folks will promise to try to help Antonio and then conveniently never get around to doing anything."

"I'm afraid so. I tried to get Fred and Aurelia to understand that without being quite so blunt about it."

"So it's still left up to us to protect him."

"For right now. I'll keep working on it, though."

"Thanks, Hallie," Stark said. "I appreciate the effort."

"Maybe you could show your appreciation by taking me out for a nice dinner some night."

Stark wanted to chuckle, but he suppressed the impulse. Hallie was about ten years younger than he was, but there were enough generational similarities between them for him to know that she probably thought she was being too forward by practically asking him out.

Yet she had done it anyway, and he was touched by the gesture. He was tempted to accept—hell, a part of him wanted to accept without hesitation, he thought—but it probably wasn't a good idea. He would have enjoyed having Hallie around even more, having someone as nice as her to share his life, but it just wouldn't work out.

He didn't want to offend her, though, so he said, "One of these days we'll do that."

She laughed.

"I'm going to consider that a promise, John Howard, no matter how hard you try to tap-dance around the question."

They said their good-byes. Stark went next door to talk to Fred and Aurelia.

"Hallie called me," Stark said when Fred opened the door to his knock.

"She said she was going to," Fred replied with a nod. "She wasn't very encouraging, John Howard."

"No, this is a bad situation," Stark acknowledged bluntly. "We'll just have to make the best of it."

"Maybe . . . maybe it'll all blow over after a while."

Stark heard the desperate hope in his friend's voice and wished he could agree with the sentiment Fred had just expressed. He knew that was pretty unlikely, though.

He had a hunch that when night fell, trouble would come calling again at the Shady Hills Retirement Park.

CHAPTER EIGHTEEN

The climate here in southwest Texas could be described generally as arid. People who lived here for very long figured out that it was best to plant trees and bushes that could get by on very little rain.

From time to time, though, thunderstorms moved in, and they were real gully washers. Stark thought that might be what was going to happen tonight. Not long after darkness settled over the landscape, the breeze picked up, and it had the faint, ionized scent of rain in it. In the distance to the west, long fingers of lightning clawed through the night sky at the gathering clouds.

Stark had moved one of his lawn chairs into the shadows between his mobile home and that of the Gomezes. He sat there now, completely enclosed by darkness, with his shotgun across his knees.

Thinking that it was unlikely anything would happen during the day, Stark had taken a nice long nap that afternoon and fortified himself with several cups of coffee. He had a thermos of the stuff propped up beside him in the chair in case he needed more during the night. He planned to stay right where he was until dawn, if need be.

If he was expecting any sort of stealth attack, he wouldn't have brought the coffee out here. The aroma might drift to somebody sneaking around and warn them that a guard was on duty.

These enemies didn't seem that sophisticated. They were more likely to come in with all guns blazing, using shock and awe tactics on the elderly residents of the park.

Here was one old geezer, Stark thought, who wouldn't be shocked and damned sure wouldn't be awed by whatever those punks tried to pull. He was going to be ready for them.

He wasn't the only one. Fred and Aurelia Gomez planned to take turns staying awake tonight. Alton Duncan was probably asleep by now, but he'd told Stark that he would be prepared in case of trouble, with a rifle by his bed. Not the .22 he'd brought out the night before, either, but a more high-powered deer rifle that ought to prove equally effective against drug smugglers.

Once a fella learned to sit quiet and motionless and wait—a lesson that Vietnam had taught Stark, and one that had saved his life more than once—he never forgot it. The ability came back to him, as it did with Stark now. His breathing was shallow and even, and every sense was on alert.

Of course, in the end it didn't much matter. A blind and deaf man could have seen and heard the convoy of low-riders and pickups that came roaring into the retirement park. Stark heard them on the highway before they ever got there, and his instincts had him on his feet and ready by the time they tore through the entrance with squealing tires and booming stereos.

That racket allowed Stark to track the intruders' progress through the grid of streets in the park. He thumbed his cell phone and sent the text messages he'd had ready to send to Fred and Alton, warning that trouble was on the way. Then he slipped the phone back into his pocket and raised the shotgun to his shoulder, holding it ready to fire.

He listened for shots but hadn't heard any so far, just the bellowing engines and blasting noise that passed for music. With tires still screaming, the big pickup that was leading the invasion slid around the corner and immediately accelerated along the street. Four cars came behind it, followed by another pickup bringing up the rear.

Nacho Montez and his friends had brought reinforcements this time.

Stark didn't care how many of them there were, he wasn't going to be intimidated. He stayed in the shadows, ready to open fire if they stopped and charged out of their vehicles.

Instead, the first pickup slowed down as it reached the Gomez house. A light flared, flame from the rag stuffed into the neck of a bottle that flew from the truck bed.

Someone crouched back there had just thrown a Molotov cocktail at the mobile home where Fred and Aurelia lived.

Stark's shotgun was already at his shoulder. He let his instincts and muscle memory take over. He'd done plenty of skeet shooting in his time, and this was similar. He squeezed the trigger and the shotgun kicked heavily against his shoulder as buckshot blasted from its muzzle.

The bottle filled with gasoline burst apart in midair as the charge struck it. The volatile stuff ignited as it sprayed around the still burning rag. Some of it fell on the lawn, but some was blown backward into the first low-rider. The speeding pickup where the Molotov cocktail had originated was already past the Gomez house.

The car's windows were down. Someone inside yelled

as the burning gasoline splattered them. Stark pumped the shotgun and fired another round, tracking the car and aiming low. Tongues of flame licked through the darkness as the invaders returned the fire with handguns and automatic weapons.

Stark dived behind the shelter of some concrete blocks he had stacked up earlier in the day. He thrust the shotgun over the makeshift barricade and let fly again at the other vehicles whipping past in the street. They had slowed down slightly, but they didn't stop. In fact, they began to speed up again.

Stark heard the *whump!* of another Molotov cocktail going off somewhere else in the park. That surprised him a little. He had thought that the invaders would confine their attack to the Gomez place, and maybe to his mobile home as well.

Guns chattered in the distance. Stark went cold inside at the sound. The smugglers had started their assault here, but now they were continuing it elsewhere in the park, targeting innocent people who had nothing to do with Antonio Gomez or the incident the night before. Stark hadn't anticipated hostilities escalating this far, this fast.

The pickup in the rear of the convoy wheeled around a corner, its taillights vanishing. Stark felt frustration boiling inside him. Why didn't they come back here and fight? Why attack the other residents of the retirement park?

Terror.

The word sprang into Stark's mind, and he knew he had the answer to his questions. Antonio Gomez's defiance of the cartel, even at such a low level, might have started this trouble, but it had turned into something else. The invaders hadn't come here to grab Antonio or to strike back at John Howard Stark for humiliating them, although they would have gladly taken either of those outcomes.

No, this was a terrorist attack.

Stark didn't fully understand the motivation, but clearly this raid was designed to strike fear into the hearts of the park's residents. He could only hope that too many people hadn't been hurt in that barrage of gunfire and the Molotov cocktail's explosion.

The front door of the Gomez mobile home slammed as Fred burst out onto the porch, brandishing his .45.

"John Howard!" he called. "Where are you, John?"

"Here!" Stark shouted back. "They're gone, Fred. Stand down."

Fred hurried down his front steps.

"That was an awful lot of shooting," he said worriedly. "What were they doing? I thought they were just after Antonio."

"It may have started out that way," Stark said as he stomped out the few places on the front lawn that were still smoldering from the burning gasoline, "but I've got a feeling that things have changed somehow." *And not for the better*, he thought.

"Hey, fellas!" Alton Duncan sang out as he trotted toward them, which was smart because as keyed-up as Fred was, he might have taken a shot at anybody who surprised him, Stark thought. "Anybody hurt?"

"Not here," Stark said. "But we don't know about the rest of the park."

"Maybe we'd better go check," Fred suggested.

Stark nodded grimly and said, "Good idea. But Alton and I will go, Fred. You stay here in case this was just a feint of some sort to draw us off."

"You really think they're that tricky?" Fred asked.

"I don't know what to think anymore," Stark said, "except that this shows signs of being even worse than any of us expected."

CHAPTER NINETEEN

The shooting had stopped by now, and the roar of engines had dwindled and disappeared. People were emerging from their homes, calling questions to each other in confused, frightened voices. Some of them carried guns, baseball bats, axes, hoes, and anything else they had on hand that could be used as a weapon.

Porch lights had been turned on all up and down the streets, so Stark and Alton were visible as they strode determinedly toward the front of the park. They drew quite a bit of attention, and men came out to ask then what was going on and then fell in step with them. Some of the women came along, too. By the time Stark reached the first signs of real damage, he had a force about two dozen strong with him.

Flames leaped from one end of a mobile home, the unmistakable result of the Molotov cocktail. People were gathered around it using portable fire extinguishers to put out the blaze. Residents in this part of the county had to rely on a volunteer fire department that took at least twenty minutes to respond to a call, so they had learned how to battle fires themselves.

Stark was glad to see that the situation wasn't any worse. Instead of striking the middle of the mobile home, the bottle of gasoline must have landed right at the end, and alert residents had been able to contain the fire and appeared to be keeping it from spreading to the rest of the home.

Stark's momentary relief gave way to horror when a woman suddenly screamed, "My babies! My babies are still in there!"

She pulled away from the man trying to comfort her and charged up the smoldering steps. The man hurried after her, yelling, "Vicky! Vicky, wait! You can't go in there!"

It was too late to stop her. The door banged behind her as she disappeared into the mobile home.

Tense moments stretched by, punctuated by the spurting hiss of the fire extinguishers as they continued to pour chemical foam on the fire. Flames were still visible inside.

Stark was about to hand his shotgun to Alton and go in there himself when the woman and her husband emerged, each of them carrying a small dog. The woman was sobbing in relief as she stumbled down the porch steps to the ground.

"They were all right, thank God!" she said as her friends closed in around her to make sure that she hadn't been hurt.

Stark looked around at the crowd and asked in a booming voice, "Everybody all right here?"

He got a volley of questions in response as people wanted to know what was going on and who the invaders had been. Stark didn't have the time or patience to lay out all the details, so he just said, "That was a drug gang," and the residents of the park gathered around him nodded knowingly.

Several more armed men joined the group as Stark

and Alton moved on toward the entrance. Stark saw some shot windows, but most of the bullet holes seemed to be high up on the mobile homes, as if the gunmen had aimed that way on purpose. He began to have some hope that no one had been killed.

A white wooden fence ran along the highway for a quarter of a mile, marking the front of the retirement park. In the middle of that fence were a couple of brick pillars flanking the entrance. An arched sign giving the name of the place was above the opening in the fence. Stark looked at it and realized there had been nothing to stop the pick-ups and low-riders from driving right in.

That problem might have to be addressed in the future.

Stark looked toward the town of Devil's Pass and saw flashing lights in the distance, speeding closer. For the third time in the past thirty-six hours, the sheriff's department was responding to emergency calls from Shady Hills.

The deputies might not like it if they found a group of armed people waiting for them at the entrance. That sort of thing made law officers assume that they had run into a mob. Stark said, "You should all go on back to your homes. There won't be any more trouble tonight."

"How can you be sure of that?" a man asked.

"They made their point already," Stark replied.

Whatever that point was, he added to himself.

The crowd broke up as the flashing lights continued drawing closer. Stark handed his shotgun to Alton and said, "Head back to your place and check on Fred, will you? Let him and Aurelia know that the law's on the way."

"If they're outside, they can probably hear the sirens," Alton said. "What are you going to do, John Howard?"

"I'll wait here and meet the cops, let them know what happened."

Alton nodded and trotted off. Stark stood beside one of the brick columns at the entrance and waited.

He didn't have to wait for long. A sheriff's cruiser skidded to a halt on the side of the road near him, and both deputies had their weapons drawn tonight as they popped out of the vehicle. One of them shined the cruiser's spotlight on Stark, who held his empty hands up in plain sight as he squinted against the glare.

"Stay where you are!" the other deputy called.

"Wasn't planning on going anywhere," Stark said.

"Who are you?"

"John Howard Stark. Sheriff Lozano knows me."

"What happened here? We had reports of shots fired and some sort of explosion."

"That about sums it up," Stark drawled. "A gang of thugs came in, shot the place up, and threw a couple of Molotov cocktails."

"The volunteer fire department is on the way."

"That's good," Stark said, "but the fire will probably be out by the time they get here."

The deputy at the spotlight angled it down as two more cruisers pulled up behind the first one.

"Come over here, Mr. Stark," he said. "Are you some sort of spokesman for the residents of the park?"

"No, I just thought somebody ought to meet you fellas and let you know what was going on."

"Are you people at war out here?" the second deputy said in a disgruntled voice. "Human heads, gunshots, explosions . . . I thought retirement was supposed to be peaceful!"

"I reckon we all make mistakes, Deputy," Stark said.

* * *

By midnight, deputies were still canvassing the residents of the park, but the details had become relatively clear, Sheriff George Lozano explained to Stark.

"They drove in, came straight here, and then started raising hell," Lozano said. "They kept it up all the way out of the park. So it's pretty obvious that their anger was directed at you, Mr. Stark, and at you and your wife, Mr. Gomez."

Lozano looked over at Fred as he added that part.

"It's because of last night, when they tried to rob me," Fred said.

"Possibly," Lozano said, but he didn't sound convinced. "They brought an awful lot of firepower with them to get even for a simple home invasion gone wrong, though."

"Those fellas don't like to do things halfway," Stark said.

Lozano just grunted. The three of them were standing outside Fred's mobile home. Burned spots in the grass were visible in the glow of the headlights from Lozano's sheriff's department SUV.

"Are you sure you've told me everything you know about this?" the sheriff asked.

"We're as baffled as you are, Sheriff," Stark said.

That wasn't exactly true, but Stark *was* puzzled at the sudden escalation of violence. If the thugs had shown up and made an attempt to get Antonio out of Fred's house, that wouldn't have surprised him. From the looks of things, though, he wasn't sure they even cared about Antonio anymore.

"Well, if you think of anything else, you be sure to let me know," Lozano went on.

"Here's something else, Sheriff," Fred said. "What are you going to do about this?"

"I'm doing everything I can. My men are getting descriptions of the suspects' vehicles. We'll try to track them down."

"What about protecting us from something like this happening again?"

"And how am I going to do that, Mr. Gomez? This is a big county, and I'm like everybody else in the world. I've had to deal with budget cuts. I don't have the resources I once did."

"If the government would just quit wasting money on a bunch of politically correct crap, there'd be plenty left over to pay for law enforcement," Fred snapped.

"You're talking to the wrong man. Tell it to the politicians."

"Sheriff's an elected office," Stark pointed out. "You are a politician."

"Not like the ones who dole out the funding and don't have a clue what they're—" Lozano stopped short and took a deep breath. "You didn't hear me say that."

Stark shrugged.

"You've got problems. So do we. What do we do if that bunch comes back?"

"Call 911," Lozano said curtly. He turned and walked toward his SUV.

Fred stood beside Stark and asked as the sheriff drove away, "What *are* we going to do if they come back, John Howard?"

Stark's mouth was a tight, grim line as he gave Fred the only answer that was left.

"The same thing that folks have been doing for a long time when the wolves start howling in the night," he said. "We stand up for ourselves. We fight back."

CHAPTER TWENTY

"Miraculously, no one was seriously hurt in the incident. We spoke with Sheriff George Lozano about it."

A close-up of Lozano's weary face appeared on the screen as he said, "At this point we have a pretty good idea who's responsible for this outrage and expect to make several arrests shortly."

A couple of guttural grunts came from Gabir Patel. After a moment, Tomás Beredo realized that the Lebanese man was laughing. The two men sat in the dining room of Beredo's ranch house enjoying a leisurely breakfast and watching the news on a flat-screen TV hung on the wall.

"You hear that?" Patel said. "He says they're going to make several arrests."

Beredo waved an impeccably manicured hand.

"We have nothing to fear from Sheriff Lozano."

"In your pocket, eh?"

"Strictly speaking, no. But he fears us. He fears for his family's safety if he becomes too zealous in his actions toward us."

"He would fear you even more if you took his son or daughter and cut off a finger," Patel suggested.

"If it becomes necessary," Beredo agreed blandly.

The camera had cut back to the host of the local morning news show, a Hispanic male almost as handsome as Beredo himself. He was saying, "We have a crew out at the Shady Hills Retirement Park this morning, and our own Tiffany de la Garza spoke to some of the residents."

A live shot of an impossibly beautiful field reporter appeared on screen. She was holding a microphone as she said redundantly, "We're here at the Shady Hills Retirement Park, the scene of some shocking violence last night." She turned to one of the people standing near her. "How did you feel when the shooting started?"

The elderly man seemed a little overwhelmed by having the microphone thrust into his face, but he recovered and said, "Well, I was scared. It sounded like a war. I was in Vietnam, you know, and it sounded like the Tet Offensive all over again. Not quite that bad, of course, but you get the idea."

The reporter, who hadn't been born until long after the Tet Offensive was over, just gave him a blank smile and said, "What about you, ma'am? Were you frightened?"

The woman she had spoken to said, "You bet I was. Guns were goin' off everywhere, and then there was this explosion. Why, I was so scared I almost—"

"Thank you," the field reporter cut in before the woman could go into detail about how she had almost reacted to the raid. The reporter turned away and the cameraman swung to follow her as she spoke to another man standing nearby. "How about you, sir? What do you think about what happened her last night?"

The park resident, a tall, powerful-looking man with thick, gray-shot dark hair and a mustache, said, "What do I think? I think it's a shame such things can even happen in this country. There was a time when a bunch of lawless thugs wouldn't dare attack innocent folks like this because they knew if they did they'd be met with hot lead. Maybe it wouldn't be such a bad idea if that was the case again."

"Sir, are you advocating vigilante justice?" the reporter asked breathlessly, as if sensing controversy and higher ratings.

"I'm advocating something that goes way back in this country, the idea that people have a right to protect themselves, especially when the government can't—or won't—do it. That's not vigilante justice, that's just justice . . . and common sense."

"So you're saying the residents of the park should fight back if they're attacked again?"

"Some of us already did," the man said. "Next time there'll be more of us standing up to those punks."

The field reporter was starting to look a little uneasy. This interview was straying into a politically incorrect area that could be dangerous.

"You almost sound like you're daring them to come back," she said.

The man shook his head.

"No. I hope they don't ever show their faces around here again. We're peace-loving folks here at Shady Hills and just want to be left alone. But we won't be bullied, and if we're hit, we're gonna hit back . . . hard."

"Would you mind telling me your name, sir?"

"Not at all." The man looked directly into the camera with eyes that were as hard as flint. "It's John Howard Stark."

The answer didn't surprise Beredo. He had thought that the man looked familiar, and now he realized that he recognized Stark from newspaper pictures dating back to Stark's previous clash with the cartel. He had known that

Stark lived at Shady Hills, of course; Jalisco had told him that much. And now he had seen Stark, the man filled with arrogant defiance, for himself.

"Stark," Patel said. "The one you were talking about a couple of nights ago."

"Yes," Beredo said with a nod.

"I don't like him. Like the girl said, he dares you to act."

"He will regret that," Beredo vowed. "He will die screaming, but only after he knows that he is responsible for the deaths of everyone he holds dear."

"Yes," Patel said. "Like all the other Americans, he must be taught that he cannot defy our glorious cause."

Beredo didn't give a damn about any "cause" other than his own ambitions, but he didn't see any point in saying that to Patel. If Hezbollah and the cartel were to come to an arrangement, it would be because the deal was beneficial to both sides, not because either side really cared about the other.

Beredo took out his phone and called one of his lieutenants.

"I want to see Ignacio Montez," he snapped. "Right away."

This John Howard Stark could not be allowed to live. If Montez wanted to protect his own place in the scheme of things, let alone move up in the cartel, he would see to it that Stark was dealt with, and that the problem of Shady Hills Retirement Park was taken care of.

Otherwise heads would roll, and none of them would belong to Tomás Beredo.

CHAPTER TWENTY-ONE

The president was flipping through the pages of his morning briefing: gas prices nearing five dollars a gallon, more saber-rattling in the Middle East, protesters wearing Nike T-shirts, drinking Starbucks coffee, and Web surfing on their iPhones while waving signs and loudly proclaiming that all corporations are evil and should be abolished . . . all business as usual, in other words.

Then he stopped and his eyes narrowed as he read the report from Texas.

"What's this?" he asked his chief of staff. "Doesn't the president of the United States have better things to do than worry about some minor disturbance in a state full of conservative yahoos? Why should we give a damn what happens down there? Our party hasn't carried Texas in the past thirty years!"

"That fellow Stark is involved," the chief of staff explained. "His name is flagged, just like you ordered, sir."

"Oh, yes," the president said with a frown. His predecessors had all kept track of John Howard Stark, so he'd thought it would be a good idea for him to do the same.

"Wasn't there something a few months ago about a possible civil rights violation . . . ?"

The chief of staff shook his head and said, "Nothing ever came of that. No matter how Justice spun it, there was just too much evidence that Stark was defending himself. The three defendants in the case are still awaiting trial."

"So what's this about?"

"Some sort of gang attacked the mobile home park where Stark lives. We don't really know why."

"Do we know who's involved?"

"DEA says there are indications that it was one of the cartels."

The president shook his head in confusion.

"Why would they be interested in attacking a bunch of trailer trash?"

The chief of staff winced.

"I wouldn't use that term to describe the residents, sir."

"Well, of course not," the president snapped. "What sort of fool do you think I am, Ron? But that doesn't change the fact that's what they are, and I don't understand why one of those drug cartels would even bother with them."

"From what I understand, in situations like this a lot of times the cartel wants to use the land as a drug-smuggling route. Maybe they're trying to scare off the residents."

"Don't they have enough ways to bring in their drugs?" The president snorted in disgust. "To hear some people tell it, our southern border is wide open anyway!"

The chief of staff looked like he was trying not to say something. After a moment he responded, "The Border Patrol has had to make quite a few budget cuts—"

"We're still spending too much money on law enforcement that ought to go to social programs. You know that, Ron."

The chief of staff sighed and said, "Yes, sir. At any rate, that's why that item was included in the briefing summaries, because of Mr. Stark's involvement. Is there any action you'd like to take regarding it?"

The president frowned in thought and finally shook his head.

"Not right now. But alert the Justice Department to keep an eye on the situation. If Stark is involved in this, there's always a chance it could escalate. There are certain news organizations that would love to distort the situation and make it look like he's some sort of hero again."

"Yes, sir." The chief of staff decided it might be a good idea to nudge the president on to another matter. "If you'll look at the latest economic numbers, you'll see that another three million people have given up and stopped looking for a job, so that means the unemployment rate will be going down again."

A broad smile wreathed the president's face as he said, "Ah! Good news. And those shortsighted fools in Congress say that our stimulus policies aren't working! The numbers don't lie, do they, Ron?"

Elsewhere in Washington on this hot, miserably muggy summer morning, a man was working out in his private gym. Despite the fact that he was in late middle age, he looked somewhat younger. Close-cropped gray hair and a certain weathered cast to his skin were the only outward signs of his years. He was bare to the waist, wearing only a pair of workout pants. His body was still lean and strong as he went through his martial arts routine. He kicked, punched, and easily defeated the opponent he could see in his head, and when he was finished a fine sheen of sweat covered his face and chest. He wasn't breathing hard, though.

"Bravo." The comment came from a woman who'd been standing at the side of the room, leaning on a pommel horse as she watched him. She was half his age, about thirty, and beautiful with a supple, curved body revealed by the spandex leotard she wore and long red hair pulled back this morning in a ponytail. "You're a remarkable specimen, Simon."

"You make me sound like an insect pinned to a board," he said.

"Not at all. You're more like something that should be on display in a museum. There aren't many like you around."

"Then that makes you doubly lucky to be with me, doesn't it?"

He slid his arm around her waist, pulled her against him, and kissed her.

When she pulled away after a long moment, she said, "There's a phone call for you. I told him he'd have to wait, that I couldn't interrupt you while you were working out."

"Who is it?"

She shook her head and said, "He didn't give me a name. But how many people have your number?"

Not many, he thought without replying. And the ones who did have it were generally worth talking to.

He went over to the bar where she had set his phone down. He picked it up with his left hand. His right was missing the thumb and index finger, both of which had been shot off cleanly several years earlier.

"Ryan," he said into the phone.

That was his real name. He still used it despite the fact that officially Simon Ryan was dead and had been for a number of years. Making that true hadn't been all that difficult, considering the help he'd had from friends in high places. Certain people in the government were more than happy to lend him a hand when he needed it, and in return he cleaned up the messes that they couldn't clean up themselves. It was an arrangement that had made him comfortably wealthy.

"Hello, Simon," a familiar voice said in his ear. "Have you seen the news this morning?"

"I don't keep up with the news," Ryan said. "The people I work for tell me all I need to know."

"There was some trouble in Texas last night."

"That doesn't have anything to do with me."

Although he had been born and raised in El Paso and had spent quite a bit of time in Texas, he didn't remember any of it particularly fondly. He had spent time in a lot of other places, too, and he didn't miss them. In the case of Texas, he hadn't been there since the incident that had cost him those two fingers on his right hand.

"An old friend of yours was involved."

"I don't have any friends in Texas."

"What about John Howard Stark?"

Ryan's left hand tightened on the phone. Stark wasn't the one who had maimed him, but it wouldn't have happened if not for the rancher. Ryan felt a little grudging admiration for Stark—the man had gone against the odds, taken on something much bigger than himself, and somehow survived—but he felt a deep and abiding hatred for Stark that was much stronger.

Over the years, Ryan hadn't tried to keep up with what Stark was doing. He'd been busy with other things, busy carving out this new life for himself. He had heard about Stark being there at the Alamo when everything had gotten crazy and bloody, and that hadn't surprised him.

But since then . . . nothing. Ryan hadn't even known whether Stark was still alive.

"He's no friend of mine," Ryan told the man on the phone.

"He's no friend of anybody in power in this town," the man said with a harsh note of anger creeping into his voice. "He was on TV this morning spouting some sort of drivel about how Americans should stand up for themselves. He's getting on the nerves of a lot of people, Simon. Important people."

"And you're calling on their behalf to ask me to do something about it." Ryan paused. "You know my price."

"Maybe you'd consider giving a discount, since you have your own score to settle with him."

Ryan laughed. He was genuinely amused.

"They don't mind spending the money they gouge out of the taxpayers, but it's a different matter when it comes out of their own pockets, isn't it?"

"Be reasonable, Simon—"

"No, you be reasonable," Ryan broke in, his voice slicing across the other man's. "The price is five million. You and I both know good and well that's nothing to the people we're talking about."

"My God, it's not like he's a head of state or something! He's just an ignorant redneck from Texas!"

"Fine."

Ryan thumbed the phone off.

It rang again less than thirty seconds later. He was ready for it. "Do we have a deal?"

"We have a deal. The money will be in your Cayman Islands account by the end of business today. When will your part of the arrangement be taken care of?"

"I don't give timetables, you know that. It'll be done when the time is right."

"That had better not be long."

"I don't care for threats, either," Ryan said.

"It wasn't a threat," the man said hastily. "Our friends are just very anxious to have this over and done with. Stark's a dangerous man. People tend to rally around him."

"Don't worry," Ryan said. "Pretty soon the only ones rallying around John Howard Stark will be his pallbearers."

CHAPTER TWENTY-TWO

"Well, here's the TV star now," Hallie said as she opened the door of her father's mobile home in answer to Stark's knock.

Stark grimaced.

"What was I supposed to do?" he said. "That gal stuck a microphone right in my face and asked me what I thought about what happened. I told her."

"You sure did, John Howard," Alton said from his chair. "You told her real good. Come on in here."

Hallie closed the door behind Stark. She said, "It almost seemed like you were daring them to come back here."

"That wasn't my intention. But I wasn't going to sugarcoat things. If there's more trouble, we need to be ready for it."

"That's why there's going to be a meeting at the community building tonight," Alton said. "We have to talk about what we're going to do."

"That makes it sound even more like you're forming a vigilante group," Hallie said. "You know what'll happen if the media gets wind of this, don't you? They'll paint you as a bunch of gun-crazy, right-wing, racist nuts. They'll say you're prejudiced against Hispanics—"

"Half the people whose homes got shot up last night are Hispanic," Stark pointed out.

Hallie shook her head. "That doesn't matter. They'll still accuse you of trying to form an anti-Hispanic vigilante group, and politicians all across the state will condemn you. Maybe all across the country."

Alton snorted and said, "You think any of us care what some politicians think of us?"

"Maybe not. But then you'll have the ACLU down on your ass, and some actors will fly in from Hollywood on their private jets to condemn you and declare themselves supporters of the common man, and every left-wing website and blog will be fanning the flames against you."

"They say you can judge a man by the quality of his enemies," Stark drawled. "Sounds to me like those are pretty good enemies to have."

"Morally, I agree with you, John Howard. Legally, you may be setting yourselves up for trouble."

Alton declared, "I'd rather take my chances in court than get my butt shot off by some drug-smuggling punk."

"You may get the opportunity to do just that," Hallie told him.

"And you'll represent me if I do, won't you?" her father asked with a grin.

Hallie just sighed and then smiled back at him.

Other than a few satellite trucks from various TV stations cruising around the streets, the park had been quiet today. Stark was grateful for any peaceful respite. They might not get too many in the future.

"What time's the meeting?" he asked Alton.

"Seven o'clock. That's why I asked you to come over.

I thought maybe you'd have dinner with us, and then we'd all walk over there together."

"Sounds good," Stark replied with a nod.

"Better bring your guns, too. Everybody I've talked to says they're going to go armed from now on."

Stark smiled and said, "That'll probably make a few liberal heads explode if they get wind of it."

"Like I said," Hallie told him, "they'll call you gun-crazy lunatics."

"I think you said nuts before."

She shook her head and rolled her eyes.

"This is serious, John Howard. You're going to stir up all sorts of trouble."

"I know it's serious. There's nothing more serious than people standing up for their rights. And it's a mighty sad day in this country when people have to worry about getting in trouble for doing that."

"You're right," Hallie said softly. She put a hand on his arm. "You're right. I just don't want to see anything bad happen to you."

"I can take care of myself," Stark said. "There's no reason to worry about me."

There was more truth to that than either Hallie or Alton knew, he thought.

Being summoned back to Señor Espantoso's head-quarters wasn't something Nacho Montez really wanted to get used to. Despite his sleek appearance, the señor reminded Nacho of a rattlesnake.

On the other hand, the life that Señor Espantoso lived was exactly the sort of life Nacho wanted for himself: the women, the luxurious surroundings, only the finest things for the señor.

One day, Nacho vowed, *he* would be the señor, the hombre everyone feared and wanted to please. When he told himself that, it calmed his nerves and allowed him to keep his voice steady as he said, "We did as you ordered, señor. We went to frighten the old people who live in the retirement park."

"That bastard Stark didn't sound frightened when he was on television this morning talking about how they would fight back next time."

"Stark," Nacho muttered. The spark of hatred glowed a little brighter within him.

"Did you think that shooting a few guns in the air would cause everyone there to flee? You didn't even kill anyone!"

"We tried to burn down two of the trailers. The fire might have spread to even more of them—"

"But it didn't happen that way," the señor broke in. "One mobile home was damaged by fire, some others have bullet holes in them. That's all."

"I didn't think you would want us to commit mass murder—"

Again Señor Espantoso interrupted him, saying, "Why not?"

"Señor?" Nacho asked with a puzzled frown.

"Why would you hesitate to kill anyone who is in the way of the cartel?" Espantoso demanded. "Do you think we fear the American law?"

"No, but—"

"The local authorities are afraid of us. They know that if they incur our wrath, they and their families run the risk of dying. Horribly. Painfully. And the ones who run the American government? Ha!" Scorn dripped from the señor's words as he continued, "They fear something even worse. They fear being accused of not being tolerant. They

fear being accused of not being sensitive. They fear
being accused of being racist! And worst of all . . . they
fear not being reelected. Because of that, they issue rules
under which their DEA and their so-called Border Patrol
have to operate, rules that make certain those agencies
have little or no chance of ever accomplishing anything.
They spend less and less money on enforcing the law
and more on giving handouts to bankers and insurance
companies and sending tax money to people who never
paid taxes in the first place. They say they are trying to
control guns, and yet they *give* guns to us. To us!" He
shook his head. "Your old grandmother is more dangerous
to us than the toothless American government, Montez.
This is *our* day! We do what we want."

It was a stirring speech, and Nacho was in awe of Señor
Espantoso at this moment. The man deserved his name.
The horrible one. The dreadful one. The phantom who
came in the night and brought death. Tomás Beredo was
all of those things and more.

"What is it you want us to do, señor?" Nacho asked, his
eyes wide.

"Your job is simple, Montez. . . . Gather as many men
as you need. Take them and wipe the Shady Hills Retirement Park off the face of the earth."

Nacho took a deep breath and risked saying, "It may
take time to get together enough men and guns—"

"A week," Señor Espantoso snapped. "And when that
week is up, no one will ever dare to defy the cartel again."

CHAPTER TWENTY-THREE

The community center, a large, metal-walled building, stood near the front of the park next to the brick home that Jack and Mindy Kasek, the owners, had built when they first bought the property to develop. There was a small parking area in front, but most of the residents walked there that evening for the meeting. Stark didn't know who had arranged the assembly, but it was a good idea. The people who lived here needed to talk about what was going to happen next.

From the looks of the crowd sitting on folding metal chairs, just about everyone from Shady Hills was here, Stark thought as he looked around. Jack Kasek, a silver-haired man with a certain gawkiness that made him look like what he was, a retired engineer, stood at the front of the big room talking to several people. He caught Stark's eye and motioned for him to come join them.

"Hello, John," he said as Stark walked up. "Glad you could make it. You know these fellas? Nick Medford, Henry Torres, Doug Jacobs, Grant Reeves."

Stark nodded to them. He was acquainted with all four

of the men, although they lived in different areas of the park and he didn't know them well.

"I was thinking we could divide the park up into different sections and have somebody be responsible for taking care of each section, sort of like a captain," Jack went on. "I'll take one area, these guys have each agreed to take one, and we'd like you to be our sixth captain, John."

"That sounds like a good idea, and I'd be honored to help out," Stark said. "I didn't know you were a military man, Jack."

Jack smiled and shook his head.

"I'm not. I never served. I'm just trying to approach the situation logically, and with some common sense. One man can't be everywhere at once."

Stark nodded and said, "Here's something that occurred to me. If everybody's here tonight, then nobody's watching for trouble."

Jack's eyes widened, and the other four men looked shocked, too. Henry Torres said, "Good Lord! You're right, John. We need to get some guards posted."

"You really think those savages will come back tonight?" Nick Medford asked.

"They've been here three nights in a row," Stark said. "I wouldn't rule it out."

"You're absolutely right," Jack said. "We need some volunteers." He turned toward the crowd, lifted his hands, and raised his voice. "Everybody, could I have your attention? Could I have your attention, please?"

The hubbub of conversation died down in the room as everybody looked at Jack and waited for him to go on.

"You know why we're here tonight," he addressed them. "We have to talk about the threat that seems to be facing us and what we're going to do about it. But before we do that, I'd like several of you men to step up here and volunteer to stand guard at the entrance to the park while the meeting's going on."

A man in the front row of folding chairs said, "Whoever does that will miss out on what's being decided."

"I know that," Jack said. "That's why I'm asking for volunteers. I know you all want to have a voice in the discussion, but if those troublemakers come back, we'll need some warning."

No one could dispute that logic. Slowly, several hands rose. Jack nodded in satisfaction and motioned for the men to stand up.

"Are you guys armed?" he asked.

Two of the men were carrying pistols. The other three were unarmed.

Jack looked at Stark and asked, "What do you think?"

"We want them to stand watch and warn us if trouble's coming," Stark said. "Nobody expects them to fight off an army. I think it'll be all right."

Jack nodded and said to the volunteers, "All right, fellas, thank you. Head out to the front gate and keep your eyes open. Maybe spread out along the fence a little."

The men left to carry out those orders, and the meeting moved on to its main agenda.

"We all know what happened last night—" Jack began.

"Yeah, Kasek, we know," one of the men interrupted him. "And we want to know what you're gonna do about it."

A chorus of agreement came from the crowd.

Jack motioned for quiet and said, "I've spoken at length to Sheriff Lozano, and he's promised to increase patrols in this area—"

"That's not going to do any good!" another man protested. "A cop car driving by every hour or two won't stop those punks. They'll just wait until the deputies aren't around."

Stark knew that in all likelihood, that was true. The

sheriff would have to station several deputies at the park full-time in order to deter another attack, and George Lozano lacked the resources to do that.

Anyway, those drug smugglers were so brazen, even the presence of law enforcement personnel at the park might not be enough to stop them. The cartel members were in the habit of thumbing their noses at authority.

"Why don't you call in the Texas Rangers?" someone suggested.

"The assistance of the Rangers has to be requested by local law enforcement agencies," Jack explained. "I already covered that with the sheriff."

"Did he agree to ask for help from them?"

"Not at this point," Jack said with obvious reluctance.

"Then how about the Border Patrol?" another man asked.

"We're not on the border."

"It's less than thirty miles away!" a woman exclaimed. "Why doesn't the government *do* something? It's supposed to protect us!"

Jack was running this meeting, so Stark didn't say anything, but he wanted to tell the woman that the government had very little interest in protecting its citizens these days. The government's real interest was in collecting taxes from the people who were still willing to work, so that the politicians could turn around and "redistribute" that money to the people who couldn't, or more often wouldn't, work, the ones who kept voting those politicians into office. It was blatant graft on a national level, and there wasn't much average citizens could do to stop it. They could vote, but it was hard to prevail against rampant election fraud covertly sponsored by one segment of the political system, and they could make their voices heard by protesting, but then they were shouted down by the puppet media forces of that same segment. It was damned frustrating, especially for people like Stark who genuinely, passionately believed in democracy, people who had risked their lives again and again to protect the system, only to see it twisted and distorted into something its founders had never intended for it to be.

So people like Stark and his friends tried to live their lives as best they could and make small differences here and there, in the hope that someday those efforts would snowball into something larger and the country would regain its reason. Their struggle was probably doomed to failure . . . but they were not the sort of people who found it easy to give up.

"Listen, I'm going to be in touch with everybody, with every agency, that might be able to give us some help," Jack was saying. "But in the meantime, we might as well face it. Right now we have to be responsible for protecting ourselves."

"How are we going to do that?"

Jack smiled and said, "I'm glad you asked that question." He turned to Stark. "I'm going to let someone who's better qualified than I am answer it. You all know John Howard Stark."

Somebody in the crowd started to clap. The applause quickly spread, causing embarrassment to well up inside Stark. He was a modest man by nature, without a shred of pretense about him. But he had been a celebrity of sorts—even though some of the bleeding-heart crowd probably considered him a villain—and in America, once a celebrity, always a celebrity.

As most of the people in the room continued to clap, Jack Kasek turned to Stark and said, "John, will you take over?"

Stark nodded. He had no great fondness for being in

charge of anything except his own life, but somebody had to do it and he supposed Jack was right about him being better qualified.

He raised his arms and motioned for quiet. After a moment he got it.

"Jack says we have to be responsible for protecting ourselves," he told the crowd. "He's right about that. In order to do that, though, we need a couple of things. How many people here own guns?"

He was glad to see that hands shot up all over the room.

"Some of you probably brought those guns with you tonight—no, I don't need a show of hands for that—and the rest of you have them at home. I'm not saying that you need to be armed twenty-four/seven, but if you have weapons they ought to be handy. Nothing's more useless than a gun you can't get to when you need it. But there's something else we need that's even more important than guns."

He paused to let that sink in, and when the room was quiet and everyone was looking at him, he asked, "How many of you are willing to fight?"

Again, hands went up all over the room. Stark figured that everyone who had answered his gun question in the affirmative was declaring their willingness to use those weapons.

The problem was, it was easy to do that in a crowd.

"What I mean," Stark said, "is how many of you are willing to pull the trigger knowing that you're probably going to kill somebody? Can you do that? Can you end a human life? Are you absolutely sure?"

Some of the hands went down, and a murmur of confusion went through the room."

"John, what are you doing?" Jack Kasek asked quietly.

"Making certain," Stark said. He waited.

A man stood up. He had a white crew cut and thick glasses. Stark didn't know him. He said, "If somebody's threatening me or my wife, if he's trying to take away everything I hold dear, then damn right I can pull the trigger."

Several other men called out, "Yeah!" and another said, "Count me in!"

Stark nodded.

"Good. Because if it comes down to a real fight against those drug smugglers, that's what it's gonna take. Each and every one of you will have to decide what's worth fighting for, and if you're willing to fight for it. And if you are . . ." Stark drew in a deep breath. "If you are, then Shady Hills belongs to us, and by God, they're not gonna take it away from us!"

CHAPTER TWENTY-FOUR

The meeting continued for another hour, and during that time Stark settled, however uncomfortably, into the role of general of this elderly army.

His "troops," despite being past retirement age, weren't ready for the rocking chair or the rest home. In fact, most of them were still pretty spry, keeping fit with gardening, yard work, handyman chores, and regular workouts. A number of them still worked part-time, many at the Mega-Mart in Devil's Pass. Not surprisingly, there was also a high percentage of veterans, some of whom had seen combat in Vietnam or Korea. One of the men, Bert Loomis, had even gone into Berlin with Patton at the end of World War II and declared that he was still ready, willing, and able to live up to the legacy of Old Blood and Guts. Stark took one look at Bert and wasn't just about to deny him that chance.

Nor was it just the men who volunteered to patrol the park and protect it if trouble loomed. A couple of dozen women, who said they had experience with guns, volunteered as well. Despite the chivalry bred into him, Stark didn't turn away the women, either. Shady Hills needed all the help it could get.

The volunteers were split up among the six captains, depending on where in the park they lived. Jack Kasek had drawn up a map clearly marked off into sections, and it was spread out on a table at the front of the room. The volunteers gathered with their captains, and then Stark addressed the entire group.

He did a quick head count before he started talking. There were seventy-two volunteers, but they weren't spread out equally among the captains. Some had fewer people to work with. Stark decided that he would speak with each captain individually and urge that they talk to their friends and try to come up with more volunteers. It was best to delegate that job, though, since they knew their neighbors better than he did.

"This is a mighty fine start," Stark told them. "Each group will provide a couple of volunteers every night to guard the front gate in shifts. There'll also be two-person patrols moving around each section of the park from dusk to dawn. The captains and I will get together and work out schedules, and they'll pass along your assignments to you."

"We'll be armed?" one of the men asked.

"Yeah, like I said earlier, you'll need your weapons with you. But even though I told you that you had to be prepared to fight, you'll need to guard against getting trigger-happy, too. The last thing you want to do is shoot one of your friends and neighbors. That's why nobody stands guard alone or patrols alone. There'll be at least two people working together at all times. That way you'll be less likely to panic and start shooting when you don't need to."

The other residents who had come to the meeting had

stood up and gathered in smaller groups to talk. Many of them had begun to drift toward the door.

"Hold on, folks!" Stark called to them. "We're not done here."

A man said, "But you've got your volunteers, Mr. Stark. What do you need us for?"

"We all need each other," Stark said firmly. "You're all old enough to have heard that saying about hanging together or hanging separately. It's true. These men and women up here may be on the front lines, but they need support from all of you. You can provide coffee and sandwiches for the gate guards and the patrols. You can make sure we've got plenty of ammunition. And you can write and call and email your representatives in Congress and tell them exactly what's going on here. They may not be willing to do anything to help, but we don't want them to be able to claim they didn't know anything about it, either. Get on the Internet and use all the social media you can to get the word out about what we're facing. Public opinion is mighty important these days."

"I don't know anything about that stuff," one man said.

"Better learn," Stark told him. "The people who don't want us to be able to stand up for ourselves are mighty good at it. They can twist the truth or tell an outright lie and spread it all over the world just by tapping a few keys. It's up to us to get the facts out there and keep on doing it until people start to see the truth again."

Most of the residents still looked dubious about that, but several of them nodded. It was a start, Stark thought. And things had to start somewhere.

When the meeting broke up, Hallie and Alton Duncan came up to Stark, along with Fred Gomez.

"You were just about the youngest person here tonight," Stark told Hallie with a smile.

"Yeah," she said wryly. "Do you know how long it's been since I was the kid of the bunch?"

"You're always the kid as far as I'm concerned," Alton said.

"Where's Aurelia?" Stark asked Fred.

"She stayed home. She said I didn't need her along, and that she knew I wouldn't do anything foolish. And she didn't want to leave Antonio there by himself."

"How's he doing?"

Fred shrugged. "He still feels like this is all his fault. He's the one who brought Shady Hills to the attention of the cartel."

"Maybe so," Stark said, "but this has turned into something a lot bigger than that. I don't think they're really interested in Antonio anymore."

"Then what do they want?" Hallie asked.

"The whole place. They want to run us off, probably so they can transport their dope through here." Stark paused. "That's just an excuse, though. The real reason they've got it in for us is because we stood up to 'em. They're able to run things because so many people are scared to death of them. If folks see that they can fight back against the cartel and win, that weakens the cartel's grip on everything."

"People who fight back against the cartel usually wind up dead," Fred said.

"Usually. But that's not gonna be the case here, and that's going to make a difference."

"Do you really think you can win?" Hallie asked.

"I do," Stark said. "That bunch is arrogant. They're gonna think that we're just a bunch of helpless old farts, and they're going to underestimate us. That's half of winning the battle right there."

"For your sake—and the sake of everybody else in Shady Hills—I hope you're right, John Howard."

Nothing had happened to interrupt the meeting, and the night continued to pass quietly. Guard and patrol schedules hadn't been drawn up yet, but some of the men offered to take their turns right away, so the park wouldn't go unprotected.

Stark didn't know all the guards, but since he was going to have to trust them sooner or later, he figured he might as well start now.

He went home and got a good night's sleep.

The next day he and the other five captains met at Jack's house to work out their schedules and plans, then spread out through the park to talk to each of the volunteers individually and make sure they understood their responsibilities. It went well, and Stark picked up a few more volunteers who had thought it over after the meeting and decided to get more actively involved. That was good, because even though there wouldn't be any roaming patrols during the day, Stark and the other captains thought it would be a good idea if at least a couple of guards were on duty at the gate around the clock.

"I could get one of those security gates put in," Jack had said when they got together that morning. "You know, the kind where you have to punch in a code to get it to open."

"No offense, Jack," Stark had said, "but those are designed to keep out salesmen and discourage amateur burglars. They won't stop anybody who really wants to get in. Neither will the wooden fence along the front or the chainlink around the rest of the property. You'd have to build a stone wall, top it with barbed wire, install bunkers at the gate, and lay mines around the outer perimeter if you want to stop anybody who's really determined to get in."

Jack had grinned and replied, "Well, maybe that's just what I'll do," but Stark knew it wasn't. Jack didn't have that kind of money. If everybody in the park pooled their funds, it might not add up to what would be needed for measures like that.

Besides, even with the local authorities on their side—something Stark wasn't convinced of—they would probably balk at the idea of a minefield.

Of course, there were some measures that residents of the park *could* take that wouldn't be quite so extreme. . . .

Several days passed in preparation, but when nothing happened, Stark sensed the atmosphere of urgency that had gripped the park following the raid was beginning to weaken. People were starting to hope that the trouble had blown over and that everything would be all right now.

Stark knew better than to believe that. He was convinced the drug smugglers were just biding their time.

Either that, or they were busy getting ready, too.

And that was the most worrisome prospect of all.

CHAPTER TWENTY-FIVE

The fifth morning after the raid, a sheriff's department SUV pulled up in front of Stark's mobile home. Sheriff George Lozano got out and came toward the porch.

Stark saw him through the window and met him on the porch with a pleasant nod, asking, "What brings you out here this morning, Sheriff?"

"Rumors, Mr. Stark," Lozano said.

"What sort of rumors?" Stark asked, even though he figured he already knew the answer.

"That you've turned this park into an armed camp. I see by the guards at the gate the rumors are true."

"A couple of fellas standing around chewing the fat doesn't make this an armed camp," Stark said.

Lozano snorted.

"It does if one of them is holding a deer rifle and the other one has a shotgun," he said.

"Both perfectly legal weapons," Stark pointed out.

"Are you saying that if I searched this place, I wouldn't find any assault rifles?"

"I don't have any idea what you'd find, Sheriff," Stark said. "I've only been in a few of the houses. I know you'd need a mighty broad search warrant to search the whole park, though. Not sure a judge would give you that much leeway."

As a matter of fact, Stark was relatively sure there *weren't* any assault rifles in the park. The residents who owned guns had their hunting rifles and shotguns, along with handguns they had bought after Texas began issuing concealed carry permits. Maybe there were a few weapons that had been modified illegally, but not many, Stark thought, because the people who lived at Shady Hills were law-abiding citizens.

And as usual these days, there was a good chance they would get penalized for that.

"Why did you come to see me, anyway?" Stark went on. "Jack Kasek and his wife own the park."

"Because I knew you'd be the ringleader of any militia that was forming out here," Lozano replied. His voice was hard and blunt.

"Militia's a buzzword, Sheriff. It conjures up images of wild-eyed domestic terrorists, which is exactly what the people who throw it around want it to do."

"Are you denying it?"

"Damn straight I'm denying it," Stark said. "We don't have any militia out here. Maybe we're being a little more watchful these days, but after what happened, can you blame us?"

Lozano didn't answer that. Instead he looked at Stark for a long moment and then asked, "How many people have moved out of here in the last five days?"

Stark's mouth tightened. That was a troubling aspect of the whole situation. There had been close to two hundred mobile homes in the park on the night of the raid. But since then, starting the very next day, trucks and work crews had shown up to move some of them out. Only about a dozen so far, but the owners had given up their leases, found other places to live, and moved out, lock, stock, and barrel. If trouble erupted again, Stark felt sure that more of the residents would leave. If the trouble was bad enough, it might cause a mass exodus.

"What's your point, Sheriff?" he asked.

"My point is that the people who have left did so because they were afraid. They know something's coming, and they don't want to be here when it happens."

"If that's the way you feel, then I'd think you'd be trying to give us more protection out here."

"I'm giving you all the protection I can," Lozano said. He took off his Stetson and ran his fingers through his thick dark hair. "Look, Mr. Stark, I hate those drug smugglers as much as you do."

"I sort of doubt that," Stark said quietly.

Lozano ignored him and went on, "I'd like to put a stop to all their activities in this area, I swear I would. But I have limited resources, and not only that, I have lawyers watching my department with eagle eyes, just waiting for us to violate some poor criminal's civil rights. I work for the county commissioners, and they've made it clear. If I or my deputies do anything to open the county up to a federal lawsuit, they'll take it out on my ass."

"So we're supposed to pack up and get out and let the cartel have this land so the county won't get sued?" Stark didn't bother trying to keep the disbelief and scorn out of his voice as he asked the question.

"That's not what I said, damn it! But arming yourselves . . . turning any little thing into a bloodbath . . . that's not gonna help anything, Stark."

"If there's a bloodbath, it won't be us who causes it," Stark said grimly.

"But some of your people will die," Lozano shot back at him. "Have you thought about that?"

Of course he had. He had lost sleep over it, in fact, lying awake and thinking of the violent end that some of the residents would likely come to if there was another confrontation with the drug smugglers. The very idea sickened Stark.

But he had a hunch that if the people of Shady Hill didn't try to defend themselves, things would be even worse. It wasn't beyond the realm of possibility that those cartel gunnies would storm in here and try to wipe out the whole park.

Talk about your bloodbath.

"Sheriff, I don't know what to tell you," Stark said. "There's no militia, we don't have any assault rifles—or bazookas or tanks, either, although under certain circumstances I wouldn't mind—and we're not going to start any trouble. We'll fight if we're forced to in order to defend our loved ones and protect our homes, but probably ninety-five percent of the people in the state of Texas, outside the city limits of Austin, would tell you the same thing."

Lozano clapped his hat back on his head and snapped, "Fine. Consider yourself warned. Step outside the bounds of the law and you'll be treated like any other criminal."

"You mean the media will talk about how I'm just a misunderstood victim of a heartless American society and a bunch of Hollywood actors will come and wave protest signs about how I should be released because I'm a political prisoner?"

The sheriff just made a frustrated noise deep in his throat and turned to stalk back to his SUV. Stark had to chuckle as he watched Lozano walk off.

Then his expression grew more serious. Every instinct in Stark's body warned him that a storm was brewing and that it would break soon with all the ferocity of a cyclone. But that might not be the worst of it. Those who survived could face an even greater ordeal when it was over, if what Lozano was saying was true.

Having a Mexican drug cartel gunning for you was bad enough.

Stark had good reason to know that having the federal government on your ass was even worse.

CHAPTER TWENTY-SIX

The residents of Shady Hills preparing themselves for an armed invasion probably would have drawn more attention from the media if not for another story that broke that week, the unexpected (by some) revelation that the former president who had ordered the nerve gas attack on American citizens opposed to his policies had had extensive ties in his youth to an Islamic terrorist group in the Far East. Evidence had surfaced to indicate that he had taken part in the planning of a bombing attack on an American embassy, an attack that had never taken place because the CIA had discovered it in time to stop it. The network pundits and news anchors were having a field day ganging up on the former chief executive, no doubt in the hope that that would make everyone forget they had been his biggest cheerleaders for years and years and were largely responsible for getting him elected to high office in the first place.

Rats, sinking ship, etc., etc., Stark thought as he watched the near-hysterical coverage day after day. But at least it kept attention focused somewhere else other than the Shady Hills Retirement Park.

As dusk settled in on the day Sheriff Lozano had paid his visit to the park, Stark drove his pickup out to the gate to check with the guards there. Four men were on duty. He didn't recall their names, although he remembered talking to them at the organizational meeting. They introduced themselves to him again and shook hands.

"Something wrong, Mr. Stark?" one of them asked. "You don't normally come out here in the evening, do you?"

"No, I'm just feeling a little antsy today," Stark replied.

"You think something's going to happen?"

Stark shook his head and said, "I don't know. Maybe I'm just feeling my age. But I've got a hunch you fellas need to keep your eyes and ears open extra wide tonight."

"We'd be doing that anyway," another of the men said. "Hey, I heard that the sheriff came out to talk to you today, Mr. Stark. What did he want?"

"He was warning us not to do anything illegal," Stark replied dryly. "And telling us again that we're on our own."

"Those things seem rather self-contradictory." The man who made the comment had been a philosophy professor in college before he retired, Stark recalled. "Of course, if you subscribe to an existentialist belief system—"

"What Phil means," one of the other guards interrupted with a grin, "is that we're screwed either way."

That brought laughter all around.

The gate guards were connected to the roaming patrol and to all six of the captains by walkie-talkies. While Stark was there they ran a comm check on the units, all of which were working perfectly. Stark said good night to the men.

"And good luck," Phil the philosophy professor added. "That's what you mean, isn't it?

"We can always use good luck," Stark said.

He drove back to his house and found Hallie Duncan

sitting on the porch steps. He had seen her car parked at her dad's earlier, so he'd known she was in the park, but he hadn't expected her to pay him a visit.

"Good to see you, Hallie," he said. "What brings you here tonight?"

She patted the step beside her and said, "Sit down, John Howard."

"Uh-oh. Something about that doesn't sound good."

"What, me asking you to sit with me?"

"Not that, just your tone of voice," Stark said as he settled onto the step beside her. "You've got some bad news."

"I got a call today from my friend who works at the Justice Department."

Stark drew in a deep breath.

"Go ahead," he told her.

"He discovered that your name is flagged in Justice's computers. They monitor just about everything—TV, radio, the Internet—and every mention of you on any news outlet anywhere generates a report that goes straight to the office of the attorney general."

"So they're keeping an eye on me," Stark said with a shrug. "That doesn't surprise me."

"No, what they're doing is waiting for an opportunity to pounce on you, John Howard. They want to come down on you with both feet as hard as they can, and they'll do it if you give them the least excuse."

"I don't doubt it. But that doesn't change anything, does it? The folks here are still in danger. They have to be able to protect themselves, and I'm willing to help 'em."

"There's more, but I don't really understand it. Josh is a pretty good hacker. He's really risking his neck poking around in computers where he's not supposed to be, but he found a link from your name to a file called 'Silence.'"

He couldn't get in there. The encryption was too good. Do you have any idea what that might be about, John Howard?"

Stark shook his head.

"Nope. Not a clue."

"I think they've got your name on a list of people to be silenced."

"You mean killed?" Stark asked in surprise.

"It's certainly a possibility."

Stark frowned in thought for a moment, then said, "I don't know, Hallie, that seems pretty unlikely to me. Sure, there are folks in Washington who wouldn't mind making my life a living hell, but they're more likely to set the IRS on me again, or file some civil rights suit against me and try to bankrupt me, or just generally harass me. Seems hard to believe that the attorney general would have his own private assassin working for him, rubbing out anybody who disagrees with the administration."

"Is it really that hard to believe, John Howard? Is it really? Think about the things they've pulled over the past ten years."

"Different president now," Stark pointed out.

"Does that matter? He's just as self-deluded and power-hungry as the rest of them. He and his allies know better than you do when it comes to your money, your health care, your religion, and everything else about you. They want to control everything you do from the moment you're born until you're lowered into the ground. But it's all for your own good, of course, so that justifies any means they want to use to grab more power."

Hallie had a bitter edge in her voice as she spoke. A raw, bleeding edge, Stark thought. The whole country was being drained dry by the politicians and bureaucrats in Washington, and none of them cared how badly the average Americans were hurting.

"I didn't know you were so political, Hallie," Stark commented. "You've never said much about things like that."

"I work in the justice system," she said with a shrug. "It's full of people who firmly believe in the things the other side is doing, even though the evidence that it doesn't work is right in front of their eyes every day, over and over again. But I still have to work with them and get along with them, so mostly I just keep my mouth shut."

"Just like people who work at universities."

"Yeah. Those bastions of diversity and tolerance . . . as long as you agree with them one hundred percent."

"None of which means that the attorney general is planning to have me killed."

"No, but you'd better be careful anyway."

"I always am," Stark said, smiling.

"No, I mean it." She reached over and took hold of his hand, squeezing it warmly. "I don't want anything to happen to you, John Howard."

She didn't let go of his hand. After a moment Stark said quietly, "Hallie . . ."

She leaned over and rested her head against his shoulder.

"Damn it, John Howard," she said in a voice little more than a whisper, "I know you've got it in your head that the two of us have to stay just friends, but there's no reason it has to be that way."

"Yeah, there is," Stark said. He tried not to sound harsh as the words came out, but he was afraid he did anyway.

"Why? Because you were married? I never knew your wife, John Howard, but if she loved you, and I'm sure she did, she would have wanted you to move on and have some warmth, some happiness, in your life."

"I reckon that's true," Stark said, remembering what he'd had with Elaine. What Hallie had just said was right, there was no doubt about that.

"Then why are you being so blasted stubborn? Tell me one good reason why the two of us shouldn't go inside your mobile home right now and give each other some happiness."

Stark could tell her one good reason, all right, and he was about to when the walkie-talkie clipped to his belt crackled into life. A voice he recognized as Phil the professor's said urgently, "Mr. Stark! Everybody! Come in, come in! Vehicles headed for the gate, and they're coming fast!"

CHAPTER TWENTY-SEVEN

Stark lunged to his feet and grabbed the walkie-talkie from his belt. As he started toward his pickup, he keyed the unit and said, "Stark here, Phil. On my way. How many incoming?"

"How many?" Phil asked someone else, then told Stark, "Four sets of headlights!"

"Four—"

Stark came to a sudden stop before he reached his truck. Something wasn't right. He turned and called to Hallie, who was on her feet as well, "Get in your dad's house! Stay there!"

"I can fight—" she began.

"No, just get inside!"

He didn't look back to see if she followed his orders or not. He hoped she would, but there wasn't time to make sure. Instead he ran around the front of his pickup, threw himself behind the wheel, and cranked the engine. When it caught he threw the truck into gear, tromped the gas, and sent it screeching into motion as he called into the walkie-talkie, "Red alert! Red alert!"

He didn't speed toward the gate, though. Instead he

careened around a corner and headed for the rear of the park.

The cartel wouldn't attack the retirement park with only four vehicles. Stark was sure of that. Which meant what was happening at the front gate was only a feint. The real strike would be somewhere else, and the most likely place was along the chain-link fence that ran across the back of the property.

The window of Stark's pickup was down. Even over the roar of the truck's engine he could hear the sound of air horns going off all over the park as word of the potential attack spread. Every house had one of the horns. The residents had pitched in to buy them, and if anybody couldn't afford one, the others picked up the slack.

That was the way things were supposed to work, with people helping out not because government forced them to but because it was the right thing to do. As soon as the captains started blowing their air horns, everybody else picked up on the signal and started spreading it as well. Nobody in Shady Hills was going to be taken by surprise tonight.

Or maybe they would be, Stark thought as he accelerated around another corner, if the real attack came from a direction they weren't looking.

He steered with one hand and brought the walkie-talkie to his mouth with the other. His thumb pushed the talk button.

"Nick! Doug! Bring your crews to the back of the park, repeat, the back of the park!"

"John Howard, is that you?" Nick Medford's voice crackled back at him.

"Yeah! Did you get my orders? Head for the rear fence!"

"But they're attacking the gate!" Nick protested.

"It's a trick! The rest of them are coming in the back!"

Stark hoped his hunch was right. If it wasn't, then he was splitting his forces for no good reason and the guards at the gate might be overwhelmed. Stark didn't really expect them to hold off the attack and prevent the cartel thugs from getting into the park, but he wanted them to slow down the assault long enough for everyone else to get ready for it. That shouldn't take long. They had been running drills for days now.

Stark turned another corner into a cul-de-sac that ended at the rear property line, and as he did the pickup's headlights washed over the chain-link fence. He was just in time to see a pickup running without lights crash through that fence, sending the tautly strung links snapping back crazily.

Stark slammed on the brakes and spun his truck's wheel. It turned and went into a slide that left him sitting broadside to the pickup that rumbled toward him. His shotgun was on the seat beside him. He picked it up, thrust the barrel through the open passenger-side window, and fired a load of buckshot at the onrushing vehicle. The windshield exploded into a million razor-sharp shards.

But the pickup kept coming, and Stark had no choice but to bail out. He threw his door open, dived from the pickup, and scrambled to his feet with the shotgun in both hands.

Behind him, the invaders' pickup T-boned his truck and knocked it over on its side. Gasoline splattered and burst into flame, and an instant later a fireball blossomed and engulfed both vehicles. The concussive force of the blast struck Stark in the back and made him stagger.

He caught his balance and whirled around, wincing slightly at the terrific heat that came off the flames. More engines roared. A couple of low-riders swerved around the inferno in the middle of the street, one to the right and the other to the left. Muzzle flashes stabbed from the windows of both cars.

Stark ran across the corner of a yard and dived behind a row of trash cans as bullets slammed into them, causing a lot of racket. He looked toward the fence and saw more cars and pickups coming through the gap the first pickup had rammed in it.

The attack wasn't proceeding without resistance, though. Windows from which the screens had been removed flew up in mobile homes on both sides of the street. Stark knew that inside those windows were homemade barricades that would protect the residents as they fought. More shots blasted as the defenders opened fire on the raiders with shotguns, deer rifles, .22s, and an assortment of handguns. The cartel's thugs suddenly found themselves in a cross fire.

Windows shattered in the vehicles. Some of them shuddered to a halt with steam and smoke pouring from under their hoods. Tires exploded as bullets pierced them, and sparks flew up from the asphalt as some of the cars were suddenly running on their rims.

Stark reached to the holster at the small of his back and pulled out his .45. He came up on one knee and drew a bead on a man who burst from one of the stopped vehicles with a chattering machine pistol in his hand. Stark fired a couple of well-aimed rounds and saw the gunner's head explode from the impact of the two heavy slugs. The machine pistol fell silent abruptly as its owner flopped to the ground.

Stark turned a little and fired again. This time his bullet cored through the chest of a thug yelling incoherent curses and firing a pistol. The invader stumbled, fell to his knees, and then pitched forward on his face to lie motionless.

Tires screeched as reinforcements for the defenders arrived. Cars and SUVs crowded into the far end of the cul-de-sac, and the volunteers led by Nick Medford and Doug Jacobs poured out of them. The men spread out across the yards of the homes along the short street, taking cover behind trees, garbage cans, and vehicles as they opened fire on the intruders.

Stark stayed where he was and continued lining up shots. So many bullets were flying around in the air that it would be dangerous to try to change position unless he had to. He squeezed off a shot and was rewarded by the sight of a cartel thug's arm jerking and then flopping loosely with a shattered elbow. The thug reeled behind a pickup, screaming in pain.

When Stark's .45 was empty, he ejected the clip and reached into his pocket for a fully loaded one he had stuck there earlier, before he knew there would be an attack tonight. As he slid the new clip into place, he glanced toward the front of the retirement park. He could hear shots from up there too and knew the battle was going on in both places.

A trio of thugs, each wielding a pump shotgun, burst from the cover of a low-rider and charged the volunteers blocking the street. Load after load of buckshot erupted from the shotguns, but the raiders made it only about ten yards before they were scythed off their feet by the deadly return fire from the defenders.

A second later, Stark realized that the foolhardy charge had been a diversion when he saw one of the cartel men kneeling next to a pickup with something balanced on his shoulder. Stark's eyes widened in shock. He had been joking when he'd mentioned a bazooka to Sheriff Lozano, but he saw now that the invaders were armed with something more up-to-date but equally dangerous.

The thug was aiming a grenade launcher at the defenders' vehicles blocking the entrance to the cul-de-sac!

CHAPTER TWENTY-EIGHT

Stark fired, the bullets from his automatic hammering into the man and knocking him to the side just as the rocket-propelled grenade erupted from the launcher, spewing a brilliant trail of fire behind it.

The launcher had been jolted into an upward angle as the man fell, however, so the grenade rose steadily as it flew through the air. It detonated high in the limbs of a cottonwood tree across the street, sending splinters flying everywhere.

Another man darted out from behind a car, making a try for the fallen grenade launcher. Stark was ready for him and drove him back with a couple of rounds. The man staggered back into cover, clutching a broken shoulder.

The nerve of the invaders was broken as well. Thanks to Stark's quick action and the timely arrival of the volunteers, the cartel thugs had been bottled up here in the cul-de-sac and were unable to spread their terror attack through the rest of the retirement park. Their attempt to break out using the grenade launcher had failed.

Now it was time to cut their losses and run.

That was what they did, falling back toward the fence

as they kept up a heavy covering fire. Their vehicles were disabled with bullet-shredded tires and blown engines, so they fled on foot. Stark and his fellow defenders hurried them on their way with buckshot and bullets. The cartel's retreat, orderly at first, quickly turned into a full-blown, panic-stricken rout as the invaders abandoned the attack and ran for their lives.

The shooting gradually died away. Stark stood up from his crouch and surveyed the scene. Every porch light on the block was on, except the ones that had been shot out, and a number of floodlights mounted on the mobile homes blazed as well, casting plenty of illumination over the carnage in the street.

More than half a dozen bodies lay sprawled and motionless around the cartel's pickups and low-riders. Stark's own pickup, along with the vehicle that had slammed into it, were charred husks. He was sure there would be more bodies in the cartel pickup, too. He estimated the invaders' losses at ten or twelve dead, along with at least three times that many wounded. No telling what the toll had been at the gate, but the shooting from there had stopped, too, Stark noted.

Sheriff Lozano had warned him about causing a bloodbath. This came pretty close to fitting that description. But he and his friends hadn't caused it, Stark thought. All they had done was defend themselves from vicious, well-armed, ruthless invaders. No doubt they had paid a price to do that.

And no doubt they would continue to pay a price, Stark mused grimly. The battle was over . . . but not the war.

The first order of business was to check on the fallen invaders and make sure they were either dead or injured badly enough not to put up any more fight. Some of the volunteers helped Stark with that while others went door-to-door to check on the defenders and summon medical help for those who needed it. Several doctors and a number of nurses, all retired, lived in the park, and they had offered their services as medics until ambulances could get here from Devil's Pass.

The death toll among the invaders was slightly higher than Stark had estimated. They found fourteen corpses, including three in the burned-out pickup. Another five men were wounded and unconscious. Stark figured some of them would succumb to their injuries.

He used his walkie-talkie to check in with the forces at the gate.

"Nick, how are things up there? You copy, Nick?"

Nick Medford's voice came back, and Stark was relieved to hear that the man sounded like he was all right.

"We drove them off, Mr. Stark," Nick reported. "They managed to get inside the gate, but then we shot out their tires and pinned them down, just like you talked about, and after a while they all piled into the two cars that were still running and got out of here."

"Good job," Stark told him. "Any casualties?"

Nick's voice became thick with emotion as he said, "José Alvarez was killed."

Stark drew a deep breath in through his nose as his jaw clenched. He didn't know his neighbor José Alvarez well, but any loss affected all of them.

"Any others?" he asked.

"A couple of bullet wounds, but nothing too bad. We were lucky."

Stark knew that was true. The invaders had spread around a lot of lead. Fortunately, they didn't seem to be very good shots. They had never had to be. They'd usually had the advantage of numbers and superior firepower.

Not tonight, though.

Except for that grenade launcher, of course.

Stark told Nick to let him know when the emergency vehicles got there from Devil's Pass, then went and picked up the launcher. It was U.S. military issue, of course, stolen from somewhere by the cartel.

He supposed they were fortunate that the invaders *hadn't* shown up tonight with a tank.

With things under control, Stark took out his cell phone and thumbed the speed dial number for Alton Duncan's house. When his next-door neighbor answered, Stark said, "Hey, Alton, everybody all right there?"

"John Howard!" Alton exclaimed. "Man, it's good to hear your voice! We were all worried about you."

"Did Hallie stay there with you like I told her to?"

It wasn't Alton who answered the question, and as he heard Hallie's voice he realized that she had taken the phone away from her dad.

"Yes, I stayed here, but don't get used to giving me orders, John Howard," she said. "Are you all right?"

"I'm fine," Stark assured her. "Think I might've twisted my knee a little when I jumped out of my truck, but it's nothing to worry about." He paused. "My truck, on the other hand, is a total loss."

"I'm sorry."

"Don't be. I can replace it. You're sure everybody's all right there?"

"The fighting never got anywhere close to us," Hallie said. "Is it over?"

"For now. Those fellas the cartel sent to run us off have done some running away themselves. The ones who still could, that is."

"John Howard . . . were some of them killed?"

"More than a dozen," Stark said flatly.

He heard Hallie sigh on the other end of the connection.

"You know this is just getting started, don't you? It's really going to hit the fan now."

"I figured as much," Stark said. "But what else were we gonna do? Let those animals bust in here, slaughter half of us, and send the rest running for the hills? We couldn't do that."

"No, I know you couldn't. I'm just saying to get ready for more trouble, and it won't be the kind you can fight with shotguns and rifles this time."

Stark smiled, even though she couldn't see him.

"I'm not worried," he said. "I've got a good lawyer."

CHAPTER TWENTY-NINE

The apartment building was old but well kept up, and its location near Dupont Circle meant that it was also expensive. There was never any shortage of tenants, however, despite the high rent. A number of very well-paid lobbyists lived here, along with various legislative aides and deputy assistant undersecretaries from the different cabinet departments, most of whom came from wealthy families that had paid for their educations at Harvard and Yale and helped them secure their positions in the government, where they could help pass legislation that raised taxes and spending in a never-ending spiral and implemented regulations that made it virtually impossible for small businesses to comply and generate any profit at all.

But that was all right. As long as the middle class made any money at all, the government could just keep on taking it.

And foolish sheep that they were, the average citizens would allow the government to keep on doing just that, Ryan thought as he rode up in the elevator with a couple of young men who looked barely old enough to be out of the exclusive prep schools they had no doubt attended.

"Senator Bascomb's going to introduce the bill next week," one of them was saying to the other.

"What's it going to do again?"

"Create a commission to study the commission on equitable distribution of healthcare benefits and also empower the secretary of health and human services to establish new guidelines to cut off coverage for non-viable patients."

"Non-viable meaning?"

"Anyone over the age of seventy. Although I'm trying to persuade the senator that he can get away with a provision lowering that to sixty-eight."

The second legislative aide laughed.

"And we used to accuse the other side of wanting to turn Granny out into the street to let her die."

"I know! And people actually bought it!"

As the two of them snickered, Ryan thought about how easy it would be to reach over and snap their necks, one at a time. He would be doing the world a service, he told himself.

But if he left their bodies in the elevator, he ran the risk of having them discovered, and that might interfere with the job that had brought him here. He didn't want that.

So when the elevator stopped on the third floor and the two young men, still telling themselves with smug satisfaction how smart they were, stepped out of the car, Ryan just smiled and said, "You fellas have yourselves a good night now."

They glanced back at him, obviously wondering why some middle-aged nobody was even talking to *them*, the best and the brightest of yet another generation of self-proclaimed best and brightest, and walked off never knowing how close they had come to death.

The door closed and the elevator rose smoothly toward the fourth floor, where Ryan's target lived.

His employer hadn't been happy that he was still in Washington instead of in Texas dealing with John Howard Stark, but Ryan operated on his own timetable, always had and always would. Anyway, it was a lucky break that he was here, because there was another little mess that needed to be cleaned up.

And cleaning up was his specialty, after all.

The elevator stopped again and announced in a sleekly modulated, recorded female voice, "Fourth floor." The door opened and Ryan stepped out.

His footsteps made no sound on the thick carpet in the hallway as he looked for apartment 407, finding it four doors up on his left. Before he could knock on it, the door of one of the other apartments on his right opened behind him. His first impulse was to look back and make sure he hadn't walked into some sort of setup. Probably some of his contacts in the government lost sleep at night from worrying that he knew too much. They might have decided it would be better just to get rid of him.

But if the door opening was entirely innocent, as it probably was, then he didn't want to show his face to whoever was back there.

He kept walking, going past 407 so that no one could testify that he'd stopped there. He heard footsteps receding behind him. A man said, "We've got plenty of time to make it. The reservation isn't until nine."

"Sure, plenty of time," a woman said. "If nobody else is on the streets of Washington tonight. That's *bound* to happen."

"Why don't you just let me worry about it, okay?"

"Fine." The woman's voice was chilly. "You won't hear me say anything else about it."

Ryan smiled faintly as he heard the elevator door open. That was going to be a tense ride down to the lobby, he thought.

When the elevator closed, he swung around and started back toward 407. The corridor was deserted now. He'd already made sure there were no security cameras in the hallway itself. While he was in the elevator he had kept his head turned so that his face would be partially obscured from the camera in there, without being too obvious about what he was doing. The same was true in the lobby downstairs.

The two legislative aides he had ridden up with might remember him, especially since he had spoken to them. That had been a dumb move, he told himself. They had annoyed him, though. Anyway, a couple of self-centered brats like that might remember him vaguely, but they wouldn't be able to describe him. Ryan knew from experience that eyewitnesses were notoriously unreliable, even when they supposedly were paying attention.

Ryan stopped in front of the door to 407, took a pair of skin-colored latex gloves from his coat pocket, and pulled them on. He knocked on the door.

Ten seconds later, the target opened it. Ryan recognized him right away from the photo that had been emailed to him. The man had been young and handsome once, with thick, unruly dark hair. Now that hair was thinning and shot through with gray, his waistline had thickened considerably, and there were pouches of weariness under his eyes. He said, "Yeah? Can I help you?"

Ryan reached under his coat and took out a manila envelope.

"Josh Mumford?"

"That's right."

"I've got a delivery for you."

Ryan was too old and too well-dressed to be a messenger, although in today's ruinous economy, you never could tell. People took whatever jobs they could get.

Everybody liked to get packages, though, and since Mumford worked at the Justice Department, he probably had documents delivered to him fairly regularly. He said, "Oh, thanks," and stuck out his hand to take the envelope.

Instead of handing it over, Ryan dropped the envelope and grabbed Mumford's wrist. He jerked the man toward him, at the same time taking a syringe and hypodermic needle from his pocket. He stabbed the needle into Mumford's neck just below the jawline and shoved the plunger down. It should have been an awkward maneuver with Ryan's missing thumb and finger, but he had done this often enough that he had no trouble with it.

Death happened so fast Mumford's eyes barely had time to widen in surprise before they began to glaze over.

Ryan pulled Mumford closer and got an arm around him to hold him up. He kicked the envelope into the apartment and wrestled Mumford out of the doorway, then heeled the door closed behind him. He pulled the needle out and put it back in his pocket.

The computer on Mumford's desk was on, and the swivel chair in front of the desk was turned toward the door. Ryan carried the dead man over and lowered him into the chair. Mumford's head sagged forward. Ryan turned the chair so that Mumford was facing toward the monitor again.

A top-notch medical examiner might notice the needle mark, but given its location the chances were that it would be mistaken for a tiny shaving nick. Ryan saw several similar tiny marks on Mumford's neck. Anyway, there wouldn't be any reason for anybody to be suspicious. The drug in the syringe mimicked a heart attack so closely that it was almost undetectable. Just looking at Mumford, he appeared to be a prime candidate for cardiac arrest, and he would be found in front of his computer, where a lot of people were found dead these days.

Facebook was up on the monitor screen, Ryan saw. He patted Mumford lightly on the shoulder and said, "Should've updated your status while you had the chance, amigo. And you shouldn't have hacked into things that were none of your business."

He looked around, made sure he hadn't left any signs of his presence, and left the apartment, setting the lock on the door and easing it closed behind him. He was just starting to turn away from it when the elevator door opened a few yards down the hall and a man charged out of it.

He wasn't attacking Ryan, though. He was muttering to himself instead, saying, "If she wouldn't pester me all the time, I wouldn't forget my damn wallet—"

He looked up and saw Ryan standing in front of the door to Josh Mumford's apartment.

Ryan reached into his pocket, took out a small automatic barely bigger than the palm of his hand, and shot the man twice in the forehead. The shots halted the man's momentum in midstep, and he wavered before pitching against the wall and sliding to the floor. Blood began to pool under him and soak into the carpet.

Ryan uttered a heartfelt curse. This was an unlucky break. Even unluckier for the guy who was going to miss his late dinner reservation after all.

The man didn't have his wallet, clearly, because he'd left it in his apartment and come back to get it. But he had keys to a Lexus in his pocket. Ryan took them to make it look as much like he could as a robbery. Having a guy killed in a mugging almost right outside the door of another guy who'd died of a heart attack about the same time might set off a few flares, but the cops wouldn't be able to prove anything.

Nobody emerged from any of the other apartments. The gun didn't have a noise suppressor on it, but it was pretty quiet to start with. Ryan walked along the hall to the stairs. No cameras in the stairwell. He shook his head. For a building in the nation's capital, they didn't take their security seriously enough. Of course, that worked to his benefit, so he wasn't going to complain.

Five minutes later he was driving back toward his own place in Georgetown, somewhat irritated that the night's work hadn't gone perfectly. Life was full of unexpected developments, though, and all a man could do was adapt to them.

CHAPTER THIRTY

Stark hoped there were no other law enforcement emergencies in the county tonight, because every available deputy was here at Shady Hills, along with Sheriff George Lozano himself.

"I warned you this would happen, Stark," Lozano said angrily as they stood beside his SUV that was parked not far inside the gate. "Damn it, I warned you!"

"It sounds like you're more worried about those men who tried to kill us than you are about the law-abiding citizens of this park," Stark snapped back at him. He had just about lost all his patience with Lozano. He didn't believe the sheriff was in bed with the cartel, but with the politician's instincts that had gotten him elected in the first place, Lozano didn't want to rock anybody's boat too much, either.

Ambulances moved back and forth steadily from the retirement park, transporting bodies to the morgue. The first thing the EMTs had done was to stabilize and load up the wounded to take them to the hospital in Devil's Pass. Deputies went along to guard all of them, including the residents of the park. An outraged Sheriff Lozano had declared that until a full investigation had been conducted, he was going to consider everybody here a possible suspect in numerous crimes. Hallie had protested that the residents had been acting in self-defense, but Lozano had told her to take that up with the district attorney.

"Don't worry," she'd told him with an angry snort of her own. "I will."

Now Stark and Lozano were meeting one on one, and the air was thick with anger on both sides. Even so, Stark wasn't expecting what happened next.

"You're under arrest," Lozano said. "Put your hands behind your back."

Stark's eyebrows rose in surprise.

"Under arrest?" he repeated. "What the hell is the charge?"

"Inciting a riot, for one thing. This bloodshed might not have happened if you hadn't armed these people and stirred them up into a killing frenzy."

"You've got to be joking," Stark snapped. "Those thugs showed up and started shooting at us first. We just returned their fire."

Lozano shook his head and said, "That's not how the survivors tell it. According to them, they were just driving by the park—on a public road, I might add—when the residents opened fire on them. That's on you, Stark."

"First off, that's a blasted lie, and second, what about the ones who came in the back? They drove a pickup right through the fence. That's *trespassing*, at the very least," Stark said with a thick note of scorn in his voice.

"And that may be all we can prove against them. Again, you can't work up a bunch of old geezers so they start shooting at somebody for knocking down a fence."

Stark knew that Lozano was being willfully obstinate. The sheriff wasn't stupid; he knew what had happened here. But for reasons of his own, he was bending over backwards to give the benefit of the doubt to the invaders.

Maybe he *was* being paid off, Stark thought.

Or else Lozano was just scared of what might happen if he openly defied the cartel. The sheriff had a teenage daughter and son, Stark recalled, along with a very attractive wife. He had seen a picture of the whole family in the newspaper after the last election.

Stark could feel a little sympathy for Lozano if the man was frightened about what might happen to his family. But that didn't excuse Lozano's failure to do his duty. If you were going to be in law enforcement, some risk always went along with the job.

"You're really going to arrest me?" Stark asked.

"Damn right I am. Now turn around." Lozano rested his hand on the butt of the holstered revolver at his side. "Or are you going to resist?"

"I'm a law-abiding man," Stark said. He turned away from Lozano and put his hands behind his back. He felt metal bite into his skin as the sheriff snapped old-fashioned handcuffs onto his wrists.

"Hey! Hey, what the hell are you doing?"

That shout came from Hallie, who had gone off to check on some of the residents of the park. Stark looked over his shoulder and saw her running toward him and the sheriff.

"Stay back, Ms. Duncan," Lozano told her. "Mr. Stark is under arrest, and you don't want to be interfering with me right now."

"Under arrest?" Hallie said, obviously flabbergasted. "What in the world for?"

"We'll decide that later after I've talked to the DA." Lozano took hold of Stark's arm and turned him toward the SUV. "Come on."

"Wait a minute! He's my client!"

"You can see him after he's been booked." Lozano opened the rear door and told Stark, "Get in."

"John Howard!"

"It's all right, Hallie," he told her. "I'll see you at the jail."

"But . . . but this is crazy!"

"These days, it seems like everything else in the world is, too," Stark said. "So I suppose we shouldn't be surprised."

Stark was booked into the jail in Devil's Pass. Instead of putting him in the holding tank with the drunks, Sheriff Lozano had him placed in a cell by himself.

"No need to put you on suicide watch, is there?" Lozano asked through the bars of the door after it slid shut and locked.

Stark snorted and said, "Not hardly."

"Fine. You'll have a chance to talk to your lawyer and post a bail bond in the morning. It's too late to take care of that tonight."

Stark nodded. He sat down on the bunk and tested the mattress with his hand.

"You may not know this, Sheriff," he said, "but I've spent the night in places that were a whole heap worse than this."

Lozano started to turn away, but he paused and said, "You brought this on yourself, you know."

"I suppose you could look at it that way. But the way I see it, I didn't have much choice in the matter. Somebody had to help those folks at Shady Hills. If it hadn't been me, it would have been somebody else."

Stark wasn't sure that was completely true, though. He

wasn't certain anybody else would have been so blasted stubborn. His wife, Elaine, had told him more than once that he could give any mule in the world a run for its money when it came to hardheadedness.

Lozano grunted and said, "I'll see you in the morning." As he walked away from the cell his footsteps echoed from cinder-block walls painted an ugly, institutional green.

Stark leaned back against the wall and closed his eyes. He hadn't been frightened, but he'd been concerned about being placed in with other prisoners. It probably wouldn't have been too difficult for the cartel to send somebody after him in those circumstances. Lozano must have known that, too. Stark was the sort of man who was willing to rely on himself and take his chances no matter where he found himself, but it didn't hurt anything to decrease the odds against him.

The lights dimmed but didn't go out. He stretched out, rolled onto his side so that he was facing the wall, and went to sleep.

By ten o'clock the next morning he was walking out of the jail a free man, at least for the time being, with Hallie at his side. The judge had set his bail at two hundred and fifty thousand dollars, but several bail bondsmen were champing at the bit to write the bond for him. Paying the bail for John Howard Stark was good publicity, Hallie had explained.

Because Stark was news this morning. Big news.

She showed him the huge headline on the local paper: BATTLE AT RETIREMENT PARK. Stark's picture was on the front page, along with an even larger photo of the two burned-out vehicles. They really did look like something from a war zone, Stark thought.

"What did they wind up charging me with?" Stark asked.

"Inciting a riot, disturbing the peace, assault with a deadly weapon, and attempted manslaughter," Hallie said.

"And bail was only a quarter of a million? I got off light."

"Oh, it's not over. The DA hasn't decided whether to charge you with manslaughter or murder in the deaths of those fourteen thugs."

"Wait a minute," Stark said. "I didn't kill all of them myself."

Hallie shook her head.

"It doesn't matter. According to the law of parties, you planned the whole thing, so you're just as responsible for their deaths as whoever actually killed them."

"Which nobody really knows, since it was in the thick of battle."

"That's right. But Jack Kasek and the other volunteer captains are going to be arrested and charged, too, under the same statutes."

"Blast it, that's just not right!" Stark said.

"No, it's not," Hallie agreed. "But from the looks of things, John Howard, you'd better get used to the insides of courtrooms and jail cells, because you're going to be seeing a lot of them."

CHAPTER THIRTY-ONE

"You don't have to tell me," the president said as the chief of staff came into the Oval Office. "I saw it on the news for myself. That bastard Stark's raising hell in Texas again."

"What I came to tell you, sir, is that the attorney general wants to see you."

"When?"

The chief of staff hesitated, then said, "He's outside now."

The president sighed.

"All right. Bring him in. And you're sitting in on the meeting, too."

"Of course, sir."

A minute later the three of them were alone in the Oval Office, two grim-faced men in front of the desk and another behind it. The president clasped his hands together and asked, "Do you think we need to bring federal charges for civil rights violations against Stark?"

"I don't see how we can avoid it," the chief of staff said. "He masterminded this whole thing. Not only that, but the secretary of state has asked for a meeting with you as well.

We've got the Mexican government raising hell because half a dozen of those dead men were Mexican nationals."

"In Texas illegally, I might add," the attorney general said.

The president waved that off and said, "What does that matter? For all intents and purposes, the border's open anyway, and it'll stay that way as long as the wetbacks are so good at getting phony Social Security cards, registering to vote, and voting for us."

Both of his subordinates winced.

"You, uh, can't use that word, sir," the chief of staff said.

"And you can't condone voter fraud," the AG added.

The president snorted in disgust.

"Are either of you secretly taping this meeting?" he asked.

Both aides reacted with vehement denials.

"Then don't worry about my choice of words," the president went on. "I know what I can say in public and what I can't. As for the other, half the shining lights in our party never would've gotten elected in the first place without a little judicious ballot box stuffing, so let's not be hypocrites among ourselves." He looked at the attorney general. "I suppose you should launch a full-scale investigation right away—"

"No, sir."

The president looked shocked that the attorney general had not only interrupted him but had disagreed with him as well.

"Did you say no?"

"We're still hurting over that nerve gas business. Half the country hates us to start with, and the other half was pretty shaken when that news broke. Sure, we were able to spin it as one inexperienced politician breaking under the strain of the job, and there are quite a few people who have convinced themselves that it never even happened, that the right-wing extremists made up the whole thing. But Stark is still widely regarded as a hero. Back when he first came to Washington's attention with that raid on the drug cartel in Mexico, there was an attempt to use the IRS to bring pressure on him. It had to be dropped because public opinion ran so high against it. All federal charges against him were dropped, in fact. I think we might be wise not to even bring it up this time."

"But for God's sake, if he's some rabble-rousing, right-wing racist, we have to do something!"

The chief of staff said, "You know, I saw something on the Internet about how the Nazis surrendered the day after Stark was born and there had to be a connection."

"That's a joke, for God's sake!" the president burst out. "Anyway, that's Chuck Norris. Stark wasn't even born yet when World War II ended."

"That doesn't change anything, sir," the attorney general said. "There's a certain folklore growing up around Stark. We'd be risking a big drop in the polls if we went after him."

Those words, "a big drop in the polls," got through the president's annoyance and shook him.

"You think so?"

"Definitely," the chief of staff said.

"What are the numbers this morning?"

"Forty-five percent approval rating, sir."

"Well . . . it could be worse." The president sighed. "All right. No federal charges against Stark."

"And it would probably be good if the local district attorney dropped any state charges against him, too," the AG said.

"Can you make that happen?"

"Of course."

"So he gets off scot-free," the president said bitterly. "He goes around acting like *we're* the bad guys, and he gets away with it."

"For now." The attorney general smiled. "But things always catch up to that sort in the end, sir."

"I suppose." The president looked at the chief of staff and went on, "Tell the secretary of state to schmooze those damn Mexicans and get them to calm down. Promise them a few billion dollars more of aid or something. Whatever it takes."

"Of course, sir."

The two men got to up to leave, but the president said to the attorney general, "Oh, by the way, I heard that one of your staffers passed away. My condolences."

"Thank you, sir. It was quite unexpected. Heart attack, you know." The attorney general shook his head. "A real shame."

Stark could tell that Hallie had been crying as soon as he answered her knock on his front door that afternoon. Her eyes were red and puffy. But she managed to put a smile on her face as she said, "I've got some good news, John Howard."

"You don't look much like it's good news, whatever it is," Stark told her. "Come in."

She wiped at her eyes as he closed the door behind her.

"I know," she said. "But this is because of something else. I'll get to that. First, I wanted you to know right away that all the charges against you have been dropped."

Stark drew in a deep breath. He couldn't have been more surprised.

"Dropped?" he said.

"Yes. The district attorney himself called to tell me. Also, he's not going to pursue those more serious charges against you like he said this morning that he was."

"What in the world changed his mind?"

"I don't know," Hallie said, "unless it's the fact that there's been an outpouring of support all across the country for you and the residents of Shady Hills."

"Yeah, I had to quit answering the phone because so many newspeople wanted to interview me. But that's not all that's going on," Stark said. "Half the country may think we did the right thing by standing up to those cartel thugs, but the other half thinks *we're* the thugs."

"Oh, John Howard. You've been reading the blogs again, haven't you?"

"I like to see what people are saying about me and my friends. Or at least I thought I did. I swear, you'd think that we went out last night and clubbed a bunch of baby seals instead of defending ourselves from bloodthirsty criminals."

"I know. It's crazy, isn't it?" Hallie smiled again. "Anyway, that's the good news."

"But that's not all the news, is it?" Stark guessed.

"No. Some of the people here in the park will be facing weapons charges. They didn't have permits for their guns, or they'd let the paperwork lapse. They'll be fined and have their weapons confiscated. The district attorney wouldn't budge on that. I think he felt like he had to have *something* to show for all this."

"That's a shame. I guess I should've checked with everybody and made sure their guns were legal."

"You couldn't think of everything, John Howard. And it wasn't your responsibility to do that."

Stark nodded. He and the other residents could pitch in

to see to it that anybody who needed help with their legal problems got it.

He said, "That's still not all of it, Hallie. Those weapons charges might make you mad, but they wouldn't make you cry. There's something else going on."

She swallowed hard and nodded.

"I got a call from a woman named Jennifer Wesley. She's Josh Mumford's sister."

Stark didn't know who that was; then something jogged in his memory.

"Your friend in Washington is named Josh. The one who works for the Justice Department. Did something happen to him?"

"He . . . passed away last night. A heart attack."

"Aw, hell," Stark said quietly. He moved closer to Hallie and rested his hands on her shoulders. "I'm sorry. He was somebody more important than just an old study buddy, wasn't he?"

"Well . . . there was a time that he was. I hadn't seen him in years, but . . . we were pretty close, back in those days."

Stark drew her against him and put his arms around her. They stood there like that for a long moment with him comforting her as best he could.

Something was nagging at his brain, though, and finally he said, "Hallie, you told me something a few days ago about this fella Josh hacking into some Justice Department computers . . . ?"

She moved back a little and lifted her head so she could look up at him.

"The same thought occurred to me. But you don't think there could be any connection between that and . . ."

"How sure was your friend's sister that he died of a heart attack?"

"I don't think there was any doubt. When he didn't

show up for work this morning his office called him but didn't get any answer. One of his coworkers went to check on him and found him sitting at his desk, in front of his computer. The computer was still on. It looked like he . . . like he was sitting there when the attack hit him and died before he could get up."

Stark nodded. "That's probably just what happened. For a second there I just wondered, that's all."

"I don't blame you," Hallie said. "I thought the same thing. But we don't want to go looking for conspiracies where there aren't any."

"No," Stark said, "we don't want to do that."

But despite his words, he wasn't completely convinced. As soon as got the chance, he told himself, he was going to do some searching on the Internet himself and see what he could find out about the death of Josh Mumford.

CHAPTER THIRTY-TWO

"It's vigilante justice, that's what it is, plain and simple, and it's illegal!"

"You mean people don't have a right to defend themselves in this country anymore?"

"The people in that trailer park weren't defending themselves. They ambushed those poor men."

"Some of those poor men, as you call them, actually *were* committing a crime. They were in this country illegally."

"Now you're just splitting hairs. This country was built on immigration. Since when is wanting to better yourself and provide for your family a crime?"

"Well, when you do it by entering a country illegally and smuggling drugs—"

"There's no proof of that."

"Every member of the cartel gang who was killed at Shady Hills had a record as long as your arm filled with violent charges against them. Some of them were suspected of multiple murders."

"Suspected, that's the key word. In this country you're innocent until proven guilty in a court of law."

"You're *considered* innocent. That doesn't mean you really are. And that doesn't hold true for conservatives, does it? You consider them guilty just because of their political beliefs. You accuse them of being vigilantes, and yet you're ready to lynch them for their so-called crimes."

"I never said anything about lynching anybody! Don't you, of all people, put racist words in my mouth!"

"Of all people? What does that mean? Oh, never mind, I understand. That's your way of accusing *me* of being racist just because I stand up for people's right to defend themselves against evil."

"It's funny how this so-called evil seems to have brown skin in your eyes."

"Let me read you a list of names: Gomez. Rodriguez. Torres. Hernandez—"

"If you're reading off a list of the victims, you're just proving my point for me."

"I'm reading a list of some of the residents of the Shady Hills Retirement Park. I can go on if you want. There are more than thirty names on this list. And since you brought up racism, how about these names: Medford. Wilson. Parker. Stanton. Bell."

"White people's names."

"No. They're all African-American. What about Trinh? Nguyen? Chang? Mujabar? All residents of Shady Hills Retirement Park."

"So it's a freakin' U.N. out there! What does that matter? They have guns!"

"Which the Second Amendment gives them every right to possess. An amendment which has been under constant attack by you and your cohorts for decades now, but somehow you haven't been able to get rid of it yet."

"They acted outside the law!"

"Evidently not. The local district attorney has dropped

all the charges against the residents except some weapons-related offenses having to do mostly with paperwork, and the Justice Department has declined to open an investigation of so-called civil rights violations."

"Just because certain people in Washington are scared to do what's right and are basing their decisions on public opinion polls doesn't mean those decisions are correct."

"Don't you trust the opinion of the public?"

"If we did that, we'd have anarchy!"

"Instead of being ruled by a bunch of elitists who think they know better about everything from what you can give your kid to eat to how and when you should die."

"Well, what if the government really does know best?"

"If you actually believe that, I'm not sure there's any point in continuing this conversation."

There was no point in continuing to watch it, Stark thought as he pushed a button on the TV remote and banished the two talking heads.

Several days had passed since the Battle of Shady Hills, as some were starting to call it, but people all across the country were still talking about it. Arguing about it, rather, because there seemed to be no middle ground on the issue. Either the residents of the park were courageous American heroes, or they were bloodthirsty racist vigilantes, depending on the political outlook of whoever was offering an opinion.

And opinions, Stark had reminded himself more than once, were like a certain portion of the anatomy: everybody had one.

He didn't fool himself into thinking that just because he and his friends had repelled one attack, the danger was over. He knew the cartel wouldn't accept such a stinging defeat. Sooner or later they would be back, and because Stark knew that, he had pressed the residents to continue guarding the park just as they had done before. Everyone went along with that without complaint.

Except the ones who had moved out. Six more mobile homes had been packed up, the skirting taken down, water and electricity connections taken loose, and trucks brought in to haul them away to some other location. Stark couldn't really blame those people for wanting to leave the danger behind and go somewhere safer, but he didn't really understand it, either.

He supposed the Good Lord just hadn't included any backup in his nature.

Along with the continued vigilance among the residents of the park, the other matter occupying Stark's attention these days was the death of Hallie's friend Josh Mumford. He had kept up with the stories about it in the online editions of the Washington newspapers, and he had spent hours searching the Internet for everything he could find about Mumford. The man had had his law degree but was a career bureaucrat, having worked for the Justice Department for more than twenty years. He was divorced, with a couple of grown children, and seemed about as bland and non-threatening as he could possibly be. There was nothing to suggest that his death was anything other than what it appeared to be, the natural result of a life spent drinking too much and working too hard.

Except for the fact that he'd been helping Hallie and had found that mysterious computer file named "Silence."

Every time Stark thought about that, something prodded his brain, some elusive memory that told him the name should mean something to him. But it didn't, and he had given up thinking about it in the hope that whatever it was would pop into his brain. So far he hadn't had any luck with that.

He was about to start pondering what to fix himself for supper when he heard footsteps on the porch stairs. A moment later someone knocked on the door.

Stark picked up the .45 automatic from the little table beside his recliner as he stood up. These days he didn't go to the door or much of anywhere else without at least one gun handy. He tucked the automatic behind the waistband of his jeans at the small of his back.

The gun wasn't necessary, he saw as he opened the door. Hallie stood there, along with her dad, Fred and Antonio Gomez, and Jack Kasek.

"Looks like somebody sent me a delegation," Stark said. "What for?"

"Why, John Howard, aren't you glad to see us?" Hallie asked with a smile.

"Sure." Stark stepped back. "Come on in. Can I get you folks something to drink?"

"This isn't a social call, John Howard," Alton Duncan said as the group walked into the mobile home. "We're here because Hallie's had an idea."

"I'm sure it's a good one. Sit down and tell me about it." Stark nodded to Antonio. "How are you doing, son? Haven't seen much of you."

"I know, and I'm tired of hiding, Mr. Stark," Antonio said. "There's no need for it anymore. Nacho and the others know I'm here. They've known ever since that first night they showed up. I don't think they're interested in me anymore."

"Probably not," Stark agreed. "Oh, they'd come after you fast enough if they got the chance, but this has all gotten a lot bigger now than you witnessing what you did and running out on them."

Antonio grimaced.

"Don't remind me. I never should have run."

"Then you would have died with those other two young people," Fred said. "We've talked about this before, Antonio. You shouldn't feel guilty."

"Maybe not, but I always will. That's why I want to do whatever I can to help everybody here. It'll be a start on making up for what I did."

Alton said, "We've gotten off the track here. Hallie, tell John Howard your idea."

"It's pretty simple, really," Hallie said. "What's the main complaint that certain people have with what happened here? What have they been calling us ever since that night?"

"Vigilantes," Stark said. "I'm getting pretty tired of it, too."

"We all are," Alton said. "That's why Hallie's idea is such a good one."

She went on, "They say we didn't have any authority to do what we did, and technically, I suppose they're right. Although we were able to justify our actions as self-defense, we weren't really legally empowered to do that."

Stark frowned in thought and slowly nodded his head. He said, "I think I see what you're getting at."

Hallie smiled.

"I thought you would, John Howard. What we need to do is incorporate Shady Hills as a town, and once we've done that you can have your own police force with the legal authority to defend the citizens. That way no one can accuse you of being vigilantes anymore."

"It's a fine idea," Stark agreed. "I'm not sure why you came to see me about it, though. I can't really help much with the effort. I'm not a lawyer."

"But you *are* a hero," Jack Kasek blurted out, "and that's why, once Shady Hills is an actual town, we want you to be its mayor!"

CHAPTER THIRTY-THREE

Stark's eyebrows rose in surprise as he leaned back in his chair.

"Mayor?" he repeated. "I think you've got the wrong man, Jack. I'm about as far from being a politician as you can get."

"You're not afraid to tell the truth," Jack said. "Isn't that what we need more of in our politicians today?"

Hallie said, "We're getting ahead of ourselves here. It's true, John Howard, that your name came up as a possible candidate for mayor, but we have to get the town incorporated first. Which means an election for that before we have an election for mayor and city council."

"So I don't have to make up my mind today?"

"Not at all."

"Okay, in that case I'm all for the idea of making Shady Hills a town. It's a good way to shut up all the people who are yelling about us being vigilantes."

"Exactly," Alton said. He beamed with pride as he looked at Hallie. "My little girl is pretty smart."

"Dad, I haven't been a little girl for forty years."

"You'll always be my little girl. Don't you know that by now?"

Stark asked, "So what's our next move?"

"We're going to form an organization called Incorporate Shady Hills and hold a press conference to announce our intentions. Then we'll have to collect signatures from a sufficient amount of registered voters on a petition for incorporation that we'll present to the county judge. He'll have to certify the petition, but once he's done that, he'll set an election date." Hallie smiled. "Then we'll have to hope that incorporation wins."

"It will," Jack Kasek said. "I can practically guarantee it."

"There are no guarantees where politics is concerned," Stark said. "Except that no matter what you do, somebody won't like it."

Stark was right about that. The news conference announcing the formation of Incorporate Shady Hills was well-attended, with representatives of the media from all the major cities in Texas, plus correspondents from *The New York Times*, *The Washington Post*, *The Los Angeles Times*, a number of cable news networks, and even an influential blogger or two.

And the coverage, also not surprisingly, was overwhelmingly negative.

TEXAS VIGILANTES TRY TO MAKE IT LEGAL, screamed one headline. Another proclaimed, A CITY BORN IN VIOLENCE AND HATRED. Pundits on the news shows explained that what Shady Hills was trying to do was in fact legal under the laws of the state of Texas but left no doubt that they thought it was wrong. Editorialists noted solemnly that this movement was likely to lead to still more violence.

Meanwhile, the residents of Shady Hills couldn't sign the petition drawn up by Hallie fast enough. In less than twenty-four hours after the news conference, the document already had enough signatures on it to be submitted, but Hallie advised the committee to wait a few more days. The more signatures they collected, she said, the more public opinion would be on their side. Having to worry about things like that instead of simple right and wrong annoyed Stark, but he knew they had to deal with the world as it was, not how they might like it to be.

An unexpected development cropped up a couple of days later. Stark was at the community center with Hallie and the rest of the committee, going over the signatures to make sure all of them were legitimate. The ACLU had already demanded to see a copy of the petition when it was turned in to the judge, to "make sure there was no effort to disenfranchise minorities," as they put it. Since the signatures included a large percentage of Hispanic names, along with a number of residents who were black, including one of the volunteer captains, that effort to interfere with the process wasn't likely to fly, but Stark and the others wanted to be sure it wouldn't.

Several men Stark didn't recognize came into the building. They were roughly dressed and he tensed for a moment, thinking that they might be there to cause trouble, but then the spokesman smiled and said, "Howdy. We're lookin' for the people who want to turn this into a town."

"That would be us," Stark said as he got to his feet. His friends were wary, too, and he figured most of them had their hands close to the guns they were carrying. "What can we do for you?"

"We want to be part of the town of Shady Hills, too," the stranger said. "We're from the Dry Wash community."

Stark was familiar with the area a couple of miles farther on up the highway, going northwest from Devil's Pass. There was an old mission there, along with the arroyo that gave the place its name, and probably two dozen houses and mobile homes.

Jack Kasek said, "We figured the boundaries of the town would be the mobile home park—"

"But there's no reason they have to be," Hallie put in. "There are different requirements for incorporation depending on the size and population of the proposed town, but there's no reason Shady Hills couldn't take in more than just the park."

"You think that's a good idea?" her father asked.

The spokesman for the visitors said, "Look, my name's Ben LaPorte. Ever since y'all had that trouble up here with those drug smugglers, a bunch of us have been gettin' together and sayin' that we wish we could've been down here to give you a helpin' hand. I'll be honest with you. We're not a fancy bunch. Just good ol' hardworkin' common folks. We try to abide by the law. And we have trouble with smugglers and illegal immigrants all the time. Everything that's not bolted down gets stole. And the sheriff . . . well, I ain't sayin' that Sheriff Lozano's a bad fella, but I don't think he cares overmuch about what happens to folks in Dry Wash, neither. We'd be happy to pay some city taxes if it meant we'd get some honest-to-God police protection out here."

Stark stood up and went over to shake hands with Ben LaPorte and the other men in turn, then said, "I'm glad you boys came to see us today, Ben. I can't make the decision myself, but I can sure promise you we'll discuss your suggestion."

Ben looked at his companions, then nodded.

"That sounds fair enough, Mr. Stark."

"You know who I am?"

"Pretty hard not to," Ben said with a smile. "Your face has been all over the TV for the past few days."

Stark chuckled and said, "Yeah, and I'm not too fond of it. For some reason those folks seem to think I'm newsworthy."

"Somebody standin' up for what's right, after so many people been apologizin' and excusin' what's wrong for the past thirty or forty years, yeah, I'd say that's newsworthy."

Stark put Ben LaPorte's number into his cell phone and promised to call when a decision had been reached. The men from Dry Wash nodded and left the community center. Stark went back to the table where they had been going over the petitions and sat down.

"What do you think?" he asked the people gathered around the table.

"I don't know," Jack Kasek said. "Dry Wash is a pretty rundown area.

Alton said, "Not really. It's just old. The community got its start as a way station on the old Butterfield Stagecoach Line, back in the 1850s. There's never been a town there, just a church or two and some houses, and they even had a little one-room school for a while, but there was never any reason for the area to develop much. People take care of their places pretty well, though. I saw that when I was handling insurance claims in this area."

"They don't cook meth in some of those trailers?"

"Now you're jumping to conclusions, Jack," Alton said. "Everybody here in the park lives in a mobile home except you and your wife. Nobody here cooks meth."

"Yeah, but we're all a bunch of old geezers," Jack protested.

Stark said, "Yeah, and with the economy the way it is, there might be some young men from Dry Wash who'd jump at the chance to be cops. I don't see a problem with including them. We can draw the boundaries of the town any way we want, can't we, Hallie?"

"As long as the area included doesn't exceed nine square miles," Hallie said.

"There are a lot of towns in Texas bigger than nine square miles," Fred protested.

"Not at the time they were incorporated, which might be well over a hundred years ago."

Fred nodded and said, "Yeah, I guess that makes sense. So after Shady Hills is incorporated, we can annex more land if we want to?"

"As long as we do it legally." Hallie looked around the table. "Shall we put it to a vote? Do we want to include Dry Wash in the city limits? There would be that many more signatures to put on the petition."

"I suppose that would be all right, if the rest of you think so," Jack said.

They didn't need a formal vote. Everyone nodded and spoke up, voicing their support for the idea.

"But the town's still going to be called Shady Hills, right?" Jack asked.

"That's all right with me," Stark said. "Something I've always wondered about, though, Jack . . . how come you to call this place Shady Hills?"

Jack grinned and said, "Would *you* want to live in a place called Flat and Blistering Hot?"

CHAPTER THIRTY-FOUR

It didn't take long for the news to spread about the community of Dry Wash being included in the proposed boundaries for the new town of Shady Hills. Once the media got hold of it, they blew the story out of proportion as usual, blaring headlines such as VIGILANTES SEEK TO EXPAND LAWLESS EMPIRE. Stark just shook his head in disbelief at that one, and Hallie commented wryly, "I guess once the town's incorporated you'll have to run for emperor instead of mayor, John Howard."

"If I was emperor there'd be some changes made, that's for sure," Stark said.

"You remember the story about the emperor's new clothes? He was naked, as I recall."

Stark changed the subject in a hurry.

The story wasn't done evolving, of course. A few days later, Stark got a phone call from a man named Carlos Arizola, who introduced himself as the principal of Joseph P. Gonzalez High School, which was down the highway between Shady Hills and Devil's River. Stark had passed the school dozens of times, but he had no idea what the principal wanted with him.

"What can I do for you, Mr. Arizola?" he asked.

"I'd like to meet with you and your friends, Mr. Stark, and talk about this new town of yours."

Stark managed not to grunt in surprise.

"Just what is it you want to talk to us about?"

"You may not be aware of this, Mr. Stark, but the school isn't in the city limits of Devil's Pass."

Stark hadn't ever thought about it, but he knew that Gonzalez High was a couple of miles north of town. It had been built there to accommodate new growth in the area when the school district's student population got to be too big for the original Devil's Pass High School. School districts in Texas never liked to split their students between two or more high schools, because the new schools always dropped into a lower classification athletically. But sometimes the numbers made it impossible to do otherwise, and that was the case in Devil's Pass. The new high school, Gonzalez High, had opened several years earlier, before Stark moved to the area, but he had heard about it.

Principal Arizola went on, "The new housing developments that have grown up in this area aren't in the city limits, either, but Devil's Pass has its eye on annexing all of us. We don't want that, Mr. Stark. If we're going to be part of a city, we'd rather it be Shady Hills."

"Shady Hills isn't even a real town yet," Stark said. "What in the world could we offer folks like you?"

"You intend to have a police department, don't you?"

"Well, sure. To be honest, that's the main reason we decided to incorporate."

"What about a fire department?" Arizola asked.

"I don't know when we'd be able to afford a real fire department. I imagine we'll have to rely on a volunteer department for a while, just like we do now."

"With a greater tax base, you could at least afford some equipment of your own. Taking care of a town costs a lot of money, Mr. Stark."

"I know," Stark said. That very subject had been weighing heavily on his mind. A lot of little towns contracted with the county in which they were located or with larger municipalities nearby to provide vital services like police and fire protection. That wasn't really going to work in the case of Shady Hills. Stark couldn't imagine George Lozano or Dennis Feasco agreeing to such an arrangement.

"We had a meeting here at our school last night," Arizola went on. "Almost a thousand people showed up, and they were overwhelmingly in support of approaching you about being included in the boundaries of Shady Hills. What it boils down to, Mr. Stark, is that we're going to be paying city taxes to *somebody* in the next few years, no matter what we do. We'd rather it be Shady Hills, where at least you're trying to do the right thing and stand up to the drug cartels. I tell you, some of the things we see in high school . . . well, it's frightening, that's all. I'm convinced that the cartels have agents right here in the school among our students."

"Wouldn't surprise me a bit," Stark said. "But I'm sorry to hear it."

"Anyway, that's what I want to talk to you about. I'd like to present my case to the leaders of your community and propose that we join forces."

"I think you already have," Stark said with a chuckle. "But if you'd like to do it face-to-face, I'm sure that would be fine. We can meet with you whenever is convenient for you. We're all retired, after all."

Arizola suggested that he come speak to the committee

that evening. Stark told him that was fine and promised to call him back if anything changed.

The people of Dry Wash wanting to be part of their cause had been a surprise, and this was an even bigger one. But it would instantly increase their credibility, Stark thought. The people who lived in those new housing developments were well-to-do, although they were suffering some like everybody else in the weak economy Washington's poorly thought out, ham-fisted policies had created. Principal Arizola was right about being able to do more with a larger tax base.

If they weren't careful, Stark told himself with a smile, Shady Hill might just wind up being a real town.

INTOLERANCE HAS A NEW HOME.

IT'S NOT THE WILD WEST ANYMORE.

NO VIGILANTES.

NO LYNCH MOB JUSTICE.

SHADY HILLS = RACISTS.

"Where did all the idiots come from?" Fred Gomez asked as he and Stark got out of the pickup Stark had bought to replace the one destroyed in the battle. Fred waved a hand at the protestors gathered on the sidewalk across the street.

"Those charter buses would be my guess," Stark said. He nodded toward two buses parked at the curb not far from the entrance to the county courthouse.

Hallie had parked behind Stark's pickup. She and her father got out of the car and joined them. Jack and Mindy Kasek were here, too, along with Ben LaPorte from Dry Wash and Principal Carlos Arizola from Gonzalez High School. All of them were going to deliver the signed petitions to County Judge Steven Oliveros. The petitions contained almost three thousand signatures of registered voters who supported the incorporation of the town of Shady Hills.

Some of Chief Feasco's uniformed officers were standing along the edge of the sidewalk to keep the protest contained. Hallie smiled and said, "I guess we shouldn't have announced when we were going to be delivering the petitions. We got some unwanted attention."

"Any publicity is good publicity, right?" Jack Kasek said.

They were getting some publicity, all right. News vans with satellite dishes on their roofs were parked along the street, and several field reporters were standing in the heat, trying to look dignified and handsome as they talked into their microphones. From time to time the cameramen turned to pan across the crowd of protestors, getting plenty of good footage for the evening newscasts.

"I've lived around here most of my life," Alton Duncan said. "I don't think I recognize any of those people who're shouting and waving signs around."

"I'm not surprised," Stark said. "Somebody brought them in from San Antonio, or more likely Austin or Houston, and is paying them to make a scene. That way when the footage shows up on the news, they can claim that public opinion is against us."

"That's just not right," Fred said.

"That's the reality of the way things are today, though," Hallie said. "The left likes to accuse fat-cat billionaires of running the country—and ruining the country—when in reality they have more fat-cat billionaires bankrolling them than our side ever did. And they're willing to spend whatever it takes until everybody in the country thinks exactly the same way they do."

"Somebody needs to put a stop to money running everything," Principal Arizola said.

"Might as well try to stop the earth from turning while you're at it," Stark drawled. "Come on. Let's get these petitions turned in."

They walked up the steps into the courthouse. Reporters and cameramen charged alongside them. Stark and his companions ignored the shouted questions. At the top of the steps, a couple of deputies halted the media members. Stark and the others went on inside, glad to be out of the commotion.

Judge Oliveros was expecting them. He met them in his outer office and took the stack of petitions that Stark handed him.

"I have to say, I don't support this effort," he told them with a stern frown. "But I give you my word I'll examine these petitions personally, and if the signatures are verifiable and in sufficient quantity, I'll certify them and set an election date as soon as possible. I'd like to see this matter settled so maybe the county won't be in such an uproar all the time."

"We appreciate that, your honor," Hallie told him.

Oliveros smiled slightly.

"You've appeared in my court before, Ms. Duncan. Since these people have such a competent attorney handling things for them, I'm confident these petitions will prove to be in order. I'll contact you as soon as I've gone over them."

As they left the courthouse, Stark asked quietly, "That's all there is to it?"

"That's all there is to it," Hallie confirmed.

The demonstration was still going on across the street. The sign-waving protesters shouted curses and insults at the people from Shady Hills as they headed back to their vehicles.

"If you asked any of them," Stark commented, "they'd tell you how much they believe in tolerance and free speech . . . until somebody who disagrees with them wants those same rights."

"Yeah, then all their high-flown talk goes right out the window," Fred said.

They had just reached Stark's pickup but hadn't gotten in yet when a particularly loud and aggressive shout made them look around.

One of the protesters had gotten past the cops somehow and was charging toward them with a crazed look on his face and his wooden sign lifted over his head and poised to use as a weapon.

Stark had time just to glimpse the words painted on the sign—PEACE AND JUSTICE FOR ALL—before it came slashing down at him and Fred.

CHAPTER THIRTY-FIVE

Stark shoved Fred to one side and twisted his body the other way. That took Stark out of the way of the sign, which whipped down between him and Fred and smashed into the hood of his pickup with a resounding *clang!*

The missed blow threw the protester off-balance. Stark thought about decking him, but he knew the news cameras were pointing at him by now and didn't want to do anything in front of the whole country that would just be twisted to make him look bad. He stepped back as the man swung the sign at him again.

A couple of police officers arrived then and grabbed the protester from behind. Another cop wrestled the sign away from him.

"Let me go!" the man yelled. "We're here to strike a blow against racism!"

"Racism!" Fred shouted back at him. "You nearly bashed my Mexican brains out, you idiot!"

The cop who had taken the sign away from the protester pointed a finger at Fred and warned, "Watch it with that hate speech, mister."

"Hate speech!" Fred's face was flushed with fury. "Can't you people get it through your heads—"

Stark took hold of his friend's arm and urged him toward the pickup's passenger side.

"Come on, Fred. We've done what we came here to do. Let's go home."

Fred pointed at the protester and said, "I want to press charges against him. What he did was assault with a deadly weapon!"

"We'll let Hallie handle it. She can talk to the district attorney."

The cops led the protester away. He was still practically foaming at the mouth with hatred. But it was hatred in the name of tolerance and diversity, Stark thought, so it would be celebrated by certain factions, by people who were blind to the utter illogic of their political positions.

Stark's other companions had started toward them when the trouble broke out, but they had stopped when the police stepped in. Stark waved at them now to let them know that he and Fred were okay. Everybody got back into their vehicles and headed back toward Shady Hills.

The knowledge that he hadn't even thrown a punch at that nutty protester gnawed at Stark as he drove. There was a time when he would have put the fella on the ground in the blink of an eye. Maybe he was getting too old for this sort of dustup. Or maybe he had just thought better of it and tempered his reaction.

But Lord help us all, he thought, when John Howard Stark was the voice of reason.

Not surprisingly, the protester who had attacked Stark and Fred wasn't arrested or charged with anything. The district attorney declined to prosecute, saying that the man, who gave an address in Austin as his place of residence, had acted in the heat of the moment and no one had been hurt. Stark had a pretty good ding in the hood of his truck where the sign had hit it, but he wasn't going to bother suing the guy in small claims court for the price of getting it fixed. He could tap it out and touch it up himself without much trouble.

Two days later, Hallie showed up at Shady Hills to deliver the good news in person.

"Judge Oliveros has verified the signatures and certified the petitions," she told Stark, her father, and the Gomezes as they sat in Stark's living room. "He's set the election for September seventh."

"That's only three weeks away," Alton said. "Will that give us time to campaign?"

"We don't need to campaign," Fred said. "Everybody who signed the petition in the first place will vote for incorporation. It'll be a landslide."

Hallie said, "Don't be so sure. There'll always be people on the other side, as well as people who don't want to incorporate because they don't want to pay city taxes."

"You can't blame them for that," Stark said. "Lord knows, we're already taxed almost to death in this country. People forget that the 'tea' in Tea Party stands for Taxed Enough Already."

"Let's not muddy the issue," Hallie suggested. "We'll keep it simple, have some signs and flyers printed that make it very clear what the benefits of incorporation are, and hope for a good turnout. The weather should be nice for the election, anyway, and that'll help get the voters out."

They began making their plans for the campaign leading up to the election, but Stark's mind wandered. This wasn't the sort of thing he was good at. Alton, Fred, and Aurelia seemed to think this was a major hurdle, that once

Shady Hills was incorporated things would be better. Stark wasn't convinced of that. His gut told him there was still plenty of trouble ahead.

For one thing, he wasn't convinced that the election would go off without a hitch. Shady Hills had become a symbol, a symbol of people standing up for their rights against not only vicious criminals but also against a "do nothing but tax, spend, and regulate" government. Because of that stance, Shady Hills would always have enemies because it threatened the status quo. It threatened the hold on power by an overreaching federal government and the rule by fear of the Mexican drug cartel.

No, things were not going to go smoothly, Stark thought, no matter what his friends might hope.

It was just a matter of trying to figure out where and how hell was going to break loose next.

For several weeks now, Nacho Montez had been smarting from the defeat at Shady Hills. He had known that those old gringos would be armed and ready for trouble, but he had expected the feint at the front gate to fool them, and he had been convinced any resistance would collapse quickly once he and his men were inside the retirement park.

Who could have guessed that the residents would fight back so fiercely and so effectively?

It was all Stark's fault, Nacho had thought more than once as a bitter, sour taste filled his mouth. Stark was their leader, the one from whom those old people drew their inspiration. Who knew he would fight like such a devil?

Kill Stark, and it would be like cutting the head off a snake. The problem was, killing Stark would not be easy. Nacho had people watching him, and Stark was always armed when he went anywhere. Not only that, but he usually had several well-armed companions with him. Nacho didn't want to take a chance on failing again. He was already worried that Señor Espantoso might be losing confidence in him.

The señor had summoned Nacho and Jalisco to the ranch today. Chuckie was at one of the cartel's safe houses on the other side of the border, recuperating from wounds he'd received during the fighting at Shady Hills. For a while there, Nacho had been very worried that his brother was going to die.

If that had happened, it would have been just one more score to settle with that gringo bastard John Howard Stark.

Now it looked like Chuckie was going to recover. He had the best medical care available, of course. The cartel could afford it. Not that they had to pay, because everyone was so frightened that they were eager to help in any way they could.

The Arab was still here, Nacho saw with distaste as he and Jalisco were shown into the sumptuous living room by Señor Espantoso's bodyguards. Nacho didn't like the man and didn't see why the cartel was so eager to do business with strangers from the Middle East. Although born and raised on the Texas side of the border, Nacho considered himself a Mexican. He could tolerate the presence of Colombians in the cartel—they provided most of the product, after all, and at least they were Latino—but getting involved with the Islamic terrorist groups seemed like a mistake to him. The cartel could get along just fine without their help.

No one asked his opinion about such things, though, so he simply ignored the Arab and said to Espantoso, "You honor us with your invitation, señor."

"Never mind that," the señor snapped. "The people at

Shady Hills are going to get their election. It was just on the news."

Nacho felt a surge of anger. This whole business of the retirement park trying to become a town was just another slap in the face of the cartel. Nacho knew that, and his wounded pride wanted to strike back at them.

He forced himself to remain calm, though, as he said, "It means nothing, señor."

"It means they will be able to hire their own police force. I want that land, Montez, and yet they continue throwing up obstacles to obtaining it."

"Even if Shady Hills becomes a town, it will be tiny and poor. What sort of police force can they afford?"

"They defeated you and your men without a police force," Señor Espantoso pointed out ominously.

Again Nacho struggled to control his anger.

"Only because they took us by surprise," he said. "I promise you, we will never underestimate them again. When we strike at them the next time—"

"And when will that be?" the señor cut in.

Nacho thought fast. He said, "They have to hold an election to become a town, no? That would be a good day to teach them a lesson they will never forget."

Espantoso frowned, and Nacho knew that the señor was considering the idea. But after a moment Espantoso shook his head.

"There is more to what we do than just simple killing," he said. "We are not like bandido warlords who just crush anyone who defies us."

And that was sort of a shame, Nacho thought. The legends of those simpler times held a great appeal to him. He had often thought that he would have liked to ride with Villa.

"We proceed tactically," Espantoso said in an annoying

lecturing tone. "And one such tactic is to let our enemies do our work for us."

Nacho had to shake his head.

"I don't understand, señor."

"We are not the only ones opposed to the idea of Shady Hills becoming a town," Espantoso said with a wolfish smile. "Perhaps we should just sit back and let their other enemies do our work for us."

CHAPTER THIRTY-SIX

The president, his chief of staff, and the attorney general sat in the Oval Office, and the latter two men looked distinctly uncomfortable as their boss slapped a folded newspaper down on the big desk.

"This has gone on long enough," the president said. The headline on the paper read: ELECTION APPROVED FOR TEXAS TERROR TOWN. "What sort of judge would approve an election to create a haven for gun-toting, Bible-thumping, racist vigilantes? Who appointed him, anyway? It couldn't have been one of us."

"He, uh, wasn't appointed by anyone, sir," the chief of staff said. "He isn't a federal judge. He's a local county judge. He was elected."

The president rolled his eyes.

"And that's why we don't trust the voters in this country. They make mistakes like that all the time!"

"What do you want me to do, Mr. President?" the attorney general asked.

"I know you both said we ought to stay out of this as much as possible." The president's finger stabbed down at the newspaper. "But this can't be allowed to stand! I want a federal injunction against this election, ASAP."

"I'm not sure about jurisdiction—" the AG began.

"Screw jurisdiction! We're the federal government! We can do whatever we want!"

The chief of staff said, "Maybe it would be better to let them have their election . . . and lose."

The president leaned forward with a frown.

"Can we do that?" he asked.

"You just said it yourself, sir. We're the federal government. We can do what we want."

The attorney general said, "The Justice Department can send observers to make sure the election is conducted fairly and to guard against voter suppression and voter fraud."

"And there can be organized demonstrations to protest the election," the chief of staff added. "That ought to keep turnout down."

"But I thought we just said we'd guard against voter suppression—" The president stopped short, then said, "Ah, I understand. Never mind. It's not voter suppression when we do it, now is it, boys?"

All three men smiled.

"There are other things we can do as well to influence the outcome," the attorney general said. "And it's certainly true that it's an even bigger win for us if they hold their election and then fail. We can spin that as a triumph for equal rights."

"Do it," the president said decisively. "Do whatever you need to do, just make sure those people come off like the racist yokels they are."

"One thing," the chief of staff said. "There are quite a few Hispanics and blacks living in Shady Hills who actually support the idea of turning the place into its own town. If people see them on the news, they're going to start asking how we can portray this as a racist effort."

"Well, that's easily taken care of, isn't it?" the president asked. "Just make sure nobody ever sees them on the news."

"I'll do my best, sir, but it's not like we completely control the media in this country. Almost, maybe, but not quite."

The president leaned back in the big chair and folded his hands on his stomach.

"Well, perhaps that's something we should work on another day, gentlemen," he said.

Ryan opened his cell phone and said, "What is it?"

"You're still in Washington."

"And how do you know that?"

"Do you think we're not keeping an eye on you?" the voice asked angrily. "You're here, and that bastard Stark is still down there in Texas causing problems for us."

"John Howard Stark will be dealt with in the proper way, at the proper time," Ryan said.

"And who decides how and when that is?"

"You know the answer to that," Ryan said. "I do."

Silence came over the phone for a few seconds before the man on the other end of the connection heaved an exasperated sigh.

"I swear, if you hadn't gotten results for us so many times in the past—"

"But I always do, don't I?"

"Yes," the man admitted. "You do."

"This time won't be any different. But I have to admit, I'm sort of enjoying watching the show down there in Texas. It must be driving you and your friends crazy to see a bunch of people refusing to knuckle under like that. Don't they know they're supposed to be good, proper American sheep and do whatever their betters tell them to do?"

"You let us worry about the political end of it," the man snapped. "You just take care of the job you've been hired to do."

"I've never let you down before," Ryan said. "I won't this time, either."

He broke the connection without saying good-bye because he was annoyed by the call. He didn't like being doubted or having his methods questioned.

Of course, the caller had a point, Ryan thought. To be fair, he *had* been dragging his feet on this Stark job, and he wasn't sure why that was the case. He had no fondness for John Howard Stark. All he had to do was glance at his maimed right hand to remind him of why he hated the former rancher.

But you had to sort of admire the man, Ryan realized. Stark, despite having served in Vietnam, wasn't a lifelong military man, wasn't a trained commando. Bigger, stronger, faster than the average man, maybe, but when you got right down to it, still a common man, not a superhero.

Yet he'd had the audacity to challenge the cartel once before and, after that, the Mexican army during that trouble at the Alamo. Now he was up in the cartel's face again, making a nuisance of himself. A deadly nuisance, if what Ryan read in the papers and on the Internet was true. Ryan still had some contacts south of the border, even though he didn't work for the drug smugglers anymore, and he wondered who was running things along the Rio Grande now. Whoever it was had to be getting mighty tired of hearing about John Howard Stark.

The thought suddenly occurred to Ryan that he ought to reach out to the cartel. Maybe he could get a bonus from them for killing Stark and still collect his fee from his regular employers. It was an intriguing idea. Double-dipping, so to speak.

He set the phone on the nightstand beside the bed and then reached over to slap the delectably bare rump of the young woman sleeping beside him. She stirred a little, then asked in a voice thick with drowsiness, "Is it time to go to work?"

"It's the middle of the morning, my dear," Ryan said. "You were late for work two hours ago."

She bolted upright and yelled, "Oh, my God! Why did you let me sleep so late? Why didn't you wake me up?"

"Because you looked so adorable lying there."

"You don't understand—"

"Don't worry. They found some cute young thing to fill in for you on the morning show, and they didn't say anything about you not showing up. They just said you had the day off."

"Was it that little bitch Carly? I'll bet it was her! She's been after my job for six months! I'll claw her eyes out! Damn it to hell, Simon—"

He shut her up by closing his hand around her jaw. Not tight enough to cause any pain, but plenty firm enough to let her know that he wanted her to stop yammering at him. He leaned closer to her and whispered into her ear. At the same time he began to caress her, and despite his grip on her jaw, she responded to his touch as she always did.

The single word he whispered to her was the same one his father had shouted at him when he was growing up in El Paso, an angry bellow that usually was followed by a slap, or if his mother tried to intervene, a beating for her.

Ryan had grown to hate that word, but that hatred hadn't stopped him from adopting it as a nickname later in life, a highly appropriate nickname considering his line of work and how very, very quiet graves were.

"Silencio."

CHAPTER THIRTY-SEVEN

Most news stories are true "nine-day wonders," fading from the public consciousness after a while. Nine days is just an approximation, of course. A story can disappear in two or three days or hang around for months, especially if there are new developments in it.

The election to determine whether or not Shady Hills would incorporate as a town had "legs," as old-time journalists would say. It might not have been on the front page every day, and sometimes it was relegated to the second or even third segment of the newscasts, but it was always there somewhere, usually with a sentence or two cleverly designed to make the public think the only motivations of the residents were racism, greed, and intolerance . . . without ever coming right out and saying that, of course.

Stark was getting tired of it. He was ready for September 7, which was a Saturday, to arrive, so the election would be over with, one way or the other.

Every day, buses full of protesters arrived at the park. They didn't try to come in. Shady Hills was private property, after all. Not that they really cared about that, but these were professionals. They knew exactly how much they could get away with. So the buses parked on the side of the highway and the protesters got out with their signs and started trooping up and down the road, staying off the shoulders so they couldn't be accused of trying to block traffic. They carried their signs and shouted slogans and bellowed through bullhorns. They didn't try to stop anybody from entering or leaving the park.

The first day it happened, Jack Kasek called the sheriff's department. A cruiser with a couple of deputies came out, sat there for a little while, then turned around and headed back to Devil's Pass. More complaints got the same results. A car came out, the deputies watched for ten or fifteen minutes, and then they left without doing anything.

Accompanied by Stark and Hallie, Jack went to see the sheriff. George Lozano kept them waiting for half an hour; then they were shown into his office.

"Sheriff, you've got to do something about those blasted protesters!" Jack began.

Lozano held up a hand to stop him.

"Are you talking about the people exercising their constitutional rights to freedom of assembly and expression?" he asked.

"You know good and well what I'm talking about!"

With a blandly neutral expression on his face, Lozano shook his head.

"My department has responded to your calls and checked out the situation, Mr. Kasek," he said. "As far as I know, the people who are demonstrating outside your retirement park—on publicly held right-of-way, I might add, not private property—aren't breaking any laws."

"They're a nuisance," Hallie said. "They're creating a public safety hazard."

"Not in my judgment, they aren't."

"Someone's going to get hurt out there."

"If they do, we'll take appropriate action against whoever starts the trouble." Lozano paused, then added with heavy emphasis, "Whoever that might be."

Jack Kasek let out a disgusted snort.

"So if we do anything to try to get rid of them, you'll arrest us," he said. "Is that what you're telling us, Sheriff?"

"I'll arrest anybody who breaks the law."

Stark said, "I don't remember that fella who attacked me and Fred Gomez being arrested."

"You'll have to take that up with Chief Feasco and the district attorney, Mr. Stark," Lozano said. "That incident didn't occur in my jurisdiction."

"We're wasting our time here, aren't we?" Hallie asked.

Lozano leaned forward in the chair behind his desk and clasped his hands together.

"Look, I sympathize with you people, I really do. If you incorporate and have your own police force, that's that much more territory I don't have to cover with limited man power and a limited budget. I hope you win your election. But I can't do anything about those protesters as long as they're not breaking the law." The sheriff sat back and shrugged. "I guess you'll just have to get used to them."

"Nobody could get used to vermin like that," Jack snapped.

Hallie took hold of his arm.

"Come on, Jack," she urged him. "We're not going to do any good here."

Jack looked back over his shoulder as he and Stark and Hallie left Lozano's office.

"Someday we'll have a real sheriff in this county again!" he said.

Once they were outside, Jack, still incensed, said, "John Howard, how about we run you for sheriff in the next election?"

Stark gave a curt laugh.

"For starters, Jack, I don't have any law enforcement experience and don't know a blasted thing about being sheriff. And don't forget, you wanted me to run for mayor of Shady Hills once it's a real town. I think that's a big enough job for me, assuming that I get it."

"Why wouldn't you? Nobody would vote against John Howard Stark!"

"Sure they would. There are bound to be people out there who don't like me, even in Shady Hills. And the incorporation question has to pass first."

"It will," Jack said with equal confidence. "Unless they somehow manage to steal the election."

"With that bunch we're going up against, I wouldn't put anything past them."

There had been news coverage all along, of course— satellite trucks parked beside the highway with the buses that brought in the protesters, field reporters with their microphones and cameramen, print journalists from all over the country writing stories on their laptops and tablets and emailing them in.

Things got worse when the Black Panthers showed up.

Stark didn't know about it until Hallie knocked on his door one afternoon a few days before the election.

"You won't believe what's happening now, John Howard," she told him.

"Oh, in this day and age, I'll believe just about anything," Stark said dryly.

"The Black Panthers are out there at the gate, demanding to be allowed in so they can pass out anti-incorporation literature to the residents."

Stark stared at her for a second, then gave a little shake of his head.

"You're right, I didn't see that one coming," he said. "What does this have to do with the Black Panthers? The only black people in this mess are the ones on our side, like Nick."

"I know that and you know that, but they say they're trying to demonstrate solidarity with their Hispanic brothers. 'Racism toward one is racism toward all,' one of their signs said."

Stark thought about it for a moment, then said, "Somebody sent them here."

"That's exactly what I was thinking. Several senators from the president's party have had ties with the Black Panthers in the past. I think the White House called them and got word to the organization through them that it might be a good thing to show up here."

"Because the president doesn't want to come out against us himself. He's still a mite leery from everything that happened in the last administration. He doesn't want to come across as being that extreme in his views."

Hallie nodded.

"That's the way it looks to me."

"Are the guards at the gate letting them in?"

"Not so far. Nick Medford happened to be up there, and when I drove in I saw that he was in a real jawing match with the leader of the group. Half a dozen news cameras were getting the whole thing."

Stark smiled and said, "That didn't work out too well

for them. I'm sure they would've rather had some white fella yelling at them. Would've looked better for their cause that way."

"Oh, they'll spin it the way they want it, one way or another."

Stark didn't doubt that.

"If they try to force their way in, there'll be trouble."

"I know. I already called the sheriff's department on my cell phone, but I don't think we can look for much help from Lozano."

"Nope," Stark agreed. "You go on over to your dad's place, Hallie. I'll drive up to the gate and see what's going on."

"Forget it. I'm coming with you. You're still my client, after all."

"I'm not facing any charges right now," Stark pointed out.

"You have me on retainer."

That was the first Stark had heard about it, but he supposed it wasn't a bad idea. He just didn't want Hallie anywhere near the gate if a fight broke out.

Arguing with her would be a waste of time, though. He said, "Come on, we'll take my pickup. At least it's got some actual metal in it, instead of that little plastic foreign car of yours."

"Don't be jingoistic, John Howard," she scolded him, but with a smile.

As they drove toward the front of the park, Hallie went on, "Did you know the Justice Department has investigators in the area?"

"First I've heard of it."

"They say there have been reports of voter registration irregularities. My hunch is that they'll claim some of the people here in the park aren't properly registered to vote."

"We know better, don't we?"

"Of course, but there's no telling what they'll dig up . . . or manufacture."

"You're saying our own Justice Department would be capable of voter fraud?"

"There were plenty of accusations of fraud and voter suppression a couple of elections ago, with a ton of evidence supporting them, including video, and the Justice Department refused to act on them. If they'll rape the law one way, they'll rape it another."

"Pretty harsh talk," Stark said.

"The truth is sometimes harsh."

Stark couldn't argue with that.

"And of course the ACLU is keeping every motel and restaurant in Devil's Pass in business right now," Hallie went on. "This is going to be one of the most closely watched elections in a long time."

"Good," Stark said. "That way the whole world will see that everything is being done legal and proper."

Stark turned a corner and they came in sight of the gate to the retirement park. Several cars and pickups belonging to the volunteers on guard duty were parked near the gate, inside the park.

The gate itself was packed with a roiling knot of people, Stark saw as alarm welled up inside him. Fists were flying as the crowd surged back and forth.

From the looks of it, a good old-fashioned riot had broken out at the entrance to Shady Hills.

CHAPTER THIRTY-EIGHT

"Oh, my God!" Hallie exclaimed as Stark sent the pickup racing closer to the fight. He jammed on the brakes just before he reached the battling mob and flung his door open.

"Stay here!" he told Hallie as he got out. He didn't know if it would do any good or not, but he didn't have time to wait and see if she did what he said.

As Stark ran toward the riot he spotted Nick Medford trying to trade punches with two men at the same time. The Black Panther members were all dressed the same, in dark jeans and black T-shirts, so it wasn't difficult to spot them. As Stark reached them, Nick went down, and the two men started kicking him.

Stark grabbed one man's shoulder and hauled him around. The man just had time to let out a startled curse before Stark's fist crashed into his nose and flattened it with a crunch of cartilage. The man howled in pain as he flew backward, tripped, and fell.

Meanwhile Nick caught hold of the other man's foot and heaved, upending him. As the second Black Panther crashed to the ground, Nick leaped on top of him and started hammering punches down into his face.

With all the yelling going on, along with the thud of fists against flesh and bone, Stark didn't hear the rush of footsteps behind him, but some instinct warned him anyway and he wheeled around just in time to duck under a roundhouse punch thrown at his head. He grabbed the man's T-shirt and pulled hard. As he was already off-balance, the man's momentum carried him forward, and Stark was able to flip him in the air with a neat judo throw he had learned in basic training, which seemed to him like a thousand years ago. The man slammed down on his back, knocking all the breath from his lungs and stunning him.

"John Howard, look out!"

The warning cry came from Hallie. Stark wasn't surprised that she hadn't stayed in the truck like he told her. He glanced over his shoulder and saw one of the intruders swinging a protest sign at him. He didn't have time to duck or twist out of the way. All he could do was throw his left arm up to block the blow.

The piece of lumber to which the sign was attached struck Stark's arm and made it go numb all the way to the shoulder. His right arm still worked just fine, but before he could throw a punch Hallie appeared behind the man and jabbed the prongs of a stun gun against the side of his neck. The man's body jerked and he arched his back as the shock hit him. His eyes widened, and then his knees came unhinged. He fell to the ground with all the fight shocked out of him.

Stark took hold of Hallie and pushed her toward the pickup.

"You don't need to be in the middle of this ruckus!" he told her.

"If I hadn't been, that guy might have busted your head open with that sign!"

Stark couldn't argue with that, but he still didn't want Hallie staying in harm's way.

Before he could do anything else, two more of the Black Panthers rushed him. He whirled to meet their charge and traded punches with them. Both men were young and muscular, and if they felt any qualms about attacking a man old enough to be their father, they sure didn't show it. Stark was also at a disadvantage because his left arm was still partially numb and didn't want to work right. He had to give ground, with Hallie retreating right behind him.

"Wah-hoooo!"

The battle cry came from a young Hispanic man Stark didn't recognize. He leaped into the fracas and tackled one of the men, driving him off his feet. That left Stark facing just one man. Stark managed to parry a couple of punches, then stepped in and drove a hard, straight right to his opponent's jaw. That blow staggered the man. Stark swept his leg around and knocked the man's feet out from under him. As the man fell, Stark caught him with an uppercut to the chin that stretched him out on the ground, momentarily senseless.

There was no respite from the violence. Someone grabbed Stark from behind and put a choke hold on him. Stark tried to break free but failed. He drove an elbow back into the man's stomach, but that didn't do any good, either. It was like ramming his elbow into a wall. Stark couldn't get any air, and bright-colored sparks seemed to be exploding in his brain.

The terrible pressure on his throat went away suddenly. He stumbled forward and gasped for air. A strong hand closed around his arm. The young Hispanic man who had helped him earlier appeared beside him and asked, "Are you all right, sir?"

"Yeah, thanks to you, son," Stark said, his voice hoarse from the near-strangulation. He looked down at the unconscious man on the ground at his feet. "I reckon it was you who cleaned this fella's clock?"

The young man grinned.

"You looked like you could use a hand," he said. He was about to say something else when Stark suddenly shoved him aside and threw a punch at the Black Panther who'd been about to bring a protest sign crashing down on his rescuer's head. The blow landed solidly and sent the protester reeling off his feet.

"Thanks," the young man said. "Looks like we're even."

"Getting there," Stark said. "Look out! Here come some more of 'em!"

Stark and his newfound friend wound up standing back-to-back, slugging it out with several of the intruders. Stark's rawhide-tough form absorbed the punishment, although he knew he would ache like the devil the next day.

The banshee wail of sirens tore through the Texas air but didn't stop the fighting. That took a dozen sheriff's deputies wading into the riot, tackling the combatants, and slapping plastic restraints on them. Park residents and intruders alike were taken down. Anger surged through Stark when he saw his friends being manhandled, but he supposed the deputies were just trying to bring the battle to an end as quickly as they could, before anybody else got hurt.

He hoped there hadn't been any serious injuries. People could get trampled to death in chaos like this.

The fighting came to an end before Stark and his new ally were taken into custody. They were able to step back, gathering with the park residents who were still free on one side of the entrance while the deputies herded the Black Panthers and other protesters who hadn't been arrested to the other side of the road. Although Stark had issues with the way Sheriff Lozano had handled things, he didn't envy those deputies being stuck between two hostile forces like that.

Lozano himself was on hand, shouting through a bullhorn, "Settle down! Back off, damn it! Everybody stop fighting, or you're going to jail!"

Jack Kasek stepped forward and pointed at the park residents who were lying on the ground with their hands fastened behind their backs.

"You can't arrest our people!" Jack yelled. "We were just defending ourselves!"

Lozano lowered the bullhorn and said, "That's always your story, isn't it, Kasek? You're just defending yourselves."

Jack started to protest, but Lozano overrode him.

"Nobody's under arrest yet," the sheriff said. "The only reason anybody is restrained is to put an end to this riot."

"A riot that those people started!" Jack said, pointing to the Black Panthers.

"Those people?" one of the black-clad intruders repeated in an indignant shout. "You racist motherf—"

Lozano brought the bullhorn to his mouth again and boomed out, "All right, that's enough!" He lowered the bullhorn and instructed his deputies, "Escort these visitors out of the retirement park."

It was Jack Kasek's turn to be indignant. He said, "You call them visitors? They attacked our security people, forced their way in here, and then attacked more of our residents."

"We were exercising our right to free speech!" the spokesman for the Black Panthers shot back. Some of the others took up the chant. "Free speech! Free speech!"

"Get 'em out of here," Lozano snarled at his men. He turned to the Shady Hills residents and went on, "Get your friends on their feet and back off. Go on about your business. Looks like you've got some cuts and bruises that need attention."

"You're not going to arrest any of them?" Jack demanded incredulously.

"Not right now, and I'm not going to arrest any of you, either. Nobody's getting arrested until my department has conducted a full investigation of this incident."

Stark had a hunch that so-called investigation wouldn't be very thorough, no matter what Lozano said. Clearly, the sheriff wanted to just sweep everything under the rug.

"By the time you get around to doing anything, they'll all have gone back to Dallas or Houston or wherever they came from," Jack said.

Lozano ignored him and turned away as the deputies herded the Black Panthers out of the park. Some of the other protesters were mixed in with them. They had avoided any real trouble so far, but in their liberal zeal they had gotten caught up in the heat of the moment and rushed in to join the battle. Like their sixties counterparts, who they admired so much, they believed in peace and love . . . and they'd kill you if you didn't agree with their version of those things.

Lozano turned and called, "Stark!" He motioned for Stark to join him.

"What do you want, Sheriff?" Stark asked as he and Hallie came up to Lozano.

The lawman looked at Hallie and said, "I didn't ask to talk to you, counselor."

"I represent Mr. Stark," she snapped.

"It's true," he said with a smile. "I think she's on permanent retainer. What can I do for you, Sheriff?"

"You seem to be the most level-headed of this bunch." Lozano inclined his head toward the residents of the park. "Tell them that I'm going to have a car here at the gate twenty-four/seven until that damned election of yours is over."

"I thought you didn't have the man power for that."

"I don't have the man power to put down any more riots like this, either," Lozano said. "It's only a few days. I'll manage somehow."

Stark nodded and said, "Well, Sheriff, we appreciate that." He could have said something about the gesture being too little, too late, but he didn't see any point in that.

Lozano studied Stark with narrowed eyes and went on, "Yeah, you're the most level-headed . . . but I wonder if that makes you the most dangerous of the bunch, too."

"I'm a peaceable man, Sheriff," Stark said.

Lozano just grunted and turned away again.

Stark and Hallie returned to the other residents. Stark passed along the sheriff's message. Jack Kasek said caustically, "*Now* he does something, after we've got more people hurt."

"Any serious injuries?" Stark asked.

"There don't seem to be. Just cuts and scrapes and bruises. We're too old for all that rough-and-tumble, though. There'll be some sore muscles in the morning."

Stark laughed and said, "Darned right there will be." He turned to the young man who had pitched in to help him during the fight. The stranger was standing with Henry Torres. Stark held out his hand and said, "Much obliged to you for your help, amigo. I'm John Howard Stark."

"I know who you are, sir," the man said as he shook hands.

Henry spoke up, saying, "This is my boy Reuben, John Howard."

"I'm mighty glad to meet you, Reuben. You visiting your dad?"

Henry said, "Actually, he's staying with me for a while until he finds a place of his own."

"That's right," Reuben Torres said. "You see, I just got out of jail."

Stark's eyebrows went up a little in surprise. Reuben Torres was about as clean-cut a young man as he had seen in a while, and he sure didn't look like the type who would have run afoul of the law.

Stark said, "I've got a hunch there's a story that goes with that. Why don't we go in the community center, get some Cokes out of the icebox, and you can tell us about it if you want to."

CHAPTER THIRTY-NINE

"I was a Border Patrol agent for five years," Reuben Torres said as he sat at a table in the community center with his father, Stark, Hallie, Jack Kasek, Nick Medford, and several other Shady Hills residents. "I was hired right out of college."

"It was all he ever wanted to do," Henry said with a note of pride in his voice. "He was smart enough he could have done anything, but he wanted to do something that would help the country."

"I thought about joining the military," Reuben said, "but it seemed to me that we have plenty of enemies closer at hand. Right in our backyard, so to speak. Like anybody else who lives near the border, I've seen the way crime has risen in these parts over the past twenty years. Once I was in the Border Patrol, I started to understand why that's happened. There are certain elements in Washington that want us to fail. They keep the Border Patrol around for show, so they can pretend that they're doing something about the drug smuggling and the illegal immigration, but they keep cutting our budget and tying our hands so that we can't succeed. Too many good agents get fed up and quit because they're so frustrated."

Stark nodded and said, "If I was them, I'd probably feel the same way."

"I doubt that, John Howard," Hallie said. "You're too blasted stubborn to quit on anything once you've made your mind up about it."

"That describes most of the agents who are left, ma'am," Reuben said. "Too blasted stubborn to know when they don't have a chance. So they keep on trying to make a difference."

Henry said, "You did everything you could. None of it was your fault. It was all Washington."

Reuben shrugged.

"Maybe so. That didn't change anything, though."

"What happened?" Hallie asked.

"I was out with three other agents, making a sweep along a section of the border where the smuggling traffic had been particularly heavy lately. It was night, so we were using infrared to locate suspects. We came across a group of eight illegals . . . two grown men, and six boys ranging in age from ten to fourteen. All of them were carrying such heavy packs full of drugs that they were just staggering along."

"They were using children to carry drugs?" Jack asked.

"That's right, sir."

"Those animals!"

Reuben smiled faintly and said, "I won't disagree with you about that." He paused, then went on, "We closed in on them and told them to halt. They scattered, of course. We took the two adult suspects into custody first, secured them, and then pursued the kids. Since we were tracking them by infrared, it didn't take long to round them up. They were all pretty scared, so I don't think they were that upset about being caught. There wasn't any trouble until we got to the last one. We pinned him up in a little wash, and he said he wanted to surrender. One of the other agents, Luiz Garcia, and I went in there to get him. The kid had put his pack on the ground. Luiz reached down to get it while I held my flashlight on the boy. That was when he reached behind his back and came out with an Uzi."

"An Uzi?" Jack repeated. "Like, one of those machine guns?"

"That's right," Reuben said. "He was swinging it up toward Luiz. I had my gun in my other hand. I could have shot him. Maybe I should have. But he was fourteen years old. I didn't want to kill him."

"What did you do?" Hallie asked.

"I threw my flashlight at him. They're pretty heavy, you understand. They're made that way so you can use them as a weapon if you have to. It smacked him across the face and knocked him down. Broke his nose. Luiz took the Uzi away from him." Reuben drew in a deep breath. "As it turned out, the gun wasn't operational. He couldn't have fired it."

"But you didn't know that at the time," Stark said.

"No, I didn't. I acted to save the life of a fellow agent, and I'd do it again in a second. But as soon as we brought the kids in, some lawyer who works for the cartel showed up and started yelling about how we'd beaten them and violated their civil rights. The kid I'd walloped was actually the only one who was hurt, but he had that broken nose and a couple of black eyes and looked really pathetic when he was photographed. It didn't take long for the Mexican government to lodge a formal complaint of brutality with our Justice Department."

"And they actually prosecuted you for that?" Hallie asked in amazement.

"Not at first. My supervisors investigated the incident and issued a report clearing me of any wrongdoing. Homeland Security looked into it, too, and decided that I hadn't done anything wrong. I.C.E. said the same thing. The attorney general himself, though, decided that the complaint had merit and took it to a federal grand jury. They indicted me for assault and civil rights violations, and then a jury convicted me. I was sentenced to three years in prison."

A stunned silence hung over the table for a long moment after Reuben stopped talking. Finally, Jack Kasek said, "That's the craziest thing I've ever heard!"

"We were devastated," Henry said. "His mother and I didn't believe Reuben had done anything wrong. We still don't. But he went to prison anyway."

"I served eight months before I was paroled," Reuben said. "It was pretty bad, but I made it through. Now I'm an ex-convict, though, with a felony conviction hanging over my head. It won't be easy finding a job."

"We'll just see about that," Jack said. "I can make some calls."

Reuben smiled and said, "I appreciate that, Mr. Kasek, but I don't know anything about aerospace engineering. All I know how to do is be a cop, basically."

"Don't worry, son," Stark told him. "Something will come along. In the meantime, I suspect you're welcome to stay here at Shady Hills as long as you want. As long as your folks go along with that."

"We're thrilled to have him home," Henry said. "As far as we're concerned, this is Reuben's home, too."

Everyone around the table nodded in agreement.

"Of course," Stark said, "if you want to take a turn at guard duty . . ."

"Yes, sir," Reuben said with an eager smile. "I'd be glad to do that."

Hallie said, "I still can't believe you were prosecuted and convicted."

"Well . . . the Justice Department gave the kid immunity from the drug-smuggling charges and for crossing the border illegally. That way they could bring him in to testify against me. By the time of the trial they'd fixed his nose and his bruises had gone away, and when they brought him into the courtroom he looked like a sweet little altar boy. Then they showed these huge close-up photos of his face after that flashlight hit him, and you could just see the jury sympathizing with him. It didn't help that the gun he had wouldn't work, although there was no way in the world for us to know that at the time."

"The government got what it wanted," Stark said. "A sacrificial lamb to shut up the complaints from Mexico, and a case they could point to as evidence of how sensitive they are to the plight of minorities."

"Hey, what about me?" Reuben said. "I'm a minority."

"You sure are, son. You're an honest, hardworking citizen who was doing your best to fight the evil that's trying to take over this country. These days, that's the only minority our government just doesn't give a damn about."

CHAPTER FORTY

As Hallie had predicted, the weather on September 7 was gorgeous. At that time of year in Texas, the temperatures can still be blistering hot, soaring to more than a hundred degrees, but instead the predicted high was eighty-two, the blue sky was streaked with feathery white clouds, and there was just enough of a breeze to keep things comfortably cool.

Stark hoped the weather was a good omen and that the election would proceed without any trouble.

He knew better than to expect that, however.

The story had picked up steam in the media again as Election Day approached. The regular protesters had been there every day, although the Black Panthers hadn't shown up again. With the sheriff's deputies posted at the gate, the protesters were on their best behavior, which was still pretty danged obnoxious and annoying as far as Stark and the other residents of Shady Hills were concerned. No one liked being accused of the things they'd been accused of, even if they knew it wasn't true.

Election judges appointed by Judge Oliveros would run the actual election, which was to be held in the community center. In addition, officials of the Justice Department had shown up early that morning, before the polls opened at seven o'clock, demanding to be allowed to monitor the election as well. Jack Kasek had told them that they were welcome and to go right ahead, although the "welcome" part of that was stretching the truth.

Representatives of the media were on hand, too. Previously they hadn't been allowed inside the retirement park, since it was private property, but as Hallie had explained, holding the election in the community center meant that they couldn't enforce those limits today.

"All the registered voters inside the proposed boundaries of the town have a right to come in and vote," she said in a meeting of the community's leaders early that morning. "So we have to let everybody else in too, although we can keep the protesters back two hundred feet. Also, we're within our rights to allow only those registered voters into the community center. Anybody else will have to stay outside. There won't be any electioneering or intimidation inside the polling place."

"We could make sure of that if we posted a few fellows with shotguns in prominent places," Jack suggested.

Hallie shook her head.

"That could be interpreted as intimidation, too. Sheriff Lozano has promised to have deputies on hand to make sure everything is peaceful. We'll just have to hope for the best."

They would be using old-fashioned paper ballots, and one large metal box with a sturdy lock and a slot in the top would serve to hold them all. That box was at the end of the table where the election judges sat. When the deputies arrived, one of them planted himself behind that box to keep an eye on it and make sure no one tampered with it.

Sheriff Lozano showed up with the deputies. He came

into the community center, looked around, and nodded to Stark.

"I hope everything goes well today," Lozano said.

"Thanks, Sheriff. We do, too."

"I've said all along that I support you folks, even when there was nothing I could do to help. I still feel that way."

"Just make sure there's no trouble outside," Stark told him. "Everything ought to take care of itself, one way or another."

"I hope so." Lozano looked at his watch. "Five minutes to seven. I guess you're about to get started."

"That's right. Election Day's finally here."

And so it was. At seven o'clock, the main doors of the community center were swung wide. The polls were open.

Before the first voters could come in, the thunderous beat of rap music exploded outside. Stark looked out and saw a sound truck parked down the street, beyond the two-hundred-foot limit. It was surrounded by Black Panthers, all of them wearing dark sunglasses and carrying baseball bats. More of them spread out on both sides of the street.

Jack Kasek came running up to Stark.

"Look at that!" Jack said. "People will have to walk or drive right past them to get here and vote! That can't be legal."

Stark looked around for Sheriff Lozano but didn't see him. The lawman was already gone.

"Hallie, what do you think?" Stark asked, raising his voice above the pounding beat of the music.

"They're not actually blocking the sidewalks," she said. "And those are baseball bats they're carrying. Technically they're not weapons. This isn't my area of expertise, John Howard, but I'd lay odds they know exactly how much they can get away with legally. They've done things like this before."

Stark figured she was right. He thought quickly and said, "We need to get some people up to the gate. There's nothing wrong with us escorting anybody who wants to vote, is there?"

"Don't ask me. Like I said, I'm not an authority on election law."

Stark glanced at the observers from the Justice Department and muttered, "I'd ask those folks, but somehow I don't think I'd get an unbiased answer." He turned back to Jack Kasek. "Spread the word to the volunteer captains, Jack. We'll provide escorts for anybody who wants one."

Jack nodded, but he sighed and said, "This is gonna be a long day."

Stark had a feeling his friend was right about that.

As soon as Stark had cast his own ballot, he joined the volunteers escorting voters to the polls. Many of those who lived in the retirement park could walk to the community center. They were joined by several volunteers who formed a buffer between them and the Black Panthers and the other protesters. Some of the demonstrators shouted angrily at the people coming to vote, calling them racists and fascists. The Black Panthers didn't say much, just leveled hostile glares at the voters.

"Don't worry about those folks," Stark told his friends and neighbors as he walked alongside them, shielding them from potential harm. "They've just got a lot of poison inside them, and it has to come out some way."

When the trouble started, it wasn't on the street but rather at the entrance to the community center. Several pickups full of men had pulled into the parking lot, and their passengers, a dozen in all, piled out of the vehicles and lined up at the doors to show their voter registration cards to the election judges posted there.

One of the judges said to the first man in line, "There seems to be something a little off about this card, sir. Do you have any other ID on you?"

"Why should I have to show you anything else?" the man demanded. He pointed at the card in the election judge's hand. "You got my card right there. That's all I'm supposed to need to vote, ain't it?"

"Yes, but it's not signed, and the printing on it is a little smeared, like it's been photocopied."

"Well, that's just a bunch of bull! That's my card, sent to me in the mail proper-like."

"It's the law that we can ask you to produce a photo ID if there are any doubts about your eligibility to vote," the judge insisted. "If you can't do that, I'm afraid I'll have to ask you to step aside and let someone else come in."

Stark had walked up in time to hear most of that exchange. He stood nearby, watching intently, as the would-be voter grumbled some more but pulled a wallet from his hip pocket and produced a driver's license.

The election judge compared it to the voter's registration card and then said, "The addresses don't match. I'm sorry, sir—you're not eligible to vote. The address on your driver's license doesn't fall within the proposed boundaries of the new town."

"I moved!" the man insisted. "I live in Dry Wash! We all do!"

He waved a hand to indicate the men who had arrived at the community center with him.

"That's not true!" Ben LaPorte said loudly as he walked up. "I've lived in Dry Wash for fifteen years, and I don't recognize any of these fellas."

The first man in line sneered at Ben.

"Are you sayin' that you know everybody who lives there?" he asked.

"As a matter of fact, I believe I do," Ben replied in his characteristically mild voice.

"Well, you're either wrong or a damned liar, and either way I'm goin' in to cast my vote against this phony town!"

The man snatched his card and driver's license back from the election judge and started forward, obviously intending to bully his way in. His companions crowded up behind him.

Ben reached out and grabbed the man's arm. He was six inches shorter and at least forty pounds lighter than the troublemaker, but he didn't hesitate.

"No, you're not," he said. "This is an honest election, and it's gonna stay that way."

With a bellow of rage, the poll-crasher whirled around and swung a sledgehammer blow at Ben's head.

CHAPTER FORTY-ONE

The punch might have torn Ben's head off, but it was too slow and ponderous. Before it could land Ben ducked under it, stepped in, and hooked a powerful punch of his own to the man's midsection. The man doubled over, turning a little green as his eyes bugged out, and Ben hit him again with blinding speed and enough force to send him sprawling under the feet of the men who had come into the park with him. They had already started toward Ben, yelling and cursing, but the ones in front stumbled over their fallen comrade.

That slowed down the charge long enough for Stark, Reuben Torres, Nick Medford, and several other men to meet it.

They got between the troublemakers and the entrance to the community center. Stark ordered, "You men back off!"

They ignored the command and started throwing punches. Stark blocked a fist coming at his head and counterpunched, slamming his fist into the man's midsection. The man staggered back, looking as green as if he'd been kicked in the belly by a mule.

The fight didn't last long. Deputies ran up and got

between the Shady Hills residents and the men who claimed to come from Dry Wash.

"They're frauds," Ben said. "Check their IDs and their voter registration cards. The cards are phonies."

"That's a damned lie!" one of the men blustered. "You're just tryin' to disenfranchise us!"

"What's that? What's that?"

The excited cries made Stark look over his shoulder. Justice Department observers and ACLU lawyers were practically stepping on each other in their eagerness to reach someone who claimed that their rights had been violated. A couple of the deputies were having a hard time keeping them back. One man shouted, "I'm from the federal government! Get out of my way! A disadvantaged citizen needs help!"

Stark's mouth twisted in disgust.

One of the deputies asked wearily, "Can somebody who actually knows what he's talking about tell me what's going on here?"

The election judge who had challenged the first man's voter registration card spoke up, pointing to the offender and saying, "That man attempted to vote with a fraudulent card. If I can examine the cards of the other men, I can tell you whether or not they're legitimate."

"You heard the man," the deputy told the men. "Let's see those cards."

"We don't have to show 'em to you," a man insisted.

"You don't have to vote, either. You can turn around and go back where you came from."

Across the street, the protesters began to chant, "Disenfranchisement! Disenfranchisement!"

Stark wondered just when and how he had wandered into an insane asylum without noticing.

Or was it just that the whole country had gone crazy

over the last few decades as the government and the news media had force-fed the population one perverted idea after another? Those perversions didn't have to do with just sex, either. Everything, from schools to business regulations to courts, had been twisted almost beyond recognition in the pursuit of so-called progressive ideas that didn't add up to anything except class warfare and taxing the "rich"—which included practically every small businessman and entrepreneur in the country—into oblivion, while at the same time spending so much and regulating so much that the national economy was always in danger of crashing down in flaming ruins. None of it bore any relation to anything resembling good old common sense.

It was all just plumb loco, as the old Westerners would say, and anyone who tried to change it ran the risk of being crushed. Stark had seen it time and again. He had been the victim of it himself.

And he greatly feared that nothing short of violent revolution would be able to change it now.

But that didn't mean he and those who believed like him were going to quit trying. Not as long as they believed in the ideal of America.

That was never going to change.

The deputies weren't backing down, Stark had to give them credit for that. After a moment, the leader of the group of poll-crashers sneered and said, "None of this matters anyway. Let's get out of here."

"Yeah," another man said. "I didn't want to vote anyway."

Still casting hostile glares at the deputies and the Shady Hills residents, the men turned and walked back to their pickups. They got in and drove away, tires squealing on the pavement.

Stark turned to Ben LaPorte and clapped a hand on the smaller man's shoulder.

"Glad you were here to step in and stop those fellas, Ben," he said.

"Like I told you when I first came down here, we may not be fancy in Dry Wash, but we're law-abidin' folks," Ben said. "I don't like it when trash like that claims to be from my home." He smiled. "I guess after today I can tell people my hometown is Shady Hills."

"And we'll all be proud for Shady Hills to claim *you*," Stark told him.

With the skirmish over, the election proceeded. After a while the protesters got bored with shouting, "Disenfranchisement!" and went back to their other chants and slogans. Stark had learned how to pretty well tune those out, the same way he did with the rap music from the Black Panthers' sound truck. He and his friends went back to escorting voters to the community center.

One thing worked in the residents' favor as the day went on: not many things were more boring than an election. There was nothing glamorous or exciting about watching voters troop in and out of the community center. The reporters and cameramen withdrew to their satellite trucks. Some of the protesters put their signs down and sat on the ground under the few shade trees along the road. Even though the day could have been a lot hotter, once the temperature hit eighty degrees and the sun was shining brightly, standing around out in the open got pretty warm, pretty fast.

Sheriff Lozano showed up again in the middle of the afternoon. He said to Stark, "I got a report that there was a little fracas out here this morning."

"It didn't amount to much," Stark said. "Your deputies

did a good job of stepping in to break it up before things got out of hand."

"I'm glad to hear it. How's the turnout been so far?"

"Good," Stark said. "I think most of the people who live here in the park have already voted."

"The polls close at seven o'clock?"

Stark nodded.

"That's right. In accordance with Texas election law."

"Did you have any advance voting?"

"Weren't required to," Stark said. "Today is the whole shebang."

"All right. I'll have deputies on hand as long as the polls are open and until all the votes are counted."

As it turned out, that wasn't really necessary, although Stark was glad to have the law enforcement personnel around. By six o'clock, with still an hour of voting left, the protesters had trudged back out to the buses and driven off. The Black Panthers had shut down their sound truck and likewise disappeared. The actual voting had slowed down to a trickle. Stark and his friends gathered on folding chairs outside the community center to wait for everything to be over.

"It went pretty well, I think," Jack Kasek said. He looked at Hallie. "Nothing happened that can be used to challenge the results in court, did it?"

"Not that I saw," she said. "Those people from the Justice Department and the ACLU have been in there all day, watching everything like hawks. I can tell by their expressions that they're frustrated because they haven't seen anything they can pounce on. It's driving them crazy."

"So now we just hope for the best on the vote count," Stark said.

"I don't think we have anything to worry about," Reuben Torres said. "Earlier some of those reporters were interviewing voters when they came back out, doing what they call exit polls. Nearly everybody was willing to answer when the reporters asked them how they voted, and I didn't hear a single person say that they voted against incorporation."

"I'm sure some people did," Hallie said. "But I think the question is going to pass in the affirmative."

Aurelia Gomez and some of the other women showed up with sandwiches and iced tea, and there were soft drinks in ice chests. It was sort of like an old-fashioned church supper on the grounds, Stark thought, and that put a good feeling inside him. No matter how crazy the world got, no matter what personal trials he went through, he still had his friends, the good people who surrounded him now. He still had beautiful Texas evenings like this one. And he still had hope that everything would turn out all right.

Night had fallen and it was close to ten o'clock when the Justice Department observers and the ACLU lawyers trudged out of the community center looking depressed. That was enough right there to tell Stark the outcome of the election. But a moment later one of the election judges came out and announced, "Here's the final tally, folks. Four thousand three hundred and sixty-seven in favor of the incorporation of Shady Hills as a legal town, and five hundred and ninety-eight against."

Several hundred people had gathered in front of the community center by now. As they heard those results, a loud, excited cheer went up. People slapped each other on the back in congratulations. Husbands and wives embraced. Reuben Torres and Antonio Gomez, who had been talking to each other most of the evening, high-fived.

Hallie threw her arms around Stark and hugged him.

"We did it, John Howard," she said. "We won. Shady Hills is a town now."

"That it is," Stark agreed. He wasn't sure how much real difference the election's outcome would make, but it was a symbolic victory, for sure, and a first step in the right direction to restoring law and order in the area.

"So, don't you think you could unbend enough to share a victory kiss with me?" Hallie asked as she looked up into his face.

Stark wasn't sure it was a good idea . . . but how the hell could a man refuse a suggestion like that one?

Good idea or not, he kissed her.

CHAPTER FORTY-TWO

No one paid any attention to the man standing toward the back of the crowd. Despite being very fit, he looked old enough that he might be retired. As the people around him whooped and cheered at the announcement of the election results, he was more restrained. But he smiled and applauded, just so no one would notice a lack of reaction and think it odd. People tended to remember things that were odd.

From where he was standing, from time to time he caught a glimpse of John Howard Stark through gaps in the crowd. His smile widened as he saw Stark kissing a tall blond woman who looked considerably younger than him.

"Why, John Howard, you old dog," Ryan murmured to himself. "I guess you're not in mourning for your wife anymore."

In fairness, it had been several years since Stark's wife died, and anyway, Stark's personal life was Ryan's business only to the extent that it might affect the job that had brought him back here to Texas. If he could use Stark's relationship with the woman to help him accomplish his goal, he wouldn't hesitate to do so.

But what, exactly, *was* his goal? Over the past few days Ryan had been forced to ask himself that question. He knew what he'd been paid to do, of course: kill John Howard Stark.

So why hadn't he done it before now? Ryan couldn't answer that, unless it was simply that he was curious to see what Stark would do next. The man was unpredictable, a wild card, just the sort of loose cannon that Ryan's employers hated.

But a game with a wild card—or two—in it was the most interesting and exciting kind, wasn't it?

Ryan smiled and clapped softly and bided his time.

"What is it?" the president asked in a surly voice. He was in his residence quarters now, not downstairs in the Oval Office, but when the word had come that the attorney general wanted to see him, the president had said to send him on up. His children were all grown, and the first lady had long ago stopped giving a damn whether he spent his evenings with her or not.

"We just got word from Texas," the AG said. "Stark and his friends won their election. That trailer park of theirs is now a separate town, along with some of the surrounding area. I'm not sure exactly what the boundaries are—"

"That doesn't matter, does it?" the president interrupted him. "What's important is that they won. Didn't you have people there to watch for voting irregularities?"

"Of course I did," the attorney general said, sounding a little put out. "And there were ACLU lawyers all over the place, too. Those Texans did everything exactly the way they were supposed to. There was one minor incident where some people who wanted to vote were turned away—"

"There you go," the president said excitedly. "That's voter suppression. Disenfranchisement! File a lawsuit!"

"But their registration cards were phonies, and crude ones at that," the attorney general went on. "A suit on their behalf wouldn't stand up in court."

The president frowned.

"I must say, I'm a little disappointed in you," he told the AG. "When you're trying to bring about the proper outcome of an election, you can't take halfway measures. You have to be professional and competent about it."

"I'm sorry, I couldn't find enough corpses to vote on short notice," the Attorney General snapped.

The president pulled in a deep breath and drew himself up straighter. He glared and said, "I think you've forgotten who you're talking to."

"I apologize for my tone, sir," the AG forced out through tight lips. "But we can't just completely run roughshod over the election process. People still have to believe that we have *some* respect for the rule of law."

"I suppose so," the president agreed with a frustrated sigh, "but it's damned inconvenient. What do we do now?"

"I'll talk to my people who were there and go over every detail of the election. Maybe we can find something to justify filing a suit to overturn the results . . . but from what I've heard so far, I wouldn't count on it."

"Didn't the national committee have protesters there? They were supposed to coordinate that."

"Of course, and the Black Panthers were on hand, too. But those are tough old birds down there in Texas, sir. They don't frighten easily."

"And that fellow Stark must be the toughest one of all."

The president looked sharply at the AG. "I thought you were handling that as well."

"I don't know what you're talking about, sir," the attorney general responded instantly.

"I mean—"

"I don't know what you're talking about, sir."

This time the president got it. He said, "Oh. Yes. Of course. I don't know what I'm talking about, either. Not a clue."

"Just don't say that where the media can hear it, sir, and you'll be all right."

The president frowned. He wasn't sure if the AG was making fun of him or not. He brushed that aside and said, "You know, I wonder if we're blowing this up to be more important than it really is. So some trailer park in Texas votes to become a town. So what? Would people even have noticed if we hadn't sent in observers and if there hadn't been protests?"

"They would have noticed, because Stark is involved," the AG said. "If we hadn't stepped in to put our spin on it right from the start, the media would have built him up to be even more of a folk hero. This way we made him look more like a radical, a right-wing extremist."

"Why would they build him up? They're supposed to be on our side."

"They are," the AG said, "but they still have to deliver ratings, too. In the end, they'll always go for a big story, no matter what it is. It's up to us to control the way it's presented."

"I suppose you're right." The president sighed, then brightened. "But if Stark were to go away—"

"I don't know what you're talking about," the attorney general said again.

But they both knew what the president was talking about . . . and it couldn't happen soon enough to suit them.

Like any businessman, Tomás Beredo, a.k.a. Señor Espantoso, had a lot to keep up with. The cartel's drug smuggling operation in this area consumed most of his time, of course, but there were also guns to be bought and sold, along with the recruitment of new soldiers, not only along the border but also in the major cities throughout Texas. *Human resources, the Americans call this*, Beredo had reflected wryly more than once. He was good at taking human beings and getting what he wanted out of them. Human resources, indeed.

And if those resources became used up and had to be discarded . . . well, that was the way of business, eh? There were always more resources.

On top of that, the cartel did a brisk business in taking illegal immigrants across the border. At one time, most of the coyotes had been independent operators, but now they all worked for the cartel. Sure, it was penny-ante stuff compared to the billions of dollars raked in from drugs, but it helped from the recruitment standpoint. Take a man's wife and children across the border so they could be with him, and he would be more agreeable when the cartel needed a favor in the future.

Beredo had seen the American movie called *The Godfather*. He had even paraphrased a line of dialogue from it once, telling a rival at a tense meeting, "Leave the gun. Take the enchilada." Mobsters had been amateurs compared to his organization, but they had laid useful groundwork.

So with all that going on, it was difficult for him to

keep track of everything that went on in his area of operations.

It was hard to miss the news about that damned retirement park, though. The story was all over the TV and the newspapers. SHADY HILLS WINS ELECTION, BECOMES TOWN. It was annoying.

It became even more so when Gabir Patel said smugly, "I thought you were going to make those old people run away so you can take our drugs through there."

Our drugs, thought Beredo. At that moment, it was all he could do not to take out a gun and put a bullet through the head of the arrogant Lebanese. For some reason, though, the hombres in Mexico City, the leaders of the cartel, insisted that their partnership with Hezbollah be made to work. So Beredo resisted the impulse and summoned one of his bodyguards instead.

"Bring me Ignacio Montez," he ordered. The bodyguard went away to carry out the command. Beredo went on to Patel, "My hope was that the Americans would tear themselves apart, as they always do, and that they would be responsible for their own defeat. This time that didn't happen."

"So what are you going to do?"

"Send them a message. By now they probably think that we've forgotten them." Beredo smiled. "Soon they will know that the cartel never forgets."

CHAPTER FORTY-THREE

There was still plenty of work to be done, so the organizers of the effort to turn Shady Hills into a town met at the community center on Sunday afternoon, the day after the election.

"The first thing we've got to do is call another election," Jack Kasek said. "Shady Hills needs a mayor and a city council. We've got a candidate for mayor already." He looked at Stark. "How about councilmen? How many do we need?"

"Four is enough," Hallie said. "Since the mayor votes, too, that ensures there won't be any ties."

"So we run John Howard for mayor and four of us for city council. Not me, though. Since I own the property, that might be perceived as a conflict of interest."

Hallie smiled and said, "I was about to point that out, Jack. I'm glad you thought of it yourself."

Kasek shrugged and said, "You don't actually live here, Hallie, or I'd suggest that you run."

"No, thanks. I'm content just to be an advisor and provide legal counsel. You can nominate my dad, though."

"What?" Alton said, looking around. "Me? Run for city council? I don't think so. I'm not a politician."

"Do I look like one of those to you?" Stark drawled.

"Well, no, but . . ." Alton looked around the table. "How about Fred?"

"Wait a minute," Fred Gomez said. "How would it look to have the mayor and one of the city councilmen living next door to each other?"

"There's no law against it," Hallie said.

"But it might be better to have folks from different parts of the park represented," Stark suggested. "Nick, how about you?"

"So I can be the black guy?" Nick shook his head. "I've got news for you, John Howard. They're still gonna call us racists whether I run or not."

"I know that. I want you to run because I think you'd be good at the job."

Nick laughed and said, "How can I say no to that? Sure, I'll run."

They threw out the names of several other residents, discussed them briefly, and soon had a slate of candidates, provided, of course, that the ones who weren't there actually agreed to run. Stark knew all of them and had a hunch that they would.

"How much time do we have to allow before the election?" Jack asked.

"I'll look into it," Hallie said. "I think a couple of weeks would be enough, though. We need to have a city government in place as soon as possible. There's business that needs to be conducted."

"Like hiring a chief of police," Fred said.

"I've got some thoughts about that," Stark said. "I guess I'd better be elected first before I start making suggestions, though. Who knows? I might not win."

"I don't think there's any chance of that," Jack scoffed. "You'll all be running unopposed."

Hallie shook her head and said, "Maybe, but we can't be sure of that. We'll have to have a period of open filing, and it needs to be announced right away. Any legal resident of the city can file to run for any of the offices."

"Yeah, but who would?" Jack asked.

"You might be surprised," Stark said. "There are always people who are ambitious, or who don't like the way things are going. I'd be surprised if somebody else *didn't* run for mayor."

"We'll see. Hallie, can you draft a press release about the filing period?"

"I'll have it ready to release first thing in the morning," Hallie promised.

Reuben Torres and Antonio Gomez had become good friends in a fairly short amount of time. That wasn't too surprising, considering that they were both staying at Shady Hills and were the only two young men in their twenties in the park. Reuben was several years older than Antonio and hadn't known him when they were both in school, but Antonio remembered Reuben, who'd been an all-district running back on the football team as well as president of the student council and salutatorian of his graduating class. They were close enough in age to have similar tastes in music, movies, and video games.

There was a certain amount of uneasiness at first because Reuben, as a former Border Patrol agent, had been in law enforcement and Antonio had been, at least for a little while, a foot soldier for the cartel. People could change, though, and Reuben knew that. Antonio had put his past behind him and tried to do right.

On Monday, two days after the election at Shady Hills, Reuben stopped at the Gomez house and asked Antonio if he wanted to go into Devil's Pass with him.

"I need to pick up a few things at the MegaMart," Reuben said.

"I don't know," Antonio said as he looked past his new friend at the SUV parked in front of the mobile home. "That ride of yours looks a little too fast for me."

Reuben grinned.

"I borrowed it from my dad. I used to have a beautiful car, man . . . but I had to sell it. Legal bills, you know."

"Yeah. Sorry."

"Don't sweat it," Reuben said. "So, you comin' or not?"

Antonio hesitated. He said, "I haven't been out of the park since . . . since that business with the murders happened." He swallowed. "And the heads."

Reuben nodded knowingly.

"Yeah, pretty grim stuff. My dad told me about it. I'm sorry, man. You got put in a bad position."

"You don't think I should have done something different?"

"Like not getting mixed up with those sleazebags in the first place? Yeah, that would have been the smart thing to do. Once that ship had sailed, though. . . . Hey, you turned out not to be like them after all. That's gotta count for something."

"Maybe."

"So, you coming to town with me or what?"

Antonio reached a decision and nodded.

"Sure. Let's go."

The radio in Henry Torres's SUV was tuned to a news and talk station. Reuben left it there as he and Antonio pulled out of the park and started toward Devil's Pass.

As a newscast came on, Antonio reached for the controls, saying, "I'll see if I can find some good music."

"Hold on a minute," Reuben said. "They're talking about Shady Hills."

The newscaster was saying, "A spokesman for the Justice Department said today that despite some concerns, it appears there were no significant voting irregularities in Saturday's election to determine whether or not Shady Hills would become an incorporated city. When asked why the federal government was monitoring such a minor local election, the spokesman replied that this administration is always concerned with seeing that the rights of the people are protected."

Antonio said, "Yeah, but they're the ones our rights need to be protected from!"

Reuben nodded solemnly in agreement. It was a shame, he thought, but most of the time Antonio's statement was absolutely correct.

"Meanwhile, County Judge Steven Oliveros confirmed the results of the election and stated this morning that Shady Hills is now a legal municipality of the state of Texas. He also announced that another election will be held three weeks from this past Saturday to fill the positions of mayor and four city councilmen for what seems to be the most newsworthy little town in the state. Filing is now open for legal residents of Shady Hills above the age of eighteen who want to run, and it will remain open for ten days."

"That's a waste of time, man," Antonio said. "Nobody's gonna run against Mr. Stark."

"I hope you're right. He seems like a good man."

"The best," Antonio said. "He saved my life, no doubt about it."

They reached Devil's Pass a few minutes later and

parked at the big MegaMart on the outskirts of town. The store was busy, as it always was, but not as busy on a Monday morning as it was during the weekend. Reuben was able to park fairly close to the entrance.

The two young men came back out about forty-five minutes later. Reuben was carrying several plastic bags containing the clothes he had bought. He had lost weight while he was in prison, and a lot of the things he'd had before no longer fit. His dad had given him the money to buy the new clothes, which bothered him. He was too old to be taking charity from his parents. It was bad enough they were giving him a place to live. But he would pay them back when he got a job, and in order to get a job, he needed to be able to dress decently when he went on interviews.

As if it would make a lot of difference, considering that he was an ex-con, he thought in those moments when he gave in to bitterness.

As they walked back to the SUV, Antonio was saying, "You know, if we could both get jobs, maybe we could rent an apartment together, you know, be roommates." He added with a grin, "We're a little too young to be retired."

"That's not a bad idea—" Reuben began.

Before he could go on, a pickup pulled through the rows of parked vehicles ahead of them and accelerated with a screech of rubber, going the wrong way in a one-way lane. That wasn't unusual—some people didn't seem to have any concept of why arrows were painted on the pavement—but this pickup was shooting along so recklessly that several people had to scurry to get out of the way, including a young mother who had to drag her kids to safety.

"Look at that idiot!" Antonio said.

Alarm bells went off inside Reuben's head. He reached for his friend, intending to grab Antonio and throw both of them between the parked cars beside them, but he was too late.

The snout of an automatic weapon poked out the open passenger-side window in the pickup and began to chatter as flame spurted from its muzzle.

CHAPTER FORTY-FOUR

The high-powered rounds stitched across Antonio's chest, their impact making his entire body shudder. Reuben dropped his bags and tackled Antonio around the waist to drive him to the ground, out of the line of fire. They fell to the pavement side by side, between two cars.

The pickup roared past and kept going. More shots blasted. People began to scream.

Reuben's eyes widened with horror as he looked at his friend. Blood welled from at least half a dozen bullet holes in Antonio's chest. Antonio's eyes were wide open, too, and filled with pain and shock and disbelief. He opened his mouth to try to say something. Nothing came out except a strangled sound and a spout of blood. Antonio lifted a shaking hand and clutched at the sleeve of Reuben's shirt.

"Hang on, man, hang on!" Reuben said desperately. "I'll get help—"

But there was no help to get. Antonio said, *"Madre—"* and then his head fell back. His eyes were still open, but there was no life in them.

Reuben heard tires screaming again, but this time the

sound was fading. The killers were fleeing, putting as much distance as they could between themselves and the scene of their brutal crime.

Reuben squeezed his eyes shut to keep tears from coming out. He pushed himself to his feet and looked around. There was nothing he could do for Antonio now, but maybe somebody else needed help.

He broke into a stumbling run and followed the screaming he heard. Broken glass that had sprayed from shattered windshields crunched under his boots. A moment later he found a screaming woman crouched behind a car. He didn't see any blood on her clothes, but he asked, "Ma'am? Ma'am, are you all right?"

"Don't shoot me!" she cried as he reached for her.

"I'm not going to shoot you." Reuben kept his voice as calm and level as he could, but it wasn't easy. "The shooters are gone. They left. Nobody's going to hurt you. Are you injured?"

She looked up at him and blinked wet eyes. A hard swallow, and then she shook her head.

"I . . . I don't think so. But there were all those shots, and bullets hitting the cars. . . ."

She was all right, Reuben decided, other than being scared out of her wits. He left her there and hurried along the aisle in the parking lot. From the looks of the vehicles, the gunner in the pickup had hosed them down in a pretty indiscriminate fashion.

In the distance, sirens wailed. Nobody came out of the store. The shoppers in there had heard the shooting and the screams, and they were staying put where they hoped they would be safe. Reuben couldn't blame them for that.

He found plenty of damage to cars, pickups, and SUVs, but no more bleeding people except for a couple who had been cut by flying glass. He was standing in the middle of the aisle where the devastation had taken place when police cars careened into the parking lot and screeched to a stop several yards away from him. Cops popped out of the cars and covered him with their pistols. Reuben made sure his empty hands were in plain sight.

"Get down!" one of the uniformed officers yelled at him. "Down on the ground!"

"There's too much broken glass, man," Reuben told the cop. "And the guys who did this are long gone. They were in a gray F-150, maybe five years old. License plate starts with DF. That's all I got."

He was a little surprised he'd been able to dredge that much out of his memory, considering how quickly everything had happened.

"You need to get an ambulance here, too," he went on. "There's a man down." He didn't add that it was too late for an ambulance to do Antonio any good.

"What the hell happened here?" one of the other cops asked. "Was this some sort of random shooting?"

Reuben didn't answer. They could try to figure it out for themselves.

But he had seen it all, and he knew this shooting wasn't random. The man with the gun had had a definite target, and the rest was just bloodthirsty exuberance and collateral damage.

That target had been Antonio Gomez.

When Stark answered the knock on his door, he found Henry Torres standing on the front deck with a stricken look on his face.

"Henry, what's wrong?" Stark asked. "You look like you've heard some mighty bad news."

"I have, John Howard," Henry replied. "I just got a call

from Reuben. He's in Devil's Pass. He and Antonio went into town a little while ago."

"They get into some sort of trouble?" Stark didn't like to think that Dennis Feasco would order his cops to harass people from Shady Hills, but the way things had been going the past few weeks Stark wouldn't rule anything out anymore.

Henry shook his head and said, "No, they were in the parking lot of the MegaMart when they were . . . when they were attacked. Somebody opened fire on them . . . with an automatic weapon." Henry swallowed hard. "Reuben's all right, but Antonio was killed."

Even before those words came out of Henry's mouth, Stark had gone cold all the way down to the core of his soul. He had known someone was dead. The fact that Reuben had survived the attack was some small consolation, but it didn't make the grief Stark felt over Antonio's brutal murder any less.

"Was anybody else hurt?" he asked in a flat, hard voice.

"Not seriously. They shot up a bunch of cars and even the MegaMart sign, but that's all. According to Reuben, they were after Antonio."

Stark nodded.

"The cartel," he said. "Has to be."

"That's what I thought, too." Henry's face twisted in anger and sorrow. "The first time the boy sets foot out of here in weeks, and he's killed an hour later. Who else could it be but that damned cartel?"

Stark took a deep breath and wearily rubbed a hand over his face.

"Do Fred and Aurelia know?"

"Not unless the cops already called them, and Reuben didn't think they had. They've been questioning him, but they took a break and he called me because he thought it might be better if somebody who knew the Gomezes broke the news to them."

Stark nodded and said, "That's a good idea. Come with me, Henry?"

"Sure. Although I'd give anything in the world not to have to."

"So would I, amigo," Stark said. "So would I."

The next few minutes were every bit as bad as Stark had expected them to be. Aurelia broke down, wailing and sobbing in her grief. Fred turned so ashen that for a second Stark wondered if he was having a heart attack. Fred had a lot of strength, despite his mild-mannered appearance, and he was able to pull himself together and ask Stark and Henry what happened. Henry filled in what few details he knew.

Fred cursed in Spanish and said, "Those drug smugglers. Those . . . those animals he ran with! If we'd just been able to keep him away from them . . . !"

"Don't blame yourself," Stark told him firmly. "I know you think of him as a boy because he's your grandson, but Antonio was a grown man. He made his own decisions. And when it finally came down to choosing between good and evil, he at least tried to choose good. That's no comfort now, but maybe someday it will be."

Stark and Henry were still standing on the front porch of the Gomez mobile home when a Devil's Pass police car pulled up at the curb. Chief Feasco himself got out and paused in surprise when he saw Stark.

"You've already heard the bad news, haven't you?" Feasco asked as he came across the yard toward the porch.

"Reuben Torres called me," Henry said. "I'm his father."

Feasco nodded.

"All right," he said. "I suppose there's no harm done, although things like this are really the job of the police."

"The real harm was done in that parking lot," Stark said. "You have any leads on the shooters, Chief?"

"Torres gave us a description of their vehicle, including a partial plate. We haven't turned up anything yet, though. Chances are the pickup was stolen and so were the license plates, but at different places."

Stark thought that was pretty likely, too. There was a good chance somebody would find the pickup out in the desert during the next few days, burned to a hulk so that no evidence would be left inside it.

"You know who's responsible for this, Chief," Fred said as he pushed forward between Stark and Henry. Aurelia was still wailing in the living room. "It was the cartel! You have to go after them! They have to pay for this! And if you don't make them pay, I will!"

Stark took hold of Fred's arm and felt how his friend was shaking with rage. He said quietly, "Aurelia needs you right now, Fred. You'd better go inside and do what you can for her."

Fred looked like he wanted to argue, but Stark's firm, compassionate words must have gotten through to him. He nodded and turned to go back into the mobile home.

Stark went down the steps and faced Feasco.

"You know he's right, Chief," Stark said in a voice that wouldn't carry into the house. "The cartel's to blame for this."

"There won't be any proof of that. If we ever do find the shooters, chances are they'll be dead, killed so they can't talk."

Stark nodded and said, "Yeah, probably. But you've got to try."

Feasco bristled.

"I never said we wouldn't try," he snapped. "We already have an APB out with the pickup's description, and I've spread it all over this part of Texas. And that's a pretty big part. In the meantime . . . you people out here already have a reputation as vigilantes. You'd better not try to add to it."

"By going after the cartel ourselves?"

"Mr. Gomez was pretty upset."

"Of course he's upset," Stark said. "But he's not a fool. He's not going after the cartel by himself."

"That's not what I said. What about you, Mr. Stark? Just how big a fool are you?"

Right now, that was a question Stark couldn't answer.

CHAPTER FORTY-FIVE

Almost the entire population of Shady Hills went *en masse* to Antonio's funeral, packing the church in Devil's Pass. In this time of sorrow, the upcoming election had been forgotten for the most part, although Janis Albert, who had worked as a city secretary before her retirement, had volunteered to fill the same post in Shady Hills and went to the community center every day in case anyone wanted to file to run. Stark, Nick Medford, and the other candidates had already turned in their paperwork to be on the ballot come September 28.

As Stark expected, a Border Patrol helicopter spotted the burned-out pickup in a desolate area about twenty miles up the Rio Grande. There was nothing left in it to provide a clue to the identities of the men who'd killed Antonio Gomez.

For now, the protesters and the media were gone from Shady Hills. Stark fully expected that they would be back before the election, but considering the somber mood that gripped the park these days, he was glad for the break from that annoyance.

Then one day Janis called him and said, "You've got

some competition for the job of mayor, Mr. Stark. Someone's just filed to run against you."

That came as no surprise to Stark. From the beginning, he had expected someone to run against him. He asked Janis, "Who is it?"

"Mitchell Larson."

The name meant nothing to Stark.

"Does he live here in the park?"

"No, he's from one of those housing developments down by the high school." Janis sounded a little tentative, as if she might have done something wrong, as she went on, "I Googled him. He has a real estate agency in Devil's Pass."

"Well, I guess now that he's a citizen of Shady Hills, he wants to do his civic duty."

"Maybe," Janis said. "But I've got a funny feeling about him, Mr. Stark."

Stark didn't know Janis well enough to have any idea whether one of her "funny feelings" meant anything at all, so he said, "I'm sure we'll get to know a lot more about him during the campaign."

"Maybe."

"What about the council positions? Anybody file for them?"

"Not yet. Those candidates are still running unopposed."

Stark thanked Janis and hung up the phone.

That night, someone drove by on the highway and fired random shots into the park. No one was injured, but that was pure, blind luck. One of the bullets shattered a window and came within a few feet of an elderly woman watching TV in her living room. More windows were broken out, and slugs punched holes in walls.

The volunteer guards at the gate didn't get a good look at the vehicle involved, although they were able to send a few shots after it as it sped off; they knew only that it was an SUV. Since Shady Hills didn't have a police force yet, the sheriff's department responded to the 911 call, but the deputies weren't able to do anything except take some reports.

"We'd better get used to it," Stark told his friends when they got together the next day to discuss the matter. "The cartel laid low for a while, but they're back now. Killing Antonio was likely just the first blow in a campaign of terror."

"You think they want us out of here?" Jack Kasek asked.

Stark nodded and said, "That's what it's starting to look like. Have you had anybody else tell you that they're moving out?"

"I got three calls this morning," Jack said grimly. "People are willing to break their leases and take the loss just to get out of here."

Alton Duncan said, "Bullets flying around tend to make people worry less about money. If John Howard is right and this is just the start . . . if this keeps up every night . . . Shady Hills will be a ghost town before too long."

"We can't let that happen," Stark said. "Tonight we'll post guards all along the fence. If anybody comes along and starts shooting, they'll get some hot lead in return."

"I like that idea," Jack said. "I'll spread the word. I don't think we'll have any shortage of volunteers."

They didn't. As night fell, two dozen armed men were posted in the shadows behind the wooden fence. They were armed with shotguns, deer rifles, and .22s, and they were ready to fight back if the park was attacked.

Nothing happened. The cartel thugs were too smart to make a move two nights in a row. They planned to keep the park residents nervous and off-balance instead. But it didn't matter how long they waited before striking again. There were enough volunteers to man the positions along the fence every night from now until the election.

Two nights later, traffic on the highway was light in the hours after midnight. The moon was only a tiny sliver providing a faint glow. Because of that, nobody saw the car running without lights until it was roaring alongside the fence. Flame jetted from the shadows inside the vehicle as automatic weapons stuttered. Then, with a whoosh of fire, a rocket of some sort exploded from the backseat. The volunteers on the other side of the fence had already started returning the fire, but several of them had to leap frantically for cover as the rocket zoomed between them. A second later it slammed into a mobile home and detonated. The concussion shook the ground and shocked the defenders so much that their shots dwindled away to nothing as the attackers sped off into the darkness.

Flames leaped high from the burning mobile home.

Reuben Torres was among the volunteers near the site of the explosion. He dropped the rifle he had borrowed from his father for this duty and ran to the front door of the mobile home. A kick shattered the lock and sent the door flying open.

Thick black smoke boiled out. Reuben drew back for a moment, tore a large piece of cloth off the T-shirt he was wearing, and pressed it over his mouth and nose as he plunged forward again. The smoke stung his eyes and blinded him for a few seconds, but then it began to clear and the leaping flames provided enough nightmarish light for him to see where he was going.

He was in the living room of the home. He spotted an elderly man lying motionless on the floor, with a woman about the same age trying futilely to pick him up and drag him. Reuben ran to her and caught hold of her arm.

"Ma'am, you've got to get out of here!" he shouted over the crackling roar of the inferno that was leaping toward them. "I'll get your husband!"

For a second the woman fought him; then she seemed to realize what he'd said. She turned and stumbled toward the door, coughing heavily. Reuben bent, got his arms around the unconscious man, and heaved him up.

At least, Reuben hoped the old man was only unconscious.

He turned and hurried toward the door. The rush of superheated air from the house was pulling the fire along with it. Reuben felt the heat pounding against the back of his head almost like a fist and knew better than to look back. He cradled the old man, who probably didn't weigh more than a hundred and thirty pounds, against his chest and made a run for it.

Flames practically exploded out the door behind him as he emerged from the mobile home. He dived off the porch and twisted in midair so he would take the brunt of the impact when he and his unconscious cargo hit the ground.

As soon as he landed on the lawn, men gathered around him and strong hands lifted the elderly man from him. Some of the other volunteers grabbed Reuben and hauled him to his feet. They all moved away from the burning mobile home as quickly as possible.

"Did you see anybody else in there?" somebody yelled in Reuben's ear.

He shook his head and glanced toward the mobile home. It was completely engulfed now, and he prayed that the elderly couple were the only ones who'd been inside.

If anybody else had been in there, it was too late for them now.

CHAPTER FORTY-SIX

As it turned out, Mr. and Mrs. Roy Devereaux lived by themselves, without even any pets, so no lives had been lost in the attack. Their mobile home was a total loss, but insurance would cover it. The money wouldn't replace everything that had gone up in smoke, of course, but it was sure better than nothing.

As soon as they were both released from the hospital in Devil's Pass, where they were treated for smoke inhalation, they moved to Houston to live with their daughter and her family. Jack Kasek offered them a special deal on their lease if they wanted to start over again in Shady Hills, but they were adamant about getting far away from the lunatics who were making it impossible for good people to live there.

"The bad part about it," Jack told Stark later as they stood and surveyed the ruins of the Devereaux home, "is that I wasn't completely sure if they meant the cartel . . . or us."

"Some people consider us lunatics for fighting that bunch, all right," Stark admitted. "Sometimes the only right thing to do seems crazy, though."

"I'm just glad that rocket hit the utility room in the back of their house," Jack said. "If it had hit the living room where they were sitting . . ."

"It didn't. And we can be thankful for that."

Over the next week, there were no more attacks on the retirement park. The damage was done, though, and not just to the Devereauxs' mobile home. A dozen more couples moved out of the park, taking their mobile homes and everything they owned with them. The transport companies were doing a brisk business these days.

The filing period for the election was over. Mitchell Larson was the only other person to file for the mayor's position, but Nick Medford and the other candidates all had opponents now, from the area outside the park that was taken in by the city limits. They had a real election on their hands, Stark thought as he looked at a sample ballot pushpinned to the bulletin board outside the entrance to the community center. He wondered why those five men had decided to run.

He didn't have to wait long to find out. Ten days before the election, a forum to introduce the candidates and allow them to state their views was held in the community center.

Despite the fact that a number of people had moved out of the retirement park, the rows of folding chairs in the center's main room were packed that evening. As Stark stood at the back of the room with Hallie, he saw Ben LaPorte and some of the other people from Dry Wash. A lot of people in their thirties and forties were on hand, too, and Stark knew they had to be from the housing developments around the high school.

Several men stood beside the table at the front of the room where the candidates would sit. One of them, a tall, lanky man with graying brown hair, looked vaguely familiar to Stark. He leaned over to Hallie, nodded toward the man, and asked, "Is that Mitchell Larson?"

"That's right," she said. "How do you know him, John Howard?"

"I don't. But I've seen his picture in newspaper ads for his real estate company."

"Well, that's him, all right. Why do you think he decided to run against you?"

Stark shook his head and said, "Beats me. But I wouldn't be surprised if he tells us tonight."

Jack Kasek called the forum to order and motioned for all the candidates to take their places at the long table, which was actually two folding tables pushed together. A podium was set up at one end of it.

"If no one objects, I'll be acting as moderator tonight," Jack began when the candidates were seated and the audience had quieted down. "As you know, we're here to meet the men who are running for mayor and city council of Shady Hills. I'm not trying to be sexist by saying that, by the way. It just so happens that no women are running in this election. I'm sure there'll be plenty of female candidates in the future."

A few reporters and cameramen were in the back of the room, covering the forum for their media outlets, but overall it hadn't drawn much attention. The same wasn't true of Antonio Gomez's murder, the random shots fired into the park, and then the all-out attack that had destroyed the Devereauxs' mobile home. That violence had gotten exhaustive coverage, nearly all of it slanted to make it seem as if none of those things would have happened if the citizens of Shady Hills weren't a bunch of bigoted vigilantes. On the other hand, a candidates' forum for a municipal election, even one in Shady Hills, wasn't nearly as sexy and ratings-grabbing as all that death and destruction.

"We'll start with the candidates for the office of mayor," Jack went on. "And in the interests of fairness, we'll do it alphabetically. That means the first candidate to speak will be Mitchell Larson."

Jack waved Larson to the podium. There was polite applause from the audience as Larson stood up, certainly not an overwhelming reception but not hostile, either. Larson looked a little uncomfortable as he gripped the sides of the podium and nodded to the people gathered in front of him. A lock of brown hair fell over his forehead, and he let go of the podium long enough to raise a hand and brush it back.

"Thank you," he said. "I'm very glad to be here tonight. Some of you already know me, but for those who don't, my name is Mitchell Larson. I own the Larson Real Estate Agency in Devil's Pass and have for the past five years. My wife Jeanne and I live in the Amber Trails development down by Joseph P. Gonzalez High School. We have two children, a son who attends the high school and a daughter who's in junior high. I'm a member of the Devil's Pass Chamber of Commerce."

So far Larson seemed about as normal as normal could get, Stark thought. Downright boring, in fact.

"You're probably asking yourselves why I want to run for mayor of Shady Hills," Larson continued, which of course was exactly what Stark wanted to know. "The answer to that is very simple, actually. I *don't* want to be the mayor of Shady Hills."

That drew a confused murmur from the crowd. Stark frowned, and so did quite a few other people.

"The reason I don't want to be mayor of Shady Hills," Larson forged ahead when the audience had quieted down again, "is that I don't believe the town should exist at all. I was against incorporation, and I still am." He had to raise his voice because people were muttering again. "We don't need a bunch of extra taxes, and we don't need to have the course of our lives determined by a bunch of racist, gun-toting, geriatric vigilantes!"

CHAPTER FORTY-SEVEN

By the time those last words came out of Mitchell Larson's mouth, his voice was booming and filled the room like that of a brush arbor, hellfire-and-brimstone preacher. Stark wouldn't have thought that the man's skinny body had that much volume and power in it.

But even that wasn't enough to drown out the outpouring of angry shouts and boos that came from the audience. Larson fell silent and just stood there holding on to the podium, looking as mild and boring as ever despite the inflammatory sentiments that had just emerged from his mouth.

Only part of the audience was booing, Stark realized. Some of the others were on their feet applauding and cheering. They agreed with Larson. All of them were younger, residents of the housing developments closer to Devil's Pass.

Stark knew from the number of votes in favor of incorporation that the majority of the people who lived down there had been on the same side as the residents of the retirement park. Which meant that quite a few of the people cheering Larson now must have supported incorporation before. What had happened to change their minds? The attacks on the park? The news media coverage?

Or had Larson been doing some quiet but intense campaigning down there since filing to run for mayor?

Either way, Stark realized, this could be a problem.

Jack Kasek got to his feet and slapped his open hand on the table until he got the audience to quiet down a little.

"Stop it!" he shouted. "There aren't going to be any demonstrations like this here tonight!"

It was a little late for that, Jack, Stark thought wryly. The demonstration was already going on.

"Everybody sit down and be quiet!" Jack went on. "Sit down, do you hear me?"

Mitchell Larson lifted his hands and motioned for his supporters to do what Jack said. Gradually, the audience got back under control. It helped when Stark stood up and said, "Take it easy, folks." The residents of the retirement park all respected him too much not to do what he said.

When it was reasonably quiet in the room again, Jack asked the man at the podium in a taut, angry voice, "Do you have anything else to say, Mr. Larson?"

"As a matter of fact, I do," Larson replied. He faced the audience again. "You can see for yourselves, right here in this room, how divisive it is to establish a town that's a sanctuary for those who hate people who are different from themselves."

"That's not—" a man in the audience began.

"Let me speak!" Larson's voice boomed out again. "We have rights in this country, rights that apply to everybody, no matter what color their skin is or what language they speak. Over the past few months, incident after violent incident has taken place here at Shady Hills. Why, just a few nights ago, a couple's home was destroyed. All this because a bunch of reactionary old people have declared this area off-limits to everyone they disapprove of. And now they want to drag the rest of us into that cycle of violence they've caused!"

Nick Medford surged to his feet and yelled, "Those are lies, all lies! We didn't start this trouble! It was the cartel—"

"That's right," Larson broke in with a condescending look on his face. "Whatever's wrong, blame it on the Mexicans."

"That's crazy!" Henry Torres called from the audience. "That's not what we're doing. Half the people who live in the park are Hispanic! The only prejudice any of us feel is toward that bunch of drug-smuggling criminals!"

Larson shook his head smugly.

"You're just blinding yourself to the truth, my friend," he said. "Just because you're Hispanic doesn't mean you can't be just as bigoted as anybody else."

The room was starting to get loud again. Jack said, "You still haven't told us what you plan to do if you get elected, Larson."

"No 'mister' now, eh? Well, I can't say I'm surprised." Larson raised his hands. "You want to know what you'll get if you vote for me and I'm elected mayor? Here it is, plain and simple. My friends who are running for city council and I will hold one vote at our first official meeting . . . and that vote will be to abolish the town of Shady Hills."

Stark wanted to ask Hallie if they could do that legally, but he would have to wait to get her opinion until after the forum.

"Vote for us and things will go back to being the way they were before all this trouble started," Larson went on. "We enjoyed excellent police and fire protection from the county. Now what services do we get? Nothing! It's anarchy, people, anarchy! It's the Old West all over again, every man for himself and if you've got a problem, well, just solve it with a gun! I don't want to live like that. I don't want to raise my children in a place like that. I want to live in a place where they're safe and protected, and if there's a problem, the government takes care of it, not some crazed vigilantes! If you feel the same way, then vote for me and my friends . . . the sane, reasonable choices."

To a deafening mixture of boos and cheers, Larson left the podium and moved back to his seat. He sat down on the folding chair looking pleased with himself.

Jack Kasek turned to Stark and said, "Do you want to try to follow that, John Howard?"

"Somebody's got to," Stark said.

He got up and moved to the podium, and the cheers and the boos switched places. Stark motioned for quiet. It took a couple of minutes to get it, but the audience finally settled down again.

"Most of you know me," Stark began. "For those of you who don't, I used to have a ranch, farther out in West Texas. I moved down here because keeping up with the place had gotten to be a little too much for me, and I wanted to spend my retirement in someplace quiet and peaceful. I sure didn't come looking for trouble . . . but I'm not the sort of fella to run away from it, either."

That brought applause and cheers from his friends, along with scattered boos from Larson's supporters. The reaction didn't last long, though.

"It's no secret that some bad things have happened here," Stark went on. "The trouble came to us; we didn't go to it. Once it was here, we've dealt with it as best we could. Remember this: this country was founded by folks who didn't take kindly to being pushed around. When somebody tried to hurt them, they stood up and fought back."

More cheers came from the audience.

"I've heard it said that nobody hates war more than a soldier, because he knows the true price people have to pay for it. Well, nobody hates trouble more than those who are forced to deal with it, like we've been during the past couple of months. All we want is to be left alone to enjoy our lives, and the only reason Shady Hills is now a legal town is to help us do that."

Stark's voice rose as he continued, "Mr. Larson there said we want to keep out anybody who's not like us. That's just not true. There are quite a few vacant places here in the retirement park right now, and I've got a hunch that Jack Kasek would be glad to lease them to anybody who comes along who can afford it and is willing to be a good neighbor. Black, Hispanic, Asian, or white, it just doesn't matter, does it, Jack?"

"Not at all," Jack said.

"What about restrictions and zoning requirements that keep out minorities?" Mitchell Larson asked. "I've seen those used time and again for racist purposes."

"I didn't know this was supposed to be a debate," Stark said with a smile.

"If you're afraid to answer the question, Mr. Stark—"

"That's not what I said." Stark addressed the audience again. "Shady Hills doesn't have any ordinances or restrictions or zoning requirements . . . yet. We probably will, at some time in the future, because to be honest, folks, you can't run a town without some sort of rules and regulations. You all know that. It's just common sense. But will they be used to treat people unfairly?" Stark shook his head. "Not while I'm the mayor, and I'd be willing to bet that the other residents of the park who are running for city council feel the same way."

Nick Medford and the other candidates nodded in emphatic agreement.

"As for the drug cartel being behind the trouble we've had, do any of you doubt for a second that the cartel exists? You think they're just some racist boogeyman that a bunch of bigots dreamed up?" The audience was quiet now as Stark shook his head. "You'd have to be blind to believe that if you've spent more than a day or two within a hundred miles of the border in the past ten or twenty years. You *know* the cartel is out there. You *know* they're bringing drugs across the border into this country every day, three hundred and sixty-five days a year. You *know* they've smuggled in terrorists who want to destroy our nation. Even the people in Washington, D.C., who insist on leaving our borders open for their own political reasons will acknowledge that."

Stark turned his head and looked along the table at Mitchell Larson, who was sitting there red-faced, obviously seething but silent for the moment.

"And speaking of the government, which Mr. Larson did . . . there's a big difference between wanting to restrict the powers of the government, as this country's founders did, and wanting to do away with it completely. The question is, who knows the best way to handle a problem? Some bureaucrat more than a thousand miles away in Washington, or somebody who lives right here, somebody who has to deal with those problems every day? Nobody in Shady Hills is advocating anarchy. All we're asking for is the freedom to deal with our problems efficiently, in a way that works. Mr. Larson said that we had police protection from the sheriff's department. Ask Sheriff Lozano himself and he'll tell you that he doesn't have the money or the man power to cover the entire county the way it should be covered. That's not his fault; it's just the way things are. Most of the time, the best the deputies can do is show up after the trouble is over. Sometimes well after.

That's the real reason we wanted Shady Hills to be a real town, so we can hire a police force of our own to stop some of these problems before more people are hurt. That's not anarchy, folks. That's the farthest thing from anarchy. And that's what we'll do if the slate of candidates from here in the park is elected. Our first job will be to hire a police chief and some officers for him to lead. After that, we'll see, but I can promise you this . . . the city government of Shady Hills will do its level best to *leave you alone*. If that's the sort of government you want . . . you know how to get it." Stark smiled again. "That's the most I've talked in ten years, so I think I'm gonna go sit down."

He did, and even some of the people who'd been applauding for Larson earlier were clapping for him now, he saw.

"Lord, that was a great speech, John Howard," Nick leaned over to say to him. "You're a born politician . . . and I mean no offense by that."

Jack Kasek stood up and said, "All right, we'll hear from the council candidates now."

After the fiery verbal clash between Stark and Larson, the comments from the other candidates were rather anticlimactic. As if sensing that, all the men on both sides of the issue kept their remarks short and to the point, the candidates from Shady Hills promising to support the positions laid out by Stark while the others backed up Larson's call to abolish the city.

Nobody could ever say that the voters didn't have a clear choice to make in this election, Stark thought.

When the forum was over, a lot of people came up to Stark to shake his hand and tell him that they appreciated what he'd said and the stance he had taken. Gradually the room cleared out, leaving Stark and his group of friends and supporters.

"Can Larson and his bunch do that, Hallie?" Stark asked. "Can they have one vote and do away with the town?"

She shook her head and said, "I don't think so. I believe there would have to be another election, this one to vote on whether or not to disincorporate. But for all practical purposes, they could accomplish their purpose just by doing nothing. If they refused to hire a police force or set a tax rate or conduct any other city business, it would be like Shady Hills isn't a town at all."

"We can't let that happen," Jack Kasek said.

"We can campaign, but in the end it's not up to us," Stark said. "The voters are the ones who'll have to decide what they want."

"You're right, John Howard, but heaven help us if they don't make the right decision. Heaven will have to, because Larson and his bunch sure won't."

CHAPTER FORTY-EIGHT

Over the next few days, fliers went up on telephone posts and campaign signs sprouted in yards in Shady Hills, Dry Wash, and the housing developments around the high school. Stark was glad to see that most of the signs in the retirement park supported him, although there were a few bearing Mitchell Larson's name. The same was true in Dry Wash, although Larson had a little more support there. In Amber Trails, where Larson lived, the situation was reversed and he had most of the support, but in the other areas the voters seemed to be about evenly split between the two mayoral candidates.

The city council races seemed almost like an afterthought. It was a foregone conclusion that everybody, or nearly everybody, who voted for Stark would also vote for the other candidates from the retirement park.

The protesters showed up again several days before the election, and with them, naturally, came the news media. The whole traveling circus had returned. Stark did his best to ignore it, but it was hard to shut out the racket coming from the front of the park.

He had a number of requests from the media for interviews. Most of them he turned down, but he accepted a few of them, although he knew that the reporters would probably try to ambush him and would distort the answers he gave to their questions. He surprised his friends by accepting the requests from some of the most notoriously liberal TV networks and newspapers.

"I'm not ashamed of anything I have to say," he explained, "and you never win anybody over if you only talk to people who agree with you to start with."

"They'll use this against you, John Howard," Hallie warned.

"They'll try, I suppose."

"And they're experts at it." She smiled. "But John Howard Stark doesn't run from fights, does he?"

"Never have," he said, "and I'm a little too old to start now."

The interviews went like he expected them to: cleverly worded questions designed to make him give inflammatory answers that could be used for sound bites, all of which he deflected by speaking the simple truth. It was sort of amusing, he thought, to watch the reporters growing more frustrated but trying not to show it.

Then one of them surprised him by asking, "What about the allegations that your opponent, Mitchell Larson, is just a puppet of the drug cartel that hates you so much?"

The interview was taking place in the community center. Stark leaned back a little in the folding chair where he sat and frowned.

"I hadn't heard anything about that," he said. "To tell you the truth, I'm not sure I believe it. I disagree with Mr. Larson's views, of course, but they seem genuine enough to me."

"Mr. Larson is a small businessman, though," the reporter insisted. "When was the last time you heard a small businessman support the government?"

"Well, I'd say it was the last time we had an administration in Washington that didn't seem bound and determined to make it impossible for small businesses to turn a profit," Stark said. "But that doesn't have anything to do with this little local election."

"Doesn't it? You've been a thorn in the side of the federal government for years now, Mr. Stark, just by being yourself: a homegrown American hero who won't take being wronged by anybody."

Stark shook his head and said, "I'm no more a hero than any average American is. You think it's not heroic just to get up in the morning and go about your business, do your job, and take care of your family, when all the while you're being belittled by the elitists and crushed by a tax burden that you'll never get out from under? Shoot, I'm retired. The real heroes are the folks who are doing their best just to get by from one day to the next and hoping that someday their kids will have it better. As for the federal government, if the people running things in Washington really are worried about who wins an election for mayor in a little ol' town in Texas . . . then the whole country's got something to worry about."

"Stark's right," the chief of staff said as he sat across the desk from the president in the Oval Office. They had just watched the interview, which had aired uncut and in its entirety.

The president frowned and complained, "Can't the FCC do something about that? They were only supposed to show selected clips from it."

"I guess the network decided the whole thing would

play better and get bigger ratings," the chief of staff said. "They've been plugging the hell out of it."

"Even though they're supposed to be on our side!"

The chief of staff sighed.

"We've talked about that before, sir. There's only so much we can control what the media does."

"Yes, I know, and I'm getting damned sick of it." The president shook his head. "So you think we should leave Stark alone?"

"Yes, sir, I do. His fifteen minutes of fame will be up sooner or later."

"It's gone on a lot longer than fifteen minutes," the president said caustically.

"Yes, sir. But it *will* run out. You can count on that."

The president sighed.

"All right. It'll be hands off, at least for now. Spread the word."

"Yes, sir."

"This fellow Stark, though . . . he's damned annoying. If something were to happen to him . . ." The president stopped and held up his hands in surrender. "I know, I know. I'm not supposed to even talk about such things."

"You're not supposed to even *think* about such things, sir. You're the president of the United States, and you represent a party that would never, ever resort to anything resembling such . . . such . . ."

"That's enough," the president snapped. "Don't presume to lecture me."

The chief of staff took a deep breath and nodded.

"Of course not, sir. Sorry."

Anyway, it didn't really matter, he thought. He suspected that the attorney general had put a plan in motion weeks ago to deal with John Howard Stark. To tell the truth, the chief of staff was more than a little surprised that

Stark was still alive . . . although such things were never to be discussed, of course.

"Besides," the president went on, "those drug smugglers have to be getting pretty annoyed. It won't take much more for them to declare open warfare against Stark and his cronies, will it?"

"Probably not, sir."

The president leaned back in his big chair and smiled in satisfaction.

"Let Stark win the damned election," he said. "We'll just see what it gets him."

"I wonder if there's a chance Larson is working for the cartel," Hallie mused as she and Stark sat in lawn chairs on Stark's front deck the night before the election, enjoying a beautiful fall evening.

"I suppose it's possible," Stark said. "He might not be actually *working* for them, though. I think there's a better chance he's scared of them."

"How do you mean?"

"He said he's got a boy in high school," Stark pointed out. "We both know the cartel has kids working for it. If somebody threatened Larson's son and passed the word that it would be a good thing for Larson to run against me and win . . . well, I can see something like that happening."

"So can I," Hallie agreed. "It's terrible, though."

Stark shrugged and said, "Or it could be that he's just like a lot of other folks. He's listened to the media go on and on about how anybody who's a conservative is bad and all their ideas are evil until he actually believes it. It must be hard not to get brainwashed like that, the way things are today."

"The way things have been for a long time, you mean.

The media has *never* told the complete truth in my lifetime, John Howard. I can look back on it now and realize that. Back in the sixties and seventies, they crowed about how the anti-war protesters ended the Vietnam War, when the North Vietnamese officials themselves admitted that the war went on longer *because* of the protests. They said over and over again that George W. Bush lied, when what Bush really did was act on faulty information from an intelligence apparatus gutted and hamstrung by Bill Clinton. And you know what they said about the president who wanted to use nerve gas on American citizens—"

Stark held up a hand to stop her. Hallie laughed and said, "I know, I'm preaching to the choir, aren't I? I just get so frustrated sometimes when people just refuse to open their eyes and really see the truth, beyond the little bits that they're spoon-fed by the newspapers and the TV networks."

"I understand," Stark said, "but fixing that is a bigger job than any of us can take on by ourselves. What we can do for starters is to win this election tomorrow."

"We're going to, John Howard. I can feel it in my gut. Then you can hire a chief of police."

Stark nodded slowly and said, "I've been doing some thinking about that."

CHAPTER FORTY-NINE

Election Day was cool and cloudy, but any rain was supposed to hold off until that evening, after the polls were closed. Stark arrived at the community center early to cast his vote. The protesters were already on hand, chanting and singing and waving signs. The Black Panthers, though, appeared to be sitting this one out. Stark supposed they were somewhere else protesting some other perceived injustice that probably had no basis in fact.

Mitchell Larson walked up while Stark was standing in front of the building with some of his friends. Stark gave him a polite nod and said, "Morning, Mitchell. How are you today?"

Larson didn't answer the question. Instead he said, "Can I talk to you for a minute, in private?"

"I don't see why not," Stark said.

The two of them walked over to a small area at the side of the building, where several picnic tables were located. Some of the reporters tried to follow them, but Stark motioned them back. Somewhat to his surprise, they stopped. The cameramen still had their cameras trained on him and Larson, though. No doubt they were hoping that the two mayoral candidates would start throwing punches at each other. That would be great footage to lead a newscast with.

When they were out of earshot of the others, Stark said, "What can I do for you, Mitchell?"

"Why are you being nice to me?" Larson asked, sounding a little annoyed. "I've said some pretty raw things about you during the campaign."

Stark shrugged.

"Things get said in a political campaign," he replied. "Maybe they're sincere, maybe they're not, but I'm not going to hate a man just because of his politics. It takes more than that."

"Well, then, you're a very rare creature. I don't know anybody on my side of the argument who doesn't hate all of you. Some of them even think that the world would be better off if all of you were to die."

"I feel sorry for anybody who thinks like that," Stark said. "On either side."

"Well . . . what I wanted to say . . . I'm only doing what I felt like I had to do. You understand?"

Something about the man's voice, some tiny note of desperation, made Stark search Mitchell Larson's face. He saw what might have been fear and was definitely worry in Larson's eyes, and that made him wonder if the theory he had expressed to Hallie was right. The cartel might have pressured Larson through his family. Stark still thought that Larson was sincere in the beliefs he had expressed, but that would have just made it easier for the cartel to make use of him.

"Look, Mitchell, when this is all over—"

"Don't say we'll be friends," Larson broke in. "I think you're a dangerous man, Stark. Dangerous to yourself, dangerous to those around you, dangerous to this whole country if so many people actually look up to you. But . . . it's just an election. I don't wish you any ill. That's all I wanted to say."

"Fine," Stark told him. "We'll leave it at that."

"Yeah." Larson turned and walked away.

"What was that about, John Howard?" Hallie asked when Stark rejoined his friends.

"A man who's realized that the world's too big for him, and he doesn't know what to do about it," Stark said.

There were no instances of would-be voter fraud in this election, no disturbances at all other than the continuing irritation of the protesters and a reporter who occasionally got too pushy when it came to interviewing the voters leaving the community center after casting their ballots. The polls closed on schedule at seven o'clock. A gentle rain began to fall about eight, and the protesters disappeared instead of waiting to find out the outcome.

Stark thought that they probably weren't being paid enough to stand out in the rain.

A little before ten o'clock, one of the election judges came out of the meeting room where the votes were being counted and said, "Congratulations, Mayor Stark. You won by a three-to-one margin."

Stark felt no real elation at winning, only a sense of relief that the election was over. He asked, "What about the city council races?"

"All that candidates from the retirement park won as well," the election judge said. "The percentages were about the same as the mayor's race."

The people who had gathered to wait along with Stark and his friends broke out in cheers and applause. Stark smiled, looked at his newly elected city councilmen, and said, "We'll have our first meeting Monday evening, if that's all right with you fellas."

"That's fine, John Howard," Nick Medford said. "What's the first item on the agenda?"

"Hiring a police chief," Stark said. "It's time we had some real law and order in Shady Hills."

According to the Good Book, Sunday was supposed to be a day of rest, but it was a busy one for Stark as he kept fielding interview requests. He figured his plain talk was at least partially responsible for his victory in the election, so he wasn't going to stop speaking plainly now. He hadn't been completely forthcoming about his plans, though, despite the fact that reporters kept badgering him to tell them exactly what he was going to do now that he was the mayor of Shady Hills.

The first-ever city council meeting was held at the community center, which for now at least would serve as the unofficial city hall. Further down the road they would have to consider moving to a modular building that could be a permanent home for the city offices. Since the meeting was public, as required by law, the main room was packed again, although not quite as much as it had been for the candidates' forum. Now that the election was over, some people had lost interest.

The first item on the agenda was to certify the election results and have Stark and the rest of the council sworn in. Judge Oliveros took care of that, then turned the meeting over to Stark, who said, "Thank you, your honor. And thanks to all you folks for turning out tonight to see what we're going to do. I hate to disappoint you, but we're going to go into closed session now to discuss personnel matters."

That brought mutters of surprise and disappointment from the crowd. Stark raised a hand to quiet them and went on, "If you'll be kind enough to wait a few minutes, we might have an announcement for you."

That mollified the audience a little. Stark and the other four councilmen, along with Hallie, who was now officially the attorney for the city of Shady Hills, withdrew into one of the small meeting rooms.

"Is this about the police chief, John Howard?" Hallie asked when the door was closed.

"That's right. I've got a good man for the job, if the rest of you will go along with the idea. Reuben Torres."

Nick Medford frowned and said, "I like Reuben, John Howard, and I think he got a raw deal. But he's a convicted felon. Can he even be a police officer?"

"He can," Hallie said with a nod. Obviously she had researched the matter. "His service with the Border Patrol meets some of the qualifications. If he's hired as chief, he'll have to complete some other courses within a certain amount of time, but he can do that. But here's the thing: he can't carry a gun. That would be illegal."

"No rule saying the chief of police has to carry a gun," Stark said. He was well aware that Reuben had carried a rifle while he was volunteering for guard duty, so technically he had been breaking the law then. From here on out, though, if Reuben was hired he would adhere strictly to the letter of the law.

Hallie smiled and said, "No, there's no rule like that. Just be sure the other police officers you hire can carry guns legally."

"I'm hoping Reuben will have some ideas about that. He told me he knows quite a few former Border Patrol agents and other peace officers who've given it up and gone into private security work. With any luck, he can talk some of them into coming and working for us."

"Shady Hills probably can't match what they're making in the private sector," one of the other councilmen said.

"Yeah, but these are cops who'd rather be doing actual police work instead of being bodyguards and things like that," Stark said. "Somebody want to make a motion that we hire Reuben Torres as police chief?"

"I'll make that motion," Nick said. Stark and Hallie seemed to have won him over.

"Second," one of the other men said.

"All in favor?" Stark said.

Five hands went up.

"It's unanimous, then. We'll move back into public session now."

As they left the meeting room, Hallie commented, "You seem to have a knack for this, John Howard."

Stark grimaced. "People keep accusing me of being good at this politics business," he said. "I'm not sure I like that."

"Better get used to it. You're in charge now."

Stark thought about that and muttered, "Lord, what's the world coming to?"

CHAPTER FIFTY

Once everyone was seated again, Stark called the meeting back to order and announced, "The council has voted to offer the job of chief of police of Shady Hills to Reuben Torres."

Reuben was sitting in the audience with his father, not really paying much attention until he heard Stark say his name. Then he lifted his head and said in surprise, "What?"

Stark smiled.

"You heard me, Reuben. The job of police chief is yours if you want it. Unless you had something else lined up . . ."

"No," Reuben said quickly. "No, I don't. But . . . I don't understand. I was in prison—"

"And fair or not, that disqualifies you for a lot of things The town's legal counsel says you'll have to take some courses, but I figure you can handle that. What do you say, Reuben? You don't have to give us an answer tonight . . . but the sooner you say yes, the sooner you can start doing your job."

Reuben looked over at his father. Henry nodded and

said, "It sounds like a fine idea to me, son. I know the town couldn't get a better man for the job."

A dubious frown appeared on Reuben's face.

"I can't carry a gun anymore," he said.

"We know that," Stark told him. "Can you lead men who are armed?"

The frown disappeared, to be replaced by a look of resolve.

"I can," Reuben said. "And I know some hombres who might be happy to sign up."

"That's exactly what we were all hoping to hear you say, Reuben," Stark said. "Nobody here has forgotten how you went into that burning mobile home and saved Roy Devereaux." He stood up and started to applaud. Within seconds all the citizens in the room had joined in.

The members of the news media who were on hand, standing in the back of the room, took it all in, obviously glad they had been there to get this story.

"In a surprising move, the newly elected leaders of the town of Shady Hills, Texas, have voted to hire a convicted felon as their chief of police. Former Border Patrol agent Reuben Torres was sent to prison for violating the rights of a suspect he was arresting. On second thought, maybe it's not so surprising that a town founded because its citizens believe in vigilante justice would hire such a man to enforce their laws."

Hallie glared at the TV and said, "Damn it, that's not reporting the news. That's editorializing! It's rabble-rousing, that's what it is!"

"All the same thing, this day and age," Stark told her. "I wouldn't worry about it. The media's made fun of us and condemned us every step of the way, and they haven't stopped us yet. They haven't even really slowed us down."

"I know it. It's just so infuriating, listening to their lies."

"Then don't listen to 'em. Go for a walk. Read a book. There are plenty of things that'll be better for your blood pressure than listening to them spout their claptrap."

"I know," she sighed. She moved closer to him on the sofa in Stark's living room. "Or you and I could make out."

"If we were thirty years younger."

"The hell with that," Hallie said. "There's no rule that says people our age can't make out."

"Except that it grosses out the young people."

"I don't see any young people here. Do you?"

"No," Stark had to reply honestly. "Come to think of it, I don't."

By the time a week had passed, Reuben had hired four police officers. Since the city hadn't collected any taxes yet, their salaries would be paid by a group of the citizens who had banded together to provide some operating funds for Shady Hills. For the moment, the police department's communication system consisted of walkie-talkies and cell phones, and the officers provided their own vehicles, although the city was able to afford detachable flashing lights of the sort that were placed on the roofs of unmarked vehicles in larger cities.

It was far from an ideal situation, but the officers, all of whom were friends of Reuben's, were willing to put up with the disadvantages for the time being if it meant they would be able to do some real police work with the actual backing of their employers.

"We don't have any city ordinances yet," Reuben

explained to them, "so we'll concentrate on enforcing the state laws."

"What about the speed limit on the highway?" one of the new officers, Dave Forbes, asked. "Will it be lowered?"

"So Shady Hills will get a reputation as a speed trap?" Reuben said. "No way. As far as I'm concerned the speed limit stays sixty, like it always was."

In addition to Forbes, the other officers were Miranda Livingston, Luiz Garcia, and Keith Hamlin. Forbes, Hamlin, and Garcia were former Border Patrol agents like Reuben. Miranda Livingston had worked for the San Antonio PD and the DEA. All of them were looking forward to working in a small town and maybe making a real difference, as well as to working with Reuben as their boss.

With such a small force, the shifts would be long and the officers would have to cover quite a bit of ground. From the high school in the south to the Dry Wash community in the north was about seven miles. The city limits were shaped somewhat like a dumbbell with a bulge in the center, that bulge being the retirement park itself.

They were all considered to be on-call twenty-four hours a day, to serve as backup for each other if needed. Hamlin and Forbes rented a trailer in Dry Wash together, while Livingston and Garcia both lived in Devil's Pass.

The first week on the job, all the officers did was stop a few speeders on the highway. Then Livingston answered a burglary-in-progress call in Dry Wash. She happened to be fairly close, and she got there in time to see the suspect running across a field in an attempt to escape. Livingston drove after him, cut him off with her car, and then tackled him. She had him restrained and in custody by the time Reuben got there to help.

"I've got this, Chief," Livingston said as she manhandled the suspect into the backseat of her car. She was a petite blonde who looked about as dangerous as a high school cheerleader, but Reuben knew better. Miranda Livingston had a gung-ho reputation, and she lived up to it.

"Good job, Officer Livingston," Reuben told her with a grin. "You can take the prisoner to Devil's Pass and turn him over to the sheriff's department. I'll talk to the people who called in the complaint and handle the paperwork up here."

"Really?" Livingston said. "But you're the chief."

"Yeah, but I've got to have something to do to keep from sitting on my butt all day and getting fat."

Livingston grinned and shook her head, as if she thought that possibility was pretty unlikely.

Despite the easy start, worry nagged at the back of Reuben's brain. He knew things weren't going to stay so calm. It was only a matter of time. . . .

And he was right, of course.

He was at the community center about ten o'clock one night, sitting in the meeting room that was serving temporarily as his office and working on a proposed budget to be delivered to the city council, when the walkie-talkie lying on the chair beside him gave its familiar chime and then crackled to life. He heard Keith Hamlin say, "Got a suspicious vehicle out here on the highway, Chief. I'm going to check it out."

Reuben picked up the walkie-talkie, keyed it, and asked, "Suspicious how, Keith?"

"It's stopped on the side of the road. Looks like four passengers. All male, I think, but I'm not sure of that."

Reuben came to his feet and asked, "What's your location?"

"Three-quarters of a mile north of the park entrance."

Reuben was already headed for the door.

"Do not approach them until backup arrives, Keith," he said. "Repeat, do not approach—"

"Too late, Chief, I'm right behind them—"

A sudden discordant racket make Reuben's hand clench hard around the walkie-talkie. He said, "Keith! Keith, do you read me?"

Nothing but static came back at him.

Reuben burst out of the community center and ran for his dad's Jeep, which he'd been borrowing for police work until he could get something of his own. The car he'd had before he went to prison had been sold, along with just about everything else he owned, to help pay for his legal bills.

As he piled into the Jeep, Reuben said into the walkie-talkie, "Miranda! Luiz! Dave! Anybody copy?"

"I heard Keith's call," Luiz Garcia responded. "I'm on my way!"

"So am I," Dave Forbes said. Reuben heard the fear in Dave's voice, fear for Keith, who was his best friend.

Reuben was glad that two of his other officers were responding to the potential emergency, but it would take them several minutes to reach Keith's position.

He, on the other hand, was less than a mile away and could get there in a matter of seconds.

He cursed that felony conviction under his breath. He'd feel a lot better about charging into trouble if he had a shotgun or a revolver. Maybe the approach of more flashing lights would scare off anybody intent on causing trouble, he thought as he clamped the magnetized light on top of the Jeep.

In this flat country, a person could see a long way. Reuben spotted the lights on Keith's car as soon as he pulled onto the highway from the retirement park. His foot came down hard on the gas and sent the Jeep surging forward. He saw more flickers of light up ahead and knew they were muzzle flashes. There was a gunfight going on.

That meant Keith was still alive, anyway, Reuben thought desperately. The suspects wouldn't still be shooting if he were dead.

As he came closer Reuben saw that the driver's door of Keith's car was open. Keith hadn't taken cover behind it, though. He had retreated all the way to the back of the car, where he crouched now, occasionally leaning out to send a couple of rounds at the other vehicle.

With a shower of sparks, a bullet *spang*ed off the hood of Reuben's Jeep. They had seen him coming and at least one of them was shooting at him now. He swerved the Jeep back and forth to make it a harder target to hit. The aluminum baseball bat that lay in the passenger seat— something that it *was* legal for Reuben to have in his possession—rolled from side to side because of the violent movement.

A cloud of dust billowed into the night sky as Reuben skidded the Jeep to a stop on the shoulder behind Keith's car. He grabbed the bat and rolled out on the passenger side, then scrambled to his feet and went in a crouching run to join his besieged officer.

"Reuben, what are you doing here?" Keith asked as Reuben dropped to a knee beside him.

"Backup," Reuben said.

"No offense, Chief, but I don't think that slugger's gonna do much good against four guns."

"They opened fire on you just as soon as you pulled up, right?"

"Yeah."

"They're bound to have something in there they didn't want you to see." Reuben turned his head to look over his shoulder toward Devil's Pass. He saw flashing lights in the distance.

"Luiz is on his way. He'll be here in a couple of minutes."

"They're not gonna wait that long," Keith said. "Here they come now!"

CHAPTER FIFTY-ONE

Reuben rose up enough to glance through the bullet-shattered front and back windows of Keith's car and saw that his friend was right. Three of the gunmen were charging while the fourth hung back and sprayed the car with shots to keep the police officers pinned down.

It wouldn't do any good to sit there and wait for death to come to them. Clutching the baseball bat, Reuben rolled out from behind the car. A bullet kicked up dirt close beside him. Footsteps slapped the ground. He twisted and rammed the bat up into the groin of the dark figure looming over him. The man screamed and the gun in his hand roared, but he had already started to clutch at himself and the bullet went almost straight down, smashing through his right foot and making him howl even louder.

Reuben came up swinging the bat. It slammed into the man's head with an resounding *clang!*

As the man went down, Reuben scooped up the gun he'd dropped. The letter of the law didn't mean a damned thing when it was stacked up against survival. Reuben came up and fired through the car's open windows at one of the menacing shapes on the other side. The man grunted and went down.

More shots had been blasting while that was going on. Keith and the third gunman were trading bullets. Reuben dived for cover again as the fourth man, the one who had stayed back, sent a slug whipping past his ear.

"This one's down!" Keith called. A surge of relief went through Reuben at the sound of his friend's voice. "The guy behind the other car is the only one left!"

The fourth gunman knew that, too. He broke from cover and dashed toward the open field at the side of the highway, firing as he ran. Clearly, he intended to flee on foot.

Reuben threw the bat. It spun through the air and struck the running man's calves, getting tangled up between them. With a startled cry, the man lost his balance and pitched off his feet to go sprawling facedown in the dirt. Reuben charged toward him, grabbed up the bat again, and brought it down on the man's wrist as he reached for the gun he'd dropped when he fell. Bone broke with a sharp crack.

Tires squealed as Luiz Garcia reached the scene. He jumped out of his car, revolver in hand, and ran to join Keith. Together they covered the gunmen while Reuben kicked the men's weapons well out of reach. Three of them were either unconscious or dead, and the fourth lay on the ground cradling his broken wrist and whimpering.

Breathing slightly hard, Reuben asked Keith, "Do you have any idea what this battle was about?"

"Not a clue," Keith replied, "but like you said, Chief, I bet if we look in that car we'll find something they didn't want us to see."

* * *

The "something" turned out to be a trunk full of cocaine, more than a million dollars' worth. Reuben waited until he had a properly executed search warrant to open the trunk. He didn't want any sort of procedural glitch to taint this bust.

All four of the men who'd been in the car were illegals. Two had been killed in the shootout, and the other two were in the hospital in Devil's Pass under police guard. An examination of the car turned up more than just the cocaine and some assorted weapons. It also found a busted water pump, which explained what had happened. The car had broken down. Reuben figured the frantic mules had called their bosses for instructions and been told to wait there until somebody could come to pick them up along with the drugs. Unfortunately for them, Keith had come along first and they had panicked and opened fire.

The story made headlines all across the state. A million-dollar cocaine bust might have anyway, but its location, in the notorious town of Shady Hills, made it even more newsworthy.

"You were lucky," Stark told Reuben the next day after Reuben finished filling him in on all the details. "You and Keith were outnumbered and outgunned. That ruckus could have ended very badly."

"I know," Reuben admitted. "Maybe I was a little reckless going out there that way."

"No, I'd say it was a lot reckless, since you were unarmed. It's a good thing Keith was able to shoot those two fellas himself."

The look Stark gave Reuben made it clear that he had a pretty good idea what had really happened. The official report didn't say anything about Reuben using a gun, though, and that was just fine with Stark.

"From now on, it might be a good idea if you didn't get

mixed up in things like that," Stark went on. "Since you can't be armed and all."

"I swing a mean bat," Reuben said with a faint smile.

"That you do, but most of the time a bat's not gonna do any good against a gun."

"You're right, Mayor, but I'm not going to leave one of my officers hanging out to dry, either."

For a moment Stark didn't say anything. Then he chuckled and said, "Between you and me, son, I probably would have done exactly the same thing. And I mean everything."

Reuben nodded, understanding what Stark meant. He said, "You realize that much cocaine meant this was a major run. It had to belong to the cartel."

"I agree," Stark said. "And they won't be happy that they lost it, either."

"You send that much cocaine north in a car that's going to break down?"

Nacho Montez managed not to wince as Señor Espantoso's angry words lashed at him.

"There was no way to know in advance that the car was going to break down, señor," he said, hoping that it wouldn't sound too much like he was making an excuse. "It seemed to be in good working order."

That was the truth, but clearly the señor didn't seem to care. He stalked back and forth across the expensively tiled floor in the living room of the ranch house he had taken over as his headquarters and said, "Those gringo police never should have even been there. The sheriff's department never patrolled that stretch of the highway that closely. This was the doing of those old dogs in Shady Hills!"

Nacho nodded.

"Sí. But the police they have hired are not old. My sources tell me that several of them are former Border Patrol agents. They know what they're doing, señor."

"So do I," Espantoso snapped. "I am being frustrated at every turn! That town should not exist! Those old people should have fled! Now they are more entrenched than ever. We'll never get them out of there!"

Jalisco had been hanging back, letting Nacho do the talking, but now the lean, pockmarked man from south of the border stepped up and said, "There is a way, señor."

Espantoso glanced at the Arab, who was sitting off to the side watching, watching like a hawk as he always did. Nacho could tell that the señor hated the Arab and felt like he'd been saddled unfairly with this outside interference. Espantoso couldn't afford to displease the Arab too much, though.

"Tell me," the señor snapped at Jalisco.

In a surprisingly strong, assertive tone, Jalisco said, "You have waited for the gringos to defeat themselves, to weaken themselves and tear themselves apart because of their politics the way they always do. This time it has not worked, señor, so you must go back to the old ways. You must strike fear in their hearts, such fear that they will never dare to defy you again."

"Do not presume to lecture me," Espantoso snapped. "You are a mere soldier in this cartel, while I am one of its leaders."

A true leader would not be afraid of some camel-humping Arab, Nacho thought . . . but of course he was too wise to ever say such a thing.

"Still, a true leader cannot be unwilling to listen to the counsel of those below him," Espantoso went on, unwittingly echoing part of the thought that had just gone through Nacho's head. "What is it you think we should do, Jalisco?"

The smile that curved Jalisco's thin lips was enough to make even Nacho shudder a little inside.

"Strike at them through their weakest link, señor," Jalisco said. "Strike at them through their children."

Someone once said there are really only two sports in Texas: football . . . and spring football. Texans' devotion to the gridiron wasn't quite that fervent, but it was certainly true that they took their football seriously. So the home stands of the stadium were packed with students, faculty, and some visitors during the late afternoon pep rally before Joseph P. Gonzalez High played its opening district game of the year against Cibolo High School.

The marching band was in the stands, playing the school fight song. Cheerleaders in short skirts did high kicks and backflips along the track that ran around the field. The members of the football team stood along the sideline wearing jeans and their uniform jerseys, waving at the crowd. In a minute, when the fight song was over, the head coach would step to the microphone that was set up at the edge of the field and give a rousing speech about how they were going to beat Cibolo that night, a victory that would be the first in a string of district wins carrying them all the way to the play-offs.

Before the band could finish, before the coach could utter one inspiring word, before the football players could do more than get started good on their lecherous fantasies involving the cheerleaders, shots rang out and people began to scream.

Figures with dark ski masks pulled down over their heads charged up the ramps into the stands, whirled to face the crowd, and sprayed automatic weapons fire above their heads. Shrieking in terror, students and teachers alike dived for cover, cowering between the long benches and trying to make themselves as small as possible. More gunmen rushed through gates in the chain-link fence around the field and surrounded the football team and cheerleaders, menacing them with guns.

One of the teachers, a former Marine, grabbed an invader and tried to wrestle the gun away from him. Another of the masked figures stepped up and fired a short burst into the teacher's head at almost point-blank range, blowing it apart like a watermelon.

Out on the field, a couple of coaches tried to fight back as well and were gunned down for their trouble. Several of the football players started to make a run for it, only to have their legs cut out from under them by bullets.

An engine roared and a dark-colored, nondescript van plowed through the fence, making its own gate. Two more similar vans followed behind it as it cut across the track and onto the football field. More men, also wearing ski masks, piled out of the vehicles as they came to a stop. They grabbed football players and cheerleaders, seemingly at random, dragged them kicking and screaming to the vans, and threw them in.

Then, without a word ever being spoken, the attackers fled with their prisoners, leaving behind several bloody corpses and a stadium filled with terror.

All in broad daylight.

CHAPTER FIFTY-TWO

It was one of those terrible things that stuck in the mind. You never forgot where you were when you heard about it.

In Stark's case, he was in the community center, talking to Jack Kasek about how they were going to pay for the city's expenses until they determined a tax rate and sent out notices.

"You can't keep paying for so many things out of your own pocket, John Howard," Jack said. "I know good and well you couldn't have gotten top dollar for your ranch when you sold it. Property values within a hundred miles of the border are way down and have been since the cartels moved in. That's true all the way up and down the Rio Grande."

"Maybe, but I got enough to keep myself comfortable for the rest of my life with quite a bit left over," Stark insisted. "I'd just as soon that extra go to help out Shady Hills. I've enjoyed living here and getting to know everybody. This is sort of paying that back."

"And we're probably lucky there are enough people in the park who feel the same way you do and have some extra financial resources," Jack admitted. "That way the city can keep going for a while—"

A car door slammed outside. Stark and Jack looked around as Fred Gomez practically ran into the building.

Fred and Aurelia had been keeping mostly to themselves since Antonio's murder. Stark saw them occasionally, but he didn't push himself on them, figuring it was better to let them deal with their grief in their own way.

He could tell that Fred was upset about something now. His friend's face was set in shocked, horrified lines. Stark jumped to his feet and hurried to meet him.

"Fred, what is it?" Stark asked. "Aurelia—"

"No, no, something's happened," Fred said. "Down at the high school—"

"Gonzalez High?"

"Yeah. There was a shooting."

"Oh, no," Jack said. "One of the kids went on a rampage?"

Fred shook his head.

"They were having a pep rally. . . . Some masked men came up. . . . They shot some people . . . and took a dozen of the kids!"

The words spilled out of Fred in bunches, and as Stark grasped what he was saying, a chill went through him. It seemed unbelievable, but he knew Fred wouldn't make up a terrible story like that.

"Maybe you heard it wrong," Stark said, grasping at that hope.

Fred shook his head again and said, "It's on all the TV channels."

"Come on," Jack said. "We'll go to my house and check it out."

Jack and Mindy's house was next door to the community center, so it took the three men only a moment to get there. When they came into the living room, Mindy was sitting on the edge of the sofa, staring at the television with tears rolling down her cheeks. She looked at the men and said in a choked voice, "It's awful, it's just awful. . . ."

The TV showed a long shot of the school's football field with the flashing lights of emergency vehicles all over it. Stark knew when he saw them that Fred hadn't gotten confused about what he'd heard. The terrible tragedy really had taken place.

They sat down and watched, listening to the breathless newscaster describe what had happened, as best it could be pieced together from the fragmentary reports that had come in. Six people were dead, three teachers and three students, and a number of others had suffered minor wounds and injuries during the violent incident, which had occurred while the school was holding a pep rally for that night's football game.

Eleven students, six boys and five girls, were missing. According to eyewitness accounts, they had been kidnapped, thrown into the vans that had crashed through the fence onto the football field. So far the authorities had not been able to locate any sign of the vehicles.

"It's Reuben," Jack exclaimed as their young chief of police appeared on the screen. A graphic at the bottom of the screen identified him.

"Because this case involves kidnapping, we've already requested assistance from the Texas Rangers and from the FBI, and Sheriff George Lozano and Devil's Pass Chief of Police Dennis Feasco have pledged any help they can give us," Reuben was saying. "We're going to find the people who did this and bring them to justice, and more importantly, we're going to find those kids and bring them home safely."

Reuben had a slightly shell-shocked look in his eyes, but

his voice was strong and firm as he made that promise. Stark knew that he meant it.

"I've got to get down there," Stark said.

"What can you do, John Howard?" Jack asked.

"I don't know, but I'm the mayor of Shady Hills and the school is part of our town. I need to be there."

Without waiting for anybody to try to talk him out of it, he left the Kasek house, got into his pickup, which was parked at the community center, and headed south on the highway toward the high school.

As he drove, his hands tightened on the steering wheel until it felt like they might tear it off the column. Nobody in a position of authority was saying anything about it yet, but they knew who was responsible for this.

They all knew.

The Texas Rangers were already on the scene when Stark got there. One of them stopped him when he tried to get close enough to the football field to find Reuben.

"Damn it, I'm the mayor of Shady Hills," Stark said. "I've got a right to talk to my police chief. You can ask Sheriff Lozano or Chief Feasco about me, too. They'll vouch for me."

"All right, hang on, amigo," the Ranger said. He stepped a few feet away and talked to someone quietly on a handheld radio, then came back to Stark and said, "Come with me."

The Ranger was either arresting him or taking him where he wanted to go, Stark thought, and either way that was better than standing around out here unable to do anything.

Reuben was standing beside the gaping hole in the fence where the kidnappers' vans had burst through the chain link, talking to several uniformed men. When he saw Stark, he finished the conversation and hurried over.

"Mayor Stark," he said after he nodded to the Ranger accompanying Stark that it was all right for him to be there. "What are you doing here?"

"I came to help," Stark said simply. "These folks down here are citizens of Shady Hills."

Reuben sighed.

"There's nothing you can do," he said. "I'm not sure there's anything any of us can do, despite those big promises I made on TV."

"You don't have any idea where they went after they left here with those kids?"

"Anybody who might know is too scared of the cartel to talk," Reuben said grimly.

"So there's no doubt that the cartel's behind this?"

"Was there ever any doubt about that?" Reuben looked disgusted. "Nobody will come out and admit it, least of all the sheriff and the chief of police, but everybody knows the cartel is behind this outrage."

Stark had thought the same thing. It was nice to know they all agreed with him, he supposed, but that didn't really accomplish anything.

"We've got to find them and go after them," he said quietly.

Reuben frowned and said, "What are you talking about, Mr. Stark?"

"Somebody's got to know where the cartel headquarters are. Some of your old contacts in the Border Patrol, maybe, or the DEA."

Reuben thought about it for a second, then said, "They'd be risking their jobs to help an ex-con."

"You're not just an ex-con. You're a police chief, remember?"

"I'm not sure that would make any difference. But I suppose I can give it a try. The problem is, you'll never get the authorities to cross the border into Mexico. The feds will insist on appealing to the Mexican government for help, and the Mexicans will insist that they be the ones to deal with the situation. But they won't. Half the government down there either works for the cartel or is too afraid to rock the boat. They'll say they're going after those kids, but they won't do it."

"I know," Stark said. "That's why we've got to start thinking about something . . . unofficial."

Reuben looked intently at him for a long moment, then said, "I didn't hear you just say that, Mr. Stark."

Stark smiled.

"I didn't figure you did, son. But that doesn't really change things. If those kids have any chance in hell, it's probably gonna come down to somebody who doesn't give a damn about breaking the rules."

CHAPTER FIFTY-THREE

Despite the coast-to-coast, probably even worldwide, news coverage, despite the multitude of law enforcement agencies—local, state, and federal—throwing their resources into the investigation, despite the offers of rewards that poured in, despite the tear-streaked faces of desperate parents making televised appeals . . . by the next morning no one had any idea where the bloodthirsty kidnappers had taken their victims.

Then the sun came up on horror.

On a shallow bluff overlooking the Rio Grande on the Mexican side of the river, a short distance upstream from Devil's Pass, three crude crosses made of heavy wooden beams were set up. Lashed to those crosses were the nude, battered bodies of three teenagers, two boys and a girl, each with a gaping chest wound where the heart had literally been cut out of them. Someone on the American side of the river noticed the crosses as reddish-gold sunlight began to spread across the landscape and trained a pair of binoculars on them, then threw up violently before making a frantic call to 911.

Mexican police from the sister city to Devil's Pass on

the southern side of the border retrieved the cartel's grisly trophies. Reuben Torres was on hand when ambulances brought the bodies across the bridge linking the two cities to turn them over to the American authorities. The Mexican officer in charge of the detail came up to the grim-faced Reuben and said, "Chief Torres?"

"Yes?" Reuben forced himself to say. He felt sick from the knowledge that he had failed at least three of the kidnapping victims.

"I remember you from when you were in the Border Patrol. You have my sympathy, señor. This is a terrible thing."

Anger welled up inside Reuben. The man sounded sincere, and maybe he really was. But Reuben also knew there was a good chance the officer had either taken payoffs from the cartel in the past or had been intimidated into doing their bidding, even if it was just looking the other way when something criminal happened.

"Thanks," Reuben said curtly. "Is there anything else?"

"This, señor," the officer said, holding out a piece of paper that had been slipped into a clear evidence bag. "We found it on the ground in front of the bodies, weighted down with a rock."

Reuben looked at the paper, on which Spanish words had been written in a bold hand. The message was shocking, but it came as no real shock to Reuben.

The words threatened that if the town of Shady Hills was not dissolved, and the retirement park vacated, then the remaining prisoners would be killed as well. There was one other condition as well.

John Howard Stark was to be turned over to the cartel.

That last part was something of a surprise. Clearly, whoever was in charge of the cartel in this area felt a personal animosity toward Stark. Old grudges, maybe. Stark had frustrated the cartel's plans in the past and been responsible for the deaths of some of their leaders. Or maybe it was just that Stark was a symbol, Reuben thought, a symbol of an America that used to be, that wasn't afraid to stand up to evildoers. That didn't apologize to those who wished to destroy it. That didn't throw its defenders into prison just for doing their jobs and let the criminals walk free, sometimes even arming them. Stark stood against all of that. He was a symbol, all right.

"I'll take that," a man's voice said.

Reuben looked over at one of the FBI agents. The man stood there with his hand out. He nodded toward the piece of paper in the evidence bag.

"It's a message from the kidnappers—" Reuben began.

"It's evidence, and it belongs to the FBI now. Hand it over."

Reuben shrugged and gave the paper to the fed. It didn't really matter now who had custody of the message. He had read it. He knew what it said.

And he knew what he had to do about it.

A large group of people had gathered this morning at the community center in the retirement park to pray together and comfort each other over the tragedy at the high school the day before. When the news of the gruesome discovery on the other side of the river reached them, the gathering became even more solemn. Stark was sitting at a table with Hallie Duncan and her father, Fred and Aurelia Gomez, Nick Medford and his wife Judith, and Jack and Mindy Kasek. When the door opened, he looked up and saw Reuben come striding purposefully into the room. The younger man caught Stark's eye, and Stark knew that Reuben wanted to talk to him.

"I'll be back," he told Hallie. He stood up and went to join Reuben near the entrance.

"Mr. Stark," the police chief said with a nod.

"Any more news?" Stark asked.

"Some, and it's not good."

"More bodies?" Trenches were etched in Stark's cheeks as he asked the question.

Reuben shook his head and said, "Not yet. But the Mexican authorities found a note with the ones who were crucified and passed it along to us. The cartel is taking responsibility for this atrocity."

Stark nodded slowly.

"We all knew they were responsible for it," he said.

"They have some demands, and they say they'll kill the other hostages if those demands aren't met."

"Money? Ransom?"

"No. They want the town of Shady Hills dissolved, and they want everybody to move out of the retirement park."

"Good Lord!" Stark felt anger shaking him deep inside. "All this can't be about just a piece of property! There are other places they can run their stinking drugs!"

"It's about power," Reuben said. "They're just trying to show everybody they're so big and bad, they can have anything they want. Or anybody."

"What does that mean?" Stark asked with a frown.

"Their other demand is that you be turned over to them, Mr. Stark."

"They'll release the hostages if I surrender to them?" Suddenly, Stark had to laugh. "Where do they want me? I'll go wherever they say if they'll release those kids."

"I'm sure they plan to torture you and kill you, sir."

"I'm sure they do," Stark said. "That doesn't matter."

"That's very noble of you—"

"Not one damned bit," Stark broke in on Reuben's

protest. "Nobility doesn't enter into it. It's just a matter of logic. One broke-down old geezer in return for eight kids with the rest of their lives still in front of them? I'll make that deal any day of the week, Reuben."

"I know you would, sir, but there's also the matter of dissolving Shady Hills and vacating the park."

Stark rubbed his jaw and admitted, "Yeah, that's trickier. There's something else to consider, too."

"What's that?"

"I don't want to let those bastards win," Stark said.

Reuben smiled faintly.

"I was hoping you'd say that. That thing you said yesterday that I didn't hear . . . I think it's time."

Stark nodded and said, "You let me handle that. You're a law enforcement officer."

"I'm the chief of police of a town that won't exist anymore if those animals get their way. I'm ready to stop them, whatever it takes."

"Are you sure about that?" Stark asked.

"Yes, sir, I am. As sure as anybody ever was about anything."

Stark nodded and said, "All right, then. Let me say good-bye to Hallie and the others, and then we'll go get started."

"Where are we going?"

"It's visiting hours at the hospital," Stark said. "We're going visiting."

The two drug smugglers who'd been captured by Reuben and Keith Hamlin a few nights earlier were still under police guard at the Devil's Pass hospital. They were being held in windowless rooms, and an officer was stationed outside the door of each room. Stark and Reuben went to the room of the man who'd accidentally shot himself in the foot after being hit in the groin with the baseball bat.

"I'm Chief Torres from Shady Hills," Reuben told the cop on duty at the door. He showed the man his identification. "I need to talk to the prisoner for a minute or two."

The cop shook his head and said, "I can't let you do that without permission from Chief Feasco, sir. I can call him if you want, but I'm sure he won't want you to talk to the prisoner without the man's lawyer present—"

"José Delgado, right?" Stark asked.

"That's right." The cop frowned at him. "I know you. You're that guy Stark."

"The mayor of Shady Hills," Stark agreed. "So I guess you can say I'm here on official business, too."

"All right, let me call the chief—"

Reuben put out a hand to stop him.

"Two minutes," he said. "That's all we're asking."

"Without permission from my boss? With no lawyer around?" The cop shook his head. "That'd cost me my job. No way."

"We're just trying to help those kids who were kidnapped," Stark said.

"I don't care, I can't—"

Stark didn't let him go on. His patience had run out, and since there was nobody else in the hall at the moment . . .

Stark hit the cop as hard as he could, a powerful punch that drove the man back against the door, which swung open under his weight. The cop slumped senseless to the floor, his body holding the door open.

"Well, it's official," Reuben said dryly. "I'll be going back to jail."

"At least you'll have some company this time," Stark said as he stepped over the stunned officer and bent down to grasp his shoulders and drag him farther into the room.

The prisoner lying in the bed was groggy from the pain medication being pumped into him. His eyes widened as he struggled to force himself more awake and alert as the two men approached.

Stark said, "I'd look at his chart, but all that medical gobbledygook doesn't mean anything to me."

"He's got busted balls and a hole in his foot," Reuben said. "What else do you need to know?"

"That ought to be enough to start," Stark said. He took hold of the drug smuggler's bandaged foot and twisted it, while Reuben clapped a hand over the man's mouth to muffle his screams.

Reuben leaned over the bed and said, "You're bound to have heard about what happened yesterday. There's a TV on the wall. So tell us . . . where would the cartel take those kids?"

The man's eyes were wide now with pain and fear. He shook his head as much as he could with Reuben's hand clamped to his face.

Stark twisted the wounded foot again, and the prisoner's back arched up from the bed.

"I don't like doing this," he said. "But parents don't like waiting to find out if their kids are dead, either. They sure as hell don't like burying them."

"You'd better tell us what we want to know," Reuben warned the man. "We're already gonna be in a lot of trouble. Finishing the job on you won't make it that much worse." His voice became even harder. "And it'll be worth it, you worthless piece of—"

The man started to nod, his head jerking up and down frantically.

Reuben took his hand away from the man's mouth and said, "Tell us where to find those kids."

CHAPTER FIFTY-FOUR

"You think he was telling the truth?" Reuben asked as they drove away from the hospital. They had gotten out without anybody discovering what they'd done, but there was certain to be an uproar before much longer.

Stark said, "He was too scared, and hurting too much, not to. I can understand why people don't like torture. They'd like to think that as a people, we're too good to resort to anything like that. But when lives are on the line, sometimes you have to do something you don't want to if you're going to prevent something even worse."

"You don't have to justify what we did, Mr. Stark. I'd do it again in a second."

"So would I," Stark said.

Reuben rubbed a hand over his face, then asked, "Do we tell the Rangers what we found out? The FBI?"

"I might trust the Rangers. Not the feds. But I'd just as soon we didn't tell any of them."

"That's what I figured. When you had that showdown with the cartel before, you went in alone, didn't you?"

"Not alone," Stark said, thinking about the friends who had been with him that day: Jack Finnegan and Henry

Macon, who hadn't made it out of the cartel stronghold south of the border. Nat Van Linh. Will Sheffield. And Rich Threadgill. The crazy man, Rich. Stark would have given a lot to have Rich Threadgill at his side right now, but that wasn't going to happen. There wasn't time. Any team he assembled would have to come from right here.

"You're not going alone today, either," Reuben said. "I'll be with you. I figure all my officers will be, too."

"They didn't get to be Shady Hills cops very long," Stark said.

"They won't care about that. How about the guys in the park? You know any of them who'd be willing—and able—to do something like this?"

Stark thought about it and nodded.

"There are some old vets living there who are pretty hard-nosed," he said. "Probably most of the men living in the park would be *willing* to fight, but there's not many of them I'd take into something like this. They'd just get themselves killed."

"You know, I ought to run up to Dry Wash and talk to Ben LaPorte," Reuben said. "I get the feeling that some of those old boys who live up there are pretty tough."

"That's a good idea," Stark agreed. "Ben talks quiet, but he doesn't back down from anybody, that's for sure."

Reuben didn't have to go up to Dry Wash, though, because as it turned out, Ben LaPorte and a dozen or so of his friends were waiting in the parking lot of the community center when they got back. Ben got out of his pickup and came over to intercept Stark and Reuben.

"Mayor," he said with a nod. "We've all heard the terrible news. It's all over the TV and Internet that those cartel animals want you in exchange for those kids. We're here to back you up if they try to come after you."

"Good to see you, Ben," Stark said as he shook hands

with the man, "and I appreciate that sentiment. I'm not gonna wait for them to come after me, though. I'm going to them."

"You're gonna surrender?" Ben sounded surprised.

"Not hardly."

A smile appeared on Ben's face as he nodded and said, "That sounds more like it. You're goin' after those varmints."

"That's the idea."

"You found out where they're holdin' those kids?"

"We've got a pretty good idea."

"Count us in," Ben said. "All the bunch who came with me today. We've got pistols, rifles, shotguns. . . ." He glanced at Reuben. "And maybe I shouldn't be admittin' this in front of the chief of police, but maybe a few weapons that aren't strictly legal, too."

"I wouldn't worry about that," Reuben told him. "It's not likely that I'll be the chief of police much longer. In fact, we might want to get out of here before the Rangers or the feds show up and try to take us into custody."

"I won't ask what for," Ben said with a smile. "Tell us where to meet you and we'll rendezvous there."

Stark thought about it for a moment, then said, "There's a little mesa a few miles north of Dry Wash, east of the highway."

Ben nodded.

"I know it. Highest point in these parts."

"That's where we'll be later today. Don't tell anybody you can't trust with the information, though."

"Count on that," Ben said.

"We can't hit them in broad daylight," Stark mused, "but I don't want to wait too long. I'm thinking dusk, when it's mighty hard to see anything except shadows."

"Will they wait that long to execute those prisoners?" Reuben asked.

Stark said, "I think I might know a way to stall."

Hallie Duncan said, "Meeting in emergency session a short time ago, Mayor John Howard Stark and the city council of Shady Hills, Texas, have voted unanimously to begin the process of disincorporating the town. Although this will take some time to go through legal channels, Mayor Stark—or rather, former mayor Stark—issued a statement saying that for all intents and purposes, Shady Hills is no longer a town. Chief of Police Reuben Torres and his four officers, who were the only municipal employees so far, have been discharged from those positions, effective immediately. Also, Jack Kasek, the owner of Shady Hills Retirement Park, has voided all leases in the park and has advised residents that they have one week to vacate the premises." Hallie looked directly into the camera as she continued, "These actions are being taken in the hopes that the violence and bloodshed which have plagued the area in recent days will come to an immediate end and that no one else will be harmed."

Hallie's statement went out on all the news channels, over the radio, and was posted on the Internet at the same time. It was seen in homes where people hoped desperately that it would be enough to bring their children home safe and sound. It was seen in homes where decent folks prayed for the same thing, even though they were far away and didn't know the people involved. It was seen in the Oval Office of the White House, where the president felt a certain degree of satisfaction and thought that it was all the fault of John Howard Stark and those other crazy, right-wing conservatives down in Texas.

It was also seen in an isolated ranch house a few miles north of the Rio Grande, where Tomás Beredo looked at Gabir Patel and said, "You see? They have learned not to defy us."

"They move slowly," Patel said with a scowl.

"Everything is slow in America, especially where the law is involved."

"And the American whore said nothing about Stark."

"They will produce Stark when another three bodies are found tomorrow morning."

"I hope you're right," Patel said. "My associates and I grow tired of these godless Americans and their stubbornness. The time will come when they are all wiped from the face of the earth."

Beredo sincerely hoped not. That would be the worst possible outcome for the cartel. Without the stupid Americans to buy the cartel's drugs, where would they be? It was becoming clear to Beredo that helping these Islamic thugs further their aims might not be the best long-term strategy for him and his friends.

But that was a problem to be dealt with another day. For now, the cartel had once again demonstrated its power for all to see, and that was what really mattered.

"You do plan to kill all of the prisoners eventually, don't you?" Patel went on.

"Of course," Beredo answered without hesitation. "The Americans must be punished, so they will never dare to go against our wishes again."

"Would you give me two of them?"

The request surprised Beredo. He said, "Why?"

"I wish to behead one of the males and have the female stoned to death," Patel replied. "And the whole thing should be recorded and sent back to my allies in Lebanon and broadcast as a sign to our enemies that judgment surely awaits them."

Beredo thought about it for a moment, then shrugged and nodded.

"I don't see why not," he said. "Soon, all of them will be dead anyway."

If the mesa had a name, Stark didn't know it. He hadn't lived in the area long enough to know all the details about all its geographical features. But the mesa was a signpost of sorts, the first break in the table-like landscape, the first indicator that as one traveled farther west along the Rio Grande, the terrain would become more rugged, until the mountains of the Big Bend reared their craggy heights.

There was a ramshackle gate in the fence that ran along the highway and a trail that was nothing more than a pair of tire tracks worn into the ground over decades. The mesa was located on somebody's ranch. Stark didn't know who the land belonged to, but he hoped that the owner wouldn't mind him and his friends gathering here to launch their mission of rescue—and vengeance.

They came by ones and twos all day so as not to attract attention: Dave Forbes, Keith Hamlin, Luiz Garcia, and Miranda Livingston, the former police force of Shady Hills who realized they would probably never get those jobs back; Ben LaPorte and eleven more men from Dry Wash—truck drivers, construction workers, mechanics, the sort of men whose work had actually built the country from the ground up and kept it running; half a dozen vets from Shady Hills who had fought in Vietnam or Desert Storm, men who had held themselves in combat readiness because that was what felt right and natural to them; and John Howard Stark and Reuben Torres, the men they would follow into battle.

They parked their vehicles on the other side of the fifty-foot-tall mesa, well out of sight of the road. As the sun began to slide down the western sky toward the horizon, Stark addressed them.

"Here's the situation, gentlemen. About ten miles from here is the ranch house where the rest of those high school students who were kidnapped are being held. Reuben and I got this information from one of the drug smugglers who were arrested a few nights ago, and we believe it to be true."

Dave Forbes said, "Some of us heard about that, Mr. Stark. There are a lot of cops looking for the two of you."

"And yet here I am," Stark said with a grin. "I don't know about you, but I've got a hunch some of those cops might not really be looking quite as hard as they pretend to be."

That drew laughter from the twenty-two men . . . and one woman. Stark, being from the generation he was, wasn't sure about taking Miranda Livingston along on a combat mission, but Reuben had vouched for her and warned that she might cause trouble if she didn't get to go along.

"Once we knew the location," Stark went on, "we were able to get some intel on the sly from some folks in the Border Patrol, since they're still friends with some of you. They emailed Reuben some satellite surveillance photos of the area we're interested in."

Reuben held up his smartphone with one of the photos displayed on it. The screen was too small for everybody to see it, of course, but they knew it was there.

"We've studied these photos," Stark said, "and we can estimate that although the cartel has hundreds, if not thousands of members, there are only between forty and fifty of them at the ranch right now. Which means that although we'll be outnumbered, it'll only be by about two to one. Those aren't bad odds."

"Most of the men who are there will be total badasses, though," Reuben warned. "Don't underestimate them."

Ben LaPorte smiled and said mildly, "There are some who'd say that we're a mite badassed ourselves, Chief."

Reuben chuckled. "That's true enough, Ben. And forget the chief business. Right now we're all just American citizens, trying to do what's right because the people who should be doing this job either can't or won't."

One of the men from Shady Hills spoke up, saying, "Before I left the park, I heard some senator on TV talking about how he was going to launch an investigation . . . of Shady Hills. He was blaming John Howard and the rest of us for what happened to those kids. Said we 'provoked' the cartel into doing what they did. Why is it that any time somebody attacks us, some people always act like it's our fault?"

"Can't answer that, Jimmy," Stark said. "All I can do is say that we all know that's not true, or else we wouldn't be here about to do what we're gonna do. And that's go in there, get those kids to safety . . . and kill any son of a bitch who tries to stop us."

CHAPTER FIFTY-FIVE

For the rest of the day, the rescue force checked their weapons, went over the satellite intel Reuben had gotten from his Border Patrol contacts, and made some rough strategic plans, although in an operation such as this, most strategy had to be improvised on the fly because you never knew what the situation would be until your boots were on the ground. But they could work out some basic things, like who would go where when they hit the cartel's headquarters.

They had no way of knowing where the prisoners were being held, but Stark figured they were either in the main house or in a barn set behind the house. There were a number of other outbuildings, but from the looks of them in the satellite photos, they weren't being used. They had estimated the number of people at the ranch based on the number of vehicles that were visible, but Stark knew that figure could be off by a considerable margin.

One thing they could be sure of was that they would be outnumbered. But as Ben LaPorte commented, "That's nothing new for you, is it, Mr. Stark? I read about you and those fellas who holed up in the Alamo with you. I wished at the time I could've been there to give you a hand."

"We'd have been glad to have you, Ben," Stark told him. "And most folks call me John or John Howard. All my friends do."

"I'm honored to be counted among 'em, John Howard."

The sun was just beginning to set when they moved out, leaving the mesa in a convoy now, pulling onto the highway and heading north. A mile later they turned left onto a county road that ran all the way to the Rio Grande, eight miles away, coming down from the northwest to flow all the way to the Gulf. They drove past the even smaller road that turned off to the north and led to the ranch taken over by the cartel.

The plan was to drive to the river, leave the vehicles there, and circle around on foot to come in from the north, where there really wasn't much of anything. Stark hoped the cartel wouldn't be expecting any trouble from that direction. The enemy would be alert for trouble in any direction, of course; after all, they were holding eight American teenagers prisoner and had to know someone might come after them. But they would expect any rescue attempt to be more likely to come from the south, up that narrow road.

It was a stroke of luck that the county road was paved. No dust cloud rose to mark their passing. When they reached the Rio Grande, the ground rose slightly to low bluffs on either side of the river that overlooked the slow-moving water. The river was down; in the fading light sandbars were visible poking through the surface here and there. A tall chain-link fence topped by barbed wire ran along the bank on the American side, but it wouldn't stop anybody who really wanted over it. In fact, it had been cut in places and only poorly repaired, if at all.

Reuben's mouth quirked in disgust as he got out of Stark's pickup and looked at the fence.

"If the government would build a good fence and man it properly, we could actually control this border," he said. "Instead Washington just talks about enforcement, and in reality they've swung the gates wide open."

"They don't even talk much about enforcement anymore," Dave Forbes put in as he joined Stark and Reuben. "The more illegals who come across the border, get phony Social Security cards, and register to vote, the more there are to keep voting them into office."

"That's a problem for another day," Stark said.

"Yeah," Forbes agreed. "But that day's gonna come, Mr. Stark. And then a lot of people are gonna wish they had paid more attention to what this country's becoming."

Stark had a feeling Forbes was right. It was almost enough to make a man despair. But Stark wasn't the despairing type, and right now, he had a job to do.

Earlier, while they were still close enough to Devil's Pass to connect to the Internet, they had used their phones to study terrain maps of the area and laid out a course that would take them to the ranch. With that course in their minds, they set out at an easy trot. The sun was down now, but just barely, and the western sky was still bright red with reflected light.

Small, rolling, treeless hills broke the flatness of the chaparral-covered terrain. Like the Apaches who had once roamed this land, Stark and his group avoided the crests of those hills, not wanting to be silhouetted against the sky. Because of that, their path weaved back and forth, and it took longer for them to reach their destination than if they had been able to follow a straight line. But that was all right, because Stark wanted the shadows to be nice and thick before they moved in on the ranch.

Finally, spotting lights in the distance, Stark motioned for everyone to get down. He and Reuben crawled to the top of one of those little ridges. From there, they could see the ranch headquarters.

The ranch house, stucco with a Spanish-style red tile roof, sprawled among several cottonwood trees that probably required a lot of irrigation. The barn and the other outbuildings were as Stark had studied them on the satellite photos. Off to the east was a paved strip long enough for private jets to land and take off. At the back of the house was a swimming pool and a tennis court. Stark wondered idly if the cartel boss who lived here ever played tennis. He couldn't imagine it.

"What sort of security do you think they have down there?" Reuben asked. "Infrared? Motion detectors? Lasers? Tripwires?"

Stark frowned and said, "I don't think they have any of those gizmos, Reuben. They're thugs. They've got a bunch of guns. They sit around with those guns and they think that everybody and his dog is so damned scared of 'em that nobody would dare come right up to their place and bust in. And ninety-nine times out of a hundred, they're right."

"And we're the hundredth time," Reuben said.

"You damned well betcha we are."

"So how do we play it?"

Stark turned his head to look back over his shoulder at his allies.

"You and I go for the house," he said. "I want Ben with us, and your buddy Forbes, and that Miranda gal."

"You want to take Miranda right inside?"

"Four of those kids are girls. There's no telling what's happened to them so far, but it's bound to be pretty bad. Once we get to them, they'll need to pay attention to what we're saying and do as they're told. They might be more likely to listen and more willing to cooperate if we've got a woman with us. Otherwise we're just more scary men with guns."

Reuben nodded and said, "That makes sense."

"Everybody else will spread out, clear those outbuildings, and then converge on the house. That way, if we're pinned down, they can come to *our* rescue."

"All right. I'll go over the plan with them."

"I'll stay here and keep an eye on the place," Stark said.

Reuben slid back down the ridge to talk to the others. Stark watched the ranch. After a few minutes, Reuben returned, bringing Ben LaPorte, Dave Forbes, and Miranda Livingston with him, and said, "Everybody understands their assignment. We're ready to move out if you think it's dark enough, John Howard."

"Yeah," Stark said, then added, "Wait a minute."

"What's wrong?"

Stark didn't answer right away. He raised himself a little higher on his elbows and looked around, scanning the rugged, dusk-shrouded countryside around them. He didn't see anything out of place, no sign of any danger.

"I don't know," Stark said. "For a second there, I just had a funny feeling. Almost like I was being watched. But there's nobody out here but us."

"You don't think they know we're here?"

Stark glanced toward the ranch house.

"I don't think they've got a clue. They're too arrogant for that."

"I hope you're right. Are we ready to go?"

Stark nodded and said, "Yeah, we're ready." The feeling he had experienced a moment earlier was gone. He knew they were doing the right thing. The only thing they *could* do.

But even as he retreated down the slope and pushed himself to his feet, he realized that he'd had a similar sensation come over him several times during the past few weeks. Never for long, only a second or two at a time, and any time he'd glanced around, no one was there. The feelings were so slight, so fleeting, that he'd paid no attention to them and forgotten them almost as soon as they happened. Only tonight, in the hypersensitive state that came before battle even in the most icy-nerved of men, had that tiny nagging feeling assumed any importance.

There was no time to do anything about it now, and it probably didn't mean anything anyway, he told himself.

With his shotgun in his hand, the .45 holstered on his right hip, and a combat knife sheathed on his left, he moved along the ridge until it dwindled away and he could turn and start toward the ranch house. The four people he had picked to come with him were right behind him. The others split up and took their own paths, moving in low, crouching runs through the mesquite bushes and chaparral that dotted the landscape.

Stark didn't doubt that the cartel had guards posted around the house. But there were jackrabbits, roadrunners, and coyotes—the four-legged kind—all over this part of the country. The guards were probably used to seeing occasional movements out here. He took advantage of all the cover he could find along the approach to the house, then finally, when he came closer, he dropped to his belly and motioned for the others with him to follow suit.

From there it was a crawl of perhaps three hundred yards to reach the area at the back of the main house where a tiled patio and the pool it surrounded were located. That was where Stark intended to make his entrance.

The shadows were thick now, just as he'd planned. An evening breeze had sprung up. As Stark neared the house, that breeze carried the unmistakable smell of marijuana to him. One of the guards must have fired one up. That made sense; the members of the cartel thought they were invulnerable here.

They were about to find out how wrong they were.

Stark used the marijuana smell as a guide. His eyes, still keen despite his age, spotted the guard sitting on a stool at the edge of the patio surrounding the pool. Stark crawled closer, using some palm trees growing in big ceramic pots to cover his approach. The guard had some sort of automatic weapon—Stark thought it might be an AK-47, but he wasn't sure—leaning against his leg. He couldn't afford to let the man get off a burst with that gun, or even a yell.

When he struck, it would have to be fast and lethal.

He left the shotgun lying in the grass at the edge of the patio and drew his knife from its sheath. As he surged to his feet he came at the guard from an angle, so that the man saw him from the corner of his eye. The guard grabbed the rifle and started to jump up, but Stark was on him too quickly. The knife's razor-sharp blade swiped across the man's throat, opening it up deeply.

Blood fountained from the wound, black in the fading light. The guard let out a soft, hideous gurgle. That was the only sound he could make with his throat laid open almost from ear to ear. The rifle fell to the patio tiles with a clatter. The guard dropped to his knees, then pitched forward on his face. Blood pooled darkly around his head.

Stark sheathed the knife, picked up his shotgun, and silently motioned for the others to follow him as he started toward the glass doors that opened into the house. Reuben picked up the AK-47 as he moved past it. The automatic weapon might come in handy inside.

Stark was still several yards from the doors when he

saw movement through the glass. Suddenly, lights switched on around the pool, illuminating it brightly, and the doors slid open. The sound of female voices chattering in Spanish drifted out into the night air. As Stark froze, three young women—girls, really, probably not out of their teens—stepped onto the patio wearing only flip-flops and carrying towels.

They stopped short at the sight of the five menacing, heavily armed figures and started to scream.

So much for going in quiet, Stark thought.

CHAPTER FIFTY-SIX

He lunged forward. The girls seemed rooted to the spot by terror, just outside the doors. Stark grabbed the arm of the nearest one and heaved her past him, into the deep end of the pool, where she landed with a huge splash.

That broke the spell holding the other two girls motionless in fear. They turned and ran, still screaming, but at least they weren't blocking the door any longer.

A large den, or sitting room, or whatever you wanted to call it, was on the other side of the glass doors. As Stark entered it, a man carrying an automatic rifle charged through a door to his left. Stark pivoted that direction and fired the shotgun before the man could bring his weapon to bear. The buckshot slammed into the man's chest, shredding it into a bloody mess as it flung him backward. Stark pumped the shotgun as two more guards burst into the room from the right.

Before he could swing around to deal with them, the AK-47 in Reuben's hands spewed bullets at them. The two cartel soldiers twitched in a brief, jittering dance of death as lead punched into them. They collapsed like bloody rag dolls.

In the moment of silence that fell after the shooting stopped, Reuben said, "After seeing what they did to Antonio, that felt good."

They didn't have time for revenge, no matter how satisfying it might be, Stark thought. He snapped, "Spread out. We need to find those kids."

More shots were coming from outside as the rest of the rescue force engaged cartel thugs. Stark headed for the corridor to his left, saying, "Ben, with me," while Reuben, Dave Forbes, and Miranda Livingston took the hallway on the right.

A fierce, ear-shattering firefight broke out almost immediately from that direction. Stark heard the chatter of automatic weapons fire punctuated by the boom of shotguns and the whipcrack of rifles. Obviously, Reuben, Dave, and Miranda had run right into trouble, but Stark knew he and Ben had to keep going. The most important thing right now was finding those kidnapped teenagers.

A door crashed open ahead of them. Stark dropped to the floor, saying, "Ben! Down!" Slugs racketed through the air as three men with pistols charged through that door. Stark fired the shotgun again. The charge swept the legs out from under one of the men. He fell screaming to the floor. A second later his head jerked as a bullet from Ben LaPorte's deer rifle shattered his skull and bored through his brain.

Stark drew his .45 and fired up at an angle from the floor as the remaining two gunmen tried to lower their aim. They were too late. The heavy bullets ripped through their bodies and erupted from their backs in sprays of blood. Both men went down, cluttering the corridor along with their companion, who Ben had killed.

"Stop!" The voice came from the room on the other side of the open door. "Stop or we will kill these children!"

Stark came to his feet, still holding the .45. He trained it on the doorway as he pressed himself to the wall on that side of the corridor. Ben moved over to the other wall, still holding his rifle ready to fire. Stark motioned for him to wait.

"How do we know those kids are even in there?" Stark called.

A terrified voice said, "We're here, mister! Please! They're gonna—"

The boy's voice broke off in a cry of pain. The grim lines on Stark's face settled in even deeper.

"Take it easy," he said. "There's no need for anybody else to get hurt. We just want those kids. Send 'em out, and we'll leave."

The man who had spoken before laughed.

"You expect me to believe that? This is war. There is no surrender, no quarter."

"Next thing you'll be playing the *Deguello*," Stark said.

Mentioning the song Santa Anna's musicians had played at the Alamo on that fateful morning back in 1836 might have been a mistake, he realized a second later when the man exclaimed, "Stark! Is it you?"

"That's right. John Howard Stark."

A laugh came from inside.

"I told you to come, and you came. Very cooperative of you, Señor Stark. My name is Tomás Beredo, but I am called Señor Espantoso."

The Dreadful One, Stark thought. A name applied to a ghost, to an angel of death. This fella Beredo fit the description, all right. Stark knew he was talking to the man who bossed the cartel operations in these parts.

"Let the kids go, Beredo," he said. "I don't give a damn about you."

"Ah, but I give a damn about you, Señor Stark. Step

into the doorway with your hands empty, and then perhaps I will consider freeing these children."

Another man's voice growled, "No, you fool. Kill them! Kill them all now! And if you won't—"

A shot blasted inside the room.

Stark didn't wait. He dropped the shotgun and launched himself in a long dive that carried him into the doorway. He saw a burly man with thinning hair and a thick mustache pointing a pistol at several bound, cowering figures. One boy was already dead, lying there with a red-rimmed bullet hole in his forehead, his wide eyes staring sightlessly.

The .45 in Stark's hand boomed deafeningly as he blew holes in the son of a bitch, firing again and again.

Ben's rifle cracked above him. The man from Dry Wash was in the doorway, too. His shot was directed at a darkhaired, sleekly handsome man in casual clothes. Ben had scored with his first shot. Blood showed bright red on the man's shirt. But he had a gun in his hand, too, and it spouted flame as he fired. Ben grunted and twisted backward from the impact of the slug.

He stayed on his feet and fired the rifle again. This time his bullet punched into the man's torso about halfway between his belt buckle and his chin. His gun sagged. Ben shot him again, this time in the head. The man fell in the loose sprawl of death.

Señor Espantoso wasn't so dreadful anymore.

Stark came to his feet and hurried to check both bodies. They were dead, all right, a richly deserved death as far as he was concerned.

From the doorway, Ben asked, "Should I go help Reuben and the others?"

"No," Stark said. "We're gonna get these kids out of here." He looked at the seven surviving prisoners, three boys and four girls. They were tied hand and foot, but they weren't blindfolded or gagged. Stark told them, "We're here to help you. You'll be all right. Ben, help me cut them loose. We're going out the window."

That would probably be safer than trying to fight their way back through the house. From the sounds of the shooting, there was still quite a battle going on.

The prisoners were still whimpering and crying, semi-hysterical from fear. As Stark drew his knife, several of them cringed as if they thought he was about to stab them.

"It's all right," Stark told them, trying to keep his voice as calm and reassuring as possible. "We're gonna get you out of here. You'll be safe soon."

They were bound with plastic restraints. Stark began cutting them loose. Ben had opened a pocketknife and was doing likewise. Stark kept talking in an attempt to stop the youngsters from panicking as soon as they were free. They needed to stay together and under control while they were fleeing from the ranch.

"Mr. Stark!" That was Miranda Livingston's voice. "Mr. Stark!"

"In here!" Stark called to her. The shooting in the house had slacked off a little, although it was still going on.

Miranda appeared in the doorway, a .38 revolver in each hand.

"Reuben sent me to look for you," she said. "We didn't find the kids, but I see you did."

Stark nodded, glad that she was here.

"Come help these young ladies," he told her.

The female prisoners were still wearing their cheer-leader outfits, although the garments had been ripped up so much they were little more than rags. Stark figured the girls had been assaulted, probably numerous times, and they would probably struggle for years to recover from this ordeal, if they ever did.

He was glad those two sons of bitches who'd been in here were dead. No matter how long they burned in hell, though, it wouldn't be as long as they deserved.

Miranda hurried over and slipped one of the revolvers into a holster clipped to her belt. She helped the girls to their feet, saying, "Don't worry, you're going to be all right now."

Stark switched off the light in the room, then went to the window and pushed back the heavy drapes. It was dark enough now that he couldn't see much outside. He unlocked the window, shoved the glass up, and knocked the screen out. The house had only one story, so it wasn't very far to the ground, only a few feet, an easy drop.

"Let's go," he said. "Ben, can you find your way back to the river in the dark?"

"Yeah, I think so," Ben said.

"You lead the way, then. Boys, you follow Ben here." Stark paused. "You're wounded, Ben. You all right to do this?"

"You bet I am," the man from Dry Wash answered without hesitation. "Come on, fellas. I'll get you back to where we left our cars."

"Miranda, you take the girls next, and I'll bring up the rear."

"What about Reuben and the others?" she asked.

"I'll let them know we've got the kids," Stark said. "I'll catch up to you."

Holding the .45 ready, he edged up to the door while Ben and Miranda were hustling the kidnapping victims out through the window. Miranda's presence seemed to have calmed down not only the girls but the boys as well. Stark was glad she had come along.

He looked out and saw that the hallway was clear except for the bodies of the cartel gunmen who'd fallen there earlier. Stark hurried back to the big sitting room and looked across it to the other corridor. Dave Forbes was coming along it supporting a wounded Reuben Torres. Reuben's left leg was stained with blood.

"Reuben, Dave!" Stark called. "We got the kids! Everybody get out the best way you can and head for the rendezvous!"

Reuben waved the gun in his hand to show that he understood. The shooting on the other side of the house had stopped, but it was still going on outside, although a lot more sporadically than it had been a few minutes earlier.

Stark turned and ran back up the hall to provide a rear guard for Ben, Miranda, and the escaping teenagers. He threw a long leg over the windowsill, levered himself through the opening, and was about to drop to the ground when muzzle flame suddenly bloomed in the darkness to his right. Somewhere up ahead, a female voice cried out in pain. Stark thought it was Miranda, but he couldn't be sure.

He leaped to the ground and opened fire. More tongues of flame stabbed through the shadows at him. He dropped to a knee as bullets whined past his head. A girl screamed.

The muzzle flashes retreated. Stark could tell the attackers were running away now. He leveled the .45, aiming at the sound of their rapid footsteps on the hard-packed ground, but before he could fire again, Miranda cried, "Mr. Stark, don't shoot! They've got one of the girls!"

CHAPTER FIFTY-SEVEN

Stark leaped to his feet and ran toward the location of Miranda's voice. He called her name softly, and she said, "Here!" He could hear the pain that drew the word taut.

Dropping to a knee beside her, he said, "How bad are you hit?"

"I'll be all right," she said. "A bullet nicked me on the hip and knocked me down, and then one of them came out of nowhere and grabbed one of the girls. Help me up and we'll go after them."

Stark took hold of her arm and hauled her to her feet, but he said, "You're getting out of here. I'll find the girl. Can you move fast enough to catch up with Ben?"

"She won't have to," Ben said as he loomed up out of the darkness. Stark almost shot him but held off on the trigger.

"Where are the kids?" Stark asked tersely.

"I ran into Keith and Luiz and some of the other fellas and sent 'em on to the river with them. We're missin' one, though."

"I know. I'm going to find her now. Take Miranda. Get her back safe."

"We can come with you and help—" Miranda began.

"You're both wounded," Stark said. "Now go! We're wasting time!"

He set off at a lope in the direction the fleeing gunmen had taken. Miranda called after him, "Be careful! There were three of them!"

A faint band of red light, the vestiges of the day, lingered just above the western horizon. Stark trotted toward it, and as he ran he reloaded the .45, his movements smooth and efficient even though he was working by feel.

Three against one wasn't very good odds, especially when the three were bloodthirsty cartel thugs, with a hostage to boot. But this was a job Stark needed to finish. He might not ever do anything else in his life, but this he was going to finish.

Like a runaway freight train, somebody came out of the darkness and slammed into him, knocking him off his feet. Stark twisted, knowing that if the attacker landed on top of him, the weight might break his ribs and incapacitate him. That was the same as a death sentence. He hit the ground, but whoever had crashed into him landed beside him.

Stark rolled and came to his feet. His eyes were adjusted well enough to the darkness by now that he could make out the huge shape of the other man. The big, bearlike figure was about to lunge at him again.

Stark's memory flashed back to the first night at Fred Gomez's mobile home when the three men had come looking for Antonio. He didn't think it was likely that two of the cartel foot soldiers would be this massive, so he took a chance and said, "Hey, Chuckie."

The man stopped short and said, "Huh?"

Stark shot him three times, the blasts coming so close together they almost sounded like one. At that range, even somebody as big as Chuckie couldn't stand up to three .45 rounds in the chest. He flung his arms in the air and went over backward, dying without a sound.

"Chuckie!" a man screamed not far away.

Stark whirled toward the cry, but the man was already shooting. A bullet gouged a furrow in Stark's upper left arm and knocked him halfway around. He didn't know where the girl was, so he hated to return the fire, but if he stood there and let the gunman kill him, he couldn't do her any good anyway.

So he triggered twice at the muzzle flashes and heard a shout of pain. Flame split the darkness again. Stark felt the impact of the bullet and rocked back a step. He fired again and then his strength suddenly deserted him. Without even realizing he had fallen, he found himself on his knees.

A rail-thin shape sauntered toward him, silhouetted for a second against the last of the light from the sunset. Jalisco. The gunslinger, Stark thought. Nacho and Chuckie were dead, but Jalisco was still alive.

"You and me, old man," Jalisco said as his gun came up.

Stark dived forward and fired. At the same time he thought he heard another shot somewhere nearby. Jalisco staggered to the side. The gun in his hand roared and spat fire. Stark triggered again and again until Jalisco spun off his feet and fell to the ground with a heavy thud that told Stark he wouldn't be getting up.

Stark's ears rang from all the blasts. His voice sounded odd to him as he called, "Girl! Girl, are you there?" He wasn't sure he would be able to hear her, even if she answered.

But then she came stumbling out of the shadows, whimpering, saying, "Please don't kill me, please, please . . ."

Stark struggled to his feet. He reached out for her and said, "It's all right, it's all right." His hand fell on her shoulder and she flinched and started to pull away, but he went on, "I've got you now, you'll be all right."

"You're . . . you're hurt!"

He felt the wet heat of blood on his side and his arm, but he was steady enough on his feet, especially when she slipped an arm around his waist to help him.

"Come on," Stark said. "We need to get to the river."

"How . . . how will we find it in the dark?"

Stark looked up at the sky. The stars had come out.

"We'll find it," he said. "There's somebody up there showing us the way."

They didn't have to steer by the stars the whole way to the river. With a throbbing *whup-whup-whup* from their blades, helicopters with bright searchlights flew over the landscape, lighting it up almost as bright as day. Flashing red and blue lights appeared in the distance. It wasn't long before men in helmets and flak jackets were swarming all over the area between the river and the cartel's head-quarters, rounding up Stark, his friends, and the rescued teenagers like they were stray cattle.

Stark didn't mind being rounded up, either. Everybody who was wounded needed medical attention as soon as possible, himself included. Almost before he knew what was happening, he found himself in the back of an ambu-lance, speeding toward Devil's Pass. He was headed for the hospital. . . .

But he knew that as soon as he was patched up, he'd be headed for jail. He didn't mind. Seven of those kids were still alive who wouldn't have been otherwise. Whatever the government did to him now, it would be worth it as far as he was concerned.

Anyway, he figured to have the last laugh on them.

He was mighty curious, though, if he had imagined that other shot that had helped him bring Jalisco down. And if it was real, if he hadn't imagined it, then who had fired it? One of the men who'd come with him? If that was the case, why hadn't the fella stuck around to help?

Stark would have pondered it some more, but the drugs coursing into his veins through an IV were starting to take hold, and he let the welcome darkness claim him.

"He did it again? *Again?* I don't frickin' believe it!"

"Well, he didn't actually invade Mexico this time, sir," the chief of staff said. "The battle took place on American soil."

"What about the hostages?"

"One was killed, but the other seven are all right. In remarkably good shape, in fact, and unfortunately, the press managed to get to some of them before we could slap a lid on the thing. They all talked about how Stark and his friends were like the Navy SEALs or something from a video game. And of course those interviews are all over the Internet by now. That genie's not going back in the bottle, sir."

"Screw the genie," the president said. "What are we going to do about Stark? Surely he and his friends broke dozens of state and federal laws!"

"Yes, sir, undoubtedly. They also have the Mexican government so upset there are going to be protests lodged for a week. But he's also widely regarded as a huge hero."

"Again."

The chief of staff sighed.

"And it certainly doesn't help matters that one of the bodies found at the ranch was identified as a known Islamic terrorist and member of Hezbollah. But if it's any comfort, sir, you're the not the first president Stark's caused trouble for."

"It's no comfort at all," the president snapped. "He's in the hospital, right?"

"Yes, sir."

"In the custody of the local authorities?"

"That's right. He hasn't been charged with anything yet, but the sheriff down there isn't going to turn loose of him any time soon."

"The district attorney in that county . . . he's one of us, right?"

"Yes, sir."

The president nodded and said, "Let him know, unofficially, of course, that if he doesn't charge John Howard Stark with murder, he'll never be elected again."

"What about the people who were with Stark?"

"I don't give a damn about them," the president said with a shake of his head and a dismissive wave. "They're not important. But whatever it takes . . . John Howard Stark is going to prison."

Ryan set aside the gun he was cleaning and answered his phone.

"You bastard!"

"That's no way to talk," Ryan said. "I'm hanging up now."

"Wait!"

Ryan didn't break the connection.

"You've seen the news? You know what happened?"

"I know all about it," Ryan said.

"You could have prevented this if you'd just killed Stark weeks ago like you were supposed to. Like you were paid to!"

"Only the first half of my fee. I wouldn't dream of trying to collect the other half until the job is done."

The man on the other end of the connection heaved a sigh.

"I don't suppose it would do any good to ask you why you've waited so long. You'd just give me that crap about how everything has to be done at the right place and the right time."

"It's not crap if you live your life by it," Ryan snapped. "If that's all you've got to say—"

"No. You can still do the job."

"What's the point? Stark's going to be tried for murder. I saw *that* on the news, too."

"As long as he's alive, he'll be stirring up trouble. Mark my word for it. Even in prison he'll do *something* to embarrass this administration. Some people are just too damned larger than life. But he's not larger than death."

Ryan had his own reasons for it, but he said, "Don't worry about it, amigo. I give you my word. John Howard Stark will never see the inside of a prison cell."

CHAPTER FIFTY-EIGHT

It was the trial of the century. It didn't matter that the century was less than a quarter finished. All the TV pundits and newspaper editorialists and celebrity bloggers said so. Some people even proclaimed it to be the trial of the millennium, which had barely gotten started. The trial had its own Twitter hash tag. "Who is John Howard Stark?" was a question on *Jeopardy!* There would never be a bigger legal spectacle.

Which was all a bunch of bull as far as Stark was concerned.

Hallie had begged him to bring in some high-powered firm of defense attorneys. Stark refused, saying that he had faith in her and she was plenty good enough as far as he was concerned. She told him she wanted to seek a change of venue.

"You won't get a more sympathetic jury in San Antonio or Dallas or Houston," he said, adding with a shrug, "Fort Worth, maybe. But here is fine. This is my home now, and we'll have the trial here."

The district attorney made a perfunctory offer of a plea bargain: plead guilty to multiple counts of first-degree murder and get a life sentence. That was better than lethal injection.

When Hallie passed along the offer to him, Stark just shook his head.

So they went to trial, and the prosecution called witness after witness: survivors from the cartel who had been granted immunity; the students who had been rescued, testifying as hostile witnesses because they'd had to be subpoenaed and threatened with prosecution themselves to get them into court, where their testimony might hurt Stark's case; and Reuben, Ben, Miranda, and the others who had gone in there with Stark to free the prisoners, also testifying under subpoena and the threat of jail time. Stark had told them just to tell the truth. He wasn't just about to be responsible for any of his friends being charged with perjury. Besides, he knew that if they didn't cooperate with prosecution, the district attorney would come after them next, and he would come with all legal guns blazing.

"John Howard, this is crazy!" Hallie whispered to him while they sat at the defense table during a brief break. "I'm doing what I can, but there's just too much evidence against you. Pleading self-defense when you're tackling some would-be car thieves is one thing, but when you assemble an armed group and launch an invasion—"

"We didn't cross the border," Stark said mildly.

"I don't think that's going to do you much good."

He patted her hand and said, "You're doing fine. I'm not worried."

"I'm glad one of us isn't," Hallie muttered.

The district attorney, who was handling the case personally, paraded his witnesses through the courtroom for several days until he finally rested the state's case.

Stark leaned over to Hallie and said, "You can rest, too."

She gave him a narrow-eyed look and said, "The hell I

will." As she came to her feet she went on in a louder voice, "Defense calls John Howard Stark."

Stark leaned back in his chair in surprise.

"You can't put me on the stand!"

"Yes, I can," she insisted. "Get up there."

"I won't do it!"

The judge, a stocky Hispanic man named Garza, said, "Counsel? Is your client going to cooperate? I can't force him to testify, you know."

"I know, your honor," she said. She looked at Stark. "John Howard, please."

With a frown on his face, Stark got to his feet. His wounds had all healed while he was out on bail, waiting to go to trial. He had lost quite a bit of weight during his recuperation, though. With obvious reluctance, he walked up to the witness stand and was sworn in.

Hallie stood at the defense table and said, "Mr. Stark, have you been seeing a doctor on a regular basis?"

"You know I have," Stark said. "I got shot."

"I don't mean because of your wounds. I mean have you been seeing a doctor for some other reason?"

"Hallie," Stark said so quietly that those in the back row of the packed spectator's benches had to strain to hear. "Don't."

"I don't have any choice," she told him. "Please answer the question, Mr. Stark."

Shifting uneasily in his seat, Stark glanced up at Judge Garza. The judge said, "I don't know what the relevance is, Mr. Stark, but you'll have to answer the question."

Stark drew in a deep breath and blew it out through his nose.

"I didn't know you knew about that, but . . . yes, I have been seeing a doctor."

"Tell the court why."

The district attorney came to his feet.

"I fail to see the relevance of this, too, your honor," he said. "I have to object—"

"Overruled," Judge Garza said. "For now. Mr. Stark?"

Stark grimaced, scratched his ear, and said, "I have cancer. There's a tumor in my brain. The doctors say there's nothing they can do about it."

That set off such an uproar in the courtroom that Judge Garza had to bang his gavel on the bench for a good three minutes before the noise even started to subside. The hall outside was filled with reporters, and they started shouting when the news reached them. The chaos soon spread outside, where the courthouse lawn was packed with people waiting to find out what the result of the trial would be.

"Recess!" Judge Garza bellowed. "Thirty-minute recess!"

When the trial finally resumed, Stark was still on the stand, and a bunch of additional bailiffs and sheriff's deputies had been brought in to keep order, not only in the courtroom but all over the courthouse square.

Hallie's next question was, "What's the prognosis for your condition, Mr. Stark?"

"They say it'll kill me, but they don't say when," Stark answered with a grim smile.

"They've given you an estimate, though, haven't they?"

"They have," Stark said. "The tumor's a slow-growing one. I've got a year, maybe. Eighteen months, if I'm really lucky . . . if you consider that luck. Two years at the outside, and that's *way* outside."

"How long have you known about this?"

"Since the day those three punks tried to steal my pickup."

The district attorney stood up and said, "I object again, your honor. This has absolutely no relevance to the case at hand."

Hallie began, "Your honor, the defendant's state of mind—"

Judge Garza shook his head.

"I'm afraid I have to agree with the district attorney, counselor. This isn't relevant to the facts of the case. I'm going to strike this entire line of questioning."

"In that case, your honor . . ." Hallie sighed. "I have nothing further."

Judge Garza looked at the district attorney and said, "Your witness."

The district attorney stood there for a long moment, obviously thinking, then said, "Mr. Stark, do you believe that a man's medical condition, assuming that he's of sound mind, excuses him for any crimes he may commit?"

"No, sir, I don't," Stark said. The district attorney nodded and started to turn away, but Stark went on, "But I don't believe I've committed any crimes. I acted only in defense of my own life and the lives of others."

"That's not a determination for you to make," the district attorney snapped, clearly annoyed that Stark had gotten that statement in.

"Well, who else is going to make it? I was the one who was there. You weren't, and the judge wasn't. The members of the jury weren't. I was there when those thugs were shooting at me and my friends and those kids. I just did what I had to do to save our lives."

"Objection, your honor! The witness isn't responding to a question. Move to strike!"

"Sustained," Judge Garza said. "All the witness's

comments following his answer to the prosecution's question will be stricken, and the jury is to disregard them."

Good luck with that, the expressions on the faces of the jury members seemed to say.

Hallie rested the defense's case as soon as Stark stepped down from the stand.

"I can't do any better than what you just did," she told him when he returned to the table.

"Practically everything I said was stricken from the record," Stark pointed out.

"There's the record . . . and then there's the truth. That's what the jury heard." She paused. "I'm sorry about having to spring that on you."

"I didn't know you knew," Stark said.

"Your doctor told me. He said he didn't care how much trouble he got into for breaking the confidence. He said they could take away his license if they wanted to. He wasn't going to let you go down without a fight." She rested her hand on his. Tears sparkled in her eyes. "But I'm so sorry, John Howard. So sorry about . . . everything."

"Don't be," Stark told her. "I'm not. I've sort of gotten used to the idea by now. I figure that even if we lose, there'll be enough appeals to keep me out of prison for the time I've got left."

"You're not going to lose," Hallie said with a fierce note coming into her voice. "Not after my closing statement."

She sat there, looking down at the table while the district attorney spent five minutes damning John Howard Stark for every crime in the book, or at least it seemed like it. Then, when he sat down, she stood up and walked over to face the jury.

"'Somebody ought to do something about that,'" she said. "How many times have you seen something that's unfair, or cruel, or just plain wrong, and said to yourself, 'Somebody ought to do something about that'? How many times have we all said that? And if the thing you're looking at is bad enough, you might even say, 'Somebody's *got* to do something about that.' But who does? Most of the time, nobody."

She turned and pointed a finger at Stark.

"That man sitting right there, *he* does something about it. He does whatever he has to in order to put things right. Look at him." She smiled. "Look at the way he's looking down at the table and shifting around in his chair. He's uncomfortable. He's even a little embarrassed. Because he doesn't think what he does is any big deal. He doesn't want people praising him or calling him a hero. He doesn't *believe* he's a hero. He's just a man trying to do what's right, the way everybody should. The way anybody hardly ever actually does. That's John Howard Stark for you, ladies and gentlemen. No big deal. Just a man." Her voice caught, but she got the words out. "Just a good man."

With tears running down her face, she walked back to the defense table and sat down. Stark lifted a hand, awkwardly, and patted her on the back.

The jury was out barely long enough to take a vote before they came back with a verdict of not guilty on all counts.

The district attorney stood up and said, "I'm going to ask the court order a new trial, your honor."

"Motion denied, counselor."

"But your honor—"

"The jury accepted the contention that Mr. Stark acted in self-defense, as do I. If you want to charge him with any of the myriad lesser offenses you might bring against him, feel free to do so."

The district attorney sighed and said, "I'll . . . take that under consideration, your honor."

"Do that." Judge Garza picked up his gavel. "Mr. Stark, you're free to go."

The gavel banged on the bench, and chaos erupted in Devil's Pass again . . . mostly happy chaos this time.

It took a dozen deputies to clear a path for Stark and Hallie to leave the courthouse. Cameras and microphones were everywhere. Reuben, Ben, and the rest of Stark's friends took over for the deputies, closing ranks around him. Despite that, he was still jostled quite a bit until they got to the car Hallie had hired, waiting to take them back to Shady Hills. Once Stark and Hallie were inside, the driver pulled away slowly, forcing the crowd to give way before him.

"That was quite a speech you made in there," Stark said. "I think you really did embarrass me."

"I don't care. You're free, and that's all that matters."

"Back to Shady Hills, ma'am?" the driver asked from the front seat.

"That's right, thank you."

"Pleasure's all mine, ma'am," the driver said as he sped north out of Devil's Pass. The rest of Stark's friends were following in their own vehicles, but they were quite some distance back. "It's not every day I get to drive a genuine hero."

Hallie smiled and said, "He doesn't like to be called a—"

Stark knew that voice, and suddenly he remembered from where.

"Silencio Ryan," he said.

The driver took one hand off the wheel and drew a gun from under his seat. He stuck it over the seat and covered them as his eyes met Stark's in the rearview mirror.

CHAPTER FIFTY-NINE

"It's been a long time," Ryan said.

"Not long enough."

Hallie had gasped in surprise at the sight of the gun. Now she said, "John Howard, what—"

"John Howard and I are old friends," Ryan said.

"Not hardly," Stark said. "Ryan's a killer. Used to work for the cartel. I guess he still does."

"You'd be wrong about that. I've moved up in the world. Now I work for people even more powerful than the cartel. They want you dead, John Howard. In fact, they hired me to kill you more than a month ago."

"You're talking about people in the government." A raw edge entered Stark's voice. "Our own government."

"It doesn't really matter. Hell, you rub so many people in power the wrong way, it might be just about anybody. But here's the shocker, John Howard. . . . I don't particularly want to kill you. I've been watching you. I always respected you as an enemy. Now I sort of . . . admire you."

"You've been watching me," Stark repeated. "I knew it.

I knew there was somebody out there. But with everything else going on . . ."

"Please," Hallie said. "If you really admire him, don't do this."

"He doesn't have any choice," Stark said. "If he doesn't do the job he was paid for, he'll never get any work again. Isn't that right, Ryan?"

"More than likely," Ryan admitted. The big car was going at least eighty now, which didn't really seem all that fast on the flat, straight, open West Texas highway. "They might even decide that *I* need to be eliminated. Can't have that."

"Of course not." Stark's mind went back to the night of the rescue. "So why didn't you just let Jalisco kill me? Your shot slowed him down just enough for me to get some lead in him."

"I couldn't let somebody else kill you, John Howard. That wouldn't be right. Especially some low-level Mexican thug whose brain was probably only one step above a snake's. It wasn't time yet. Besides, if I hadn't waited, I wouldn't have known that I was doing you a favor."

"A . . . a favor?" Hallie said. "By killing us?"

"Well, not you, miss, and I'm sorry about that. But John Howard here, he's going to die anyway. Aren't you, John Howard? You really want to spend the next year or two wasting away to nothing and suffering the torments of the damned, when one bullet can end it all? One second of time, one little squeeze of the trigger?" Ryan laughed. "Don't tell me you haven't thought about it yourself!"

Stark drew in a deep breath. He *had* thought about it. He didn't like to admit that, even to himself, but the thought had crossed his mind. Maybe it would be better if everything ended quickly. . . .

"You don't have to kill Hallie," he said. "She can't hurt

you. Just do what you need to, stop the car, make her get out, and drive away. I know you, Ryan. Nobody's ever going to catch you."

"That's true," Ryan said. "But it's not the way things work." He checked the mirror again, not looking at Stark this time but at the empty road behind them. "We've run off and left all your friends. They're several minutes behind us. That's plenty of time. I'll stop and give the two of you a chance to say good-bye."

"Listen, Mr. . . . . Ryan, was it?" Hallie said. "There's something else I need to tell John Howard instead of good-bye."

"What's that?"

Hallie looked over at Stark and said, "Get that son of a bitch."

She brought her briefcase up and slammed it into Ryan's wrist just as he pulled the trigger. The gun roared, but the bullet went into the car's roof. Before Ryan could fire again, Stark had hold of his wrist. He shoved Ryan's arm toward the front of the car, so when the gun went off again the bullet blew out the front passenger window. Stark used his legs to drive himself forward over the seat while he hung on to Ryan's arm. He caught a glimpse of the speedometer needle hovering just under ninety miles per hour.

Stark spilled over into the front seat. His shoulder hit the steering wheel and turned it. The tires howled like a lost soul as the car went into a skid. While Stark wrestled with Ryan, the vehicle's front and rear tried to swap places. The car veered toward the shoulder, across it. The rear wheels bit into the dirt, spraying gravel and sending dust billowing into the air.

It stayed on the ground for ten feet or so before it hit a little dip and flipped.

Stark didn't know where Hallie was, didn't know if she was all right. All he knew was that he had hold of Ryan's wrist and that they were airborne, turning over and over. With a loud rending of metal and a bone-shaking impact, the car landed on its roof and began to slide, throwing up even more dirt and dust.

Stark and Ryan were lying on the roof now. Neither of them had been thrown clear, despite the fact that neither of them had been wearing seat belts. Hallie had been, Stark recalled. Maybe she would be all right. No time to check on her. He smashed Ryan's wrist against the roof of the car. The gun came free.

Ryan's other hand locked around Stark's throat a second later. Stark hammered a punch into Ryan's face but didn't loosen his grip. Ryan leaned closer to him, snarling in an expression of triumph. Blood dripped from a cut on his forehead.

Ryan had made a mistake. Stark bunched his shoulders and summoned his strength to drive his head into Ryan's face. The head butt loosened Ryan's grip. Stark reached up with his left hand and grabbed the shoulder harness that was hanging down slightly with the car in this upside-down position.

He pulled it lower, looped it around Ryan's neck, and hung on for dear life as he tightened it more and more.

Ryan slammed blow after blow into his head and body, but Stark took the punishment. Ryan's face turned a dark red, the color of a brick, and his eyes began to bulge. His tongue came out of his mouth and he gasped desperately, but no air made it down his throat to his lungs.

With their faces no more than a foot apart, their eyes

met. As panic and desperation began to show in Ryan's gaze, Stark looked at him and said, "I want to live. I may be dying, but I'm not dead yet."

He heaved even harder. Something snapped. Ryan went limp, and the life went out of his eyes like water running out of a bucket with a hole in it.

When he was sure Ryan was dead, Stark let go of him and shoved him aside. He twisted around on the inside of the car's roof, searching frantically for Hallie.

She was still in the backseat, hanging limply from her seat belt.

Stark crawled to her and reached up to struggle with the catch. It came loose, and she sprawled down into his arms. As he cradled her against him, her eyes fluttered open.

"J-John Howard?" she asked, her voice weak.

"I'm here," he told her. "How bad are you hurt?"

"I think . . . my arm's broken. But you . . . you're alive."

"Damn right I am," Stark said. He lifted a foot and kicked the back door. It took two kicks, but the door sprang open.

Stark crawled out, then turned around to ease Hallie carefully out of the overturned vehicle as well. He'd been sniffing for gasoline but hadn't smelled any so far. That was a stroke of luck. He saw that her arm was indeed bent at a funny angle, so he was as careful as he could be as he lifted her to her feet.

A glance along the highway to Devil's Pass told him that their friends were racing toward them, still a mile or more away. He held Hallie and waited for them, and as he did, a breeze blew the last of the dust cloud away. It was autumn now and the heat of summer was gone. Even here in West Texas, the breeze held a faint hint of pleasant coolness. The sky was as blue as it could be, Stark saw when he tilted his head slightly to look up.

It was a beautiful day, and he was alive.

Stark didn't know how much time he had left. No one did.

But he knew in his heart there would be other beautiful days in his future.

And he intended to enjoy each and every one of them, as long as they lasted.